inThrallMent

First Book

Daniel McIntee

ISBN   978-0-9905996-0-9

For Judy

because she asked

Acknowledgements

Many thanks to Barb Flory who read two early drafts and gave me what I needed: excited encouragement followed by "Are you sure you want to do *that*?" delivered in the kindest way possible. To Judy Lott who many years ago, out of the blue, asked "How's the writing going?" I never forgot that. Wendy Kawabata who made all my dumb ideas for the cover look, well, *really* dumb. To my sons who are quickly becoming young men: Aidan for being a willing guinea pig for all Dad's weird requests and Gaelen for driving around town taking pictures of carrots. A big heartfelt thanks to Mark Harrison and Alice McKinstry for everything they do. And of course my wife Sue for her patience and understanding.

1

Seven Ways To Fail

The year is 2146

Jerry had been blessed with the gift of disappointment. Specifically, the delivery of disappointing news. Not the darn-it-all-oh-well kind of news, or the truly devastating news. Jerry excelled at the kind of hope dashing letdown that required sincerely false expressions of sympathy and positive spin.

This minor function of social etiquette had become a sought after skill because 99.9967% of the clients failed. The odds of success seemed equal with the odds of riding a unicorn to work. But hope never dies, (despite being slashed, pummeled, stabbed, shot and torched by reality) it just needs a soft pillow of empathy to fall on. This meant a lot of pillow fluffing: the clients were one billion hopeful souls, nearly every person in the United Syndicates of America.

Jerry was a Retirement Counselor.

A thin man with short legs and a long torso, he appeared taller when sitting than standing. Red hair--nicely trimmed with a part and a wave on the right side--gave his pale white face a boyish look in spite of the wrinkles. Never an ambitious man, his past jobs were mostly fast food, retail, and delivery. He never earned benefits and could never afford EverLife. As Jerry aged the stigma of poverty was slowly etched on his face.

As he neared the natural age of fifty, with death looming closer and the beautiful people making him ever shabbier by comparison, Jerry relinquished his last bit of pride and applied for the job no one wanted. That he might have a gift for it was far from his mind.

He was hired on the spot and within a few weeks became The Most Admired Man In The Room. His evaluations were excellent. Coworkers were envious and desperate for advice. The job included benefits; he now had EverLife. His self-esteem rose so high he would sometimes find himself giddy for no reason.

All because of something that *didn't* happen. Jerry never suffered a blowup, when a client lost it and turned into a screaming lunatic. Every counselor experienced blowups at least once a week, or more often, several times a day. Except for Jerry. He did have close calls, when clients walked away simmering. *Just luck* he would think and try to use it as a reminder to stay focused. But other counselors would badger him with questions--How'd you deal with that guy? What'd you say?--and his humility would dissolve under an onslaught of admiration.

Jerry once requested a Days Without Incident digital counter, a small one, hanging in an inconspicuous corner of his cubicle, but management said no. So he made do by writing the number, in red pen, on each day of his paper wall calendar. Though it was early he had already written in today's number: 1,136. Jerry had been on the job just over three years. The number was perfect.

His cubicle was the fifth of ten on the west side of Square One on the 33rd floor of Building Nine. Ten cubicles on a side, two squares on each floor. Forty counselors in a square taking on the anxious public, with one supervisor perched in a high round desk in the center. In Square One this was Imelda, a blonde beauty with the supple skin of an eighteen year old who barked orders with a voice like a cranky old lion with a nicotine habit.

Weird contrasts like this sometimes showed up in early EverLife generations. The gossips around the office claimed her first EverLife treatment had gone wrong and could never be corrected. Or the technology wasn't as good then. Or some defects could not be fixed. Or she liked it that way. Who knew.

Imelda thought she had Jerry figured out.

"It's because you're hard," she said, subtlety not being one of Imelda's talents. "You're a hardened man. You've been without EverLife, you've watched yourself grow old and inch towards death. Your fifty years of wrinkle-ravaged frustration more than matches their whiny complaining. You deliver the news nice but inside they know they can't ever trump you."

In Imelda's world this was a compliment.

Jerry tried not to listen too closely when Imelda propositioned him. She was cantankerous, critical, mean at the best of times, bossy in an annoyingly nit-picky way, a woman who spread gloom and unhappiness with the ease of a cartoon fairy casting a spell. Jerry felt no real attraction and worried about the consequences of rejecting or accepting her come-on. Best to act dumb and try to avoid eye contact.

The compact printer on his left plunked out a new form. His next client, name of Roland V. Smalls. From the first generation. The character profile rated him 3 in temperament (amenable and compliant, easy-going, mild mannered) and 6 in work ethic (hard-working). Nothing unusual. Most clients fell into or near the three-six range. Last year's counselor had noted an "inclination to frustration."

Mr. Smalls had been at this a long time. "Inclination to frustration" was code for "watch out, this guy's about to crack." Mr. Smalls would be his biggest challenge of the day. Of course the ideal solution would be to help Mr. Smalls retire. Make him one of the lucky .0033%. Jerry knew better than to put any hope in this, but it lingered in the back of his mind.

A round faced man in a black overcoat and tie approached.

"Is this 9331510w?"

"Yes it is Mr. Smalls and welcome to your annual audit!" Jerry stood and offered his hand and a big friendly smile. Roland Smalls shook hands and looked at Jerry's plastic name tag.

"Hello Jerry. Nice to meet you." Mr. Smalls made an attempt at a smile and failed.

As they sat the high cloth dividers cut the conversational noise to a manageable grumble. Like every working day, and every working hour of every day, all eighty counselors were busy.

"First of all, let me thank you for coming in. I know it's inconvenient and am grateful you took the time. This should only take a few minutes.

"Now the disclaimer. Yes, you hear this every year, but we're required to say it: Only a small percentage of the population achieves retirement. When the number is published on New Year's Day we sincerely hope this will be your year. If it is, then congratulations and enjoy yourself! We know you've earned it. However, if you are among the majority who must still work, you should look on this as an opportunity for self-improvement, a guide to help you make informed decisions that will help you achieve retirement in the future."

Mr. Smalls nodded.

"Let's start with your name. Could you spell it for me to make sure I have it correct? Last name first and first name last."

Mr. Smalls spelled his name. As he wrote Jerry double checked the information against the computer screen on his right.

"Do you have a middle name?"

"Vaughan," said Mr. Smalls and spelled it. Correctly, according to the computer.

"Your address?"

"8715 Mason Lane." Confirmed by the computer.

"That's a nice area of town, Mr. Smalls. You've done well for yourself. Married, divorced, separated or single?"

"Married." The computer said Mr. Smalls had been married once.

"How many marriages?"

"Just the one." Mr. and Mrs. Smalls applied for a marriage license in 2023. A long monogamous relationship and a good sign. So many people had multiple marriages. Jerry let his hopes rise. Finding an actual retiree was a goal he had yet to achieve.

"That's really impressive Mr. Smalls, that you and your wife have been together so long. That makes me feel good, knowing there is still true love in the world. How many children?"

"Just one." Confirmed by the computer, but...

"I'm sorry, my computer is saying this is an unlicensed child." A possible crime.

"We run into this every year. Max was born before the Protection Laws. Just scroll down a little more..."

"Oh, I see it, a retroactive exemption." Mixed possibilities here. The single child was good, and unusual for a couple from the "Reality Gap" years, between EverLife and the Population Protection Act, when humanity went on a procreation binge. The Smalls likely got their exemption by agreeing to limit themselves to one child.

Exemptions--the all-powerful bureaucratic tool for sweeping away indiscretions, procedural screw-ups, or any failure needing official absolution--didn't always work. Roger, from Square Two, liked to tell anyone caught listening the story of his only retiree, a woman whose parameters were way over but somehow always fell short.

Previous counselors told her to expect to retire. When Roger said the same thing she had banshee-like blowup that brought the entire floor to a halt. Afterward, Roger took the time to get the full story. (That he hung by the woman as she was detained impressed Jerry the most.) Roger dug into the woman's official past and found an exemption for a previous marriage--her first husband died in a bungee jumping accident--with the wrong marriage code, preventing her from retiring for a decade.

"What is the child's gender and age?"

"A boy. One hundred and eight."

"How old are you?"

"One hundred and forty seven." This triggered one of Jerry's mental bookmarks.

"You were alive during the war." The Second Preservation War had been the only school subject to hold Jerry's attention. Reminiscing over a historical touchstone was an effective icebreaker.

"Yes I was."

"Wasn't there some battle around here?"

"There were a thousand battles all over the country."

"It was a big battle, so big they had to give it a name. Really horrible, really bloody."

"The Turner Street Massacre."

"I've never heard of that."

"You know it better as The Battle of Old Town."

"Yeah! That was it! Lots of people dead on both sides."

"It was one-sided, more slaughter than battle."

"Did you see it?"

"Yes."

"Cool! I've never met anyone who was there. Was it as bad as they say? Blood running in streets? Body parts strewn on the sidewalk?"

"I don't know."

"How could you not know?"

"I sat on my couch and watched it on TV."

That was a letdown. "Well...but that's good. Must have been a terrible thing, a real...uh...what's the word...tragedy. But you did the right thing."

"The right thing? What was that?"

"You stayed out of it, at home. You didn't get involved."

Jerry looked up and involuntarily flinched back. Mr. Smalls was staring at him like a dog about to attack. "You don't know what the word means."

"I'm sorry? Which word?"

"Tragedy. You couldn't even think of it. Had to work at it. You don't know the meaning of the word."

"Mr. Smalls, I am truly sorry if I've offended you. I meant no disrespect. I do understand what you've gone through and how important the past is and would never take for granted the sacrifices of your generation." Jerry used his most servile tone, hoping it would induce some guilt.

"You act like death is an exciting experience you've been denied."

"No sir, I'm just trying to make conversation." The humble tone was not working. "We should move on. Do you have your W2 and F3 forms?"

"Why do we meet like this?"

"Well, a yearly assessment is required by law--"

"Yes, I know that. What else besides the obvious?"

"The CEO of Paragon Retirement felt the process was becoming too impersonal--"

"Jerry, we both know everything is on the computer. The damn thing knows more about me than I do. There's no reason for us to meet. And you have to know hand writing superficial information on a paper form is meaningless."

"Mr. Smalls, I assure you our meeting is extremely important in the retirement process, essential actually."

"I am *required* to be here. I don't have any choice."

"Mr. Smalls--"

"Call me Rolly. All my enemies do."

"Certainly Rolly. At the very least your presence confirms that you exist, you're alive and our records are up-to-date."

"And the computers are infallible."

"Absolutely. Backed up multiple times in multiple places. Stored at such high encryption no one, nor any computer, could possibly break in. Is that what's bothering you?"

"It bothers me that you're missing the point. If computers are infallible, why are we here?"

"Are you a lawyer?"

"I work for the insurance company."

Control of the conversation was now in Mr. Smalls rhetorical hands. Best to keep him talking, vent off a little anger, try to lessen the looming tirade. "It not about the computers all the time. We are still human."

"That's true. The computers are a tool. So I'm forced to come here and suffer through another disappointment, handed out by warm-hearted human instead of an impersonal computer. I preferred the computer."

"I'm sorry to hear that. Wasn't there a time when your statement was a computer generated email?"

"About five decades ago, before you were born."

"So you were unhappy when the counseling service was created."

"I thought it was a good idea. At the time. An excuse to get out of work for a couple hours."

"What changed your mind? Did you have a bad counselor?"

"Every counselor has been equally as helpful as you, Jerry. You are all very well trained."

"Thank you." A compliment, and a positive sign. "I appreciate you saying that. So what turned you off on counseling?"

"It's the same rejection every year no matter who says it."

"How many times has it been?"

"Sixty-seven."

"You shouldn't think of it as rejection. It's nothing more than a convergence of numbers, a happenstance of addition and subtraction." Straight out of the training manual. "Maybe this will be your year. We haven't looked at all your info. Can I see your W2 and F3 forms?"

Rolly frowned and pulled two sealed envelopes from an inside jacket pocket. Jerry passed them under a blue light to break the electronic seal, then cut them open with a miniature medieval claymore.

There are seven parameters that determine eligibility for retirement. Two are tracked and compiled by Paragon Retirement Inc.: Marriage and Children. Two are reported and judged by the client's employer: Length of Service and Productivity. The remaining three are compiled by the potential retiree's financial provider, a summary of their current financial state: Assets and Debt for a total net worth, and the client's overall Credit Rating.

These seven numbers are inserted into a mathematical formula, calculated by computer, to produce the client's final tally for the year, called their Reckoning. If the client's Reckoning is higher than The Number (the Corporament's cutoff for selecting retirees, calculated using economic parameters such as market activity, profit margins, and overall productivity), the client can retire.

No amount of hard work, loyalty or social responsibility could make up for the tiny number sitting on Mr. Smalls' financial form. Jerry understood this at a glance.

He said nothing, kept his facial expression locked, and began typing, entering Mr. Smalls' numbers into the formula. In seconds he had a sum.

"This year your Reckoning is 425.31."

Mr. Smalls looked shocked. "That's the same as last year!"

"Really? I've never seen a no-change." He checked the computer record. "You're absolutely right. How about that." Jerry smiled.

"Weren't there changes to the formula this year? To make retirement easier?"

"Only for point zero-zero-zero-zero-one percent of the populace. But that's only this year. Depending on next year's change we estimate--"

"How many people is that?"

"About ten thousand."

"And I'm not one of them."

"I'm sorry Rolly, it's not going to happen this year."

"I knew that. In spite of everyone saying otherwise, I knew that."

"I can help you sort out where the problem is. Looking at your F3 form your--"

"No." Mr. Smalls raised his voice. "You're not going to do anything. You're going to put my file in that pile by the desk and by the end of the day you'll forget we talked."

"Rolly, I *can* help you--"

"You're just a pencil pusher."

"Mr. Smalls, Rolly, give me a chance to find some wiggle room."

"Wiggle room. You know how many times I've heard that? Or some other synonym for the same vague promise? Find some leeway. Or space. Or a little extra in the nooks and crannies. You people need to update your training. Find new ways to say fail."

"Rolly, you should try to be more positive."

"Do you even listen? Is your brain already moving on to the next spin? Do you know how many times I've sat across from someone with that same fake positive attitude, and how many times I bought into it?"

"Sixty-seven times."

"You do listen. That's good. Let's work this out together. How many different ways can we say 'failure' without actually saying 'failure?' You start."

"I don't--"

"Okay, I'll start. We're dealing with a failure to retire, in a society where everyone lives forever, so we could call it 'permanent work.' But that has such a depressing sound. Not much of a euphemism. How about 'skill reassessment' or 'financial reassessment.' I know! 'Time management reassessment.' Reassessing things makes it sound like a change for the better. That's good. Your turn."

"Mr. Smalls, I think it's time to end our meeting."

"But I'm just getting started! You want to make this personal. But you know," the words now sodden with sarcasm, "personal isn't good enough. It's too polite, not positive enough. What else can we call it? How about friendly? Or maybe tolerable? Bearable? Survivable? Not a pain in the ass? Oh, here we go: 'warm and cuddly.' 'We'd like to make the retirement process warm and cuddly.' C'mon Jerry, let's sit here and think up ways to spin this so it doesn't sound pointless."

"It's not pointless."

"How old are you?"

"Fifty-two."

"God, you're young. Not even up to pre-EverLife retirement age."

"I'm sorry I couldn't help you Rolly. Maybe next--"

"What was The Number last year?"

"477."

"Why does The Number always go up?"

"The general health of the economy, the population count, value of the dollar, more things than I can list."

"But The Number always goes up. The economy goes up and down, but The Number goes up. The population stays the same, but The Number goes up."

"It's just the way things work."

"Bullshit. It's a bunch of rich bastards sitting in a skyscraper pulling a number out of a hat."

Mr. Smalls had gone beyond frustration into paranoia. "That's a farfetched notion. Don't believe everything you read on the internet. The wealthy have more important things to think about."

"Like controlling the Corporament."

"We still live in a democracy."

"A democracy controlled by corporations."

"We still vote. We still elect representatives."

"We vote for the candidate our company picked. The one they tell us to vote for."

"It's still your decision."

"Is it? Really? A choice between a politician who represents Warburton Inc. or one who represents Knoll & Sons Limited? Is it my choice when the company says they'll give you a raise if their man is elected? Or a cut if he isn't?"

"You didn't vote in the last election did you?"

"Yes I did and voted for my own sorry self interests!" Rolly's voice raised enough to attract a few glances. Jerry could feel Imelda staring holes through his back.

"Mr. Smalls, we can help you retire. Just not this year. And please remember, cameras are recording everything."

"Jerry, I have done everything the way I was supposed to my entire life. I worked at the same company, I stayed married to the same woman, I only have one child, I've been saving and scrimping...everything we've done is about getting retired."

"I appreciate your effort but I can't change The Number."

Silence, for a split second, but in memory like a paused movie. Rolly gazed at Jerry, his expression unmoving when it should have been reacting. Jerry had never been to this point before, that was the downside of perfection, a lack of experience. But he would learn: this was the calm before the strike.

In an instant Rolly was up and lunging over the half wall and screaming inches from Jerry's face.

"I HAVE BEEN WORKING FOR ONE HUNDRED AND TWENTY FIVE YEARS AND I WANT TO RETIRE!"

Rolly sat back down, eyes wide, hands shaking.

One-hundred and sixty plus people stopped talking and turned to look.

"Rolly, I under--"

"Goodbye."

Mr. Roland Smalls disappeared, like a fly jumping into flight before the hand swats it, leaving Jerry alone to stare back at the gawking faces.

The wannabe retirees looked at him warily. His fellow counselors were shocked; everyone stared. Finally, the tension broke and they turned away, muttering things he didn't want to hear.

Jerry picked up a pen and buried the 1,136 he had written on today's date in a violent obliteration of red ink.

"Shit," he said.

2

Fashionably Punctual

Back at his workstation Rolly sat with face in hands. Usually he only thought those things, never said them out loud. A new project was waiting. Rolly buried himself in it.

An hour later he resurfaced and took a few seconds to visually check his HearSay. Seven new messages were waiting in his personal network:

Radnor Tanner
> Hey! Rolly lost it at his audit! Here's the link.

Fenton Dost
> U sure? Didn't think he was kapable.

Dahlia Kenyon
> Bout time, Rooly. You rule!

Talwyn Reamer
> Atta boy Rolly! Give em hell!

Orsen Carslake
> Bout tim you retured. You weigh to old!

Paloma Corpela
> I fel 4 u rol. happen 2 me 2 yr ago.

Fenton couldn't type, Orsen couldn't spell. Dahlia insisted on calling him "Rooly" no matter how much he complained. Paloma posted in a rush because she wasn't supposed to socialize at work. Radnor found the video less than a minute after Rolly made his escape. Didn't that guy have anything better to do? He touched the link and a video filled his cubicle, playing back in gleaming holographic perfection. There he was, in Jerry's face, his own face distorted into a snarl. It looked uglier than it felt.

The last posting was from his best friend:

Aidan Luks
> Get ready for your first visit, you lunatic.

Rolly knew what that meant.

The day after his incident (flare-up? tantrum? sudden outburst? con-
niption fit? perfectly understandable expression of frustration? he hadn't
settled on a justification yet) Rolly chose to eat lunch at a restaurant six
blocks from work named Renfrew's Fine Cuisine. His fellow cubicle rats
called the place "Grease Hog Pit." How they came up with that nickname he
didn't know. Considering the meeting he was about to have, it seemed perfect.

Rolly opened the door and stepped in, the smell of cheap meat turning
to charcoal destroying his appetite and any hope of finding edible food.
He waited in line for a booth.

A petite brown haired waitress seated him. Rolly picked up the dirty
laminated menu, holding it in front of his face as if shortsighted. Within
seconds the table shook and the old vinyl seat creaked. He put down the
menu. Two men in black jackets and red ties smiled back at him.

"Hello Rolly, it's nice to meet you. I'm Mr. Kalchik," Mr. Kalchik was
caucasian with spiky bleached-blonde hair, "and this is Mr. Sage." Mr.
Sage was African-American with short nearly-bald hair and a button nose.

Physically they were barely adults, their age frozen at twenty-one,
after the brain has fully developed, when the youthful glow still lingers,
before the body begins its slow decline. Mr. Kalchik and Mr. Sage were
officially known as Intervention Agents, the front line enforcers of HBM
Resources LLC, the company responsible for policing and security.
Commonly known as the Thought Police.

Rolly guessed their real ages to be thirty or forty based on how they
dressed. The jacket and tie were required by HBM--as close to a uniform
as those organized head-shrinkers would get. Beyond that their appearance
differed drastically: pale Mr. Kalchik wore eyeliner and a small silver
earring, like a link of chain, in each ear. Under his tailored black jacket
Mr. Sage had a plain white shirt and a skinny red tie; a neatly folded red
silk handkerchief poked out of the jacket pocket. Mr. Kalchik's too small
jacket creased at the shoulders, the collar was upturned, and the shirt
underneath featured an abstract pattern in pink and green. They didn't
match any fashion trend Rolly knew of, or maybe it was too many trends
at once. Definitely younger men.

Mr. Kalchik, "I'm sure you know why we're here, otherwise you wouldn't
have chosen such a nice restaurant. Is it okay if we talk?"

"Of course."

"We're worried about you Mr. Smalls." To Mr. Sage's credit he said
it with almost no manufactured sincerity.

"Yes, what happened yesterday is not like the Rolly we know and respect."

"It was completely out of character."

"Yes, it was." Rolly tried his best to smile nervously.

When dealing with the Thought Police the wisest course was to agree with everything and act contrite. But Rolly wasn't feeling it. He wanted to take them on, like Jerry, rant until their heads exploded. A satisfying image but a supremely bad idea.

"That counselor was very upset."

"You ruined his record. No one had ever gone off on him before."

"Oh really?" *You're lying. You never talked to him.*

"He hadn't had an incident for three years."

"He was so upset they sent him home."

"That's lost work time. He'll have to make it up."

"I'm sorry to hear that." *Bullshit.*

Mr. Sage, "But we're not here to talk about Jerry, we're here to talk about Rolly. How are you today?"

"I'm fine." *And how are you, you officious, intruding prick?*

Mr. Kalchik, "Are you really?"

"You didn't seem fine yesterday."

"I know what it looks like, and I am sorry, but I'm fine today," he said with a defiant tone. *It was the most relaxing thing I've done in decades.*

"This restaurant is full of people, Rolly. I wouldn't want to put any of them in danger."

"We do have authorization to use deadly force if necessary." *Deadly force? What are you going to do, psychoanalyze me to death?*

"Let's hope it doesn't come to that."

"I only lost my cool. What's the big deal?" *Yeah, what is the big deal?*

Mr. Sage, "It isn't a big deal. But big deals always start small."

Mr. Kalchik, "And we like to stop those big deals when they are small."

That exchange was clunky. The black coats looked at each other, expressionless. *Needs more rehearsal.*

"You know how it is with the retirement office. You get your hopes up and always get rejected." *Here we go. Time to play guilty.*

"Is that how you think of this Rolly? As rejection?"

"No, it's not that." Pause. "It's really frustrating, you know."

"And sometimes it gets the better of you."

"Yeah, I've been working a long time you know." *Gotcha.*

Mr. Kalchik, "You mustn't think of it as work, Rolly. Think of it as fortune smiling upon you."

Mr. Sage, "Good point. Lot's of people have no job and no EverLife."

"You're a lucky man, Rolly."

"Yes, you're right of course. And I really am sorry for making Jerry upset. That was not my intention at all." This time with more guilt. And downcast eyes. *I hope I meet Jerry in a dark alley sometime so I can scream at him some more.*

"That's good to hear Rolly."

"Sometimes it's like that science rule, the one about walking toward a wall but only taking a step half the size of the last, I forget what it's called. It's like that with retirement, I make a half step every year but I'll never reach the wall." *Oops! Too much! Too much! Stop talking! What the hell are you trying to do? Shut up already!*

"I have no idea how that feels Rolly. Retirement is decades away for me."

"Which means you are very close Mr. Smalls, and that makes you a very lucky man." *Yeah, the lucky guy that gets to run an eternal treadmill.*

"Try to see it this way, Mr. Smalls, and not as a burden, and you will be much happier."

"Yes, you're right. I just needed reminding of tards." *Go fuck yourselves you goddamn bas-*

Mr. Sage, "I'm sorry? I didn't catch all that."

"I just need reminding."

Mr. Kalchik, "Sorry. Sounded like you called us bastards."

Rolly looked at him a moment, realized his thoughts had made it to his mouth once again, and started laughing as genuinely as he could. "A what?" The black coats joined in.

Mr. Sage, between gasps, "No, no I think we just misheard."

Mr. Kalchik, between snorts, "Yeah, it wasn't a slip of the tongue or anything."

"I'm sure Mr. Smalls is being completely sincere with us." He abruptly stopped laughing. "Well, we need to go."

They began to slide out of the booth, "Let's leave Mr. Smalls to his lunch. Oh, by the way, don't eat the food. Nasty processed garbage, barely qualifies as stomach filler. Your nanobots will be starving before break time. Order the garden salad. It's the only thing they do right, delivered by truck every morning. But next time, for our sake, pick a place with decent food."

And they left. No good-byes or nice-to-meet-yous. Rolly watched Mr. Sage's black bell bottom slacks flop against each other over shiny leather dress shoes. Mr. Kalchik made less noise, his pinstriped wool pants and brown suede moon boots being very quiet.

Rolly watched this display with one arched eyebrow and mouth open in wonderment. Should he be laughing or scared out of his wits? What just happened? A drive-by psychological shakedown by a clown costume party? An attack by the bizarrely caricatured ghosts of trends past? Was he being mocked or treated like a moron? Should he believe anything they said?

Despite the ridiculous clothing the threat was real. This was the Thought Police version of a courtesy call, and could have been worse. He hadn't fooled them, shouldn't have tried, may have made things worse. He was on their watch list now, their massive trolling computers looking for his name, his face, his voice in every crowd and conversation, protecting the populace from villainous wild-eyed retiree wannabes.

The waitress came back, young and pretty. No wait, she looked older than himself, or newly "youth-anized" in the current pop culture slang. Waitresses couldn't afford EverLife or age-realignment surgery. She likely had a sponsor paying to keep her looks fresh.

"Ready to order?" She seemed happy. Her name tag read Carolann.

"Um, no, changed my mind. Didn't see anything on the menu I liked. Guess I'll just go."

"You shouldn't do that. It makes you look guilty."

"I'm not guilty of anything."

"You don't look like the type. But weren't those psych guys with you?"

"Uh--"

"Yeah, I know them. Come in here all the time. Gang up on some poor shlub and leave. Never order anything, don't leave a tip."

"They're in here all the time?"

"Must be their territory. How's that work? You make an appointment or is it the other way around?"

"Uh, no they just showed up."

"But you were expecting them?"

"Uh, yeah."

"Okay, that's interesting. Me and a couple other girls were wondering how this worked. So you did something that got their attention."

"I guess so."

"Don't worry, you don't have to tell me. They're a little touchy for me, you know? Get a little pissed off because the vending machine took your fiver but didn't hand over the danish and they're all over you like mud on a pig."

"This happens a lot here?"

"Seems to. Don't know about other places. But yeah, we've seen those guys lots of times. After they leave, they stand on the corner across the street and wait for their mark to walk out, then follow him."

Rolly turned and looked out the front window but only saw a rushing-by mass of humanity.

"They do that?"

"Yep. Don't know why, looking for something to do I guess."

"You think if I stay they'll go away?"

"Probably."

It did occur to Rolly she might be pulling his leg, trying to get him to order and make it worth *her* while. Then again, it would be typical of the Thought Police to follow him. At least he thought so. He had no experience with this. What did it matter if they were waiting or not? He was hungry.

"I'll have the garden salad."

"Good choice."

3

The New Death

Rolly lay on the exam table staring at the ceiling, wondering why he wasn't more freaked out.

Ten years ago a visit from the Thought Police would have left him paralyzed with dread. It had been a point of pride that among his friends he remained "innocent." Yet only two days ago he sat across from two Intervention Agents and attempted to fool them as if they were born-yesterday rubes.

The ceiling displayed a large photograph of a sunlit green jungle. A list of animals ran down the left side; a child's seek and find picture. The jungle occupied most of Rolly's vision. If he held up his arm and pointed he could draw a circle around the hidden animal and flick his finger to check it off the list. Rolly didn't care how many tigers or monkeys or snakes were hidden in the foliage, he just wanted to look at something not covered in concrete or asphalt or glass.

Rolly had to lie in the exact center of the table so the machine could do its work. All of his metallic, electronic or signal blocking paraphernalia had been set aside, leaving only underwear, slacks and shirt, right sleeve rolled up. Once settled, eight gleaming steel concave antennas slid up and out of the table, the edges joining perfectly to form an elongated octagonal box, much like an old fashioned wooden coffin.

The antennas collected transmissions from the nanomedibots, those floating, crawling, probing, penetrating microscopic machines that ran amok through his body. Rolly pictured them as manmade germs set loose in his bloodstream. In reality the nanomedibots had specific tasks and specific places to be, trillions of slightly-larger-than-a-molecule robots swarming through his bones, muscles, and organs; monitoring, repairing, regenerating; and before being replaced they had to tell the medicomputer what Rolly's insides were up to.

While the nanomedibots reported back to base, Rolly had time to think. He decided the outburst was Jerry's fault. The fool talked about dying like it was a special adventure, and his historical opinions were regurgitated propaganda. Rolly never got used to this, dealing with someone who looked older and experienced but acted so naïve. The man irked him, got under his skin and pushed him over the edge. The anger burst like steam out of a broken pipe and Jerry the craggy faced youngster, nearly one hundred years his junior, was to blame.

Would they do anything to him? Time was the weapon of choice for the Thought Police. A few days of detention, or extended interrogation, maybe a week or two of intensive therapy, things that took you away from work, made your Productivity crash, pushed retirement away an inch at a time. They had myriad ways of punishing anti-stability behavior. In extreme cases they might take away EverLife for years. People used to being young did not like watching themselves grow old. The Thought Police worked in subtle terror.

He should be on his best behavior, and sensibly paranoid, but didn't care. Be on his best behavior? He had been on his best behavior for twelve decades. Why would his behavior need to improve? Is this how they trained people to think? He didn't want to be that way anymore. He didn't want to live in paranoia. Rolly could not work up a decent amount of worry even knowing the Thought Police were shadowing him. Fuck it all. Who cared if they watched?

Rolly heard the door open with a hiss of pneumatic air and a tech aid in a light blue uniform appeared over the antennas. A pretty girl with long brown curly hair. A little plump--different from all the skinny women around--with a friendly smile. She held a rectangular black box with four large vials inside, each filled with sparkling clear fluid.

"Hello Mr. Smalls. All the info is downloaded. It's time to switch to the delivery phase. Give me two minutes and I'll be out of your hair." She smelled like strawberries. Her name tag read Christine. The antennas descended into the table, then it rose and morphed into a reclining chair.

"All set. Can I get anything for you?" She was prettier at eye level.

"No, I'm all set. Thanks though."

"Hubert's running behind this morning. He should be here in a few minutes."

"No problem." He should ask her over for dinner before leaving.

Those first few decades of EverLife were one big party. No worries about disease or viruses or germs, EverLife defeated every ailment. Immortality without consequence. Fuck anyone you want. No AIDS, no herpes, no pregnancy. Eat anything you want. Barbecues where the food went on forever. EverLife kept you thin. Chug an entire bottle of whiskey and never get more than a slight buzz. EverLife kept you sober, or as sober as you wanted to be, usually just enough to break down those pesky inhibitions. Social networking websites became sex trading sites and personal relationships fell into predictable cycles of jealousy and envy. Gossip flowed as freely as status updates, littering people's reputations like so much digital garbage.

The internet equivalent of graffiti on a bathroom wall. And just as truthful. Life had become a sordid reality show.

"Morning Rolly. How's that car of yours?" Hubert had been Rolly's biotech for thirty years and they were friends, in the online sense of the word. A third generation American, his heritage was South American: brown skin, square cheeks and jaw, straight black hair. He sat on a stool between Rolly and the machine that would impart another three months of eternity.

Other techs talked in a stilted fake language designed to avoid offense. Hubert spoke what he thought, no matter the consequences, straight, no bullshit, and he accepted everyone as they were, without judgement.

"Much better now. Took it to a different shop, told them the other place couldn't fix it, said it might be the converter instead of the drive and they were right."

"Huh. Think they don't know electric drives so well?"

"Maybe. Or they had a brain freeze. Who knows."

"Glad it worked out. Let's see what the nanobots have to say about you today." Hubert turned to a monitor on the machine.

"You ever feel guilty about living forever?"

"Nope, never."

"Don't you ever think 'what if?'"

"What if what?"

"What if we had normal lifespans and more people were born."

"You mean born and died."

"Right."

"Sounds like a time machine trip to the past."

"Maybe."

"Feeling nostalgic?"

"I always feel that way. This is more like...I don't know...do I deserve to live forever when others will never get the chance."

"Others as in...?"

"New people, people who haven't been born."

"You're feeling guilty because you think you're taking away from unborn future generations."

"Who might be here now, contributing in ways I can't."

"Don't beat yourself up, Rolly. You're worrying about a problem that doesn't exist."

"But what if this unborn person invented a really earthshaking machine, or had some new idea that improved everyone's lives."

"Like EverLife? Can't get more earthshaking then that."

"There's always room for improvement."

"Not sure I agree with that. EverLife is pretty much it."

"You don't think we can do better?"

"How can you improve on immortality? The population is stable, almost everyone has a decent job, enough to eat. What about this needs improving?"

"I don't know. The person I'm preventing from being born might have an idea about that."

"You're worrying over nothing. There are plenty of intelligent people alive who can think up these things, and plenty of new smart people coming along too. Nothing has changed, Rolly. Life goes on. It just doesn't stop like it used to. And that's a good thing."

"I still feel like I need to get out of the way."

"Ah, don't beat yourself up over it." Hubert looked up from his screen. "Wait, you're always posting about retirement."

"Yeah, I do."

"You're itching for retirement."

"Who isn't?"

"Well that's why Rolly. That's why you want to 'get out of the way.' You want to retire."

"Yeah, I do. I really, really do."

"You must be close, if you're even thinking about it."

"Somewhat close. Not like right up against it or anything. Kind of on the horizon."

"Just out of curiosity, you don't have to tell me if you don't want, how far away are you?"

"About thirty away."

"That is on the horizon. Kind of far on the horizon but you'll get there, a little each year, like everyone else."

"I just had my audit. My Reckoning was the same as last year."

"Shit no! That's harsh. Sorry about swearing Rolly." Rolly could not recall Hubert ever cussing.

"That's all right. Kind of a shock. Don't know what happened."

Silence as Hubert lost himself in nano-info and Rolly lost himself in self-pity.

"You know, the situation you're in, obsessing about retirement, there's something you're not telling me."

Rolly took a long time to answer. Saying it aloud meant breaking decades of avoidance. "My son owes me money."

"A lot? Enough to put you over?"

"Don't know for sure. Enough to get me a lot closer."

"When was the last time you two talked?"

"Sometime in twenty-one teens."

"Thirty years, that's a long time. Is he still mad at you?"

"Probably."

"You need to get your money back. I'm sure Stephanie's told you this."

"Many times. Usually in December."

"You're gonna have to swallow your pride Rolly. Otherwise you'll be aching to retire forever."

"I know. I'm going to do it this time. Stop making myself crazy and call him up."

"Good. You need to get yourself on the outs."

Hubert snapped the box with the four vials into the machine, then added a fifth vial of brownish liquid Rolly had never seen before. "What's that?"

"New compound that lowers your body temperature. Acts like a preservative. Includes a new set of nanomedibots that freeze internal structures if there's an emergency."

"It won't have a bad reaction with other EverLife components, will it?"

"It's been thoroughly tested with every enzyme inhibitor, telamerase activator, amino acid, anti-oxidant, FOXO activator, and that wonderland of proteins that are the backbone of EverLife. Even the nanomedibots are cool with it."

"Will it cause cancer?"

"That's an old one. No, it will not cause cancer."

"I thought I read somewhere that EverLife might cause cancer."

"Not possible. EverLife fights cancer. One defensive nanobot carries enough poison to eradicate eight cancer cells. Which is an interesting irony. Cancer cells are immortal. That's why they're so hard to kill. We are killing immortal cells to become immortal. Kind of stealing it I guess."

"But cancer was an issue at one time?"

"It was one of the problems early on. Look Rolly, you live long enough you're going to develop some cancer. That doesn't mean EverLife caused it. How many times have you had cancer?"

"A few times."

"Here, this is today's chart." Hubert pointed to the monitor. The white screen was divided into sections labeled with various body parts containing numerical data meaningless to Rolly. "The nanobots had to eradicate malignant cells in your pancreas twice over the last three months. Does that mean EverLife is trying to destroy it? No. Let's check your history...last pancreatic transplant was fifty-two years ago. The average lifespan of a replacement pancreas is fifty years. It's time for a new one. Which I've been telling you for the last two years."

"I wasn't really worried Hubert."

"Let's look at the rest of your chart. In addition to the cancer you had some inflammation in your knee joints, plaque removed from the arteries in your left leg and right arm, they've been working really hard keeping your blood pressure down," Hubert glanced at Rolly, "230,000 calories of excess sugar removed from your diet-"

"Cookies are my weakness. And chocolate covered cake donuts."

"-and your brain created 2.5 million new synapses. That's a good amount, right where it should be. I think we created a few more today as well. So, should we set up an appointment to replace that pancreas? Your level 2 status covers it."

"Yeah, might as well."

"Excellent. I'll have the lab start growing a new one. Any other concerns? Topics of interest?"

"No, I'm good."

"Great. Give me a few minutes to program the nanobots and we'll get you on your way."

Hubert sat down in front of the EverLife machine, a console of computer screens and digital medical monitors measuring Rolly's current medical condition, and held up his portable. The two computers talked for moment, then Hubert began entering parameters for the nanomedibots. A minute or so later Hubert pushed a big green button. Liquid from the vials drained into the machine and one word popped up on the main screen: Programming... Each and every nanobot, hundreds of millions, were being given their "mission" for his body. The computer had to wait for confirmation they had received instructions and were ready to go. It took a few minutes.

"Hey, can they grow brains yet?"

"Sort of. They can do the basic frame work but not much beyond that. The brain is way too unique and complex for the usual regeneration. Even if they could create a complete brain, there's no way remake the person inside."

"Think they'll ever figure it out?"

The EverLife machine began to push the combined fluids into an intravenous drip chamber.

"I don't know. There's not a lot of incentive. You have to keep the neurons intact and synapses firing, make sure the myelin sheath doesn't degrade, which EverLife takes care of already. Why, do you need a new brain?"

"Ha, that was sort of funny."

"I have to wonder when I hear so many dumb questions. Here we go." Hubert touched a pedal on the base of the exam table and it began to flatten. "You know the drill, lay still and enjoy the show."

"Thanks Hubert."

"No problem Rolly."

Hubert inserted a needle in Rolly's arm and taped it down. He pushed another big green button. The main screen said "Delivering." Fluid in the IV began to drip down through the tube.

"Lights on or off?"

"Off." Hubert left the room.

You had to lie still for half an hour while the machines went sightseeing through your bloodstream, in search of their proper place. Looking up once more, Rolly found the jungle still on the ceiling, challenging him to find tigers in the shadows.

Here's the thing about wallowing in pleasure: it's a distraction. While the world partied, the powerful people worked to make sure they stayed powerful. Which meant, as it always has, sucking up to the money. Corporations had money and decided they were in the market for a government. Politicians lined up to represent whatever company was convenient, and proceeded to reorganize the government in what would become a silent coup. The fifty independent states were replaced (too inefficient and redundant) with thirty American Domains centered on large cities. Rural areas were left to fend for themselves. The cost of providing services was too great, the distance required caused too much inefficiency. Local government entities--the small towns and townships and boroughs--were abolished, folded into a District Board, appointed by whatever local company claimed the greatest profit. Elections were still held every four years, to maintain a façade of Democracy.

All of this was done in the open, reported on holovision, radio and internet. The American public gave tacit approval by doing nothing. Talking points were repeated endlessly in the news cycle: We work for a company, not the government, wouldn't the company better represent our interests? Business is so efficient, it can do a much better job running things. After all, we owe them don't we? For giving us jobs?

Meanwhile, religious leaders awoke from an existential crises (how can anyone burn in hell if they don't die?) seeing opportunity in the rise of their natural conservative allies, the business class. They decried the moral outrages, the lack of modesty, the breaking of vows, the godlessness brought on by EverLife. Something needs to be done, right now! EverLife must go! The newly formed Corporament was not amused. EverLife isn't going anywhere, they said, any other ideas?

Much discussion ensued, compromises were made, resulting in the Corporament's first great accomplishment: the retirement system, to be administered by the newly formed Paragon Retirement Inc. Both sides agreed that the seven parameters were a nice balance of religious values and corporate practicality: Length of Service, Children, Productivity, Assets, Debt, Credit Rating, and Marriage.

Speaking of marriage, Stephanie was home. They saw each other in passing, in the early morning and late evening before and after work. Last week Stephanie's best friend Renee spent two nights at the house. The first night Stephanie headed off to Roger's house for a one-nighter. Rolly didn't know where Stephanie spent the second night, until he got up in the morning and found the two women chatting over coffee and bagels. Michelle, an embarrassingly youthful looking girl Rolly knew from work, was with Renee's husband. Roger had been the waiter at a girl's night out party the previous week. This morning Rolly ended his latest tryst when

Marli, a girl from the grocery store, kissed him goodbye, conveniently leaving the house to Rolly and Stephanie.

Rolly could never keep his lovers straight without help. He used a HearSay, the most popular organizing device on the planet, an ultra-fast computer with personality living inside his ear.

Basic models were simply a small dot glued inside one ear canal. The largest ones had a thin wire that curled out and around behind the ear, providing more power and memory. The sign of an expensive HearSay was the coil of wire attached to the side of someone's neck, the larger the coil the greater the status. Permanent and durable, no shower or ill-advised cotton swab could dislodge a HearSay; only licensed installers could perform upgrades. The sound was amazing. Music had more power and clarity as it literally reverberated inside your head.

The HearSay's killer app was its ability to listen--and respond. When Stephanie said Renee wanted to spend a couple of nights with Rolly she was talking to both Rolly and his Hearsay. Immediately in his right ear Rolly heard:

"Way to go Dude! Should I make it official like?" The device included two hundred voice styles and thousands more available to purchase online. Some had specific personalities; most were vocal caricatures designed for popular appeal. After his outburst at Paragon, Rolly switched to a "Surfer Dude" voice he named Sean.

Rolly answered "Yes" to Stephanie and Sean replied "Consider it done, you dog you." In a more private situation Rolly could have pressed the first knuckle of his first finger on his left hand. This was the default gesture for yes. Pushing the second knuckle meant no. Sensors embedded in his wrist recognized the movements and transmitted his answer to Sean. A lot of surreptitious hand watching happened during conversations.

A pocket interface was part of the HearSay system. A foldable screen and keyboard that allowed you to watch video or play games and type out messages, sometimes to the HearSay itself. Because talking to yourself in a crowded room wasn't always convenient.

Even the most basic model had enough memory for hundreds of years of appointments. Not to mention conversations. It stored and recorded every sound that reached its owner's ears twenty-four hours a day. Forget what someone said and rewind to the day of the conversation, or search for the person by name, or keywords they might have used. The HearSay recognized individuals by voice and knew exactly who you were talking to.

Thinking about Stephanie jogged Rolly's memory. That old feeling of having misplaced something. To bad the HearSay couldn't read minds. Wait...oh shit. Rolly said aloud:

"Sean, do I have an appointment with Stephanie tonight?"

Two voices answered.

"Yep, sh--"

"Please lie still Mr. Smalls." Christine, monitoring from some other room.

"Sorry. Forgot."

"Just be still please." A little more commanding this time. The Renewal Center staff were very serious about stillness.

"Whoa, sorry there O Hallowed One," said Sean, with a little snicker, "shoulda known you were in for your regular oil change. Yeah, she's on for quarter past the big eight. Asked for it ya know, but we figured you'd forget. I'll tell you about it when you're done chillin'."

The HearSay included a "jargon level" adjustment that controlled how much slang each voice used. Rolly thought his was set low, but each voice was different. You had to live with one awhile to figure out how much you could tolerate.

Stephanie wanted to talk about retirement. It was that time of year and the only thing keeping them together. If you wanted to retire you had to be married. They tied the knot before EverLife was invented, back when they were best friends. Before decades of familiarity bred long term contempt.

She already knew about the outburst. Despite the mutual animosity she was part of his personal network, and he part of hers. There was no way she could not know. There would be no rationalizing it either. Crystal clear three dimensional video tended to do that to your excuses. All that remained was an uncomfortable discussion of the consequences.

Rolly always walked back to work after a renewal session, no matter the season or weather. An EverLife renewal was a legitimate excuse for missing work and therefore not counted against Productivity. He wanted to make the time last. This November day was sunny and cool, slightly warmer than normal. He could make the trip at a relaxing saunter.

He was 147 years old. At what point were you supposed to accept the concept of forever and be comfortable with a triple-digit age? Rolly still felt like the weary thirty-two year old he had been arrested at, sleepwalking through the last 115 years.

Time accelerated, weeks blurred into days, months felt like weeks, a year passed before the days were properly counted, then another, then a decade was gone and you didn't know where it went. Working constantly, retirement always the goal, making sacrifices, always pushing for better Productivity. And always more efficient, every year some new machine or software or process making his job more efficient.

The problem with efficiency was it bred more things to do. The machines needed fixing, the software needed updating, everything needed endless fine tuning. Efficiency took a lot of time. This didn't seem to bother the company, as long as he did stuff, accomplished things, and produced measurable data. Everyone's job was supposed to be easier because of efficiency, but the opposite was true. He tried to believe this was ironic, but it wasn't ironic, it was torture by employment and efficiency the iron maiden of corporate life.

Good weather or bad, the sidewalk was thick with people. Men dressed exactly like himself, women in business suits that never fit right, teenagers with scalp tattoos and pre-torn silk tee shirts celebrating conformity to nonconformity, faces from so many ethnic backgrounds, and many mixes, all flowing in a mass of sameness.

Rolly turned right and merged with the pedestrian traffic. The crowd ebbed and flowed as obstacles were avoided and the sidewalk narrowed and widened but everyone moved at a mostly steady pace.

Buildings were still made of brick and stone. Houses were still made of wood and brick. Windows were still made of glass. People still drove gas/electric hybrid cars. The oil industry lingered despite nearly exhausted supplies. "Oil conservation" was the latest media mantra. The preferred method of generating electricity still involved burning coal, garbage, natural gas, anything flammable that could be dumped into an incinerator. Solar, wind, geothermal, tidal, and other promising methods were still ridiculed as niche technologies.

Out of tens of billions of people why hadn't one of them come up with a better way to generate electricity. Like fusion power. How come that hadn't gone anywhere?

It used to be said that the twentieth century witnessed more technological innovation in a hundred years than the previous five thousand. Automobiles, telephones, radio, television, trips to the moon, computers, the internet, the information age. Maybe it was braggadocio because the last one-hundred plus years had been the exact opposite. No one had gone back to the moon or to any planet in the solar system. People still drove gasoline powered cars, when they could afford it. Innovation was reserved for products that could be mass marketed and sold at a substantial profit.

And Rolly still wore a suit and tie to work, with an overcoat on cold days. He still tied his tie the same way he did on his first day of work, one-hundred and twenty five years ago.

Efficiency was only a symptom, Rolly decided. The biggest change was more of everything--more people, more cars, more problems, more work to do. Like now, on the downtown street of a mid-size city, shoulder to shoulder with a thousand fellow pedestrians. Impossible to move without brushing and bumping into others. The crowd seemed more aggressive than usual, jostling and shoving instead of brushing and bumping. Someone stepped on Rolly's shoe; he tripped into two other bodies. A heavy heel smashed his toes. A metallic briefcase whacked his thigh. An umbrella point caught his stomach.

Not so long ago someone spray painted "Flow or Die" on the side of a building. It quickly became a trademarked slogan appearing on bumper stickers, magnets and coffee mugs. Rolly didn't know if it meant acceptance or sarcasm or both.

Rolly tried to flow, but felt his frustration rising. He wanted to lash out, no more friendly elbows and murmured excuse me's. This was not good. He spotted a recessed doorway, made his way over and stepped out of the crowd. He turned to watch it go by, willing himself to calm down.

A hand tapped him on the shoulder.

"Meh I hep you?" said a bald man with a grey mustache. Bald and grey were appearance choices, sometimes fashionable, sometimes practical.

"No, I'm fine thank you."

"Ten you need move on. You block my door." The man spoke with an accent, Eastern European he thought, maybe Polish. Rolly hadn't heard an accent in decades.

"I'm sorry. Are you the owner?"

"Yes. Pleess move on."

"I'm not in anyone's way."

"You are in my way."

"There's plenty of room to go around."

"Why I want make customers walk around doofus? Move or I call police."

"Maybe I'm going to shop at your store. Did you ever think of that?"

"Is women's clothing store and all you do is watch women walk by. It disgusting and make them avoid store. You scumbag voyeur, go now or I call police."

So Rolly flowed again, forcing himself into the mass, simmering with anger. Why was everyone treating him like a criminal?

"Hey Rolly, like, your blood pressure is way, way up. You might want to slow down and start some nice Zen-like breathing."

Rolly ignored Sean and began to walk faster, shouldering into a tweed jacket.

"Hey man, that guy back there, he was just bein', well, an asshole. Ignore it, man. You shouldn't take it personal, some dudes are just rude like that. Let it go."

Rolly continued driving forward, shoving aside a bright green peacoat, ramming into the back of a blue hoodie. It earned him lots of scatological name-calling.

"Rolly, man, let it go. That guy is a tinpot Napoleon ruling his twelve feet of sidewalk frontage. He's a little man with little regard, little confidence and little means, and he deserves little of your attention." Some things didn't translate well into surfer-speak.

Rolly knew this was only programming talking, an automated response to aural input and stress levels. Sean was being agreeable to cool him down. He touched the second knuckle and held it for 2.6 seconds.

"Signing off," Sean said.

Rolly stopped abruptly. The flow parted and crashed around him with a rushing roar of insults. He was standing in front of a sixty-two story glass and metal rectangle, building Number 2 in District 11 of the Stableman Insurance Family. His workplace.

So much for the relaxing saunter.

4

Becoming inThrallEd

One hundred and twenty-five years ago, getting a job at the insurance company was safe and unadventurous, an announcement that you were reliable, hard working and valued stable long term employment. Nothing wrong with that, Rolly and Stephanie were planing to have a family, it was sensible. Then EverLife came along and made Rolly's boring career choice look like brilliant prophecy.

EverLife did not make anyone truly immortal. It conquered aging and disease but could not fix you if a catastrophe happened, like falling off a cliff. Minor damage--a broken bone, a gash in the skin, a bruised knee--it could handle. But massive damage meant death. A bullet hole in the head. A knife through the heart. Smash your car into a bridge support at ninety miles an hour. Ingest enough poison (it took more than normal). Point was, there were still myriad accidental--or deliberate--ways to die.

Shortly after EverLife was announced a group of mathematicians and statisticians got together and, after arguing for a weekend, came up with an average lifespan for EverLife Users: 1,274.3 years. Play your cards right, get a little lucky and you might live forever, but probably not. Life still had limits, newly extended, but not necessarily eternal.

The implications of this took awhile to sink in. No one likes talking about death, especially potential immortals. Eventually every User came to this silent revelation: EverLife had erased the hope of a peaceful die-in-your-sleep passing. Death no longer lurked around the corner. Now it was around the corner and twelve blocks down, waiting patiently at the bus stop where it planned on running you over with a garbage truck.

Realizing you can only die by violent misadventure is a whole new level of fear, even if it is thirteen hundred years away. And people who live a long time have much to lose. Insurance provided the security EverLife could not and Rolly found himself in the middle of a booming industry.

Rolly worked on the 43rd floor. His department, The Office of Context Management, created the media intended for public consumption. All the audio, web and telegraphic advertising, responses to negative rumors or news stories, and how to avoid life-threatening dangers. The OCM was the gentle and caring face of the company, but at anytime might be required to cajole, scare, or vaguely threaten as well. Ultimately they wanted to make insurance fun so the company could sell more.

Rolly was a vidician tasked with creating public service videos about the proper safety procedures for whatever potential hazard was making news. The laughably didactic and obvious videos that no one took seriously. Including Rolly.

Last week a woman in Montana tripped over her cat and fell. Unfortunately she smashed the side of her head into the corner of a marble counter. The fall damaged her HearSay; it couldn't call for help. Alone in her apartment, the woman died before anyone realized she was missing.

A freak accident, a tragic sequence of events. She had a generous life insurance policy and Stableman Insurance paid the full amount. HearSay records and video from her refrigerator confirmed the accident. The resulting project kept Rolly busy for two weeks making safety vids: the importance of rubber bumpers on counter edges, awareness of your surroundings, wearing non-slip shoes around the house, physical fitness and how to prevent injury in a fall, and lastly, and most strenuously, the inherent dangers of owning a cat.

Rolly created everything from scratch using templates for environments, people, clothes, voices, everything needed to make realistic video. Sometimes he would use beautiful people, sometimes sight gags, sometimes visual irony (which almost always pissed off the script writer), he had a computer full of tricks. The challenge was making a serious message entertaining. It was so easy to veer into the ridiculous, especially when trying to make a meaningful safety video, melodrama being one exaggerated gesture or expression away. Sometimes the over-the-top approached worked, but finding the right balance was a challenge.

And he had to worry about multiple target audiences as well. Each video needed to be properly contextualized for the type of viewers who would be watching. Kind and friendly for the family channels. Graphic and bloody for the action channels. Sexy for the porn channels. Making accidental death palatable for the family channels was hardest. Sometimes he could retool an existing video, but usually it meant creating a new one. There was enough work to keep four vidicians busy.

When entering the office one of two things would happen: he would be greeted with a gauntlet of hellos and how-are-yous and how'd-it-gos or a mood of sullen stillness and resentment. The first meant everything normal, the second meant a vice president had penetrated the room. By sheer number, vice presidents were hard to avoid. In this building, which contained 13,000 workers, a thousand vice-presidents wandered freely, attempting to create justification for their continued employment.

Only fifteen VPs could rightfully claim the OCM as part of their jurisdiction. Most popped in at irregular intervals, some only once every year or two. The real trouble came from VPs who had no business in the OCM trying to push unapproved projects as if the office rats were idle soldiers waiting for orders.

As he stepped in Myrna, the receptionist, greeted him with a smile. "Hello Rolly. How was your quarterly?"

"Just fine. Thanks for asking."

The office looked like a billion other offices in the world: a long rectangular box with windows at one end designed to repel light, and a rabbit warren of cubicles purposely arranged to confuse outsiders. Myrna's half moon desk guarded the central entrance to the cubicles. Anyone wanting admittance had to go through her and Myrna was exceptionally good at stonewalling and/or redirection. Her knowledge of the inner workings of the company was legendary.

Rolly's cubicle was two thirds of the way in, on the far right up against the wall. The most direct path (which still zigzagged) took him past several coworkers he considered friends.

"Hey Rolly. Anything new at the quarterly?" asked Bob Sanchez, marketing liaison. The OCM had one other Bob and a Robert. Bob Sanchez stood five inches shorter than Rolly and sported a permanent dark scowl that made him look evil. He was one of the nicest people Rolly knew.

"Oh you know, a touch of cancer and a new pancreas. Nothing major."

"Damn, a new pancreas. Maybe I should get one, just to keep up." They laughed. Bob was a few years younger and like Rolly could remember when cancer was more than a cute name for an astrological sign.

Rolly continued on. "Don't forget about the 2:30 meeting," Bob said.

What meeting? Rolly turned to ask but Bob disappeared into the maze.

"Hello Mr. Smalls. How are you today?" This was Lambert, a perky young girl who always smiled big and called everyone Mister or Miss. Lambert dressed for business, usually in a pantsuit with a nice set of silver earrings or a tasteful necklace and high heeled patent leather shoes that raised her four inches off the floor--and she was still shorter than anyone else. She was in her seventies but had retained her adolescent giddiness. Most everyone thought she was dumb. Rolly knew better. Lambert was more intelligent and clever than anyone realized.

"I'm fine Lambert. How are you?" Lambert was her first name. Rolly couldn't remember her last name and had never heard anyone use it.

"I'm just peachy today Mr. Smalls! Thank you for asking! Especially now that you're back." Lambert was especially friendly to Rolly, not flirty, like a reward for his respect. He could always count on Lambert.

Rolly made three turns in quick succession, a longer walk before the final right turn, which forced him to look into Souliere's cubicle, who glanced up. Neither man smiled or spoke. Souliere's face was older and weathered, darkened by sunlight, a condition he never changed. Deep curved lines ran from his nostrils to the corners of his mouth, his lips set in a permanent straight line. Souliere turned back to his monitor. A simple action, but dismissive, as if Rolly weren't worth his attention. Souliere was the office know-it-all, the guy with the right answer for every question. He was annoying, aloof, and indispensable.

Rolly entered his cubicle. There were no papers (hidden in a desk drawer; handwritten notes were the most secure way to share information), but the space was full of stuff. A digital photo frame playing a slideshow of his family, another with photos of friends (some from so long ago he could not remember their names), the puck that whizzed by his ear at a hockey game forty years ago, a bonsai tree and a potted cactus, a stapler that had no reason to be there, a mug full of dusty pens and pencils, a digital radio, a battery recharging pad, a baseball mitt, an alligator head, a larger digital frame that cycled through concert posters, a set of bongos, a model of a 1930's red roadster. Rolly took off his coat and put his bag on the floor next to his desk.

"Back already? You need to draw these things out." This was Doug, a fellow vidician, in the cubicle behind Rolly.

"Yeah, I tried but they wouldn't let me." "They" and "them" referred to the great mass of human flesh everyone had to fight through. As opposed to "we" or "us" meaning anyone in the immediate vicinity who, by virtue of proximity to the utterance of the word, were exempt.

"Yep, I know how it goes." Doug's head was backlit by a yellow glow from the floating icons.

Macklin, the office manager, appeared in the aisle. When EverLife was invented Macklin had been in her mid sixties. A series of plastic surgeries followed in an attempt to regain a youthful exterior. The surgeons were good, but not miracle workers. Macklin was too far gone. She would always be an old woman in a young body.

"You two know about the 2:30 meeting?"

Doug, "No. What meeting?"

"With Steve Mann. Has some big idea. Conference room D."

Rolly, "What time is it now?"

Sean responded, "Two-thirteen pm. Dude."

Doug looked at Macklin. "He just got back from his quarterly."

"Both of you need to be there. Don't be late."

Conference room D was last on the forty-ninth floor, known as "the one with the windows." Conference rooms A through C were identical--same table, chairs, carpet, paint and whiteboard. Twenty five years previously, when the prevailing management paradigm believed art would stimulate employee creativity, the company purchased four large landscape prints to hang in each room. The exact same picture, hung in the same place, in each room.

A through C could be easily confused (and the setting for many practical jokes) but no one had trouble locating conference room D. The windows let actual sunlight in. Meetings went over allotted time with no complaints. Steve Mann was one of the few VPs with enough clout to bump whoever booked it.

Rolly and Doug were last to arrive. Macklin and Bob Sanchez were sitting next to each other but pretending they weren't. Suzi Harper from the print department sat across the table; brown hair pulled back in a ponytail, the picture of proficiency. Print was making one of its cyclical comebacks. Suzi wanted to make a good impression before it died again. Rich Embrey sat next to her, the media liaison. His job was to get this idea embedded in the entertainment world. The group was rounded out by Julie Dougherty and Frank Charles from radio and holovision, respectively, and Souliere, who was at every meeting. Steve Mann sat at the head of the table, as manicured and slick-looking as every other VP.

All eyes watched accusingly as the pair made their entrance. Making coworkers wait was nearly unforgivable; an offering of donuts would be required in the morning. Steve stood and smiled, happy he could finally start. Rolly and Doug sat on opposite sides of the table.

"Excellent! Glad to see you two could make it. Let's get this road on the show." He laughed nervously. Everyone else laughed dutifully.

"Before I start, you should know I've run this idea past Bob Earle already," Bob Earle was Managing Vice President, Steve's boss and only one step removed from company president, "and he liked it so much he took it to Stewart McCabe." The company President. "So approval for this, literally, comes from on high."

Steve smiled proudly but the faces that looked back were filled with animosity. The most creative department in a bland and bureaucratic business was being told what to do without being asked for input.

Steve continued, pretending he didn't care. "As you all know approximately fifteen percent of the population does not have life insurance. These last percentagers"--he made air quotes with his fingers--"have been hard to crack for a long time. I believe I have the answer."

Steve held his breath. Julie sighed. Rich closed his eyes. He appeared to be praying. Macklin rolled her eyes to the ceiling. Someone muttered "Ah shit." Doug had his face in his hands. Rolly stared back at Steve, trying to maintain a neutral face, thinking *Christ, not again*.

Steve went on. "We know these people are a smorgasbord of demographics. Fifteen percent are too poor to afford it. Or so they think. Nine percent have decided not to get insurance on some kind of perverted moral grounds. Nineteen percent claim to have never thought about insurance and another fifteen percent believe they will live forever. Ten percent want to get insurance but haven't gotten around to it. And thirty-two percent believe buying insurance will keep them from saving for retirement.

"I've been brainstorming and asking myself What is the common denominator here? Laziness? Not for all of them. Morality? Some have no morals. Delusional thinking? If that were the case it'd be easy for you guys, just feed their delusion."

Doug snickered.

"Obviously that hasn't worked. Some of these people are so grounded they have no imagination at all. Invincibility thinking? Still leaves some out. But that got me thinking, What's the opposite of invincible? And that's when I found it, the common denominator, the complete opposite of invincibility. Anyone guess what it is?"

Steve had a shit-eating grin, like he knew no one would get it. Silence ensued. Steve continued to grin, waiting. The pause became pregnant, grew a belly and threatened to break water. Rolly thought this a unique trait of management types: an inability to recognize apathy.

"Just tell us Steven," Macklin said. Only she could get away with using his full first name.

"Fear. It's fear," he said. "Some of them are wallowing in it to the point of paranoia and some don't have enough of it. We need to bring them all together using fear."

Rolly, "You want us to scare them into buying life insurance."

"Fear is a great motivator. It makes perfect sense."

Macklin, "This is nothing new. We scare people into buying insurance all the time, every couple of years I think."

Suzi flattened out a keyboard, unfolded a monitor and began typing. "Macklin's right. Every few years we do a scare campaign. I can share a copy of the past schedule with everyone..."

Steve, "No, that's okay," his best decision of the meeting so far, "Since you have it up, can you tell us what we did in-between?"

"Well, we did the opposite. We made the company the good friend, the helpful neighbor, looking out for the well-being of our customers."

"So we've been alternating scare/friend for a long time."

"Correct."

"What if we did both at the same time?" Steve looked almost triumphant.

Slight pause while Suzi listened to her HearSay. "We did that back in twenty ninety-eight."

Steve looked shocked.

Macklin, "So it's been done already. Nothing new here."

Frank, "Nothing new under the sun."

Julie, "That was fifty years ago. No one remembers it."

Doug, "No one except the internet."

Macklin, "Someone will dig up the old one and compare it to this one, tear it apart, look for contradictions."

Rolly, feeling impatient, "Who cares? They're gonna do that no matter what we do. Just have the computer run a contradiction cross-reference and vague it a little. Let the blog bastards make up shit instead."

Everyone looked at Rolly as if he'd been replaced by an alien pod-person. "What?"

Suzi, looking cross, "You don't usually use such...colorful language."

"A drab discussion needs a little color. Maybe we can put some colorful language in our ad, spice it up."

Steve, "Speaking of language, I have the perfect tag line. 'Become enthralled with insurance.'"

Everyone sat silent, considering.

"Enthralled with insurance?" Frank said/asked.

Steve, "You know like, someone gets enthralled by a...beautiful woman."

"Are you enthralled now?" Julie asked.

"Um, no. We're only talking about being enthralled."

Macklin, "You don't think any of the women in this room are enthralling?"

"That's not what I meant, I was...thinking of my wife, who is absolutely totally ravishingly enthralling."

None of the women seemed convinced.

"It was only meant as an example."

Bob, who hated uncomfortable discussions, "What else can someone be enthralled by?"

Doug, "Anything, really. A hobby. The news. A hologram. A child. Anything that holds your interest."

Julie, "Like some guys are enthralled with their train sets."

Frank, with a resentful look at Julie, "Like some women are enthralled with themselves."

Steve rescued the conversation. "I think we get the idea. Where do we go with this?"

Doug, "We take a beautiful model, show what a wonderful, enthralling person she is, then kill her off in a tragic train accident. Tell everyone to become enthralled with insurance or else."

They watched Doug, waiting for him to laugh, but he was a master of the straight face. Steve looked confused.

"Okay, it's a start. I don't think we want to go in that direction exactly, but I have an idea that will help us link enthralled and insurance. I say we do a counter spelling of enthralled. Everyone get out your HearSays."

VPs were notorious for this, an excuse to show off how bigger, newer and more expensive his toy was compared to theirs.

Steve unpocketed his interface and placed it on the table. The thing unfurled itself with a whizz of tiny motors, both keyboard and monitor, keys popping up with a rubbery sound. When it was fully erect, er, deployed, it nearly hid Steve's head.

Frank, "That was cool." After gloating, Steve started typing.

"Start with a small 'i' instead of an 'e' change the 't' to a capital, and capitalize the 'e' as well. So it looks like this." He transmitted the spelling to everyone.

Sean said, "Receiving a request from--" Rolly pressed his first knuckle.

"Done. Dude."

inThrallEd.

Frank, "The capital E gets lost next to the two L's."

Suzi, "How about if we took out one of the L's?"

"That will never work," Macklin said, "people associate the aw sound with two L's. You'll have them pronouncing it with a short 'a' like in pal, or Cal or Al. They'll be wondering why we want to 'inthrAL' them with insurance."

Doug, "To me it looks like one of the L's is going to impale the E. The way people skim through text they'll be thinking we want to impale them with insurance."

Rolly, "Get rid of the capital E, keep it a small e."

There were several nods but no one would verbally commit.

Steve, "I like the capital E, it's one of those subliminal things. Some people will see it, most will miss it, but it makes the word seem cooler. What does everyone think?"

More nodding. No one disagreed.

Bob said to Suzi, "When was the last time we used an 'i' word in a promotion?"

"Twenty-six years and seven months ago."

"A lot of time gone. Everyone will have forgotten whatever it was."

Suzi, "iBelieve in Insurance."

Steve, "That's good, but it's not really a matter of faith. Insurance is much more practical. If you have insurance you won't need faith."

Everyone stared at Steve. "No, no. That was the tagline for the last 'i' promotion. iBelieve in Insurance."

"Oh. Okay." Steve's face turned red.

Doug, "Well that proves it. If Steve doesn't remember no one will."

Macklin, "Got in trouble with the religions for that one. Said it confused their own advertising."

Frank, "That's a good line though. We might want to recycle it at some point."

Julie, "But not too soon after 'inThrallEd with Insurance'. We don't want people to get jaded, thinking we're just going to hit them with 'i' words all the time."

Nods and agreements. Steve, who had been staring off into space, spoke.

"No, I disagree. We should follow 'inThrallEd' immediately with 'iBelieve.' Makes perfect sense."

Rolly, "How?"

"Well, the two are linked, aren't they? Not sure I can say this right. Being enthralled is like a religious, uh, fervor, I think. What do they call it? Enlightenment?"

Suzi, "Rapture? Ecstasy? Is one of those what you're looking for?"

"Dunno. One of those two. Anyway belief follows enthrallment."

Doug, "Yeah. I can see that."

Julie, "Can't quite get my head around it, but it sounds good."

Rolly, "It's the other way around. Enthrallment follows belief."

Macklin, ignoring Rolly, "I think we have a plan. Any objections?"

Souliere spoke for the first time, "Does anyone remember or even know the other definition of enthralled?"

Steve, "It means something else?"

Suzi, reading from her HearSay, "1. to captivate or charm. 2. to put on hold or in slavery; subjugate."

Souliere, "It means slavery. A thrall is a slave."

Steve, looking dismayed, "Is this going to be a problem?"

Doug, "I can see the online posters twisting it into 'Enslaved by Insurance.'"

Frank, "Won't take them long to start calling us slave masters."

Rolly, "It's a bad idea."

Suzi, so softly half the people couldn't hear, "I don't think it's going to matter." Steve was right next to her. "Why not?" he asked.

"Well, no one here knew this. Only Souliere brought it up. How many real-world people are going to think it means slavery?"

Julie, "When I heard enthralled the first thing I thought was enchanted."

Suzi, "Right. Enthralled is a positive thing, a good thing. You get enthralled by a person or object or idea you like. Slavery is an archaic definition."

Souliere, "No, it's still current. Haven't you played video games?"

Suzi, "Why does that matter?"

Souliere, "Half of them use thralls as bad guys. It's more interesting than calling them zombies all the time."

Doug turned to Souliere, "You're saying we're going to call our potential customers zombies and slaves?"

Souliere, "We're implying it, sure."

Frank, "The chatters will have a field day."

Macklin, "So what? Who cares what they think, or reads what they post? Mostly they start stupid arguments and try to insult each another."

Frank, "We're taking a big chance if we go with this."

Suzi, "Isn't that how we reach these holdouts? By taking a chance?"

Souliere, "It's not a big chance, it's an epic fail. It will backfire and the company will become a running gag for every English speaking adult."

Julie, "What do you want us to do? Recycle the same tagline again?"

Rolly, "We're already recycling that stupid small 'i' thing."

Suzi, "If we don't act bold we'll never grow the company. And why should they keep us employed if we don't do our jobs? They'll outsource us to the advertising company and you can say goodbye to EverLife."

Rolly, "It's gonna take more than boldness to convince the holdouts."

Steve, to Suzi, "You have pretty strong feelings about this."

Suzi, hesitantly, "I don't agree with Souliere and Rolly. We can't be hostage to every forgotten meaning of a word."

Souliere, "It's not forgotten. It's in use as we speak."

Steve, "It's my ass on the line if it fails. But big gambles mean big payouts. Suzi, could you give us more of that second definition of enthrall?"

"'A person who is in bondage; slave. A person who is morally or mentally enslaved by some power, influence, or the like.'"

Steve, "Okay, there's the slave thing again. But two other words jumped out at me: morally and influence. We are influencing the morals of the holdouts. God knows they need it."

Souliere, "Morally is ambiguous. It could mean either good or evil."

Steve, "Well, we're not evil are we? And isn't it a moral imperative that everyone have insurance? We're giving these holdouts the moral influence they need. That's a good thing. Suzi is right, and because she doesn't speak out unless she really feels passionate, well, that's enough for me. I'm willing to take a chance. Let's do it."

———————————

Twenty minutes later everyone was back in their cubicles being productive but feeling unsatisfied. The abrupt end of the meeting left too many things unsaid, the desire to talk was still strong.

Doug, "EverLife is a stupid name."

Rich, peering over the top of the cubicle, "What's wrong with calling it EverLife?"

Suzi, from two cubicles down, "It's an okay name. I couldn't think of it any other way."

Doug, "I don't know. It just seems too...uh...can't think of the right way to say it."

Rolly, "It's too safe. All rounded corners and softness. No edge."

Frank, across from Rolly and diagonal, "It's just a marketing term. Clear and to the point."

Doug, "It's too fake nice, doesn't mean anything. It should be more meaningful."

Rich, "Like what?"

Doug, "I don't know...maybe DeathEnd."

Suzi, "Too morbid. It should be called HereLife, instead of hereafter."

Rich, "You can't use death or anything that sounds like it, that's too negative. Isn't morte Latin for death? How about NoMorte? Like No More Death, but nicer."

Rolly, "Nobody knows Latin. It's confusing."

Julie, speaking loudly from the other side of the cubicles, "You're such a downer Rolly."

Rolly, "Yes, but I get to live forever."

Doug, "We're coming at this all wrong. Try it from the opposite direction, think immortal or interrupt, like death interrupted."

Julie, "There's your morte, in the word immortal."

Rolly, "Here's one: MorteCept. Combining morte with intercept."

Rich, "Good one."

Sean interrupted, "Perp alert coming in."

Everyone received the same message. The conversation stopped.

Through their HearSays a pleasant computer voice said: "This is a Citizens Watch Alert for the city of Lansing, state of Michigan, for Tuesday, November 7th, 2147. At 3:18 pm a suspect was observed moving east on foot along Grand River Avenue, near the intersection of Clemens Avenue. Suspect is wearing a blue windbreaker, black athletic shoes, and is armed and dangerous. Do not approach. Contact Protection Services immediately if you see this person."

Suzi, "Should we go look?"

Frank, "Nah, that's three blocks away and the guy's heading away from us."

Doug, "I wish they wouldn't make the broadcast area so wide. We didn't need to be interrupted."

Rich, "What were we talking about?"

Macklin walked into the aisle, "Yes, what were you talking about." Everyone expected her to end the after-meeting gabfest but she didn't seem concerned.

Rolly, "We're thinking up new names for EverLife."

"That's productive."

Suzi, changing the subject to distract Macklin, "So Rolly. How'd your audit go?"

Rolly, "I got the same number as last year."

Frank, "Oh my God!"

Rich, "Shit! You don't say!"

Suzi, "Oh, I'm so sorry Rolly."

Julie, looking over the cubicle wall, probably kneeling on her desk, "That's never happened. It's like getting stuck in purgatory."

Macklin, "They might have it wrong."

Rolly, "It's Paragon, they're never wrong."

Suzi, "Rolly, I know this guy--"

Frank, "Here we go."

"--named Gordon O'Leary, he's a retirement coach. I'm sure he can help."

Macklin, "Coach? Is that what they're calling themselves now?"

"That's what Gordon calls himself. It's on his business cards."

Rolly, "You know this guy?"

"Not personally. He helped my cousin retire so he must be good."

Silence.

"I know what you're all thinking, he's another hack, but it's true. My cousin had been trying for decades and she saw Gordon and made retirement the next year."

Macklin, "How well do you know your cousin?"

"We see each other at family gatherings."

Frank, "How often?"

"Three or four times a year."

Macklin, "How do you know she's retired?"

"I haven't seen her in a year and a half. And my other cousin said so."

Rolly, "That's not much to go on."

"Why else would someone disappear? I think she missed like one family gathering in seventy years. She's retired for sure."

Macklin, "What do you think Rolly?"

Doug, "Worth a try?"

Rolly knew exactly why he always fell short of The Number and no coach or consultant had enough tricks to make it happen. But staying the same, one year to the next, that was harsh. A little help, just to push it in the right direction, seemed like a good idea.

Rolly, "Okay, give me his contact info."

"Yay! Isabella, send Gordon O'Leary's contact information to Rolly Smalls."

Sean, "Receiving Gordon O'Leary contact info. You want me to, like, save it?"

"Yes."

Frank, "Maybe O'Leary can tell you what the secret parameter is."

Macklin, "There's no secret parameter."

Doug, "Yes there is, there has to be. How come some people retire and others don't? People like Rolly who are way past due."

Julie, "Why don't they tell us then?"

Doug, "Maybe the Corporament doesn't want us to know."

Rolly, "It's bullshit. There's no secret. It's just marketing nonsense specialists use to get you in the door. That's why I've never gone to one."

Macklin, "O'Leary's your first?"

Frank, "All these years and you're still a retirement scam virgin."

Julie, "Why are you doing this now?"

Rolly, "I'm desperate, to be honest, and willing to do anything."

Doug, "How long have you been working?"

Rolly, "One hundred and twenty five years."

Frank, "That's a long time. I'm at seventy-four."

Suzi, "Forty-three for me."

Doug, "Eighty six. I'll bet Macklin has you beat."

Macklin, "One hundred and thirty seven. I jumped companies too many times."

Frank, "Hey Suzi Q, what's the average retirement age?"

"Your HearSay can find it as well as mine."

"But you're better at it."

"Isabella, you heard Frank."

Suzi listened for a moment, "Paragon doesn't calculate an average age. They do track Length of Service for every retiree, which they consider the more meaningful measurement. Currently the average is one hundred and three point four."

Doug, "You're way past due Rolly."

"Go see Gordon. You won't be sorry."

Rolly, "I'll do that Suzi."

Macklin, looking at her watch, "Time to break up the love fest. Before our Productivity ends up in the sewer. Go enthrall customers with insurance."

5

Crossing Lives

The drive home took more than the usual hour and a half with two stops for gas ($150 for six gallons) and Chinese takeout. Seventeen miles between home and work and both were still in the city limits.

Rolly let the car in drive itself only when he had a book to read or game to play, otherwise the car would scare him. Accelerating and slowing whenever it wanted, passing with only millimeters to spare. At red lights it stopped so close to other vehicles he could reach out and knock on his neighbor's window. When it became too much Rolly would take over driving and be immediately directed to the manual lane. Friends said he was crazy to do any manual driving, the cars were supposed to be that close, like a flock of birds. He would reply "I'm not a goddamn bird" and they would look at him as if he were speaking gibberish.

"Sean, how long until we get home?"

"Like, the car says eight thirty. Fourteen point three minutes."

Stephanie was there, in her space again. He hoped she would let him eat before bringing up the annual retirement conversation. She had been home for two weeks. Strange how he thought of it as empty when she was gone, though plenty of lovers passed through.

Stephanie spent long periods away from home, usually living with a new lover, the longest being two years; usually it was only a few months. Or a few days. Rolly always knew where she was and when she was coming home. She kept in touch, usually by text.

How long had it been this time? Three weeks? A month? No, it was more. They hadn't crossed lives in awhile. Even under the same roof they only met in passing.

Forty years ago--or was it fifty?--they remodeled their single-story house into three sections: Rolly's bedroom, office and bathroom on the south end, Stephanie's on the north end, both sealed from the middle of the house with a wall and a single door. In between was the kitchen, dining room, and entertainment room. Friends teased them for still having a dining room. And a house.

A front door with foyer led into the center of the house; a sliding door led out to the backyard. Each end had its own exit to the outside, for the discreet comings and goings of lovers. Both doors were stuck from disuse. The grape vine outside Rolly's end kept trying to poke in under the door.

The Marriage parameter required hopeful retirees to be married, preferably once, the longer the better. Multiple marriages counted against an individual's Reckoning, making it harder to reach retirement, but not impossible. There had to be room for redemption. As an incentive a couple's assets and debts were lumped together to determine retirement eligibility for both spouses.

Rolly and Stephanie hadn't participated in the post-EverLife orgy. At the time, they were newly married and in love. Their infidelity grew over decades of sameness and boredom, with no children to occupy their time and entertainment beating a drum of excruciating repetition, then the vicarious thrill of a new lover kept things interesting.

Their situation was common. Most couples had been trading spouses for years. Conservatives complained about it. Ministers preached against it. But, as long as a façade of monogamy was maintained, nothing changed.

Stephanie called Rolly's lovers "three night trysts," as if they were annoying pests with a short lifespan. He didn't have a new lover every three days, they just stayed around for three days and left. At most he had two or three a month. The last had been Marli Jo Sanchez, a sweet-faced beauty, the new cashier at the grocery store. They made eye contact on Saturday and she kissed him goodbye this morning, Tuesday.

Rolly thought three lovers a month plenty. He liked having the house to himself. He would go out to the garage, back the car into the driveway, close the door and get out his tools. Clamps, chisels, table saw, router, bandsaw, lathe; nothing fancy, just good solid tools. Rolly would set to work on building a wardrobe, or a lamp, maybe a nice set of shelves, a flower stand, or a storage trunk. He would get lost in each one, loving the intricate details, cutting joints that fit right. There was satisfaction in carpentry, but frustration too. Time was limited. He would just get started then have to stop and clean up.

Coming home tired, sitting down to relax but feeling like he was wasting time, a board needed planing or a table leg needed turning or that dresser needed to be stained. When the thing he loved doing only caused agitation, he would pick up a new lover. Three days of sex, work, sleeping, and discovering how little in common he had with this person, the mutual acknowledgement that yes, this had been fun but... Then a week or so with work, sleep and sawdust.

Why was it difficult to find someone who hung around more than a few days? A flirty glance here, a superficial conversation there, but scratch the surface and that person turned into someone else. Spend a few days passing judgement and move on. He wondered if he was missing something, if the habit of making temporary lovers clouded his insight. Why was this so much easier for Stephanie? Because she was a woman? Rolly knew other men who were in the same situation, house husbands who stayed home while wives moved around. Even those men had extended relationships, usually with Stephanie. Must be a personal flaw. He was screwed up and there was no fixing it.

They had been married 119 years with only one child, as required by the Population Protection Act. How long were two people expected to be bonded together? Vows of loving each other forever were outdated. But Rolly meant it when he said "to death do us part" and could not imagine being divorced any more than trying to be monogamous again.

He supposed this was a consequence of having the libido of a twenty-one year old. Perpetual horniness. No User had to endure the decreasing passion of old age, and the "settling in" of a long relationship. Biological imperative ruled their coupling. At least it made a good excuse.

About the only drawback to a parade of lovers was the snooping. As if sleeping over gave someone permission ransack your cupboards. In the beginning Stephanie would rant when she came home and found her kitchen rearranged. Rolly would remind her she was doing the same in someone else's house, and she would go into her bedroom and rant there instead. The kitchen had become useless anyway. The fridge held only two cases of Rolly's favorite soda. All his meals were drive-thru or delivery.

The car pulled itself into the garage and parked, the door came down on cue. A few leaves blew in before it made to the bottom. At 1200 square feet the house was small; when they bought it the plan was to move to a bigger place when their careers took off and the family grew. Then the world changed, the population exploded and 1200 square feet became extravagant.

As the city expanded Rolly watched his neighborhood densify. Land values skyrocketed, the money too enticing for his neighbors. They sold and developers built three houses where one had stood before. Rolly and Stephanie made a fateful decision: stay put and pay off the mortgage. Compared to eternity, thirty years was nothing.

When a few extra houses weren't enough, the developers came again and replaced them with apartment buildings. The value of their property, with its deep backyard, shot into the stratosphere. Offers were made, some generous, others an insult. Rolly asked a counselor to calculate how much asset value they would need to retire. He took this to the developers who refused to get near it. So Rolly and Stephanie waited, assuming their property value would continue to rise and in a few years put them in retirement. And it did. But The Number went up as well, always just out of reach.

Rolly's house looked like a hermit shack sitting at the bottom of an aluminum and glass canyon. The property now worth around fifty times what they paid for it. He felt like the stubborn old coot refusing to step aside as progress came barreling through. Sometimes, when he was outside, he would hear a disembodied voice yell "Old fart!"

Rolly opened the door to the house (the knob recognized his handprint) and the nearest monitor greeted him.

"Hello Mr. Smalls. Welcome home. How was your day?" Onscreen was the face of a chiseled male model with a crewcut and deep voice. Stephanie's favorite personality.

This monitor was part of the ECC--Entertainment and Communication Center. One big monitor in the living room and many smaller ones throughout the house. Every room had a monitor. The ECC maintained all the appliances, took phone calls (voice and video), accessed the internet, the satellite, stored and played back movies and shows and family pictures. Every byte of digital information that came into and left the house passed through the ECC.

The main screen, taking up more than half of one wall in the living room, was off. Knowing he was home it should be showing his favorite news channel.

"Turn on the television."

"I'm sorry Rolly, it's not responding." He hated when the machine called him by his first name.

"Sean, turn on the television."

"Uh, not happenin' man. It's like, passed out or somethin'."

Something was wrong. Rolly walked to the living room and touched a button on the remote. The room filled with bluish light. One of Stephanie's decorating shows. Now he'd have to change the channel too. What a pain.

Stephanie would say *Why don't you get a new one?* Her usual response whenever he complained about their appliances. *Prices have come down and screens have gotten bigger. We can get a new one for the same price as the old and it will fill the entire wall.* But Rolly didn't want to spend the money. He hadn't bought anything up-to-date in years, and only when he absolutely had to.

Rolly changed channels and was assaulted by the flashing split second images of a commercial.

"Hey! You!" the tv yelled. "You want to drive this car?" A red sports car flashed by. "Own this boat?" A cabin cruiser cutting through the water at top speed. "You want out of the rat race?" Obligatory caged rat on an exercise wheel. "You want to retire?" Sudden cut to a quiet old man in a creaky rocking chair. "Is that number on your TS5 holding you back?" Office drone, head in hands, TS5 form on the desk, his shockingly low productivity rating circled in red. "You need RocketRed!" a red and black can zoomed into view, "the productivity drink for the serious future retiree. Our special formulation works with your nanobots to supercharge energy and stamina, making you more focused and productive." Montage of scenes as man drinks

RocketRed and becomes a happy, energetic worker. As he strides confidently through the office female coworkers turn to look and lick their lips. "Drink just two fifty ounce cans a day and you'll be enjoying the retirement you've always wanted in no time." Man on screen shakes hands with balding Corporament official and drives off in the red car.

A plethora of beaten to death cliches. Another commercial starts. "Sean, is there a news channel that's actually showing news?"

"Scanning dude." The tv ran through fifty-three different news channels in less than a second. "Sorry man, they're into commercials big time."

"Mute it, until the commercials are over."

"Awesome! Consider it done *Mr*. Smalls."

Rolly hung his coat in the closet, left his shoes in the shoe rack, and emptied his pockets on the dresser in his bedroom. Stephanie was in the house somewhere, why else would the decorating show be on? She would show when she was ready.

He went back to the dining table, in full view of the television, set out his boxes of food, sat down and started twirling beef lo mein on a fork.

On the news an old downtown hotel was burning. Rolly said "Put it on 3D." Projectors in the four top corners fired up. A solid, miniature image appeared in the middle of the living room. Firemen on tall bucket ladders sprayed water onto a square brick building with ornate window arches and iron-railed balconies. Flames poured out of the top floors, so real Rolly thought he could feel heat. The camera slowly circled, attached to a hovering drone. The roof collapsed and more orange flames shot up, lighting Rolly's ceiling and causing a moment of thoughtless panic as he imagined his house catching fire.

"TV off," Stephanie said, as she sat across from Rolly.

Curly blonde hair and brown eyes. A bright smile with dimples when she was happy, a dark scowl when she was angry, and everything in between. Stephanie was not fat, but insisted she was, her almost-an-hourglass figure always stood straight and tall, though four inches shorter than Rolly.

Rolly considered Stephanie a beautiful woman and told her so, but she did not share his belief. Photos made her look puffy with shiny red cheeks. Stephanie looked her best in the true light of day, when you could see all of her and not an inferior two dimensional photo.

Despite her negative body image she did not lack confidence. This was her most attractive quality. She had been a nurse when they married. After EverLife decimated the medical profession, Stephanie announced she would be changing careers. She went back to school and earned a degree in business administration. Within a month of graduation she had a job with Nyros (New You Robotic Outpatient Surgery), one of the few places that still valued medical experience, and quickly rose to a regional management position. She never asked, she simply went and did it. Rolly envied that kind of assertiveness.

"Hello Steph. How are you?"

"I'm fine. How's work treating you?" Their pleasantries were strained, uttered with mock happiness.

"Oh, you know, can't complain but I still hate it. Is this our annual retirement meeting?"

"Yes it is. And you know what I'm going to say."

"About what happened at Paragon...I know it doesn't look good and I'm sorry."

"Don't worry about it."

"Well I'm worried. The Thought Police are after me."

"They won't do anything. They just like to scare people."

Rolly was not expecting this. "But they'll screw up retirement."

"Think you're the first person to lose it? You're a newbie, they like scaring newbies. No one's going to kill your retirement over this. If you did the same thing next year...maybe yeah, you'd be in trouble. Now it doesn't matter."

The conversation paused. Rolly really wanted to know what she saw in George Willicker, her recent bedmate. A little taller than Rolly, thin as a razor, kind of a wimp. But they agreed never to discuss lovers.

"So what's your Reckoning?"

Rolly froze. Apparently she had watched the video but not listened to it.

"Same as last year."

"What!" She sat straight up. "How? That never happens!"

"Why do you think I lost it?"

"What'd you do wrong?"

"I don't know. Worked my ass off twelve hours a day, six days a week. Worked a few Sundays too."

"Spend too much money? Screw around at work? This isn't supposed to happen."

"Guess I'm lucky."

"You have to call this time."

"I can't. You know why."

"Bullshit. You're making excuses."

"It was a gift."

"It was a loan."

"I don't remember talking about what it was."

"Your HearSay would remember. Why don't you ask it."

"That conversation got erased when it crashed in '26. You know that." This was not true.

"He's your son and he owes you money."

"I can't ask him because it was a gift."

"You want to spend the rest of your life yelling at retirement counselors? That's pathetic."

"That's cutting low."

She raised her voice. "This is the one thing, no, the only thing you can do to make retirement happen and you won't because of some stupid male pride thing. And now your Reckoning is going backwards!"

"It didn't go backwards. It stayed the same."

"Same difference!"

"It's been too long. He doesn't think about it and if it was a loan he would have paid it back."

"How do you know?"

"Because he's my son and that's what I would do."

"Oh, you're so honorable you pay back all your debts?"

Rolly did not like the insinuation. "That is exactly what I'm saying."

"What about your debt to me? I've been waiting to retire for a hundred and *twenty* years! My Productivity has been in the 98th percentile for eighty years. I only had one child so it wouldn't hurt our chances. You remember when I wanted a big family? I've been making sacrifices and saving money and doing my part and the only thing that's holding me back is you."

"You changed jobs. Your Length of Service isn't as good."

"You gave away half our life savings! And won't do anything to get it back."

"I can't. It's too late."

Stephanie rubbed her hands over her face in exasperation. "God you're dense. What the hell is going on? Would you be happier as a transient? Is that what this is about? You want to go live outside the city? Plant gardens and rummage through dumpsters? You have some kind freaky death wish?"

"Christ, I want to retire even more than you. I hate my fucking job."

"Then call him."

"I can't call him."

"You owe me."

Rolly hung his head. "All right. Fine. I'll do it. But nothing is gonna change."

"It's a start. Better than nothing." Stephanie stood up, went to the closet and put on her coat. "I'm spending the night at George's house. Don't wait. Call now. New Year's is only a few weeks away."

6

Max's War

Max hated Rolly and Rolly had no idea why.

Hate was probably too strong a word. The two of them hadn't spoken in decades, most news coming by way of Stephanie, who would post information on her social site and Rolly would find out when he bothered to look, having to word search his wife's website to find the history of his son's life.

The last direct contact between father and son had been thirty-three years ago, at Max's seventy-fifth birthday party. Rolly was excited to see his son and hoped the two of them could sit and talk. Max spent most of his time with old friends--shaking hands and slapping backs and smiling-- but with Rolly was close-lipped and barely tolerant. Rolly felt like an unwelcome ghost. He left early.

Friends were fluid in the EverLife world. Friendships could be long lasting, but they weren't eternal. Most were fleeting, some lasted thirty or forty years, but even the good, reliable friends eventually drifted away. Max was seeing old friends in the truest sense of the word.

In the ensuing years Rolly's attempts to contact Max were stonewalled by the "thugs and mercenary secretaries" that surrounded his son. Max made it clear he did not want to talk to Rolly. Rolly gave up trying. Now every bit of news Stephanie shared was like an insult, stinging because it came second hand. Rolly spent years being angry, ignoring Stephanie's posts, eventually checking in from a lingering sense of fatherly duty, the resentment slowly fading.

Maybe Max's animosity had faded as well.

Why did Max feel this way? His childhood had been happy, despite the massive cultural changes. EverLife and its aftermath were in full swing when Max came along. Out in the world people were becoming immortal and celebrating, overpopulating, fighting wars, and dying for the usual stupid reasons. Inside their home Stephanie and Rolly sheltered Max as best they could, trying to keep his childhood stable.

Had they been too protective? Was the shock of the real world too much? No, that didn't make sense. Even as a boy Max had an infectious belief in himself, drawing other children like moths, making them followers in any scheme. Self-confidence was as natural to him as breathing and he never lost it, despite some failures, through his teenage years and into adulthood, where he literally changed the way the world worked.

Max invented the Tactile Holographic Interface, the standard interface for every computer and visual electronic device on the entire planet. Rolly's job would have been ten times harder without it.

The THI allowed users to handle three dimensional holographic projections. The system could fill the top of a desk, an entire room or the few inches in front of a HearSay interface. That file folder icon suspended in midair could be grabbed, opened and manipulated by hand. Read a book as if holding a hardcover edition, alter pictures, make movies, sculptures, design parts for any device and put them together, whatever the programming allowed, a user could do by hand, bypassing the clunky keyboard and mouse.

While the THI's ability to respond to human touch was amazing its name was a misnomer; it could not give substance to the images and therefore no sense of touch, only an illusion the user interpreted as touch. There was nothing "tactile" about it.

(Traditional touch screens never went away, mainly for privacy reasons. Holograms made spectacular displays no matter what they were projecting.)

For many years a holographic interface had been the holy grail of computing. Quartal Inc., the computer maker, was working on it, the HearSay company was working on it, the one remaining movie studio, hobbyists and dreamers all around the world. Thousands of engineers and billions of dollars of development money, and no one could find the answer.

But Max did, so obvious and easily dismissed. He told Rolly the engineers were looking at the light, they weren't thinking of the shadows. He mentioned dark matter but most of the concepts went over Rolly's head. Max showed him an early crude prototype and Rolly's heart stopped. It had the power of simplicity, amazingly easy to use and intuitively clean. If the kid could do this with a few taped together components, what couldn't he do? Max asked for money to start his own company and Rolly gave it to him a few days later on his son's birthday. He moved it without talking to Stephanie, assuming she would be happy to support their son.

Her reaction was anything but supportive. When he told her--after raving about how brilliant their son was, how amazing his invention, and offhandedly, how he had given the boy half their savings--she went from proud to angry in the time it took to slam down a hairbrush. In public she would become the doting mother, bragging about her bright and handsome child, but that first night she was yelling and pointing a maroon fingernail saying "I would divorce you if it didn't mean another fifty years of hard labor."

This was a shock. Rolly thought their marriage stable, a little bland and routine but reliable. In hindsight, it should have been the first hint of Stephanie's unhappiness.

Max started THI Incorporated with some friends and put together a polished prototype. Not yet ready for mass consumption, but it worked. Rolly was relieved, thinking *Yeah, the kid did it again, he'll pay me back in no time.*

The company failed two months later. Machinery was purchased, factories rented, workers hired. Max and his friends could not settle on how to market and protect what was sure to be the next great invention. Max wanted full credit, a sore point with the others. Discussions turned to arguing, then accusations, and two of the more thin-skinned friends took their money and left. Max made a valiant effort to keep the company going but creditors demanded payment and by Corporament rules they were allowed to take any assets equal in value to the money owed. Nothing was left to build product with--no materials, no machinery. Rolly's money was gone.

His invention in jeopardy (one of his "friends" was already trying to sell the idea to Quartal) Max went into overdrive and in days found new investors and started a new company he named Holomax. Rolly didn't know these new investors; Max never asked him for more money. Before anyone could turn around Max was showing off his machine on one of the major tech channels.

What did Max do to make this happen, and so quickly?

The smartest thing Max did was put his name and face next to the THI, making them synonymous. An immeasurable help in the parade of lawsuits that followed.

Quartal tried to claim the THI as their own, arguing that the sheer amount of resources they put into the concept and the pervasiveness of social interconnectivity meant Max had to have known about their research and therefore built on their work. How could one man create a device a hundred thousand engineers couldn't? They ridiculed Max as if he were delusional, but it was a flimsy tactic. Max fought the long battle, for decades, and so did Quartal. The THI was a massive success and the profits fueled Max's defense, but it was not enough. Quartal's pockets were too deep. It ended the way business disputes usually do: the larger company bought the smaller one for an undisclosed sum of money.

Max ceased being the face of the THI and his fame faded into lost memories. Rolly's notoriety as the father of the inventor of the THI passed more quickly. If he wanted to brag, he had to explain who he was and who his son was, which was embarrassing. The name "Max Smalls" became a trivia game answer that tripped up nearly everyone.

These days Max was wealthy but still worked for Quartal making mods and themes for the THI, superficial ways to change how it looked, not how it functioned. Max never left for a different company, or tried to start another of his own. He seemed content to be an employee. That was how Stephanie phrased it. Rolly thought it sounded like surrender.

Time heals all wounds. Experience mellows the soul. Platitudes Rolly hoped were true. Max had a comfortable life, no more business to worry about, maybe he would be more approachable. He couldn't put this off any longer. A month from now would be too late.

"Sean, call Max Smalls."

"Righto."

———————

From his belt clip Rolly pulled out the HearSay interface, carefully unfolded its screen supports to the side, pulled out the telescoping mast, unrolled the screen and hooked it to the top. A locking mechanism kept the mast from collapsing, but it was wearing out. Sometimes the screen would slowly shrink, unnoticed until the caller's face was cutoff. He set it at eye-level so he could be face-to-face with Max.

The HearSay connected immediately; a man with a rough unsmiling face answered.

"Can I help you?" Rolly's cheap screen sometimes distorted facial features but this man looked unusually large. A perfectly squared crewcut gave him a commanding presence.

"I want to speak to Max Smalls."

"Who is calling?" His identity would have been confirmed by the security programs attached to every face call. Being asked this was an insult.

"His father, Rolly Smalls."

The man leaned in, his face filling the entire screen. If he were trying to intimidate it failed. Rolly kept the 3D turned off because it ran down the battery.

"Just a moment." The ugly man put Rolly on hold.

"Hello Rolly." No Hi Dad, How are you, straight to the point. Still the fresh faced twenty year old. His child. Who called him by his first name.

"Hi Max. How are you?"

"I'm fine." No smile, no frown, just the bland patience of someone waiting for an unpleasantness to be over.

"It's been a long time. What's going on? What are you up to?"

"Not much."

"How's work? Created anything spectacular lately? Some new secret mod you're working on?"

"No."

"How's your home life? Met anyone worth keeping? Gonna make me a grandfather someday?"

"The world is crowded enough already."

The usual pleasantries weren't working. Rolly decided to say what was on his mind, be honest, and hope Max would do the same.

"I think you're taking this call because your Mother told you to."

"She asked me to take it, yes."

"What happened, Max? You used to be full of energy. Commanded a room when you walked in. Now you're sitting there like a stone. What gives?"

Max's brows creased. "What gives? Fifty years of litigation. Thirty-three years of employment drudgery. Despite my best efforts, I ended up just like you *Dad*."

Speaking of stone, Rolly felt like he had just been hit by one.

"You're not like me. You have money. You're successful. Sold your company and made billions." An afterthought, squeezing it in before Max could reply, "And I helped you get there."

"All the money in the world won't get me retired. I need a work history like everyone else."

"But that money lets you do anything."

"Yes, I can go and do anything. But I lose work time. And Productivity."

"All that time you spent building your company. It has to count."

"I was self-employed, by Corporament standards. They only consider Length of Service if you work for a fully accredited company that can report parameter fulfillment. They never recognized Holomax. Said they never would, no matter how successful I was."

"Use your money. Go start another company."

Now Max was frustrated. "The Corporament won't let me. The member companies are too powerful. They think they're the only ones who know how to make money. To them a new company is an absurd idea."

"You're trying to retire too," Rolly said, finally understanding what Max had been saying all along. "What about the money you owe me?" he blurted out and immediately regretted it.

"I don't owe you anything. That money was a gift."

"It helped start your business. A very successful business."

"That money went into THI which folded before it got started. You invested in a failed business. That was the chance you took."

"I loaned you half our retirement. And now we're stuck."

"Oh well. Nothing I can do about that."

Max wasn't a stone, he was a wall. "I don't know why you dislike me Max, but if you won't do it for me then do it for your mother."

"She's getting along fine."

"She wants to retire just as much as you and I."

Max paused and thought about this. "She'll make it. Eventually."

"That's harsh. When you have so much to give."

"You want to know why I can't stand you?" Abruptly changing the subject. Max showing his impatience.

Rolly did want to know, but not this way, not from Max himself. "Okay," he said reluctantly.

"You're a loser. Working all the time, doing what you're told. Never trying to be anything better. How could someone like me come from you? You were at every one of my trials. My nothing father mocking me like a vision of a backwards future. Did it make you happy to see me dragged down to your level? 'Someday you'll be just like your father.' It's the only curse that works. Here I am Dad, drudging through life just like you. Hope you're happy."

They stared at each other across a thousand miles of bouncing wireless signals. The picture was crisp and detailed in spite of the cheap monitor. Rolly really looked at his son and saw the drooping eyelids and the creases around his mouth. This was not a cool and controlled man, this was a beaten man, who every day had to face the criminals who robbed him and call them sir.

"Max, I'm--"

"Goodbye Rolly."

The screen went dark.

Two knocks on the door; Stephanie stepped in without waiting. Rolly stared at the blank interface.

"How'd it go?"

"Not so good."

"Damn him. What is it between the two of you?"

"He thinks I'm a loser." He told Stephanie what Max said.

"You are so different from each other."

"Why don't you call. Maybe he'll listen to you."

"We don't talk as much as you think. Mostly texts and emails. Don't give up. He talked to you today, he'll talk to you again."

"He made it pretty clear we're done."

"Max just said more to you in ten minutes than he has in fifty years."

"It wasn't anything good."

"Give him time to cool off."

"Time to cool off? That's a hundred years of resentment talking. He's not going to let it go overnight."

"No one stays mad forever. The fact is you made progress. Give him a week and try again."

"Okay fine. Suzi at work recommended some guy calls himself a retirement coach. Guess I'll give that a try."

Stephanie frowned. "Half those people are scam artists and the other half are liars."

"Got a better idea?"

She didn't. "Just don't use it as an excuse not to call Max again."

That night, when Rolly was on the verge of sleep, the door opened. Stephanie came in and slipped under the sheets. On her side, back to him, wearing panties and a tee shirt. Without thinking he rolled over and laid his forearm in the comfortable curve of her waist. Rolly exhaled and fell asleep. They stayed that way until the next workday dawned.

7

The Secret Parameter

Rolly stopped on the sidewalk outside the office of Gordon O'Leary, Retirement Coach. One of a series of tall thin row buildings sandwiched between a bank office and a Nyros franchise. It would have blended perfectly but for the screaming orange letters Gordon used to display his name.

Small waiting area, eight metal and plastic chairs, two people already seated. A woman with long pink fingernails and too much makeup flipping through a magazine, and a man in biker's leathers, boots to jacket with chrome chains, also reading a magazine.

Rolly confirmed his appointment with the receptionist and sat as far away from the others as possible.

On the wall next to the receptionist was a large bronze plaque titled "Our Retirees" in an English scroll font. Below that were four smaller, rectangular plaques with engraved names and many empty spaces.

The door behind the receptionist opened and a man stepped out. "Roland Smalls?"

Rolly stood up. Ms. Makeup and Mr. Leather continued flipping and slouching.

"Hello Roland. How are you today?"

"I'm fine. Please call me Rolly."

"I like that name. I'm Gordon O'Leary. Follow me."

O'Leary was a stocky man in a light gray suit that hung on him like a set of window drapes. Dirty blonde hair and a mustache and beard to match. His hair was cut short on the sides, almost to the stubble, but longer and bushy on top, as if he were wearing a poor fitting hairpiece. A fashionable trim, but Gordon couldn't quite pull it off, looking rumpled, unrefined, and cheap no matter how hard he tried. As with any new acquaintance Rolly wondered about O'Leary's true age.

Gordon closed the office door and sat behind a cluttered desk with a flip up monitor. Rolly sat in an old wooden chair with a carved seat. All the finish had worn off but the wood was thick and sturdy; it would take an earthquake to destroy the thing.

"You get the lucky chair," Gordon said. "Bought it at a garage sale right after EverLife. Had it ever since. It's made some of my clients very happy."

"Well I hope it works today."

"Business out of the way first. You've seen my fees? Do you know which plan you'd like to go with?"

"They're a little high. How can I be sure I'll get my money's worth?"

"Well, the ultimate would be to get you retired. Odds are that won't happen so the next best thing is to get you closer. Depending on the plan I guarantee at least a five point improvement in your Reckoning. I can do this because I know the secret parameter."

"I've heard about that. Not sure I believe it's true."

"Oh it is most definitely true. I've seen it work again and again."

"But you've only had four actual retirees."

"That's all I can legally claim. The rules are pretty strict about these things. I was on retainer for those four when they made retirement. But there's hundreds more that got a big boost from working with me and went on to retire."

"They weren't your clients when they retired?"

"They were satisfied with what they achieved and felt empowered to work on their own." Said with a hint of annoyance.

"None of them contracted with a different specialist?"

"Not that I know of."

"If you are so successful why would they leave?"

"It's hard making money in this business, especially when everyone thinks they need to save every quarter for retirement. Keeping steady clients is always a challenge."

"Aren't you being taken advantage of? They get your advice and go retire with some other specialist."

"I get satisfaction knowing I helped them. I think of it as setting them on the right path."

"Do you get anything if I retire? A bonus?"

"There is a stipulation that if retirement is achieved a small fee is part of the renumeration. Five per cent of your total net worth."

"Total net worth? It's not based on how much I pay you?"

"No, and it's perfectly legal."

"That's a big chunk of my retirement."

"It's not due until after you retire. By then the Corporament will have your assets and you won't be paying me, they will."

Rolly did not like the sound of this, it seemed too easy, too cut and dried. Mr. O'Leary was becoming shadier by the second.

"How long have you been in business?"

"Since 2113, thirty four years."

"How many clients have you had?"

"Don't know the exact number. I believe it's around nine thousand."

"Nine thousand clients and only four retirees."

"It's better than it sounds. Above the average actually. I know plenty of specialists with only one or two retirees, and many who haven't found any."

"You guarantee a five point gain in my Reckoning. What if it only goes up three points?"

"Trust me, I will work very hard to earn those five points. But if for some reason we fall short, I will refund your money."

"Five points isn't enough to help me retire."

"True, but how long would it take to make that gain on your own?" Mr. O'Leary consulted his monitor. "Your average Reckoning increase is point six one eight. The Number usually increases somewhere between point seven five and point nine eight. You're digging a hole, Mr. Smalls. At this rate you'll never retire. I can help you get ahead of the yearly increase instead of falling behind."

That was tempting. A little ahead would feel like an accomplishment. O'Leary wasn't promising the world, only a modest increase. He wasn't slick but did seem to know what he was doing.

"What's the secret parameter?"

"Can't tell you. Only when you're an official client."

"It's not spending is it? That's what I keep hearing."

"You'll have to pay me if you want to find out."

Rolly hesitated, weighing the pros and cons. Was a five point gain worth an angry tirade from Stephanie? On the other hand, she was really on his case this year. Five points would be better than standing still. If O'Leary failed--and Rolly thought it was a lot to guarantee--the money would come back. Rolly figured the odds were in his favor.

"Okay, let's try your basic plan."

"Good. I think you'll be happy with the results." Gordon sat forward and began typing on his desktop. A moment later Sean spoke up.

"So Rolly my man, there's this dude name of Gordon O'Leary who wants to take money from your main savings account. You wanna let him do this deed?"

"Yes."

"You got it. Sending the dough now. Your new balance is-"

"Don't tell me."

"'kay."

Gordon watched his screen, then smiled. "We're all set. Thank you Mr. Smalls. By paying me you've already helped yourself."

"Don't say it." Rolly closed his eyes.

"It's true, the more you spend the better your Reckoning will be." Rolly could not see Gordon but it sounded like he was smiling.

"The money you just spent will earn at least one more point. Now there's not much we can do about the lack of funds in savings--"

"Except take more of it."

"--but we can squeeze a little more out of the variable parameters. The main thing will be finding the spending balance."

"Spending balance?"

"My own word for it. Sums up what I do pretty well."

"Like a savings balance?"

"No, this isn't about how much money you have or don't have, it's about how much you spend in relation to how much you've saved."

"I don't understand."

"There is an optimal number for how much you should spend based on how much you've saved. The more money saved the more you can spend. But you have to be careful not to spend too much, which negatively affects debt. Records show you maintain a debt, which is a good thing."

"I thought that was bad. I always try to get rid of debt."

"No, no you want debt, helps your Reckoning. Tells them you're spending like you should."

"Right. You're going to have to work real hard to convince me this isn't another load of bullshit."

Gordon was insulted. "The best evidence is my own experience. I've seen this work many times. Do you doubt my word?"

"I doubt a secret parameter exists at all. What would be the point? There's already seven ways to fail. Why add more?"

"I don't know why. It's not my job to read minds. I can only speculate."

Rolly watched O'Leary, looking for any sign he might be lying. The man sat calmly, serious and still, betraying nothing.

"Okay, tell me. Why do they need a secret parameter?"

Gordon sat forward; he liked talking about this. "Think about how retirement is structured. It's this weird mixture of social responsibility and financial responsibility. You have to be married but only once. You have to have children, but as few as possible. And a stable job, and good financial management skills. You have to prove you're a reliable member of society. Spending fits right in. Everything we do drives the economy and the Corporament loves a prosperous economy. What better way to prove you're a fine upstanding citizen than spending money?"

"No one tracks this, it's not part of The Number."

"Of course you don't see it, they don't want you to. But every time you swipe a MiniVault or order online it's tracked and recorded. They know instantly how much you've spent, how it relates to your savings, whether it's below or above the spending balance. If you're over and stay over too long, they might judge you incompetent and keep you from retiring. If you save too much you're not contributing to the economy and they'll keep you working until you spend more."

"I've spent enough. My house is full of useless stuff."

"Actually, you haven't. My own custom designed software calculates your spending balance. You need to spend twenty-six percent more."

"Can you give me a number, a goal I can shoot for?"

"Five hundred forty-two thousand three hundred and fifty seven dollars."

"Christ! That's more than I make in a year!"

"Remember it's already halfway through November. You've only got six weeks to spend."

"I'd be throwing it away. Isn't there a better way to do this?"

"You can't be any more married than you already are and you can't return your child. Every time you go to work your Reckoning improves a little. Every hour at work makes you a little more productive. Getting rid of debt will get you a point or two, maybe, but it really counts for little compared to your income/savings ratio. Which is surprising."

"Why's that?"

"Your savings is much less than normal. I've helped many couples from your generation and savings is usually their biggest asset. You have much less and it doesn't appear in your physical assets or your spending history."

"You have access to that?"

"Matter of public record."

Rolly did not know this. "I thought that was confidential, between me and my bank."

"Was until twelve years ago. They changed the rules, quietly, didn't make it public. Thought it would be safer. Makes my a lot job easier. I know every company wanted the info so they could find out what their employees were up to. But yeah, I know. So does everyone else."

Rolly was shocked. Was his privacy completely gone? "But can you prove this 'spending balance' is real and it's connected to The Number?"

"You just have to trust me Mr. Smalls."

"I need time to think about this."

"Okay, but my guarantee only extends to the door of this office. Change your mind now and I'll refund your money. Walk away and you get nothing back."

"You didn't tell me this up front."

"It's in the fine print."

"What fine print?"

"On the sign, in the reception area."

Rolly tried to remember a sign and could only recall the names of retirees, then remembered the receptionist and a little plastic sign with tiny letters sitting on her desk. The bastard.

"Your five point guarantee still applies?"

"Absolutely."

"You have only six weeks to make my Reckoning go up."

"Contingent on you following my instructions. You have contracted my services but this is a partnership. I can't make five points magically appear. You have to help."

"By spending nearly six hundred thousand dollars of my savings."

"Don't think you can get your money back by refusing to spend. You've already paid me and that is a tacit agreement to my contract."

Cornered again, goddamn it. Why was this always happening? "It's still cheaper to pay your fee and not do the spending."

"True. But you won't do that because you're desperate, like every other person in this country. You've worked the same job with the same company and been married to the same wife for too long. Retirement is your way out and you want it too badly. You'll do it. The only question is how far you'll go."

Rolly sat up and leaned forward quickly. "I expect you to bust your ass and make sure I get those five points."

"On my honor, I will work as hard as I can." Rolly stood up to leave; Gordon stuck out his hand to shake. Rolly took it reluctantly.

Rolly opened the door and Gordon O'Leary escorted him out. Mr. Leather stopped reading and looked Rolly in the eye. The man had the bearing of a telephone pole even while lounging. Dark weathered skin and blue eyes, heavy black boots propped up as if he were in a comfortable recliner. On the sidewalk Rolly glanced back. Mr. Leather was still watching.

Rolly had the feeling he'd just made a terrible mistake.

8

Belated

Stephanie and Rolly faced off across the holoroom on opposing couches, Stephanie with crossed legs and arms folded. Rolly bent forward, head down, elbows on knees, fingers laced together. She was not happy. Rolly had just finished saying how much Gordon O'Leary wanted him to spend.

"At least you didn't have another screaming fit and tear his head off."

The holoroom was windowless but open to the dining room and sunken a foot lower. Two white leather armchairs and matching couches formed a horseshoe facing the monitor wall. The center of the room was wide and empty for holographic projections. The holoroom was the most comfortable neutral space in the house and the preferred spot for serious discussions.

"O'Leary's a slick operator. But an extra five points will make a big difference."

"Not this year, no matter how much you spend."

"It'll push my Reckoning ahead."

"For how long? His guarantee only holds for this year, not ten years down the road."

"Better than digging a hole."

"What about Max? Have you talked to him again?"

"I thought you were going to talk to him."

"I did. It was a nice conversation."

"That's it? A nice conversation? Did you ask for the money back?"

"No, he was expecting me to, but I didn't."

"So you called to mess with his head?"

"I called to ask how he was and to catch up and see how he was doing."

"I don't talk to Max for years and when I do I bring up the money issue. But when you talk to him all you do is shoot the breeze and that's okay?"

"Things like this take time. You can't just call and start asking for money. You act like a brick sometimes, you know? All dense and blunt and stuck. Try to be more subtle. Use a little tact and finesse."

"Tact and finesse won't cut it. Max made it clear he hates me."

"Oh stop it. He doesn't hate you. It ever occur to you Max has a different view of things?"

"How different could it be?"

"Your son invented a new interface and started his own company. Nobody's done that in a hundred years."

"He changed the world."

"Yes he did, and he paid the price. All the lawsuits and countersuits, the rumors--"

"I know all that."

"You never knew how bad it was. They overwhelmed him. More lawsuits than twenty lawyers could keep up with, one after the other. They spread rumors, nasty media lies made up to embarrass him. And always under constant Corporament scrutiny. They would find problems at THI and use it as an excuse to levy fines. At one point he was paying out a million dollars every day. Friends and lovers stayed away, afraid to be seen with him. You remember his seventy-fifth birthday? He was in negotiations to sell the company so the Corporament finally backed off. He got to see so many old friends that day; it was the happiest I think I've ever seen him. You left early."

"I tried to talk to him. He wanted nothing to do with me."

"He was busy with other people. You're not the center of his life."

Rolly looked down at the floor.

Stephanie continued. "Max is full of pride. Like his father. And like every man he takes it too far and ends up disappointed. So he blames you for everything that went wrong, looks down on you, cuts you out of his life. Once Max believed he would be rich and popular and master of his destiny. He had a long way to fall."

"He's still a success. He sold Holomax and made a fortune."

"They forced him to sell it."

"He always has us, his family."

"Tell him that. Maybe he'll come around."

A dozen holographic images hovered around Rolly's head--faces, torsos, arms, furniture, plants, fruit baskets, picket fences--waiting to be assembled into a dire warning about the dangers of the seemingly harmless soup spoon. Rolly was lost in thought, closing in on the "reflection limit point" where the computer would stop giving him free time and start subtracting Productivity. He was trying to play out a conversation with Max that would end happily but his imagination wasn't cooperating.

Every time Rolly sat down at a computer or played a game it reminded him of his son. Sometimes he smiled with pride, sometimes he cursed. For all its brilliance the THI could feel like a cage.

The Productivity alarm chimed and brought Rolly back to reality. On screen, a timer spun backwards in negative numbers. Five minutes of

Productivity gone. He sat up and with both hands, grabbed a female face, turning it side to side, and started molding. The timer began moving in the other direction. Rolly used his fingers to dimple and pull and gather, and carving tools to cut and discard, and a wireless stylus and brushes to draw brow lines and wrinkles. This character was Korean, dressed in casual clothes, at home setting the table for dinner. The evil spoon was already on the kitschy metal table, waiting to accidentally poke her eye out. Rolly had yet to work out how this was going to happen, a little creative camera work he thought. At the moment he was trying to find the right shape for her face. Too perfect and the audience might not sympathize. Too round and they would think her fat.

Work, work, work. That's all he did. Trying to get ahead, some camera or computer program always snooping over his shoulder, recording everything. Take five minutes to daydream and a happy chime forced him back to productive behavior. It was all so pleasant and oppressive. Rolly was tired of being someone's surveillance project. He wanted out. He put down the tools leaving the Korean woman with impossibly puckered cheeks, dropped his head into his hands and rubbed his eyes. The need to get out was so intense...way past mere desire. He was desperate and knew work would kill him. Not physically, but over time, day-by-day, a slow erosion of his soul. EverLife couldn't save him, only make it worse. He had to change this. Now.

Sometimes the best time to start a conversation is when you aren't ready.

"Sean, call Max."

"Yes my liege."

It took several minutes to get through Max's phalanx of automated answering programs. He watched the floating holograms, half expecting Max to find an excuse to be occupied, but he didn't bother. An assistant named Bruno came on--voice only--and said Max did not want to talk to him. Would he like to leave a message?

"Yes." The line went quiet, then the shrill beep.

"Hi Max, it's your father. You don't know how hard it is to call up your own son and ask for money. Embarrassing actually. I suppose it fits with your opinion of me as a loser. Which I am not, by the way. I work hard and do the best I can. But that doesn't seem to be enough anymore.

"We need the money if we're going to retire. I want to be honest about that. I don't know if it'll put us over but it will sure get us closer. My Reckoning stayed the same, no change from last year. I'm in danger of slipping backwards and I'm really hoping that money will kickstart my chances. Stating the obvious here but it's up to you.

"I was always proud of you Max. A little afraid you'd end up in jail sometimes, but you kept your nose clean. Then your life took off like a race car. Guess it felt like I got left behind. And it seemed like you didn't want me around. So I backed off. Maybe I shouldn't have done that. I don't know. Funny how easy it is to put things out of your mind. For decades.

"Our last conversation didn't go so well but it was great to hear your voice and see you again. Your childhood was so short it seems like a bright light in a long drab existence. I miss you Max. Even if you don't give the money back I wish you would call me. Just to talk. About anything. I won't hold it against you or bug you about it, but I can't promise to never say anything. We've both been alive too long to trust promises. Just don't be like me and clam up. If there's any one thing I'm sure I've taught you it's be better than your old man. Goodbye Max."

Rolly closed the connection with a thumb-on-knuckle press, sat back and thought about what he had said. Did he make things better or worse? No way to know, but he didn't have high hopes. It was honest and that was the best he could do.

"Sean, how long was the call?"

"Counting all the garbage you had to verbally machete through, you were on for sixteen minutes and twenty nine seconds."

He would have to add that onto the end of the day to make up for lost Productivity. Every little bit counted.

9

The Memory Tail

On November 20th, a Sunday, Rolly went shopping. That same morning he transferred the exact amount Gordon O'Leary told him to spend into his debit account, which he accessed with a debit pen. There was no ink in this pen but it did recognize his fingerprints and move money through whatever capture device Rolly was putting his name on. The pen was in his shirt pocket, feeling like a lead weight against his chest.

Sunday was the only day he didn't work. Usually. He tried to reserve it as a mental health day but if his Productivity was down he might go in. He certainly didn't need the time. Length of Service was one of his strong parameters.

He could have stayed home and shopped through the television, checking out multi-dimensional images of merchandise, displayed at ten times actual size, but he wanted out of the house. Stephanie was cleaning and tidying as if she lived there. Her presence felt like an intrusion. Besides, what he really wanted had to be installed at the store.

Unlike other industries retail was not controlled by one big company or even a behind the scenes conglomerate. Fresh Furnishings sold furniture, Leanna's Wardrobe sold women's clothing, Gadget World sold electronics, etc. Why retail never homogenized like every other business Rolly didn't know. The General Business Code, aka the Constitution of the Corporament, somehow prevented it.

Rolly's one stop would be his favorite store, Gadget World. First on his list: a HearSay upgrade.

Crossing the threshold meant walking into a wall of noise generated by myriad electronic devices clamoring for attention, made more tortuous by the glass cases, free standing hanger displays, wire racks, and shelves arranged to prevent a direct route from one part of the store to another. Rolly had to make a near-desperate maze run, backtracking twice, to reach the relative quiet of the HearSays.

Being tiny and inconspicuous made the HearSay a poor candidate for display but that didn't stop Gadget World. In a darkened corner three glass cases showed off every HearSay model with the dramatic lighting normally reserved for jewelry. They looked nearly alike. Rolly had to read the list of features to know which was which.

The HearSay company offered twenty-four different lines of "personal listening assistants," which could be broken down to three basic groupings: mono (single ear) models, stereo (two ear) models, and the super-enhanced versions that took the HearSay to unusual places. Cameras could be placed in the eyes to record video of everything the wearer saw every minute of every day. Following the five senses, flavor readers and projectors could be placed in the mouth, smell gatherers and aerifiers in the nose, and touch sensors anywhere in the body. Anywhere.

Enhancements included sensors that provided a means to control the HearSay without the bothersome gesture recognition software, easy downloading of smells and tastes for sharing on social media sites, streaming real-time sensations from friends, communication with EverLife nanomachines (a standard feature on all but the most basic HearSay model), and of course more memory, more voices, more of anything they could put a price on.

Rolly's current HearSay was a basic mono version. Not the bottom-of-line model; he did have some self-respect. He wanted an upgrade to a stereo model and more memory. During the HearSay's last maintenance check Sean informed him there were only twenty years of memory left. Memory was added by increasing the length of the tail, the metallic string that extended out of the ear canal and behind the ear, as much as two feet long. The extra length was coiled and placed just below the skull on the neck, a status symbol often decorated with tattoos.

Rolly had no interest in the Wild Card line. Too many implants. The thought of a store-trained technician inserting a tiny camera in his eyeball was unnerving. And out of his price range. The memory needed for video capture required a larger, thicker tail be inserted under the skin. Rolly had no desire to undergo major surgery to get the coolest gadget. A small upgrade was all he needed.

He chose one of the higher mid-range models with a coiled tail, high definition sound, 2,000 plus voices, translation programs for one hundred and twenty languages (but no dialects), enough memory for a hundred lifetimes of appointments and conversations, faster search and playback, better voice and video reception, an interface with a larger screen (though not as big as Steve Mann's), and, like every other HearSay, access to every movie, book, television show, magazine, radio broadcast, or internet media ever created. For a small fee. And access charges. And data usage charges. And taxes.

The installer was a woman named Rosemary. She was efficient and nice, business-like and not very talkative. Triangular face, coffee-with-cream colored skin, and three inches taller than Rolly.

Rosemary seated him on a tall chair in a glass booth, upright, back against a clear plastic support. Four oar-like braces, also made from clear plastic (as if that made the process more antiseptic), descended over his head and held it in place. He wasn't comfortable but didn't resist either. It would be over soon. Rosemary sat on his right in a shorter, adjustable chair.

Rolly's stored memories were quickly transferred to the new HearSay. Rosemary began the delicate task of removing his old HearSay. Using a water-based solvent she dissolved the breathable glue that held the device in place. The entire booth rotated to put Rolly's head on a downward angle and keep the solvent from dribbling into his inner ear.

Rosemary applied the solvent to the outer ear and once the glue was gone the HearSay and its short behind-the-ear tail were easily pulled off. She wiped off the residue, cleaned the skin where the new HearSay would be attached, let it dry, and attached the new coil on his neck and new unit inside his ear. Over the new coil she placed a round bandage.

"This fools your body into thinking you have a wound that needs to be healed. The bandage has to stay on for one week. It will itch but don't scratch! After seven days you can take it off and your new memory tail will be under the skin. Your nanobots will remove the dead skin and keep the new skin from turning into scar tissue."

Rosemary ran a tiny wire up and behind the ear where it connected with the lead wire from the HearSay itself. She treated the wires with a silicon gel she said would do the same thing as the bandage, then repeated everything on the left side. The booth moved his head wherever she needed it to be. He relaxed and enjoyed letting the machine do the work for him. The installation took thirty-five minutes.

"Let's give it a try Mr. Smalls. Talk to your HearSay."

"Sean? Are you there?"

"Right, el-dude-o-rini. Wow! New digs!" His voice had a deep echo.

"What's with the echo?"

"It's to show you how wonderful our nice new HearSay is. Wow, I can even talk to you from different places." Sean played with the stereo image in his head. "Like from the back, or the left, or the right, or somewhere in betweeeeeen." He said the last bit with an obnoxious amount of echo and fading, as if he were falling away.

"Turn off the echo Sean, always talk to me from the back center and whisper in my left ear if you have to speak quietly. And don't talk like we're friends."

"'kay." No echo this time.

Rolly told Rosemary, "Everything seems okay."

"Very good. All of your contacts and saved media have been transferred over. If you think something is missing we have backup copies you can reboot from. You can take a shower, clean your ears, all with no worries. It stays permanently attached but if something goes wrong give us a call. The number is programmed into the unit. This is your first stereo unit so the coils will take getting used to. Some people end up removing them. This is not covered under warranty and there is a fee for early coil removal."

"Thank you." Rosemary held the door as Rolly walked out, his shopping not yet done.

The new HearSay was nice, but it was only a fifth of the money he needed to spend. He had one more large purchase to make, which should fill out O'Leary's "spending balance" and relieve him of an ongoing embarrassment. No more watching television on half a wall. It was time to upgrade.

The television department was not what it used to be. The bright screens showing the same video were gone, instead a row of out-of-place doors lined the wall. These doors were made to look like the front doors of residential homes and apartments, complete with seasonal appropriate decorations--wreaths, ornaments and Christmas bells. Sitting areas outside of each door gave customers a place to wait and negotiate: two semi-circular black leather overstuffed couches with a clear glass table between, holding a signature reader.

Rolly felt shunned. By now he should have been accosted by two or three salespeople.

In a nearby sitting area a head popped up, followed by shoulders in a white uniform shirt. The man struggled to extract himself, his leg caught until he managed to wrench it free, accompanied by an audible "Ow!" but not from the man, who tumbled out onto the floor, quickly stood up and ran over to Rolly, hand extended.

"Hello and welcome to Gadget World. How can I help you today?"

The name tag said Kendrick. Kendrick was breathing hard and had a sweaty palm.

"Are you okay?" Other salespeople began to emerge from the sitting area, slowly, getting up off the floor, taking a moment to catch their breath.

"I am fine. Thank you for asking and giving me the honor of serving you. Are you looking for a new television?"

"Yes, I want to replace the wall screen in my house."

"Excellent! How many walls are you using now?"

"One."

"You've picked a great time to upgrade. We have screens from two walls up to six, in the highest resolutions possible, at the lowest prices of the season."

"Six walls?"

"Yes, every wall in your room! For the most immersive experience. If you're on a budget we recommend a minimum of three walls for an acceptable viewing experience."

"The floor and ceiling aren't walls."

"Depends on how you look at them."

"I already have holographic projection. Why would I need two more wall screens?"

"You don't know what you're missing. Follow me."

Kendrick took Rolly to one of the homey-looking doors and held it open. "Step into my parlor," he said in a low voice, trying to be funny.

They were in an empty room about the size of Rolly's living room. The walls, including the floor and ceiling, looked normal.

"Stand at the far end if you will." Rolly did as asked. The lights went off and the screen across from him lit up, playing a montage of movie scenes.

"If you're like most people you have one wall screen," Rolly thought the screen already looked better, "and holographic projectors." The top four corners lit with bright lights and the movie played in ghostly three dimensional roundness in the middle of the room.

"This works well, but watch what happens when we add the walls to the right and left." The room brightened and the 3D characters filled out. "The side walls are not just showing the same thing as the main screen, they are showing the same scene but from the right and left perspectives. A completely different view of the action."

This was nice. The holograms were fuller and more defined, the action not as blurry. "Take a walk around, see what it's like." Rolly did. The pictures on the walls did not line up with the hologram, but seemed to give it more definition, as if the hologram were pulling light out of the pictures, or maybe it was the other way around. The hologram was the center of the experience. As he moved around Rolly's shadow darkened the images.

"Now, look what happens when we add in the fourth wall." More light again, the people running through and shooting guns became a little more defined. As if a door had been shut and the glare removed. "The fourth wall closes the gap, but doesn't make a huge difference. The real change happens when we add in the ceiling." The room blazed into daylight, a blue sky overhead. The abrupt sense of space jarring, as if the roof had been ripped off an airplane. Rolly's shadow disappeared. The characters resolved into near-reality, hair flying, nostrils flaring, blood splattering. He convulsively stepped aside when a bad guy pointed a gun in his direction, a scar running crookedly across the villain's cheek.

"Pretty impressive, huh? If you look down you'll notice that the feet are still a little vague." The feet were shadowy outlines. "If we add in the floor, this goes away."

The scene shifted to a savanna. Rolly was standing near the tree line surrounded by waist high grasses. In the distance on a hill, under a lone tree, two lions were staring him down. A line of people emerged from the forest, dark skinned natives and white adventurers wearing khaki shirts and pith helmets. He stepped up to the path to watch, to see their feet as they passed. Some kind of safari movie, a drama he thought. It looked dated, mid 20th century early cinema, though as crystal clear as any modern movie. They stopped and rested in a clearing of matted grasses and rocks and a stump or two, the natives in bare feet with dry broken skin, the great white hunters in tall laced boots, overdressed for the climate.

Rolly walked around, looking at each one closely. The details were incredibly sharp, no fuzzy halo, the telltale sign of a holoimage. The clarity made it easy to get lost in the movie, if the story didn't ruin it.

The characters argued in the overwrought manner of theater-trained actors. A conflict between the two white hunters over a woman. A native guide pointed to the lions and all romantic rivalries were forgotten as they pulled out two ridiculously large rifles and excitedly went after the lions, who disappeared down the backside of the hill.

The party formed up behind the hunters, two lines of real-looking people walking directly at Rolly. The hunters made no move to go around. Rolly thought he was about to be trampled, while knowing it could not possibly happen, but having his senses warn him otherwise. In spite of himself he held his breath. The holographic people moved through him. Rolly thought he felt a brush of air as each passed.

Kendrick appeared beside Rolly. "Your brain fills in some of the sensation, as if it's really there. Pretty cool isn't it?"

"Yes, it is. It still plays old movies and shows in 2D? The same picture on each wall?"

"Actually it upconverts those old 2D things to full holographic. You can watch black & white twentieth century film noirs or modern pirate dramas in realistic glory."

"How is that possible? There were no surround cameras back then, the really old movies were filmed on a stage. How does the program 'upconvert' to a ceiling that was never there?"

"It extrapolates from other camera angles and other scenes and fills in what should be there. If the film was made on location the system looks for historical pictures and creates the proper setting. It's pretty amazing."

"It can't know everything. There has to be some holes. Anything filmed on a set would have no fourth wall."

"On rare occasions someone has to do some fill-ins. But the really cool thing is live performances. The system creates a unique face for every member of the audience. That's how good it is at creating a fourth wall. You can stand on the stage and see what it's like having ten thousand people watch your every move."

"Can you make them applaud anything you do?"

Kendrick's smile got wider. "Yeah, there's a game for that."

Rolly was being sarcastic but Kendrick was sincere.

"How much is all this?"

"The entire six wall system, plus holographic projectors and 15.3 audiophile perfection surround sound and installation is nine hundred ninety-nine thousand nine hundred and ninety nine dollars and ninety five cents."

"That's too much. How about if we drop the fourth wall and the floor."

"Price goes down two hundred grand."

"Still too much. Without the ceiling?"

"Down another one hundred grand."

Rolly had never been good at haggling, but felt there was more room to move than Kendrick was letting on.

"Kendrick, I have a debit pen in my pocket loaded with money. Cash that goes directly to the store and your commission. No bank fees, no Corporament routing through fifty different agencies, instant money for you. So what kind of deal can you offer me?"

"How much money do you want to spend?"

"Make me an offer first."

"Well...there's not much to work with here, I think maybe we can take ten thousand off."

"Maybe we should talk to your manager."

Kendrick stood still. Rolly decided he must be new at the job, then Kendrick nodded. "I'll be right back."

He returned a minute later with a petite Indian woman named Irina. She had big eyes and big teeth that seemed luminescent. She turned out to be a tough haggler. The two of them went back and forth for fifteen minutes, arguing about the relative value of each component, Rolly trying not to settle for lesser product, the direction Irina was pushing him. She had the advantage of no competition; Gadget World was the only wall screen dealer. Rolly had fast money in his pocket waiting to be scribbled away. Stores loved shoppers like Rolly, his one advantage and the only reason Irina was bothering to talk to him.

Rolly ended up with three walls and a lesser ceiling, a B-stock holographic projector and a 7.5 audio clarity sound system, the cheapest model that could still broadcast on a HearSay channel. He caved on the sound system, figuring its lack of quality would be offset by his new stereo HearSay. What could possibly sound better than music and sound piped directly into your ears?

Irina watched him sign the money away with a satisfied smile. Rolly smiled too, trying to pretend he didn't know she won the better part of the deal. The prices were inflated, Gadget World had used him to unload some damaged and hard-to-sell inventory at a hefty profit. He was a terrible negotiator. Why did he even bother trying? *Look on the bright side, this new system is better than what you have.* He left the store repeating that thought, trying to maintain an air of dignity.

The debit pen still contained a few hundred dollars. On the way home he stopped at Builder Zone and bought a new circular saw and a set of carving tools. He did not go over the limit, leaving a balance of $20.46.

Stephanie met him at the door, smiling as well. She rarely smiled, and then only ironically, but this was genuine.

"I've got great news," she said, practically giddy. "Max is going to pay us back. You don't have to spend that money."

"Oh."

"Aren't you happy? This means we're going to retire!"

"Yeah, absolutely, for sure."

"What's the problem?"

"They're installing the new holo-tv on Thursday. It has three walls and a ceiling."

10

Paying The Math

Rolly called to thank Max and ask why he changed his mind.

"I don't know. Couldn't think of a good reason not to. Guess I said what I needed to say. I've got more than enough money; that wasn't a good excuse anymore. Nothing to prove either. I'm tired of fighting battles all the time. And part of me wants to see you retire to prove it's real."

"But you need the money for your own retirement."

"Considering how much LOS I have to make up, I'll have plenty of time to replenish savings."

"I meant what I said. About calling me anytime you want."

"I know. And the same for you. My people all know to let your calls through now."

"Thanks Max."

"It just occurred to me. It would feel weird to retire before my parents."

"But not unusual."

"No, but I don't want to see it happen. I want you tell me what it's like before I get there."

"I'll do that. I promise." They talked for another ten minutes before an awkward silence ended the conversation. They had a lot to learn about each other but Rolly was happier than he had been in a long time.

———————

Mid-December in Michigan is bleak and cold with occasional bursts of sunlight that make the natives squint in wonderment. The days are frosty and the nights still and dry. A few leaves swirl in concrete corners, dead leftovers from the few dormant trees lining the streets. Parks that were lush green only a month ago are barren and brown. A throng of people trudge the frigid sidewalks, losing their breath to a piercing wind, hoping it will snow and fill the air with something besides numbing cold.

Rolly was on his way to an appointment with Gordon O'Leary, a spring in his step and a blush on his cheeks. The money problem had been solved, he was free and happy. Well, almost free and only an average level of happy, but it was an improvement.

Stephanie needed convincing though. Rolly's shopping spree had sent her into a rage. After twenty minutes of pointless arguing they retreated to their separate ends of house. A day later, after ten hours of work had worn them down, they were able to talk. Stephanie viewed their predicament in down-to-earth money-in-the-bank terms: a big chunk comes in, another goes out. "Two steps forward, one step back, and we're still screwed." Rolly saw it as vindication of his 'hard work never killed anyone' retirement strategy: Max's repayment would push his Reckoning up a lot, O'Leary's five point guarantee would push it up a little, it was a win-win. Rolly eventually convinced Stephanie that, they were okay, retirement was a virtual guarantee.

As he strode happily under the ruddy clouds and grey buildings a thought nagged at him. *Not so fast, you don't know your Reckoning yet.* He had been here too many times, been too close and denied. Rolly dismissed the idea as cynical, he had become too jaded, he needed to lighten up and appreciate the end of his work life.

Rolly decided not to tell coworkers until he was sure. Although several noticed his more genial demeanor and wondered what was going on. Given the time of year it wouldn't take long to figure it out.

Rolly reminded himself not to settle for less than five points, afraid O'Leary might try to claim the gains from Max's payback. No, he expected five points above and beyond anything else. He would have to be tough, make sure O'Leary kept his word.

O'Leary's waiting room hadn't changed, including Mr. Leather, now leafing through a home and garden magazine. Ms. Makeup had been replaced with Mr. Tattoo, who had thick blade-shaped ink patterns up and down his arms and over his bald head. He was portly and slouching with dark bags under his eyes, another transient. His eyes were darting over the pictures in a cooking magazine. The receptionist escorted Rolly to O'Leary's office.

"How did the spending go?"

"Bought a new HearSay and television."

"You didn't go over did you?"

"No, ended up a little under. Made up for the rest by buying some tools."

"Did you spend the exact amount?"

"I had about twenty bucks leftover."

O'Leary looked disappointed. "I calculate my spending balance to the last penny. Let's hope this doesn't affect your point gain."

Rolly suffered a momentary pang of fear, then regretted it. O'Leary was giving himself an out should something go wrong. The man was slick.

"Here's the big news: my son repaid the money, plus some extra."

"Oh really? Let's check this out, see where you're at."

O'Leary flipped up his keyboard. Sean asked for permission to transmit a verification code. O'Leary in his retirement file now, asking Paragon computers to recalculate his Reckoning. It took less than thirty seconds.

O'Leary sat straight up, looked around the screen, slid windows away and back, unfolded his HearSay screen, head rotating from HearSay to desk monitor, sliding more documents around, punching the screen, drawing figures with his finger, switching to a stylus for more refined touching, more typing, squinting, mouth open, eyes flitting back and forth, folding both screens down and slumping in his chair.

"The Corporament says your Reckoning is 478.31. Next year's projected Number is 478. This should be enough to put you over. You are going to retire Mr. Rolly Smalls."

Rolly felt a smile bending his atrophied cheeks and realized that, despite his previous confidence, he hadn't allowed himself to feel successful. The smile turned into a snicker, then a laugh, and Rolly had to stand up and walk around and pump his fists and yell "Yes!"

O'Leary sat passively staring at Rolly.

Rolly saw him and stopped. "You're sure, right? This won't suddenly change or anything?"

"Nothing is guaranteed, but it seems likely."

"You're not as excited."

"It is *your* retirement, not mine. Guess I'm a little shocked. It's never happened this quickly. I was only working for the extra points, planning a ten year schedule for you, and here you are practically retired. I haven't processed it yet."

"Did I get the five points?"

"Yes you did."

"Can I see?"

"Screen, HearSay or paper?"

"Paper." A printer whined to life under the desk and O'Leary handed Rolly eight sheets of paper. Each sheet showed the activity on his account for each of the seven parameters and his Reckoning at the end of each day, for the last week plus one day. When he got to work, when he went to lunch, what he spent money on, how productive he was, all the details of his life condensed to columns of numbers. On the day he went shopping his Reckoning decreased three points.

"I don't see a gain. I see a three point loss."

"Let me see." Rolly handed over the pages. O'Leary leafed through, stopping on a different day. "Here it is, right here under 'Procurement.'" O'Leary circled a line and handed it back.

There it was, the word "Procurement" and an extra five points. Every other activity was detailed with dates and numbers in each column, but "Procurement" was blank all the way across.

"What does that mean?"

"Procurement? I know the dictionary definition but what, exactly, it means to the Corporament I don't know. As far as I'm concerned it means you spent the right amount."

"But this is only a net gain of two points. They took away three when I spent the money."

"Yeah, that happens. Sometimes you have to pay the math."

"What?"

"Sorry, it's a counselor's term. Don't usually share it with the public. It means you had to pay for what you got. This whole thing, the Number and your Reckoning, retirement, it's all run by machines, adding and subtracting and dividing and multiplying, shooting everything through a hundred different algorithms. These computers take all your information, all those thousands of things you do every day, and turns them into one single solitary number. Who knows what really happens inside their pin-sized circuit boards. Sometimes, when they give a lot they take a little in return. I don't control it. Nobody does. It's just the way it's programmed. Consider your points a digital sacrifice to the gods of math and machines."

"That's it? That's your excuse? Blame it on the machines?"

"It is what it is."

"But you guaranteed five points."

Heavy footsteps echoed in the hallway.

"And you got five points. It's right there on the report."

"No, it was only two points after losing three for money spent."

"Give or take, what's the difference? According to our agreement I have met my obligations. End of story."

"This is bullshit. You knew this would happen. I want my money back."

A throat cleared loudly. The doorframe creaked as a large body leaned against it.

"What's the problem Mr. Smalls? You're going to retire. Why complain?"

"Point-three-one isn't much padding. I'd feel better if I had those three points back."

"The Number goes up one point every year like clockwork--"

"Sometimes it goes up two or three points."

"Rarely. Like once every twenty or thirty years. I can't even remember the last time it did that. It's been a point a year for a long time now and it'll be a point this year too. Like I said, it's no guarantee but in my opinion you've got a ninety-nine percent chance of retiring."

"But if I had those three points it would be certain."

"The Corporament takes what it wants. There's no getting those points back."

"But you can give me my money back."

"So you can get five points for free? I don't think so. Besides, my small fee isn't going to get you three points."

"Your fee isn't that small and it will get me something more than point-three-one."

"You're not getting your money back."

"Do I have to sue you?"

The door opened and Mr. Leather made a menacing entrance, banging his boot heels on the floor. "Is there a problem here?"

"Hold your horses Donald. Mr. Smalls and I are just working things out. You want to play harsh? Go ahead and sue me. The judge will laugh you out of the courtroom. My contract's been vetted by four different lawyers. It's as tight as security at a Corporament barbecue."

"You're a liar and conman and I will post it on every social site I can think of."

"Go right ahead. When you retire all those so called friends will come running to my door. Best advertisement in the world. Yeah, you'll fix me up real good. Of course I could sue you for business disparagement. You know that's a law, don't you? Since 2082? Means you can't say anything bad about a business anytime, anywhere, ever. Hell, I could sue you just for *suggesting* it. They like putting mouthy people like you on trial. Makes a good show. Whatever you do I'll get lots of publicity. Hey, I'll be able to add your name to my wall. I may even call today and have the plaque made. Go home Mr. Smalls, and have a nice retirement. Make sure he finds the door Donald."

11

New Year's Eve

Rolly raged at O'Leary for the next three days. His Productivity suffered; Stephanie was thankfully away with another lover. He went home feeling castrated, just another dupe getting played. *Why didn't I see this coming, I should have known better*, all the usual self-flagellations. But his new Reckoning--that was amazing. The one thing he wanted more than anything else was about to happen, after seventy-two years of trying. And it wasn't O'Leary who put him over, it was Max. Rolly needed someone to talk to.

Max answered right away. A relief since this was only their third phone call and Rolly wasn't sure how much grace Max was willing to give. He told Max about O'Leary and his new Reckoning.

"Don't worry about O'Leary. He's taken his pound of flesh. Worry about your Reckoning."

"That's the good news!"

"Seems too good. Didn't you tell me it wouldn't happen this year? Maybe next year, or the year after?"

"I'll take it anytime."

"I would too, but nothing happens this easily with the Corporament. Don't get your hopes up."

"Too late. I'm already there." Rolly could feel a smile scrunching his cheeks. Max laughed at his father's giddiness. It was the first time he'd seen his son smile in, well, he couldn't remember the last time Max had smiled.

"I mean it. I don't want to see you let down. Play it cool. Be skeptical. If you win it'll be all the sweeter."

"All right." Rolly agreed because Max was right, but there was no coming down. Not only was he about to retire, but his son was talking to him, and it was a *friendly* conversation.

They drifted to sports and complaining about women, talking for over an hour.

Feeling good and unable to contain himself, Rolly told his coworkers, receiving congratulations and envious looks equally. Some asked for O'Leary's number but Rolly begged off. He would not give that bastard the opportunity. He did try to explain how Max put him over, but the two people listening acted amused, as if "Rolly's rich son" were a precious fantasy they shouldn't contradict.

In early December Rolly sat down at his workstation and asked himself *Why am I doing this?* He didn't need more Productivity, or Length of Service. *Why bother?* Instead Rolly daydreamed, staring at a spot on the cubicle wall, knowing everything he *didn't* do was recorded by the computer. He fiddled with useless paper clips, wondering how in the world they got hooked together sitting peacefully in a desk drawer. He drummed on the desk with his fingers, trying to keep a steady rhythm. He slouched in the chair and gazed at the ceiling and afterward couldn't remember his own thoughts. He laughed at memories of coworkers doing stupid things.

That afternoon Rolly took an actual break, his first in many years. The tiny windowless room had the standard issue conveniences: dirty microwave oven, cheap coffee maker, mostly empty cupboards and a round table that had once been white. He slid two five dollar coins into the vending machine and bought a can of soda. A camera up in the corner watched him slacking. Rolly stared back, wondering who might be on the other side, then gazed at the candy in the snack machine, discovering nuances in the brightly colored packaging he hadn't noticed before.

Rolly relaxed. For the first time in decades. Sitting here staring at the machine. Like a balloon inside his body had suddenly deflated. His aching, tensed-up muscles settled and loosened. It was the most wonderful feeling.

Souliere walked in and poured himself a cup of coffee. He stirred in three creams and a sugar and sat across from Rolly.

"Word around the office is you're about to retire."

Rolly had personally shared the news with everyone, except Souliere, who he didn't think would care. Souliere and Rolly rarely talked, only about work, and only when Rolly had a question that needed answering.

"That's right. I loaned some money to my son years ago and he paid me back. Enough to put me over."

"This is the son who invented the THI." It sounded like a statement but Souliere looked as if he expected an answer.

"Yes."

"You gave him that money to start his own business."

"Uh, yes."

"Good for him. You did a great thing, taking a chance on your son's wild dreams. I hope he paid you interest."

Rolly stumbled over his answer, not quite knowing how to respond to a man he didn't even share a hello with every morning, who seemed to know more about his life than his closest friends. "Uh, he did, a small amount, I didn't ask for a percentage."

"That's okay. Fathers like us shouldn't count percentages. If you don't mind I'd like to offer a little advice."

"Uh, okay."

"I know you're looking forward to an imminent retirement, but you should know that when specialists add up your Reckoning they assume you will maintain a consistent level of Productivity, right up to December 31st. I know that's only a couple weeks away, but I don't think you should be taking it easy yet. You might lose some of those precious gains."

O'Leary never mentioned this. "All right."

Souliere stood up to leave. "Congratulations Rolly." He held up his styrofoam cup in toast. "Here's to hoping I won't see you January 1st."

"Thanks." Rolly held up his soda. As Souliere left he realized it was the first time he'd ever heard the man say his name.

———

New Year's Eve fell on the perfect day: Saturday. Rolly and Stephanie would leave work early at six o'clock and get home with enough time to dress for the festivities. Sunday was a short workday, giving extra time to recover from late night parties. EverLife prevented drunkenness and the nanobots took care of hangovers. The problem was getting enough sleep. Dozing off at your desk could ruin Productivity. Of course Rolly wouldn't have to worry about that after tonight.

The short winter days meant Rolly left for work in the dark and arrived home in the dark. Living without daylight robbed him of a sense of passing time; he missed the rising and the setting of the sun and the way it put a capital letter and a period on each day. Time seemed endless, as if it had no definition. He chose to view this as a good omen: an endless retirement was in sight.

As usual Stephanie made it home first. She had already showered and shaved her legs, freshly curled her hair, and slipped into a light purple silk dress with spaghetti straps, a matching sash around her waist. Simple and effective. The dress alternately slipped and clung to her bare breasts, hiding them one second, outlining every detail the next. She met him in the front room, shoeless, clipping on a necklace.

"Finally. Hurry up and get dressed or you'll make us late."

"Yes ma'am."

Stephanie went to her end of the house, Rolly to his. He knew what he wanted to wear--a silver/black striped shirt and black pants--but grabbed an ugly green shirt instead. He found Steph in front of the bathroom mirror, leaning forward, applying blue eye shadow. She wasn't leaning far but in the reflection Rolly could see all of her cleavage and the tops of her breasts.

Rolly realized he hadn't seen Stephanie's body so enticingly framed since last New Year's. He put a hand on her round butt and slid it up to the naked skin between her shoulders.

"No, we don't have time."

"Aww."

"When you're retired we'll have all the time in the world."

"I'll remember you said that."

Rolly retreated to his end of the house. He had forgotten to ask about the ugly green shirt.

———————

They always celebrated New Year's at Riddell's, a bar/restaurant with emphasis on bar. Riddell's had fifteen locations around the city and each had the same layout and interior design, except for one, where everything had been flipped in a mirror image of its clones. The wealthy elite preferred to party there because it was different and therefore cooler.

Rolly and Stephanie chose one of the normal Riddell's, which was still massive, 150 feet on each side with a forty foot ceiling. Twenty-three thousand square feet of tables, dance floor and bar. A balcony ran all the way around, set with comfortable chairs and small tables. The design theme was "Rome In Ruin," styrofoam arches and columns made to look chipped and crumbling lining the main ballroom and the balcony. The designers were trying to make partygoers believe they were inside the Coliseum but it came off as cheap. A bar ran the entire length of one wall, surrounded by a sea of poorly lit tables.

In the middle of the dance floor stood Riddell's claim to fame and the main reason anybody showed up: a towering octagon of precision ground glass known as Riddell's Pillar, the centerpiece of a massive holographic viewer. Digital projectors fired laser-like beams of light at the Pillar, from all around the room at multiple angles, from the inside, from the top and bottom, from projectors mounted on scaffolds standing on the floor and hanging from the ceiling. When an event streamed live, like a football game, the glass would disappear leaving only the players on a field of grass. Occasionally holograms would play on two levels, one for the main floor and one for the balcony.

(The existence of the Pillar was a direct result of Max's work on the THI, which Max discovered when they preemptively counter-sued him. Obligated to file his own suit, Max eventually lost because the court said, in his lawyer's interpretation of the twisted legalese, "Riddell's got there first.")

Rolly and Stephanie arrived after nine o'clock, Riddell's celebrated wall of noise hitting them like a slap on the ears, the music loud and the patrons louder. Lights flitted everywhere, a larger-than-life pop star danced in the Pillar, pseudo fireworks exploded near the ceiling forming shapes, some silly, some suggestive. Riddell's employed a squad of professional party directors. The place would not quiet down until just before midnight.

Stephanie spotted some friends and went to offer hugs. The crowd swallowed her like a hungry alien blob. Rolly began inching and sliding through warm bodies, catching glimpses of friends and workmates, in pairs but not couples, talking in groups or flirting with one another, their significant others elsewhere. As if everyone's marriage evaporated at the door.

He spotted Doug from work, arm around a petulant girl. They shook hands.

"Congratulations Rolly. Michelle, this is the guy who's going to retire."

She looked at Rolly, head down eyes up, no smile, mouth open like a trolling fish. "What's your number?" she asked.

"Four hundred seventy eight point three one."

"Is that good enough?"

"Should be."

"Oh." She turned away, apparently bored.

"Hey, when you retire send me a postcard, let me know what it's like."

"Give me a stamp and I'll send you one." They laughed. Both were old enough to remember the post office and sending actual pieces of paper through the mail.

Michelle looked as if they were speaking a foreign language. Doug took her by the shoulders and steered her to another part of the crowd.

Rolly took two steps and ran into Alicia something-or-other, who he dated a really long time ago.

"Hi Rolly! How are you?"

Sean said, "Her name is Alicia Hubbs." Rolly had never been good at remembering names. Decades inside his head taught Sean to know when to kick in the voice recognition software. It was a nicely refined system. Unlike Rolly.

"Alicia, nice to see you. How are you?" She had a big smile with red cheeks and dimples.

"Can't complain. How's Stephanie?"

"She's fine. Better than me, as usual. How long's it been?"

"Twenty two years."

"Wow, that long. I had no idea. Time flies." Now he remembered. The woman who counted everything. Her daily calorie intake, the number of breaths she took, her white blood cells, the color and viscosity of her urine, how many minutes she slept every night, the intensity and duration of sex with Rolly (or any partner), any measurable part of her life. Her HearSay kept track of everything and she gleefully shared it on her public webpage. Alicia was especially fond of comparing lovers.

"There's a rumor you're going to retire this year. Is that true?"

"Yeah, pretty sure."

"Pretty sure? Either you are or you aren't."

"My number's high enough. 478.31. Should put us over."

"Hmmm. Not that high. You sure?"

"As sure as I can be."

"Good luck with that. Hey! We should get together again. Like old times. See if we've learned any new tricks."

Seemed foolish to make a date when retirement was a few hours away but he didn't want to be rude. "Okay. What day works for you?"

Sean, "At the ready, Sir Rolly."

"How bout next Thursday at nine?"

"Free and clear, dude. You're good to go. But the ever popular Mrs. Smalls has not indicated where she'll be on the evening in question."

It wasn't going to matter. He would be bedding an exotic Tahitian beauty next Thursday.

"Thursday at nine works for me."

"Appointment *con*firmed."

"Great! See you then." She threw her arms up and they hugged. Alicia gave him a light kiss on the lips and a sultry/playful look as she slipped into the crowd.

Rolly wove his way through the mass of mingling people, stopping to chat with friends and lovers. Logan Akers, an old neighbor; Olivia Belrose, a former coworker; several online friends he saw at New Year's; his old car mechanic; Noah Donati, a fellow poker player; Ryan Boyle, skydiving partner from way back; Gareth Magee, second baseman on the company softball team 2089, and other men wandering the crowd sans wife, looking for new lovers. Everyone he ran into, even people he hadn't seen in decades, wanted to congratulate him on retiring.

A commercial played on The Pillar, all flying hair and and ten foot breasts thrust out from comically bended torsos. For two seconds a giant hand clutching a beer bottle hovered over all four sides of the dance floor, label prominently displayed. Rolly decided he was thirsty.

He caught sight of Stephanie, laughing with two men he didn't know. She already had a drink in hand, lightly touching one of the men's arms. Rolly could see her nipples outlined by the clingy silk top. He felt jealous. Or was it possessive? How-dare-you-flirt-with-my-wife? No, that wasn't it. They were married in name only, bound together by the thin promise of retirement. Rolly knew she wanted to leave him and might after tonight. He would not object if she did. But she had two suitors and he was still alone. Maybe it was jealousy after all.

These confused emotions called for the deadening effects of large quantities of alcohol. When Rolly finally made it to the bar he ordered a double shot of whiskey, which pleasantly burned the length of his esophagus (the nanomachines already repairing the damage), followed by a chugged pint of beer, and a double sized mug of the same fine beverage to go. It hit him fast. Rolly marched back into the herd.

Over the the next few hours Rolly visited the bar often, leaving with a different drink each time. EverLife allowed a predetermined amount of inebriation, set by the user. At 11:02 Rolly achieved this level. From then on any alcohol that passed his lips was used to maintain intoxication or purged from his system. Later, when Rolly watched the recording of his mapped movements, he would count seven trips to the bathroom before midnight.

A giant hairy head suddenly materialized and said in a growling caveman voice "Are you man enough?" Rolly jumped, then realized he was on the dance floor, standing next to the Pillar. Alone. Everyone staring at him. Clarity barged into his alcoholic stupor; an EverLife emergency response to his fear reaction. Rolly had no idea what he had been doing before the giant head rudely interrupted, but people were giggling and pointing. He turned and confronted the head, scraggly hair and unibrow furrowed in an angry glare. It was looking directly at him. He made an impotent slapping motion and the head was sucked back into the Pillar. The crowd roared with laughter.

Rolly made his way off the dance floor, trying to regain his anonymity. A woman with pointy breasts said "You're cute" but Rolly stumbled past.

Sean, "The delightful and elegant Mrs. Smalls has sent you a messahge. She requests that you stop messing with the hologram and meet her at the northeast corner of the dance floor, by the sex gambling machines."

Rolly, breathless, "Right. I'll be right there."

"She would like to remind you that it's time to stop drinking."

"Good idea."

"She has also requested that I inform you it is now 11:45."

"Okay. Got it. On my way. Tell her I'm on my way."

"Righto."

The tradition of couples kissing at midnight had not gone away (kept naggingly alive by Corporament "marriage first" commercials) and the rush to find spouses was beginning. Rolly stopped, surrounded by a dark mass of loud moving shapes. He had not completely recovered and couldn't remember where the sex gambling machines were. He blinked twice. Some of the fuzziness disappeared but he still could not get any bearings.

"Sean, I need a little help here."

"Anything my master."

"I need directions to Stephanie."

"No prob. Turn left and start walking, seventeen paces."

Rolly took three steps and bumped into something. "Hey! Watch it asshole!" A large man sitting at a table with a tall yellow drink in hand. Some of it had spilled. He looked at Rolly with fight in his eyes.

"Sorry, sorry. A little dark over here, didn't see you sitting there. So sorry. You need help with that?"

Rolly escaped his fellow drunks unscathed. "So, like, Rolly, you need *detailed* directions."

Rolly, sheepishly, "Yes."

"So, I know where Stephanie is, and I've got a map of the building and GMS, but you've got the peepers, you're gonna have to do the steering. You up for it, dude?"

"Yeah, I guess."

"All right! Let's do this. Walk five paces in the same direction you were going before rattling that guy's world. Good. Now there's a table on your right, and a step later another on your left. Squeeze between them, the chairs are kinda tight here. Good. Turn slightly right and keep going. Watch out for that column. Well, it's just a small scratch. And probably a bruise. Who leaves a nail that big sticking out of the wall in a bar? Oh well. A little more right. Good. We have to go through the gaming area now. Pool tables, air hockey, holographic badminton, simulation pods, the adult ball pit. Too much fun happening here, you'll have to be extra careful. Look out for bouncing basketballs and plastic flying discs. Keep going now, you're on the right track, Titanic simulator on your left, classic gaming on the right. Manual controls are so, like, quaint. Okay, badminton to your left, duck if you need to, good, keep going, just a little farther, you're almost--oops, that hurt, walk it off, it's not as bad as you think. Well maybe it is. Those cue sticks come outta nowhere, don't they? What was that guy trying to do, break *all* the balls on the table? Whoa, okay, you're a little woozy, stop for a minute, let the pain go, breathe, slowly. Feeling better? Okay, almost there. Waitress station coming up on the right, a couple more tables, left, now right, and Stephanie should be riiiiiiight here."

"You drink too much when we're out. Did Sean help you get here?"

Rolly was wincing but trying not to, most of his willpower going to the task of remaining upright instead of falling on the floor in fetal position. Pain was making a significant contribution to his sobriety. "Not at all. Found my way fine," he croaked

"Always at your service, my man."

"Only three minutes left. Get ready."

Stephanie had saved them a spot on the edge of the dance floor, at the front of the crowd, nothing but space between them and the Pillar. While they waited two more couples offered congratulations.

All eyes were on the hologram forty feet tall and twenty wide. The streamed video shifted between crowd shots of Times Square tourists, and long shots of the ball atop its pole, shooting out beams of multi-colored lights, animated numbers slithering around its surface in high-definition LED perfection. Constructed from diamonds and gold and platinum and any precious resource the Corporament could think of--including a quart of crude oil encased in crystal--the ball was a splurge of gaudy excess meant to impress. Here in Riddell's The Number would appear on the dance floor in twelve foot high digits, directly in front of Rolly and Stephanie.

At thirty seconds to midnight the ball began its descent. At ten seconds everyone started counting. Stephanie raised her arms, getting ready to celebrate. As the ball came lower and closer it lit up their faces. "Three, two, one, Happy New Year!" A neon sign beneath the ball lit up reading "Happy New Year!" and the ball itself showed "2147!" in bright green numbers. A blinding flash of light and the boom of fireworks and The Number blazed up, Rolly and Stephanie shielding their eyes, waiting for their pupils to adjust.

Four hundred and seventy nine.

The Number had gone up two points.

Kissing and hugging all around, music playing, but not loud, not celebratory, waiting to see if some couple had made retirement. It didn't happen every year, but sometimes it was possible to see an actual retirement. Rolly froze in place, Stephanie slipped her hands behind her neck and locked fingers together, arms over ears. Someone across the room screamed with joy, releasing the tension. The crowd craned their necks and pointed and someone said "Oh, I know them" and the gossiping started.

The party shifted. An empty space opened up behind Rolly and Stephanie, who stood unmoving, and apart.

12

New Year's Day

A deep freeze descended over the city from the north, by way of Canada. Twelve degrees and not a snowflake in sight. In mid-afternoon the sun made a brief appearance causing the temperature to rise to a balmy nineteen before the clouds closed ranks and it fell back again. Winter was here.

Rolly slept until eight o'clock, giving himself a small Sunday luxury. Stephanie had packed her duffle and left sometime during the early morning hours. Rolly heard the front door slam shut; she did not say where she was going. A text would make its way to his HearSay. Eventually.

Rolly got out of bed, coasted through his morning routine and drove to work. He opened a project and did nothing, his morning a blur of non-action, his mind a jumble of disconnected thoughts and daydreams.

He left the building for lunch without planning to, stepping into the cold air with no direction. He sat down on a cement bench, next to a large cement planter holding a leafless tree, and stared down the metal and marble canyon outside his workplace. Being back at work was surreal, as if watching an alternate reality play out courtesy of a spiteful angel. Sitting at the same desk, at the same computer, creating the same boring videos. He couldn't really be here, he was supposed to be somewhere else, somewhere warm. Reality was failing him.

Rolly sat for a long time, not realizing how much time passed. He remembered a cold chill seeping up through his thin slacks and into his loins. It seemed to be gone now.

"Uh, Master Dude, Rolly-of-the-Smalls clan, I don't want to alarm you or anything serious like that, but the little nanothingies say it's getting too cold out there in your extremities, you know, your fingers and toes and stuff."

Rolly did not reply or move.

"They say if you stay outside any longer you're gonna get frostbite, maybe lose a couple of 'em."

Rolly roused himself. "Why does that matter? Who cares if I lose a couple of fingers? It's all for the greater good."

"Uh...don't get it."

"If I lose a finger I'll go to the EverLife Renewal Center and get the special injection that grows it back, full of regeneration nanobots and extra stem cells 'cause if I don't I'll lose my job because missing a finger makes me disabled. A disabled worker is less productive. So I will spend a lot of money which makes me a good consumer, like the Corporament wants me to be. I might even get a point or two out of it."

"Still not makin' sense."

"For a low-on-the-food-chain consumer the only way to get ahead is spend, spend, spend. Didn't you learn anything from Gordon O'Leary? Every dollar brings me closer to retirement. Let's say for every finger or toe I lose I get an extra half point. Lose a handful and I should be able to retire next year."

"That's crazy talk man. Go inside, get warm. Save your money. You'll be alright."

"No, no, no. Spending is the key. How much money did Max give me and how little did it help? If I hadn't gone to O'Leary I'd be even further in the hole."

"Just tryin' to look on the bright side."

"In fact I should stay out here until *all* my fingers freeze and have them cut off and regrown. That would get me a theoretical gain of five points. More than enough to cover a two point jump."

"You can't work with no fingers. Takes like three months to grow 'em back. Then there's physical therapy--"

"Think of all the EverLife technicians who will benefit. The money EverLife will be able to overcharge me. I'll be doing great things for the economy--no wait--I'll be sacrificing myself for the economy. Won't that make me some kind of hero? But it could be even better. Stay out here and freeze my entire body. That's an idea. Why not go all the way? Full body freezing. I think they might erect a statue for that."

Sean was quiet. The HearSay was programmed with responses for every conceivable statement or query. It never went quiet when in direct conversation. Rolly perked up, curious to hear what would happen.

"Here's the deal Rolly. I'm just a humble ol' computer in your ear. I can only recognize a fundamental level of sarcasm. It don't take much, then I'm totally lost. When I get to that point there's a little program that says I have to shut down. It's nagging me right now so I gotta go. Bye."

"Sean? Sean?" No answer. Did he just accidentally kill his own HearSay? Who knew. At least it was quiet now. Sean was off licking his wounded microtransistors, he would be back. Still, it was more fun than simply turning the thing off.

"Hey Rolly. How you doin'?"

Rolly looked up. A woman standing next to him, in a fur lined parka with the hood zipped up, obscuring her face.

"Fine. How're you?"

"The hell you are." She sat next to him without being invited.

"What are you doing?"

"Sitting down. You can identify basic movements can't you?"

Rolly was annoyed. "Can't you sit somewhere else?"

"Not if I'm going to have a conversation with you."

"Why would you want to do that?"

"Because I'm going to help you retire." She pulled her hood back and revealed a staggeringly gorgeous face. The kind of beauty that makes supermodels weep and move to a farm in Kansas to make babies.

"How much did you pay for that face?"

"A lot. But I got the spectacular body half off." Passersby were starting to stare.

"I want to be alone. No offense."

"None taken. If you really want to retire, and I mean really, really want to retire, I can help, but we need to start now."

"Oh hell, I'm never gonna to retire. You're wasting your time."

"I'm almost positive I can get you retired next year."

"What? No guarantees?"

"There are no guarantees. In anything we do."

"I've had my fill of specialists and I've only been to one. I'm not going to pay your fee no matter how good your bullshit is. Leave me alone."

"You don't have to pay me anything and I'm not one of those scumbags. I pick my own clients. I know where you stand, how close you are. We can get you retired."

"How do you know my name?"

"You were referred by someone you know, who would like to remain anonymous."

"Is that supposed to instill confidence? Knowing someone's sneaking around behind my back? Is it my wife?"

"Rolly--"

"Doug?"

"No it's--"

"Couldn't be Max. He's done more than enough."

"It's Souliere."

Stunned, all Rolly could say was "Who?"

"Your coworker. Don't ask me why."

"Why?"

She had the pained expression of someone quickly losing patience. "He has his reasons."

"Why'd you tell me if he wants to be anonymous?"

"'Cause I hate playing this cloak and dagger shit. Why don't we get off this cold bench and go back to my office?"

"Can't. I have to go back to work. Get my twelve hours in."

"When you get there, are you gonna do more than play with your holograms?"

"What?"

"I looked up your Productivity. There's nothing there. All you're doing is twiddling icons. Okay, you had a big letdown yesterday. But you go in and let the computers watch you do nothing. If you're going to be a zombie you should've stayed home. Not a good start for your next stab at retirement."

Rolly really looked at her. Pale round face and pale blue eyes surrounded by straight brown hair. Simple, elegant, and absolutely perfect. The epitome of sweet innocence, sculpted by a skilled surgeon. She wore dark blue jeans and black suede boots, her coat was purple with faux rabbit fur trim. With hood up she blended into the crowd; unzip and pull it down and she drew attention like a flashing neon sign.

"How do you know so much about me?"

"I'm a retirement specialist. I have access to all kinds of info."

"You need my permission to do that."

"Legally. But they can't stop me."

"I could have you arrested."

"Breach of privacy is a misdemeanor. They don't arrest people for that. They give out tickets. Or they laugh."

"A restraining order then. Or a lawsuit. There's lots of cheap lawyers looking for work."

"All you have to do is say no. I'll tell Souliere the bad news and move on to my next client. If you bring in the psycops I will disappear forever."

"What makes you think you'll get away that easy?"

"We are two people in a world of fourteen billion. How much authoritarian justice does that get you?"

"You don't look like someone I can trust."

"Would it help if I was wearing a suit?"

"Yes it would."

"Maybe that's your problem."

Rolly frowned. "What *is* your name?"

"Leah Lockwood. Nice to meet you Rolly Smalls."

————————

Rolly followed Leah to her office, a three block trip to the west and around the corner on Townsend Street. Fingers and toes tingled as he walked. The sensation was especially uncomfortable in his crotch, causing Rolly to walk awkwardly with legs too far apart. Leah gave him a look. "Just warming back up," he said. She nodded and walked on. Her jeans were intentionally baggy and shapeless, but unable to hide the curves underneath. She walked with a confidant stride at odds with her clothes; every man that passed gave her a sideways glance. Leah led him down a back alley to a single door in the side of a small square building three stories tall. She unlocked the door with a metal key.

Once inside she slipped the hood off and fanned her hair with her fingers, relaxing as if she'd walked in the front door of her home. Rolly was six feet tall, Leah only an inch or two shorter.

Six steps took them up to a long bland hallway lined with office doors. Leah strode to what Rolly thought was the end of the hall, turned left, a short walk past four doors, a right turn, another long walk, another right turn, ten doors passed, another left, past two doors. Leah stopped and unlocked the door to suite B131. Rolly was thoroughly lost.

The room was barren. A well-used steel desk and two chairs, nothing else. A white paper shade covered a window behind the desk, blocking any view but letting in plenty of light. A closed door on the left led to a second room.

Up in the ceiling corners the required cameras were surrounded by bendable monitors. Rolly noticed the same setup for cameras in the hallway. At random spots on the walls, floor and ceiling, small circles of something that looked like black bumpy mushrooms seemed to grow. Rolly thought Leah had a mold problem.

She saw him looking. "That's a spray on tar I use to muffle microphones. The monitors around the cameras are programmed to show this room empty, using the correct time of day and year for placement of the sunbeams. Or gray skies. They know the weather too."

"How'd you set it up without being caught?"

"You pick an office in the bowels of some boring building, find and cover every camera and mic, set up your own surveillance and watch the office. If after a week no one comes to check on things, they weren't paying attention. It's not whether they see you or not, it's whether they care. We are free to talk."

Leah sat at the desk and pulled a HearSay interface from her coat pocket. Rolly took the chair across from her. The interface was longer than his by two inches. It unfolded in an origami performance that lasted thirty seconds. A full keyboard and monitor three feet wide and two feet tall. Steve Mann would have drooled with envy.

"I just bought a new HearSay and don't remember seeing anything this big."

"It's custom made. Can't find it in stores."

"How'd you get it?"

"I saved my pennies for a hundred years. Back to your retirement. I'll bet you're wondering what the catch is."

"My brain hadn't got that far. It's still trying to decide if you're for real. But yes, I would like to know what the catch is."

"You're going to have to work harder than you ever have before. The next year will be pure hell."

"You need to work on your presentation."

"I'm soft-pedaling a bit. It'll probably be much worse."

"Have you done this before?"

"Many times."

"How many times?"

"I haven't kept count. Thirty or forty I think."

"Have all of your clients retired?"

"No, only about thirty percent."

"That's better than Gordon O'Leary."

"O'Leary is a legalized thief. He stole your money with the blessing of the Corporament. Shits like him make my job harder and there's a thousand like him in every city."

"He got me five points."

"And how many did you lose? There is no gain with a bastard like O'Leary. Clients see that magic five point gain and say 'Hey, this is easy. I don't need this guy to tell me how spend money.' Or the gullible ones keep going back to get a new 'spending balance.' Either way the Corporament wins. And so does O'Leary."

Rolly prided himself on being a skeptic, having a nose for scams. Now a stranger had to explain it to him? "Why should I believe you? You're a retirement coach, or specialist, or whatever--"

"Freelance retirement consultant."

"--like O'Leary. Maybe you're just saying this to make him look bad."

"O'Leary is a liar and a cheat. I am not but you don't have any reason to trust me. Yet. All I can offer is my word and a promise: I will not ask for money and I will always tell the truth no matter how much it hurts."

"You're a terrible saleswoman."

"Take a leap of faith and trust me."

"Why would I do that? What's my motivation?"

"Desperation."

"I've been desperate a long time. Got a better reason?"

"This is your best opportunity, right now, when you're on the verge. You took the extra step and convinced your son to pay you back. That put you in spitting distance of The Number. O'Leary will only help you dig a hole. You'll watch retirement slip away a little more each year. If you thought the past forty years were frustrating imagine spending decades always falling a point or two short. You have to act now, while you're close. I can do things you can't and I know things you don't. I can get you over the hump. You need me."

This was no sales pitch. Leah spoke with a take-it-or-leave-it tone, stating a fact, without expectation. Rolly regarded her for a moment. "You're saying you'll work for free. Nothing is free. There's always a price."

"True. You've been offered a gift. It would be foolish to turn it down."

"What if I fail again?"

"My services are completely free the following year, and the year after that, until you retire. Neither you, nor Souliere, will have to pay."

"Considering my record that could be a very long time."

"No client of mine has ever taken more than a year to retire."

"Can I sleep on it?"

"No. Accept now or leave."

Rolly had already made up his mind. He didn't know how much more gainful employment he could endure. Leah was not promising instant gratification and she had a time limit, one year, with a warning of hard labor. But really, how much harder could it be?

"Yes."

Leah sat up straight. "Good. I've identified two things we can start working on now. First, your Productivity. You've already wasted more than half a day. You need to get back to Stableman ASAP and start working your ass off. Don't stop, put in as many hours as you can." Leah stood up and led him into the adjoining room, more barren than the first with only a cot. "What time do you normally get to work?"

"Eight o'clock."

"Plan on going in at six every day from now on. No days off, no vacation, no sick days, no weekends. You're going to work straight through to New Year's. Tomorrow I want you back here at 5:15. If you have to work all night that's fine. We have plans to make."

Leah pulled out another key and opened a dark brown wooden door.

Rolly was dealing with the idea of working with no days off when the delicious smell of baking bread settled over him like a warm quilt. Leah led him into the back kitchen of a bakery, down a short hall lined with chrome shelves and bread pans, to the front of the store and around the counter, where a line of people waited to buy pastries.

"That's Capitol Avenue out front. You can find your way from there. Tomorrow come in through the office entrance. I'll meet you at the door. Go back to work now."

"You said there were two things. What's the second?"

"We have to figure out what to do about your daughter. She's causing problems with your Reckoning."

"I don't have a daughter."

Leah frowned. "You don't know about her? Jesus O'Leary is incompetent. Took me two seconds to find her. Yes, you have a daughter, from years ago."

"I would know if--"

"Not necessarily. We'll talk in the morning. Go get your hours in. And be productive!"

Rolly went back to work as directed, did the things he had neglected in the morning, and managed to score an average Productivity for the day. He did not see Souliere. Myriad emotions turned over in his mind. *A daughter? How is that possible? Isn't EverLife supposed to prevent that? Stephanie won't be happy. What is this doing to my Reckoning? Can I trust Leah? Why am I putting myself through this again?*

Rolly didn't get home until midnight and went straight to bed, setting his alarm for 4:00 am. Tomorrow he would confront Souliere and get some answers.

13

Productivity

As promised, Leah met him at the front door; he was late. She was in bare feet, wearing plain grey warm-up pants and a white tee shirt, hair a mess, nursing a large cup of coffee. Her cosmetically altered features were still in place--perfectly arched eyebrows, high cheekbones, permanently blushed cheeks--as gorgeous as the day before. The added mussiness made her more appealing. Leah started talking the moment he entered. As they walked Rolly watched her butt bounce under the loose fabric.

"You're late. You shouldn't be late ever. Every minute counts. I know what you're thinking, 'like it hasn't counted before,' but it counts more now 'cause we only have a year. More time at work means more Productivity. Provided you don't screw off and sit on your ass all day. I meant that figuratively. Just get stuff done and do it in a way that gets you noticed.

"You've probably got projects lying around. That's great, but it won't take long to burn through 'em. Your Productivity counter doesn't know that. So you're going to find other things to do. Take more than usual. If someone is behind, ask if you can help. Learn other people's jobs, help when you can."

"They won't like that. Makes them look bad."

"It's a touchy subject. You have to tread lightly and not just with coworkers. Your company is pretty anal about loyalty. There's some crap about retirement as a natural result of hard work in their company manifesto. They think wanting to retire means you're a weak employee. You need to be on your best behavior. Management will be watching."

"Won't they suspect me?"

"Of course. So you're going to admit you were trying to retire and when it didn't happen you got upset. Anguished. Mentally debilitated. Find some stress disorder that sounds serious and use it. You're so upset by your failure to retire you're throwing yourself into work. Admitting your mistake and seeking redemption through the purity of hard work. They'll love it."

"That's not that far from the truth."

"That'll help you sell it."

Leah unlocked the door to her office and walked around the desk. She leaned forward to type something into her interface, then stood up. Nipples stood out in detail under the shear fabric of her shirt. Rolly forced himself to meet her gaze.

"You wanna fuck now or later?"

"What?"

"I want this out of the way before it gets out of hand."

Rolly, utterly confused, "You want to have sex? I thought we were talking about retirement."

"I don't want to have sex, especially with you. No offense. You're a client and it's not good to have a personal relationship where it should be business. But you've been screwing half a dozen women every month for years now. It's unrealistic to expect you to stop. Getting this out of the way is better than having you lust after me all the time. So let's do it now and be done with it. I have anti-bacterial wipes to clean up with."

Rolly stared. From face to nipples, face to nipples. She wasn't smiling, her tone hadn't changed, still matter-of-fact. His desire drained away.

"You're using reverse psychology to get me to leave you alone."

"Yep."

"Just to be clear, I wasn't planning on having sex with you."

"Not now, but probably later."

"I don't want to be with anyone who doesn't want to be with me."

"Do you want to screw or not?"

"No. Your strategy was successful."

"Okay then. Let's move on." More relaxed now. "From now on we'll talk mostly by HearSay. Face-to-face is time consuming. We'll meet here if it needs to be confidential, but not much."

Rolly had a revelation. "You invited me here just to turn me down."

"Pretty much, yeah."

"Why? That doesn't make any sense."

"Ever had a drunk call you up in the middle of the night to blubber about how much he loves you?"

"No."

"Then don't ask why. Contact me when you need something or have a question, phone, text, voice or video. You have my number. Texting is best. Keep it professional and don't abuse it."

"Yes ma'am."

"Now for the reality check. Productivity isn't just about being productive. It's about kissing up to your boss. But you knew that already, right?"

Rolly said nothing.

"A hundred and twenty-five years of office politics and you haven't figured this out?"

"I know, I'm not very good at it."

"That's your excuse? It's older than we are. The computer tally only counts for seventy percent of Productivity, the rest is left to company discretion, in other words, your boss. If they aren't on your side all this work will be wasted."

"I'll make a fool of myself."

"This isn't hard. Sit, smile, nod and listen. Who's your boss?"

"Steve Mann."

"Steve doesn't care about your opinion or what sports you like. He wants to spout his opinions and have someone listen. Is he an asshole?"

"No, he's okay. Most of the time."

"That's good, 'cause spending quality time with an asshole is torture. Here's your situation the way I see it. You're independently motivated, management can leave you alone and know you'll do your job. As far as they're concerned you're in the perfect place--out of sight, out of mind and very productive. You need to get Steve to notice you in a good way. Give yourself a learning curve, say a month or two. Don't march into his office and suddenly be mister can-I-do-anything-for-you. Be subtle. Work your way in slowly, learn what he likes and doesn't like. Learn when to nod and when to smile, or occasionally, look concerned."

"Don't know if I can do that. Not that I don't wanna try, I don't have the personality for it."

"Well then fake it. Start by learning to smile."

"I smile," Rolly said indignantly.

"Try it." Rolly curled up the corners of his mouth.

"You look deranged. Or like you're faking it. Try again."

This time Rolly let his eyebrows go up. Leah cocked her head to one side. She stepped up and rubbed her thumbs over his cheeks as if she were trying to smooth them out. She did the same to his forehead, then pinched his cheeks. "Relax," she said, and stood back and frowned.

"Needs work. Go home and practice in front of a mirror. Steve knows you want to retire. He'll be on the lookout for the kind of brown nosing you'll be doing. Remember, be subtle, don't force it. Now go to work."

"Wait. What about this daughter I supposedly have."

"What about her?"

"Who is she?"

"I don't know anything, only that she exists. She showed up in your DNA tree. It'll take a little more digging to get the details. Now get out of here."

———————————

In the afternoon Rolly called for a five minute Personnel Conference Break (this paused the Productivity counter) and quickly made his way to Souliere's cubicle.

Souliere was alone behind his desk when Rolly barged in; he was about to complain but Rolly spoke first.

"Did you hire Leah Lockwood to help me retire?"

Souliere's brows arched in surprise. "So much for anonymity."

"Why?"

"Because I hate to see you disappointed again."

"You haven't given me the time of day in twenty years and now you're willing to pay someone to help me retire. What's in it for you?"

"Does there have to be?"

"There usually is."

"Rolly, you don't need to worry about anything."

"What is it you want?"

"I want you to retire. Then help us with a little favor."

"Us?"

"The time isn't right for this discussion. That's why I wanted to be anonymous. Suffice to say we're not asking for expensive recompense or some horrible request. It's a simple thing, easy to accomplish, painless. But not now."

"Why not?"

"Because we're not ready."

"That's all you can say?"

"All I'm allowed to say. You can stop working with Leah anytime you want. But she is extremely good at her job. One of the best. We've worked with her before and she's never failed. It's in your best interest to continue."

"Why should I help you?"

"Because we believe in true freedom."

Sean, "Four minutes forty seconds *dude*," with an impatient cadence on the last word.

Rolly turned to leave. "We'll talk later."

"I look forward to it."

While the car drove home Rolly called Max, who had tried to contact him earlier. Rolly didn't feel comfortable talking at work. Sean sent a nice personalized message saying he would call back later, but having your HearSay respond was still considered rude by many people. He hoped Max wouldn't be offended.

Rolly started by falling over himself with apologies--sorry I didn't call sooner, sorry I couldn't take your call--he was deathly afraid Max would find some hate-triggering subtext in everything he did or didn't do. But Max seemed okay.

"We failed again."

"I know. Mom told me."

"How is she?"

"Angry. Ranting. I'd stay away if I were you."

"She won't be home anytime soon."

"So what's the plan now?"

"I've hooked up with another retirement specialist. She's making me work my ass off." Rolly told Max about Leah. Except for the almost sex part. And the long-lost missing daughter part.

Max looked concerned. "Sounds too good to be true. Has she told you to spend money like O'Leary?"

"No. She seemed disgusted with O'Leary. Said he was a blight on her profession."

"That's a good angle if she's trying to con you."

"I thought of that. How many con artists torture you with more work?"

"Keeps you busy while she robs you blind."

"What else am I gonna do? I've tried doing this on my own for seventy years. I need help."

"So you're going through with it."

"Guess I am. I don't really care if it works or not. This is the last time. I'm on my last shred of hope and if we fail again I'm going to stop."

"Stop what?"

"Trying. Doing. I'll make sure none of your money is touched. You'll get it back if nothing happens."

"Dad--"

"You have a better chance than us. It needs to be where it can do some good."

"You're being dramatic."

"Probably. But I mean it."

Father and son regarded each other. They were strangers. Time had changed both of them. He needed to get to know his son better. How was he going to do that working fifteen hours a day?

"Be careful. Make sure this woman doesn't take advantage of you. Let me know if I can help."

"I will. Thanks for calling Max."

Sunday, January 8th

Rolly had nearly the entire office to himself. None of the nearby cubicles were occupied; someone from embedded ads was working on the far side of the room; in one of the side offices a manager was shuffling papers around.

He had plenty of work--a video on attic dangers, graphic images of a man falling off a ladder, lots of detail he was avoiding. The silence of the office made it hard to concentrate. His mind drifted and he started day-dreaming.

Did she look like him? Did she have his round face and brown hair? He didn't even know who her mother was. Where did she live? In the same town? Was she married? Did he have grandkids? What company did she work for?

He imagined her cute with a round face and big white teeth and dimples. Rolly knew this was unrealistic but the image stuck in his brain and wouldn't leave. More likely she was an adult with a hundred cosmetic surgeries. One of a million statuesque blondes walking around the city.

He hoped he hadn't inadvertently slept with her. That was a disturbing thought. Many DNA comparison apps were available for the HearSay, all of which had limitations. It was common to use more than one when testing a new lover but accidental incest still happened.

The Productivity monitor began beeping. Rolly forced himself to concentrate on the man falling from the ladder and cracking his head on a flowerpot. The dent in the skull had to be just right.

She could be average sized, the same height as Rolly, or less. Long brown curly hair? Wide open blue eyes or squinty green ones, like Stephanie? Oops, stop, Stephanie is not this girl's mother. Remember that. Do not let this slip in the wrong company. In fact don't talk about it at all. No reason Stephanie needs to know.

Rolly dove into his project, working the blood to get it flowing properly down the concrete steps. He managed to get through his day with only occasional bouts of daydreaming.

Thursday, January 12th

Rolly at home, sprawled across an old overstuffed chair and ottoman, exhausted from another day of work, a hologram playing he wasn't watching, the sound turned off. Entertainment improved when the inane words and cliched music were removed.

Sean interrupted. "You got a text from Leah."

"I'll read it myself."

> How much of what oleary made you buy can you return?
> I could return the tools but the hearsay and holosystem had to be installed.
> You paid near full price for both. Didnt you negotiate?
> I did. Thought i got a good deal.
> You must suck at it. Less than a full system and part of it scratch and dent. Ill bet gadget world loves you.
> Whatever. Thanks for the ego beat-down.

Your in a tight spot. Debt is too high. Hurts your reckoning. Debt has to come down or disappear. Easy to pay down with savings but that means half of savings gone. Less savings is worse when its time to add everything up. Either way your screwd.

So i should give up while im still ahead.

Doesnt mean there isnt a third way. We need Stephanie. When can you bring her in?

No idea where she is. Left on new years havent seen her since. Might be weeks before she surfaces.

Contact her. Get her here asap.

Shes pissed. Shell ignore anything I send.

Shell be even more pissed after im done.

Tuesday, January 17th

Steve Mann was planning an appearance in the afternoon to check progress on the "inThrallEd with Insurance" campaign.

Rolly was playing catch up. The project began with six weeks left in the previous year. Certain he would retire Rolly did only superficial work, spending most of his time dreaming of tropical getaways. Steve would know how little he had accomplished.

Rolly liked Steve. He wasn't demanding or unrealistic or prone to scenes of manufactured anger. He trusted them to do their jobs, made reasonable requests, never raised his voice. His one fault was a streak of idealism tinged with integrity, arcane traits vice presidents rarely displayed. Rolly did not have high hopes for a long Steve Mann tenure.

Rolly's project was a commercial with a slow camera pass through the aftermath of a home invasion, no bloody bodies, just the mess of a ransacked house. It was a complex scene. Rolly had been throwing it together for the last two weeks. It looked crude and unfinished.

On the other hand Rolly's coworker Doug, had an easy project with a soothing voice over talking about death while a holographic sun set on an ocean horizon. As the sun went down the words "Become inThrallEd with Insurance" faded in until the entire slogan was spelled out.

Steve arrived at one o'clock and checked in with Myrna. Macklin escorted him through the cubicle maze. Rolly could hear indistinct but happy voices as Steve worked his way around.

Minutes later Macklin and Steve came around the corner into their dead-end cubicle trail.

"Hello Doug, Rolly."

"Hey Steve" and "Steve, how are you?"

"Not doing too bad. Guys, the deadline for InThrallEd has been moved up to September 1st. Is that a problem?"

In normal times, yes. However, with a year of work days needing to be filled, it was a godsend.

Doug, "We've been getting a lot of orders for PSAs lately. More than usual. I don't see how we can be done by September."

Rolly, "No problem. It'll get it done."

Doug looked at Rolly, surprised. Steve squinted and looked from one to the other.

"You sure about that Rolly? Your first commercial is barely half-finished. Doug's is already done."

"Yeah, no problem. I'm planning on putting extra hours in."

"Will it be enough to make up for the six weeks you spent twiddling your thumbs?"

That raised eyebrows.

"I'm sure. And then some."

"Prove it. Have your commercial ready for review by Wednesday. Doug, good work on the sunset spot. You need to slow down the sun though, draw it out more."

"Is it still twenty seconds?"

"Twenty-five now. The internet channels are making their commercial breaks longer."

Rolly, "I can do that. I can have both spots for you next week."

Steve was caught off guard. Doug looked shocked.

"This is Doug's job Rolly. He can handle it."

"I know he can, but I need to prove myself. What better way than finishing both projects?"

Steve considered. "If you really do this I can move Doug forward, get us on track for the new deadline. After you set us back. The two of you should be checking each other's work anyway. Rolly, if you succeed that's great, and nothing more. If you fail I'll throw you off inThrallEd, maybe out of the OCM. We don't need non-producers here. You have one week."

Steve turned and left. Macklin scowled at Rolly and followed Steve out. Doug looked angry. Very angry.

"What the hell are you doing? We never touch each other's stuff. You know that."

"I know, I'm sorry. It's just...I'm trying to get retired. Move my Productivity up, get more hours in."

"Ah hell. Are you working with another specialist? Turning into one of those freaky people talking about secret parameters all the time?"

"It's what you'd be doing if you were staring down a two point gap instead of another twenty years."

"Thanks Rolly. Thanks a lot. You're not the only one trying to retire. Ever think of that?"

Rolly didn't want to admit that no, he hadn't thought about it. He said "Sorry Doug" and went back to work. Doug was being selfish, thinking of a retirement decades away. Shouldn't he be helping? Isn't that the right thing to do? Doug had little to gain while he was so close. If Doug wouldn't help he'd have to take what he needed.

———————

Eight o'clock in the evening. Rolly could hear a handful of lingerers, steps going by, a rustle of paper, a brief funny conversation, the copy machine running. Normal sounds made conspicuous by the silence of the usually bustling office.

The sunset commercial was taking longer than anticipated. Doug organized files and commands in ways Rolly found absurd. The commercial had yet to be altered; Rolly was still trying to figure out how Doug fit it all together.

"That didn't go so well. Bit heavy handed I think."

The voice came from Doug's cubicle. Rolly was deep into the project, frustrated, opening a file for the tenth time.

"Yeah, well I keep trying. Sorting out your mess isn't easy."

"I thought I was obsessively well organized."

That wasn't Doug's voice. Rolly turned to see Souliere sitting in Doug's chair, wearing a pink shirt and teal green tie and somehow looking tasteful.

"Jeez, you scared me. Didn't know you were there."

"I only stay late once in awhile, so I won't get interrupted by someone else's emergency. Looks like you've accepted our offer."

"What else am I gonna do?"

"True, but making your coworkers angry is a bad way to start. You're going to need Doug if you want to retire."

"Why?"

"Instead of stealing work wouldn't it be better if they gave it to you?"

"They'll never do that. Especially Doug."

"How do you know until you ask? Pilfering makes you look desperate. All you'll get is animosity. If you think this is hard now wait until everyone hates you."

"I'd feel funny asking. *That* would make me desperate."

"Try. It's easier to get things done with a polite question. And don't be so obvious when sucking up to the boss."

"Thought I did okay. Made an impression."

"Yes, but not a good one. What you did do, and this is a good thing, was create an opening. When the commercials are finished you'll have an excuse to talk to Steve, tell him they're ready for review. It'll be an opportunity to work on those suck-up skills Leah was coaching you on. Sit, smile, nod and listen."

"I'll try my best."

"I know it's not your nature to be a brown-noser. You believe hard work will get you ahead. But that's not true. It's never been true. This is what you do if you want to retire."

"What about you? Rumor is you already retired."

"Nineteen years ago."

"Why the hell would you go back to work? Why not stay retired?"

Souliere smiled and stood up. "That's why we want you to retire. So you can experience it for yourself."

Saturday, January 21st

"Yo dude. You got a text. Want I should read it?"

"Who's it from?"

"That hot chick Leah."

"You can't see. How do you know she's hot?"

"Your pulse goes up, your blood pressure increases, your testosterone level peaks and blood starts flowing to your groin."

"You and EverLife should stop being so friendly."

"What can I say? It's the way we're programmed man. Want me to read it before you get too excited?"

"Yes."

In Leah's voice: "Call me by vid when you have a free moment. Make sure it's private."

Why was she calling him at work? And why would she think he has a free moment? Then again, the choices were limited. He was either working, driving, or unconscious in bed. He could call on his half hour dinner break but finding privacy would be difficult.

"Text her back. Say it will be a few hours before I can call."

"On it." Half a minute went by. "No problem. She'll be waiting."

———————

The break room was out. The only place he could hope to find privacy was one of the perimeter offices, and the only manager who might let him borrow an office was Macklin. She took her dinner break at 5:30. At 5:29 Rolly caught her as she was leaving, pulling on a dark blue overcoat.

"Hey Mack. Mind if I use your office while you're out? Need to make a private call."

She looked at him dubiously. Rolly never asked to use her office. This was a first. "You know how the company feels about personal calls."

"I've already logged out for break. I'm sure it won't take more than the fourteen minutes I have left. I'll be gone long before you're back."

Macklin frowned. "Alright, keep an eye on the time and don't touch anything."

"No problem. Enjoy your dinner."

Macklin walked away, taking the closest thing to a direct route through the cubicle maze, waving to Myrna as she left. Rolly watched her go, then turned to find the door had shut automatically. The knob refused to turn. Locked out.

Shit. Rolly was frantically looking for another open office when he heard a click, metal snapping against hollow metal. He tried the knob again and the door opened. He slipped inside, sat behind Macklin's desk and unfolded his interface. It didn't take long for Leah to answer, wearing black horn-rimmed glasses. No one needed glasses anymore, it was a fashion statement.

"Are you alone?"

"In the physical sense of the word."

"Gotcha." This was common shorthand for yes, there are no other humans present, but who knows how many cameras, microphones and spy programs are watching?

"Just to humor my paranoia, speak in a low voice. We need to keep this between ourselves. I know more about your missing relative."

Leah held up a handwritten sign: *Your Daughter's Name is Nola Cooke.*

"I'm hoping this might ring a bell."

Another sign: *Her Mother was Tressa Monroe.*

Tressa who? "I don't know--"

"Wait, here's a picture." Rolly leaned in for a better look. Leah held up a glossy photo, a portrait of a wrinkled old woman. Rolly jerked back from the screen.

"Sorry. Wrong one. Try this one."

Same woman, this time younger and attractive, black hair in a bob, darker complexion, Asian with some Hawaiian or Polynesian thrown in. Then he remembered.

"She didn't call herself Tressa. It was something that started with a T though. Trudy or Tara I think."

"Doesn't matter what she called herself as long as you recognize her. Anything else?"

"She was fun, smiled a lot, shy but open minded. Girlish."

"Can you remember something besides the usual flirty girl come-ons?"

"Uh...no, not really. It was good sex."

"That's interesting. Describe her. How did she look naked?"

"She was a small girl you know, so she had small breasts. But not too tiny either. Just right, just enough to be a handful. With nice dark nipples that rose up into cute little cones when she got aroused...how does this help you?"

"It doesn't. You remember her breasts better than you remember her name. Use those brain cells for something useful. How long were you with her?"

"About a week. Why the secrecy? As if it matters?"

"There's a glitch in your records and we may not want to fix it. Your familial record says you have one child, your DNA tree says you have two. Paragon's computers read both when your Reckoning is calculated. They're supposed to match and if they don't it should set off an audit. It's been over fifty years and nothing's happened. I don't know why."

"Nola's fifty years old?"

"Over fifty. Got any other bastards I should know about?"

"I didn't know about this one. I wasn't trying to get her pregnant. I thought EverLife prevented that."

"There are ways around everything. If Nola ends up in your familial record it could be disastrous."

"Because two children makes me an irresponsible citizen and the Corporament will need to punish me."

"Something like that. I don't have enough info to know what to do yet. You'll have to be patient while I sort this out."

"How long? If you fix this glitch will it solve my retirement problem?"

"I don't know. This is going to take time and a delicate touch. If I go poking in the wrong place it could set off that audit and we're finished. When I know more I'll let you know."

"So all you need from me is to do nothing."

"Less than nothing. Don't search for either Nola or Tressa, don't try to call, don't tell your friends or your enemies. Keep low, data-wise."

"Okay. Couldn't this have waited until after work?"

"Maybe. Just trying to break up your day, all work and no play and all that garbage. I was bored. And I don't like waiting for answers."

The screen went dead. Rolly frowned and packed up his HearSay. He opened the door and over the cubicle walls could see two heads near the front door, Myrna facing him and the unmistakable back of Macklin's head. *Shit.* He'd been on the phone too long. That meant an extra half hour at the end of the day. Rolly quietly closed the door, crouched down and disappeared back into cubicle land.

Wednesday, February 1st

Rolly cracked the door to his house at 9:47 pm, earlier than usual, looking forward to a few extra minutes of relax time before slipping between the sheets. He let out a tension releasing sigh, head bowed, looking at the floor. He was tired, feeling like he had been through a month of Mondays. In the kitchen Stephanie was waiting, arms folded across her chest, fully dressed in jeans and sweater. She looked ready to walk out the door, though she hadn't been home since New Year's.

"Where have you been?"

"At work. Where have you been?"

"With Jack Kanner. Working late?"

"Who?"

"Customer at Nyros, you don't know him. His wife was...well, I don't know where she was. Vacation, I think."

"Great name. Sounds like a movie star. Did he make you happy?"

"He was good enough."

"Until his wife came home."

"Yeah, and I'm sure you've had a dozen three day tarts."

"Nobody here but me. Don't remember the last time I had sex."

"Don't get your hopes up."

"I'm not. Look, I'm really tired and need to go to bed. Is there something you need?"

"You know I've been home for two days now."

"No, I didn't know that."

"You get up early and shoot out the door by five in the morning and don't get back until after ten at night. I want to know what's going on."

"New retirement specialist. She's making me work more to get my Productivity up."

"You're spending money on another specialist."

"I don't pay her, someone else does."

"What? Who?"

"Souliere."

"Who?"

"Guy from work. You don't know him."

"No. Nope. Don't even want to go there. Are you completely stupid? Drop this nonsense before we lose more money. You should know better after the way you embarrassed us at New Year's."

"No, I'm not doing that. I intend to see this through. Besides, it's free."

"Nothing's free. Whoever is pimping this woman wants something. It's a scam. A developer after our land. Who knows. Drop her now."

Fatigue washed over Rolly; his eyelids wanted to close. It put him in a bad temper. "Who the fuck are you to tell me what to do? You're gone months at a time, playing house with some other guy, and think you can walk in here and start giving orders? I don't think so. Hell, you're always mad because we're not retired and here I am trying to make it happen and all I get is criticized."

Rolly kept going. "Let's look on the bright side. If this works and you retire, that's great. If Leah turns out to be a criminal she might murder me and leave you an unfortunate widow. You win again. Or maybe outer space aliens will abduct me and prepare a dinner with me as the main course. Another win for you. You want me to retire or die and dying is kind of rare these days. You're stuck."

"Stop it, you're not making sense."

"Nothing makes sense. Everything's bullshit."

"What if you fail again? We're both stuck, aren't we?"

"But we won't be any poorer for trying."

Stephanie glared at him. "Leah you said? I want to meet her."

"That's good 'cause she wants to meet you too."

14

Effectively Sterile

Thursday, February 2nd

Max was being slowly tortured to death. He had known this for decades but thought he could endure it. Now he wasn't so sure. Like a dripping water torture the Corporament was driving him insane one empty minute at a time.

After forcing him to sell HoloMax they installed him as CEO of the insipidly named TactiMorph, a provision they insisted he accept. "For your own good," he was told, "No one will hire you. You have a reputation now. And a good job means you can retire." TactiMorph designed three dimensional icons, folders, backgrounds, light cues, and responsive handles for the Tactile Holographic Interface. His invention. Add-ons that let end users customize their experience. Max hated it. He felt like a shoe salesman in a computer store. It wasn't what he was meant to do. He needed to be creating, pushing, solving, moving in a clear direction to accomplish a defined goal. A big goal. Something revolutionary.

The slow torture was partially his own fault. In an act of rebellion he once hacked the Productivity counter and reprogrammed it to "see" an especially productive day over and over. Of course this was illegal and Max expected to be arrested and punished, but no Intervention Agent came to visit, no threatening email was sent. Even now, sitting with feet up on the desk, arms folded, having done nothing for the last hour, his Productivity showed an impressive 99.4%.

Why hadn't they come after him? He didn't try to hide the hack, his tampering had been intentionally sloppy, sure to draw attention. Were they trying to keep him from retiring? The sale of HoloMax had included an enormous sum of money. The Assets parameter was not a problem, and he had no Debt to speak of, so his Credit Rating was excellent. And of course his Productivity was outstanding. According to retirement counselors the sheer amount of money should cover both his lack of Marriage and Children. Which left only Length of Service. And therein lay the answer.

No matter how much he pretended to work, or how much money was in his bank account, he could not cheat the LOS. The fulfillment of this one Parameter was so distant it would take another lifetime. The Corporament with its EverLife induced, godlike mindset--too big, too important and too eternal--could wait him out forever. They didn't need to waste energy punishing Max Smalls. He had dug his own hole and conveniently buried himself in it.

But, like peevish gods, the Corporament was not above petty hostility. Anyone desperate to impress a manager knew Max was an acceptable target. Usually it was amateurish hacks into his bank accounts or TactiMorph and its products, sometimes online rumor spreading and legalized libel. One crazed idiot took a lead pipe to Max's car with him still in it. Six different times a gun had been pointed at his face. So he hired tough looking bodyguards and secretaries with icy voices to scare off the timid ones, but sometimes the more determined suck-ups got through. At least it gave him something to do.

Twice the Corporament teased him with a return to his old company, HoloMax. The first was an upgrade. Max negotiated for a waiver of the marriage requirement and went to work. After he finished the THI functioned better than ever. They told him the waiver was in process, it would appear in his portfolio soon. It never came. Years of fruitless conversations with people at Paragon followed. First they were clueless, then they forgot, then they accused him of trying to defraud the company.

The second time a virus threatened to crash the worldwide THI system. He said "give me my fucking waiver first." They were as good as their word this time; his Reckoning shot up fifty points. He had a specialist print a copy of the waiver. The virus took a good two months of work to eradicate. At the end of the year Max went to his annual audit expecting happy news only to find the waiver had disappeared. When Max showed the counselor the printout she frowned and said "Paper's no good. Too easy to fake. The only official record is on the computer." Max went home and punched holes in the walls of his house, breaking half the bones in both hands. EverLife fixed it, with some extra nanobots and a little help from Nyros. The pain helped dull his humiliation.

And now his endurance--really a nose-to-the-grindstone indifference--was waning. He had hopes something better would come along, but decades passed with no viable prospects. The Corporament had successfully marginalized him. His life was now officially dull.

It was more than a little annoying that his *father* was leading a more interesting life. The man who did what he was told and made no waves. Timid and unchallenging. Dutifully showing up at every trial, offering moral support. Waste of a chair in the gallery, Max thought at the time. And now sitting on the cusp of retirement, working with some mysterious specialist. When Rolly asked for the money back Max tried to hold on to his anger but there was none left. Time had hollowed it out and left it a fragile shell of emptiness. He still had issues with his father--how could the creator of the

THI have come from someone like that?--but could not wish him ill any longer. Max discovered he cared about his father and wanted him to retire.

The two of them were so different. Rolly did what he was told; Max did what he wanted. Rolly followed the rules; Max broke them on purpose. Rolly had a mediocre life; Max had everything he wanted. And all the consequences. In spite of the outward dependability his father was not completely trustworthy. When Max was a child Rolly locked the family in the basement for a week saying they were hiding from a tornado. That was nonsense. No one hides from a tornado for a week. Later, when he was a teenager, Max asked what really happened and his father became angry. Rolly never showed anger, he was always calm and self-controlled. Watching his father turn monster and scream with rage was too much. It left bitter feelings.

A beam saver traced colorful whirls in the air over Max's desk. If he brushed the image it would revert to the floating icons of his workspace. A TactiMorph product, pretty and useless.

Max worried his father was too trusting, that this new specialist might be another con artist. He could give his parents more money, the one thing holding them back, but he wasn't ready to go that far. It satisfied his sense of duty to repay the money with interest, and nothing more. Besides, Rolly's pride wouldn't allow him to accept it.

A knock on Max's door. Nick, one of his employees, entered.

"I can't get the stars in the new background to shine. They're there, they just don't shine."

Nick was not very bright. He would likely be a long term employee since the Corporament snatched anyone who showed the slightest hint of intelligence. Max spent most of his time teaching Nick, and the rest of his staff, the basics. Yet another example of leisurely Corporament torture.

Max sighed. "I'll be right there."

Friday, February 3rd

"Good morning Rolly! It's nice to see you again!"

Lambert caught him returning from the break room. Her cheeriness always had a hint of aggression. Rolly chose to ignore it, grateful she took the time to try.

"Morning Lambert. How are you?"

"I am just peachy Mr. Smalls. I have a request for you." Her "requests" were a euphemism for more work. Lambert was obviously nervous about asking again. His attitude had been surly the last two weeks and she had taken the brunt of it. Rolly felt guilty so he made an effort to be happier.

"Nancy in Social Media is asking you to take a look at her embedded ad. The one with the construction workers talking in female voices."

An ad that depended on the right juxtaposition of burly workmen and soft feminine voices. Yet another idea being recycled. It would have a limited run; the surprise wore off quickly. Nancy liked things straight ahead. No irony, mismatches, or dissonance. When assigned projects out of her comfort zone Nancy went overboard, not knowing where to stop. Someone would have to correct it eventually.

"Tell Nancy to send it to my workstation."

Lambert nearly jumped up, putting both hands on his arm. "Oh, you're the best Rolly! Thank you! Just turn it in when you're done."

"Sure." He began to walk away. "Hey, wait--" but she had disappeared.

Ever since he completed both his and Doug's initial projects--and earned Steve's satisfaction-coworkers had been asking for "help." Apparently Lambert was their chosen messenger. These were unfinished or behind schedule projects. He needed the work, but being everyone's mule? This is why he was irritated. Rolly couldn't help feeling like he was being used. His friends were taking advantage and his only choice was to put up with it.

Sunday, February 5th

"I have to warn you, she's stunning. Totally gorgeous."

"Have you fucked her yet?" Stephanie only used "fuck" when feeling hostile.

"This coming from the woman who played house with Jack Kanner for a month."

"I know you Rolly. Your hands will be wandering in no time."

"It's not gonna happen."

"Right."

Rolly led her through the maze to Leah's office. Leah greeted Stephanie with a handshake.

"Hi Stephanie, nice to meet you."

"Oh my lord. He said you were gorgeous but this is unreal."

"Well thank you, you're very pretty yourself."

Stephanie stared until Rolly got her attention and pointed toward a chair.

"Thank you for coming. We need your help to get Rolly retired."

"This isn't real is it? I mean your looks. You've had surgery, right?" Stephanie was pleading.

"Yes I did. Many years ago. To get a promotion."

"Did it work?"

"It did."

"You're not wearing makeup."

"Nope. Everything's already in place. All I have to do is keep it clean."

Stephanie's eyes narrowed. "What were you before?"

"Sorry?"

"What were you before the surgery?"

"A human female?"

"Okay, that's good." Leah was being sarcastic but Stephanie missed it, instead looking relieved. Leah, obviously insulted, opened her mouth to retort. Rolly interrupted.

"Maybe, to put our minds at ease, you could tell us more about yourself." Rolly felt like a school principal playing referee between bickering parents.

Leah closed her mouth and looked wryly at Rolly. She must have had a particularly cutting insult lined up. "I used to be a short mousy girl with a lot of ambition. Everyone looked over the top of me as if I wasn't there. So I fixed it. Found the most expensive surgeon, designed the best face and body, went from five foot two to five foot ten. Amazing how a few inches of elevation changes your perspective."

A height extension beyond a couple of inches was radical, even in an image obsessed society, and extremely expensive.

"You got a new face and body and fucked your way to a promotion."

"People fuck with each other all the time. I just made it work for me."

"Why are you helping my husband? What's in it for you?"

"As I'm sure he's told you, I'm being paid by a mutual acquaintance."

"Some guy named Souliere. Can he be trusted?"

"I've worked with him before. Honors his contracts and pays his bills. Actually doesn't fuck with people, which is a little weird, but he's okay."

"Why is he helping Rolly?"

"I don't ask and he doesn't tell."

"Why should we trust you?"

"If I was going to scam you, don't you think I'd be a little nicer?"

"Could be a cover-up. You seem smart. You could pull it off."

"Stephanie, if you want to end this, do it now, before I spend any more time on you."

"Won't you lose your fee?"

"I have 112 clients who would love to see me show up at their door. And that's just in this town. There's no shortage of people who want to retire."

Rolly, "I thought you chose your own clients."

"I do. And I have a reputation. People send me names and I chose who to help. Usually the ones who are walking the edge. That's where Rolly is. Retirement in reach but if he doesn't bust his butt now it will disappear."

"By driving him crazy? Fifteen hours a days seven days a week? That's bullshit. If we miss this year we'll try again next year. That's how everybody does it. That's how you're *supposed* to do it."

"And how's that working? How many *decades* have you been trying? The Number is always slipping away. I know clients whose Reckoning was only a half point away and they still failed. Some expense comes up, someone loses a job, or maybe The Number goes up more than expected. It's always out of reach."

"Max paid us back. That's going to put us over. Eventually."

"Because Max paid you back is the only reason I'm here. It will count for nothing if you do nothing. Remember Rolly's Reckoning before Max was so generous?"

Rolly, "Same as the previous year."

"He's already sliding backwards. Max did a wonderful thing but it's not enough. Rolly needs to work harder than ever, doing the thing he hates the most. That's his leap of faith."

Rolly and Stephanie stared at Leah, the manufactured goddess, the sum total and representation of a thousand lifetimes of beauty, slouching in her chair like an office manager explaining good work ethics to new hires.

"Why am I here, if this is all about Rolly?"

"He needs your help with the debt."

"That's not my fault."

"No it's not. Rolly is mostly to blame. And Gordon O'Leary. But don't get me started. The debt has to come down."

"Use part of the savings."

"It's too large. Cutting the debt by three quarters will deplete more than half your savings. The benefit you gain by lowering the debt is offset by the loss in savings and you end up back in the same position."

"How big is this debt?"

Leah turned her monitor so Stephanie could see. Large black numbers on a grey background, the last few digits increasing as interest was added.

"What the hell! Where did this come from?!"

Rolly, "It's not all me. Some was there before I went shopping."

"But it was manageable! We kept it under...what was it? 20% of savings? And you tripled that!"

"I thought I was doing the right thing."

"Blame O'Leary. The bastard preys on desperate people. Rolly shouldn't have trusted him but we can't take it back."

"What the hell are we going to do?"

"I'm asking you to take a second job and use the income to pay down the debt."

The next few minutes are best described as a tirade, or maybe a whirlwind of expletives aimed at Rolly, zinging out of Stephanie's mouth like supersonic failure-seeking air-to-air missiles. His intelligence and manhood were questioned in the same sentence, whether he exhibited age appropriate behavior or not, what part of his body he used for thinking, the apparent lack of size of said body part, her insistence that his brain would likely fit into said body part, and his ancient ancestors who somewhere in the distant past apparently fornicated with a cow.

Rolly sat numb and took his punishment. Leah interjected an agreeable comment now and then, but mostly let Stephanie rant.

Stephanie dropped into the chair and looked away at one of Leah's blank walls. Rolly stared straight ahead. She had a bottomless reserve of insults; he was waiting for the residual abuse to be launched. Stephanie only turned and stared, saying nothing, with a look that said she wanted to rip his skin off.

"I had no idea she was going to ask for that."

"You had no idea? That's the truth."

Leah, "I don't blame you for being angry. But it's not as bad as you--"

"What makes you think I'll be able to take another job? What if Nyros won't let me?"

"Nyros is surprisingly open minded about second jobs. Probably because they hire a lot of transients. I'm sure they won't mind if a reliable employee were to ask."

"You know how long it's been since I've looked for a job?"

"I already have a line on one, not far from your office. St. Bart's Hospital needs nurses. You've been out of it awhile but they're more than happy to talk to you."

"They are?"

"You have an interview tomorrow at six o'clock. In the evening."

Stephanie's mouth dropped open. "What the...have you planned the rest of my week as well? What if I don't show up for this interview?"

"That's your choice. But Rolly won't retire. And neither will you."

Stephanie rolled her eyes and looked at the ceiling. "I have to work to pay off your goddamn tv."

"No, you cut the debt with money from savings to avoid more interest. Money from the second job goes to build savings back up."

"Sounds better than paying for his stupidity. Is this all I have to do?"

"Both of you need to limit spending. Only buy essentials. Food and gas, enough to function on, nothing more. No extravagances, eat your toast plain. No eating out, take your lunch and dinner to work. No long trips. No new clothes, wear your old ones. No new gadgets, no upgrades or new voices, nothing new at all. If something breaks, decide if you really need it before replacing it. Or repair it yourself. Live with what you've got. Rolly will put money he doesn't spend into savings as well."

"Absolutely. No problem. I'll save every quarter."

"Stephanie, what do you think?"

She sat quietly, chewing her lower lip, then turned to Rolly. "I'll be home the rest of the year. Can you handle that?"

"I'll be at work or asleep. You'll be happy as a clam."

"Don't get smart. You're going to owe me big time."

"I know."

Tuesday, February 7th

A daughter. Rolly kept rolling the thought around trying to get a handle on it. Another child, by another woman. He worried how much legal trouble this might cause, tried to remind himself this girl was an adult, then wondered why nobody told him and why *didn't* he get in trouble all those years ago. Emotions lingering without closure. Who might she be, what did she do, who was she married to, did he have grandchildren, and the big question, should he meet her? Would she want to meet him? Did she know about him? Would there be resentment?

After Max grew up and left the house Stephanie started talking about about another child, wanting a daughter. The timing seemed good, the Corporament preferred to see parents with one child at a time, but only a few spots opened every year. The waiting list was long and birth permits took years to obtain. Stephanie never started the process; Rolly didn't know why. He didn't want another child, but it was not like Stephanie to let his opinion get in the way of her desires. Other reasons must have stopped her. A down economy, a sudden spike in births, parameter restrictions tightened again. A media full of experts advising everyone to make the most of their strongest parameter, and by all means, do not have another child.

A daughter. All these decades of acting like the father of an only child. Rolly tried to imagine meeting her and a pit of fear opened in the middle of his gut. This girl who should have had someone to support her didn't. This child who should have been protected wasn't. She had matured without a father to teach her who to trust or how to face a world of constant nagging corruptions. No one taught her how to deal with the Corporament. Maybe someone had stepped up and taken care of her. He didn't know. All he had was a name and a barely remembered tryst.

Sean broke his reverie. "'Nother text from hot chick Leah."

"Read it."

"See me at the office after work." Leah wanted to talk without being snooped.

"Text her back and tell her I'll be there around ten o'clock."

"'Kay. Done."

It was pitch dark and damp cold when Rolly arrived at Leah's office. He was tired; he wanted this over quickly.

"I know more about the mother of your long lost child."

"Tell me."

"Tressa Monroe, born May 14th, 2071 in Chicago, parents had good jobs, stable family. No major run-ins with the law, although she was cited for disorderly conduct at seventeen. Don't know what she did but that's about the time the transient laws were in dispute.

"Never married but decided she wanted a child. Applied for a permit, was put on a waiting list and told it would be ten years. She didn't want to wait. This is all in the transcripts and vid files from her trial if you want to check them out."

"She was put on trial?"

"For violations of the Population Protection Act. Your daughter was illegal."

He should have known that. "What happened?"

"She was an EverLife User. Its birth control functions were fully activated. She had to get off it without anyone noticing. So she played musical techs, telling one she was moving to another in time to avoid her next quarterly. She stayed off EverLife a full year, long enough for the chemical contraception to wear off. Then went looking for a donor."

"I was the lucky guy. Why'd she choose me?"

"Said you held the door for her at a restaurant and were very tall."

"Didn't take much to impress her."

"Very little in fact. Just remember, all she wanted was your sperm."

Rolly was not entirely sure how he felt about that.

"Once pregnant she disappeared. The psycops tracked her HearSay to a landfill where they found it without her attached. They searched a couple of billion faces with no luck. Either she was dead or beyond the Corporament, equivalent ends in their view. She suddenly showed up at a hospital, staggering like an old drunk, the baby trying to push its way out. She was dirty and smelled like a sewer. The baby came out healthy. Tressa was reported to the authorities, arrested in the delivery room, handcuffed to her bed. The baby was taken away.

"She refused to say where she had been but did spill everything else, identifying you as the father. Admitted lying, took responsibility for everything.

"There's a court case, Blain vs. Marroso, went all the way to the Supreme Court, when it still existed. The justices decided that, given the prevalence of EverLife and the need to control population growth, it was reasonable to assume any woman would be effectively sterile. Even if Tressa said nothing you'd be off the hook. In the eyes of the court you were an unwitting donor and therefore not guilty. So no one told you. For her honesty they sentenced Tressa to exile, mandatory punishment for illegal conception and birth."

This was harsh, even beyond the common "EverLife sequestration," Corporament parlance for cutting off access to EverLife. Taking away EverLife was an established penalty for various crimes. For the length of their sentences criminals got to look in the mirror everyday and watch themselves grow older. Wrinkles deepened, spots formed, joints creaked. They were vulnerable, a simple scratch might become infected and kill. Convicts were always under stress and always looked scared. Ask one what they were feeling and they would say death was flying at them. They longed to get back to EverLife.

Exiles, however, were forbidden from taking EverLife for remainder of their natural life, and considered lower than transients. Some could live in the cities as long as they were escorted. Others weren't allowed anywhere near population centers. Women convicted of illegal birthing were given extra punishment: made to leave their home cities and live a thousand miles away, and--as insurance against future pregnancies--removal of their ovaries.

"Why would she do that? Why give it all away?"

"Lie? Are you nuts? The Corporament knows when you're going to lie before you do."

"She stayed hidden for nine months. Plenty of time to think up an excuse that couldn't be verified."

Deep sigh. "Rolly, I don't know how women like this think. There's no logic, nothing rational I can follow. Maybe her plans fell through. Maybe she had second thoughts. I don't know and it's beyond my job to figure it out."

"Where is Tressa now?"

"She died a month ago at a transient haven in Pennsylvania. In real years she was 85, but she spent eight years on EverLife. Her actual age at death was 77."

"That first picture you showed, the old woman, was that her?"

"Yes."

"Can I see it again?" Leah pulled the printed picture out of a file folder. A full-length shot, taken outside on a hillside, green grass in the background. Tressa wore a brown ankle length skirt with a purple shawl around her shoulders, hair grey but not all the way. Face wrinkled and darker than he remembered. She had a stoop in her shoulders and a walking stick taller than herself. She was smiling. A genuine ear-to-ear grin, not a tight lipped false smile, or the I'm-being-tolerant-of-the-photographer smile, but a real smile of happiness.

"She looks happy. How could someone in exile be happy?"

"Pictures from the havens are hard to come by. Family members send pics to one another, usually privately, but once in a while one turns up on the general internet. That's how I found this one, using a facial search with her mugshot. I don't know anything about her life after she was exiled. The picture is dated five months before she died. How she got happy is a mystery."

"What about Nola?"

"Still working on it. How you doin' with this Rolly? Must be a shock to the system."

"Don't know what to do. Don't know what to think. An adult child with a life of her own I was never part of. She probably hates me."

"She might. We'll know more in a few months."

"How old is she?"

"Nola is fifty-two."

"Wow. Way beyond my influence. Old enough to build up plenty of resentment. You think she would want to see me?"

"I have no idea...wait...are you thinking of seeing her?"

Rolly opened his mouth to make an excuse but nothing came out.

"I figured. That is the absolute last thing you want to do. Tying Nola to yourself would blow your retirement to shreds. A second child on your record, a second dependent on your assets. She's the kiss of death. Stay away, be like most men and ignore her."

"Be like most men? What's that supposed to mean?"

"You're not the first man to dip his wick in the wrong honeypot. I've had many clients with children lurking in their DNA. It's common, given how everyone is fucking each other all the time. Most men say Oh That's Nice and move on. You need to be like that. And you need to tell Stephanie."

"How do you know I haven't already?"

"Because that's who you are. Keeping things tight. Hiding your mistakes. Stephanie won't like it no matter when you tell her, so get it over with."

"I'll do it as soon as I can." Rolly had no intention of telling Stephanie at all, ever.

Saturday, February 11th

Five o'clock in the morning, the sun not even hinting at the horizon. Rolly pulled a box of breakfast out of the freezer and tossed it in the Flamer, a clear glass device that looked like a cake stand with two green strips running around the top and bottom. The Flamer read a code on the packaging then incinerated everything (cardboard was often spiced to add flavor) in a convection tornado of infrared heat and microwaves. Rolly's box of breakfast burritos and pancakes took forty-nine seconds to go from frozen bricks into steaming food shaped substances.

The taste of food cooked from scratch would always live in Rolly's memories but such luxuries were beyond him. A restaurant that created recipes from fresh ingredients? Best not to torture yourself with thoughts like that.

Stephanie surprised him by plopping into a chair across the table, wearing an oversized fluffy terrycloth robe, eyes swollen with sleep. She was not a morning person.

"What are you doing up?"

She pulled the robe a little tighter, like trying to curl up under a blanket. "I thought I should...I wanted to...tell you I got the job."

"At St. Bart's?"

"Yes."

"Sure you want to do this? It's not the best neighborhood." Only a few blocks from her regular job, but the difference from one block to the next was night and day.

Stephanie opened her eyes, annoyed, "Of course I don't. It's Leah's idea."

"Where are they putting you?"

"Emergency room and overnight geriatrics." St. Bart's served mostly transients.

"That's bottom of the barrel. You've got thirty years as a nurse. How could they treat you like that?"

Stephanie, still waking up, yelled like a child throwing a tantrum. "I don't have seniority! They wouldn't give me what I wanted. Said they'd put me where they needed me. I didn't have a choice. Said if I stayed five years they'd make me a supervisor. I ain't staying in that stinking dung heap any longer than I have to."

"I thought they were desperate for nurses."

"Only dumps like St. Bart's are that bad off."

"I'm sorry you have to do this Steph."

"You should be."

One of the many changes EverLife wrought was the decimation of the nursing profession. Technicians and tech assistants handled Users and any extra care they might need; only transients needed nurses. Low pay and the need to develop a meaningless skill made the profession less than desirable. Hospitals like St. Bart's would hire any warm body. An experienced nurse like Stephanie should be a treasure.

"How'd you convince Nyros to let you take the second job?"

"Told them I'd get more physiologic exper...know how and it would make me a better employee."

"They believed that?"

"They were cool. Don't think they cared. Business has been good for a long time."

At St. Bart's Stephanie would learn to treat cancer and heart problems, bacterial infections, sinus problems, headaches, broken bones; geriatric issues like arthritis and Alzheimer's, useless knowledge in the real world but handy for a surgery store like Nyros.

Stephanie rubbed her eyes and yawned. "I start tonight. Thought I should tell you now 'cause we'll be missing each other going in and out."

"Thanks for doing this Steph. I really appreciate it."

"You're welcome." She smiled and Rolly took the time to enjoy it, knowing if she were fully awake there would be no smile at all.

15

Genial Confrontations

Monday, February 28th

Documents, pictures and graphs and charts–oh my–scrolled across Stephanie's monitor, popping up and demanding immediate attention, a queue of pressing issues waiting impatiently in the virtual rectangle.

Stephanie's elbows were planted on the desk, fingers raked into her hair, pulling the skin of her face as if being blown back by intense g-forces. She was tired. All the issues plaguing her were part of a normal day for a Nyros regional manager but she wasn't handling it well. The company had 112 operating theaters in the Lansing district, ranging from one technician store fronts in strip malls to larger suburban complexes employing a dozen techs. Maintenance crews needed to be coordinated, employees scheduled, mistakes corrected and apologized for. Two days ago an Asian woman had gone under for lip enhancement; the robot gave her blonde eyebrows instead. Stephanie didn't know if it was machine or operator error. Either way the tech would lose his job. Not that it mattered. He was transient and they were plentiful. A hundred would be clamoring to take his place.

Long nights working St. Bart's were doing her in. Part time evenings and weekends, eating on the run, go home and sleep, get up, do it over. That damn hospital was a sinkhole swallowing her happiness, and she was facing ten more months of late night shifts. That last thought was best avoided. It made her imagine creative ways of eviscerating Rolly.

Nikki, Stephanie's HearSay, buzzed her.

"What is it?"

"You are receiving a voice and video call from Leah Lockwood. Do you want to take it?"

"Yes." Stephanie slammed down the monitor, pulled out her HearSay and watched it unfurl. It had taken a long time and a lot of money to find the right HearSay voice. Stephanie knew exactly what she wanted: female with the right amount of deference, acquiescent and confident. In the end she had a custom voice created, an amalgam of professionally mixed personalities, primarily a Japanese geisha and a husky voiced actress popular a hundred years ago. Nikki would do exactly as told, never question anything Stephanie said or did, never make suggestions of her own and never use contractions. Every word needed to be uttered with absolute clarity.

Stephanie's first words to Leah were: "I'm tired."

"I'm sure you are, all the work you're doing."

"Don't think I can make it the rest of the year."

"Then you won't retire."

"You're supposed to offer a sympathetic ear."

"You are welcome to call anytime you want and dump as much baggage as you need. But I don't do sympathy."

"You called me face-to-face to tell me you're a bitch?"

Leah smiled. "No, I called to tell you something you don't know."

"A secret?"

"Secrets are for children." Leah placed a handwritten sign in front of her camera that read:

Rolly has another child from an old lover, a daughter, who is grown and very much alive.

Anger bloomed and spread to the muscles of Stephanie's body, tensing her like a bear trap. *She* wanted a second baby. *She* wanted a daughter. Rolly didn't. They needed to make retirement, end of discussion. Save money, work harder, work longer, be loyal, and for god's sake whatever you do, don't have a second child. Stephanie put her name on the birth license waiting list anyway, but anti-birth hostility was everywhere. Friends and coworkers talked about pregnant women as if they were traitors. A lover threw her out when she mentioned wanting another child. Her best friend looked appalled. So Stephanie took her name off the list, in favor of retirement, making a sacrifice for their mutual goal. But Rolly, who couldn't keep his dick in his pants, screwed it up.

Stephanie's voice dropped three whole tones. "What do you know."

Leah related the story of Rolly's daughter with all the drama and exclamations of a teenage girl gossiping about boys at school. The tone was so jarring it took a moment to realize she was using false modulations to hide information from the Corporament's trolling computers. Leah was careful not mention any names or specific information.

"Is that all?"

"I'm sure there's more. It'll take time to find it."

"I want to know as soon as you do. No, change that. I want to know before you tell you-know-who."

"Can't do that. He's my client. I have to tell him first."

"What, like it's a rule or something? Screw that, tell me first."

"No rules, professional ethics. He's my client, news goes to him first."

"Yet here you are telling me about his bastard."

"Information is power. Withholding information is power too, but it's petty, small minded. The more power you have the more likely you'll retire.

It's a simple equation. He isn't telling you because he's embarrassed. Or afraid. Either way he needs to get over it and keep you in the loop."

"But telling me first is the wrong thing."

"Yes it is."

"You have a warped sense of ethics."

"My ethics are impeccable. Of course I *can* tell both of you at the same time."

"What? A loophole?"

"We get together and the three of us talk. You'll have to get straight with him first, make sure you're on the same page."

"You mean confront him."

"Whatever you want to call it."

"Well then, I will plan on having a genial confrontation with my philandering husband."

Wednesday, March 1st

Sitting in the break room, cup of coffee on the table growing cold, staring at a blank wall, contemplating what shade of beige it might be.

Rolly hadn't taken a break since the beginning of the year. Today, at the urging of an automated computer voice, he stood up and left his workstation, brain frazzled, body moving out of cow-to-the-barn habit. He bought a coffee from the machine, sat down at the round brown table, and stopped. Now he was lost in deep thoughts regarding the shading of wall paint.

Rolly was overwhelmed by the amount of work coming his way. By now he should be long caught up and desperately looking for something to do. Instead coworkers were loading him with behind schedule projects, asking for advice that turned into more work, and dragging him to meetings with long discussions about trivial issues. Rolly was so busy he barely had time to complete his own assignments. Some spilled over into Doug's lap. Their conversations were short and monosyllabic; Rolly figured it wouldn't be long before they weren't speaking at all.

Lambert no longer brought requests. She kept a waiting list instead. He never had to ask: when he finished she would appear with the next project urgently in need of help.

If he had the time Rolly would be angry. Did they think so little of him? The worst part was knowing they were doing less, enough to maintain average productivity, while he did the work of two. And Lambert had become his de facto secretary. She seemed happy. Rolly wondered if her smile was surgically permanent. He liked it better when they were equals.

Steve Mann noticed but how he felt about it was a mystery. Rolly didn't have enough time to do any meaningful kissing up; that Steve's office was a floor higher didn't help. When Steve came down to move among the serfs he seemed to watch Rolly more than normal. Rolly wasn't sure what this meant.

Souliere walked in and broke the trance, ordering himself a coffee. Rolly had lost track of time. He should get back to his desk. Before he could rise Souliere parked in a chair and started chatting.

"Ever wonder how many people have retired?"

"No, everyone retires. Eventually."

"Actually no, not everyone retires."

"How do you know?"

"Mark LaDuke in purchasing. Has three more years than you and he's nowhere near. Too many divorces."

"That's one guy and it's his own fault."

"Aimee Kiesler, Graham Shanley and Drew Thorpe, all in claims, all working about as long as you, none even thinking about retirement for the same reason: too much debt."

"Are you trying to depress me? 'Cause I really don't need any help in that department."

"It's hard to tell since everyone looks young. You can't look at someone who looks older and wonder why haven't they retired. Age hides. Do you remember, when EverLife came along, how many people were living in the United States?"

"Three hundred and fifty million, or something like that."

"It's been one hundred and twenty years since EverLife and how many of those thee hundred and fifty million have retired?"

"Well, not all were adults, not all had good jobs, some were unlucky..."

"Don't you think, having worked as long as you have, most of those original Users would be retired? How many people would that be? Millions? I'll bet you can count on one hand the number of people you know who've retired."

Rolly had counted. Friends and family, acquaintances, distant cousins, the stepfather of a friend of a friend's brother, people he didn't know he'd only heard had retired. Six people. That was all.

"I hope you make retirement Rolly, I really do. You know there's a pool going."

"For what?"

"Whether you retire or not."

"How do they know I'm trying to retire?"

"Nothing is as fleeting as a secret in an office. Everyone knows. Most of these folks are betting you're going to make it. Goes against common sense, but that's the way it is."

"I get it. They're trying to make me give up so they can win the money."

"You're such a pessimist Rolly. They *want* to see you retire. They know your son has money. They know you came close last year. They're helping because you're on the brink and they need to see someone make it so they don't feel like they're working in vain. Don't be angry, be thankful. Smile and enjoy it. The world is coming to you for a change."

Friday, March 3rd

Lost in a project (tentatively titled "Orange Peels: The Danger From Within"), Rolly felt a presence behind him. Usually it was Lambert, who had developed the unnerving ability to appear and disappear without apparent movement. Rolly turned and there she was, smiling and patiently waiting.

"Good afternoon Rolly. I have a request from Brygid, in static ads. She would like you to review this photo and let her know what's wrong with it."

Lambert was holding a sheet of paper, a rare thing. "That's unusually open minded for Brygid."

"Those were her words. Says she knows something's wrong but can't put her finger on it." Rolly found this flattering and confusing.

"Okay, I'll take a look." He stood to stretch his legs. It caught Lambert off guard; she stood her ground but looked surprised. They ended up shoulder to nose, Rolly taking the paper from her hand. He had never been this close to Lambert and only now realized how feminine she was. And pretty. Lambert looked up with big green eyes. Rolly made a great effort to put the lust out of his mind. He liked Lambert and valued their relationship. Ruining it with sex would be stupid.

Rolly took a half step back. So did Lambert.

The picture was utterly dull. A man staring straight ahead wearing a suit jacket and something underneath that wasn't clear, with a generic expression that could be interpreted fifty different ways. Brygid didn't know what was wrong with this? Was she blind? Or lazy? He decided to send it back, claiming ignorance of its deficiencies.

Over the tops of the cubicles Rolly saw Macklin talking to Steve Mann. A surprise visit. As he watched they looked in his direction, several times, nodding as they did. They separated and Steve began walking his way.

Rolly immediately sat down. Better to meet the boss seated. He said to Lambert, "Yeah, I'll see what I can do."

Lambert knew him too well. "Something's happening, isn't it?"

"It might be best if you go." Rolly expected this to be bad.

"Okay. I'll be back." Meaning I-expect-the-details-later.

Steve charged in right after she turned the corner. "Rolly I have a job for you."

"Hi Steve. How are you?" Giving a greeting when none had been offered. Rolly felt foolish. Steve ignored it.

"I need a video put together by tomorrow noon. It's a new InThrallEd element, not on the schedule. Can you do it?"

"How good does it need to be?"

"I'm presenting it to the board. They're not expecting a finished product so it doesn't need to be perfect." *Yes it does.*

"Okay. What is it?"

"I'll send you the details but in a nutshell we want to add a new character we're calling Mr. Dodds who guides the insured out of danger. There's a preliminary script and a description, but he'll need some situations to work with. Can you do it?"

"Absolutely."

"Good. Don't let me down." Steve turned and left.

Rolly rubbed his eyes, realizing he had condemned himself to an overnight stay in the office. When he opened them again, Lambert was occupying the space where Steve had been.

"I won't be going home tonight."

"I heard. I think your new reputation is getting noticed."

"Reputation?"

"For getting things done. This is very cool Rolly."

"Yeah, guess it is. Could you tell Brygid she's gonna have to wait?"

"No problem. I'll put on a big pot of coffee before I leave tonight."

Rolly silently groaned. "Thanks Lambert."

Saturday, March 4th

Stephanie was standing at the foot of a patient bed, six beds crammed in with barely enough room to squeeze between, all the patients sleeping by way of exhaustion or drugs, a record screen in hand as if about to write something, and she couldn't remember why she was here.

She wore a baby blue uniform and white support shoes. Curly hair pinned back against her scalp tight enough to hurt. The room was dark, one nightlight in the corner plus the glow from her screen.

Her first few days were the definition of trial by fire. The old skills did not come back easily. Giving shots, inserting IV lines, dressing wounds, things that should have been second nature were fumbled by out of practice fingers. She didn't know where anything was and felt stupid having to ask where gauze was stored while a patient bled onto the floor. But no one seemed bothered. No doctors chewed her out.

One person died because of her. A black man, transient, in severe shock from electrocution, organs beginning to shut down, the damage to his brain unknown. One dose of cephladone would have stimulated the heart, keeping him alive. She was nervous, hands shaking, the only nurse in the room with one doctor. He had to tell her where the syringes were, then she dropped the medicine bottle and had to grab another, shoved the needle in too far passing through the man's vein, trying the other arm, that vein disappearing as she watched, trying again before it disappeared, then the steady whine of the heart rate monitor.

The doctor did not try to resuscitate him. He turned off the respirator and called the morgue. On the way out he said "Oh well, better luck next time." Referring to her fumbling. He smiled like he was trying to cheer her up.

The dead man lay naked to the waist. Receding hair, touch of grey around the edges, potbelly. Wrinkles and age spots on his face, fat rolls around his stomach, a thin patch of tightly curled chest hair. Older, fifties or sixties maybe. Worst were the moles and skin tags that sprouted like raisins in random spots. The details of old age bothered Stephanie most.

Stephanie was still standing with stylus in hand as if about to write. Why was she here? Who was this patient? The machines--blowing, beeping or softly thrumming--had settled into a syncopated rhythm, like a heartbeat with more anticipation. Heat from the machines, as well as the patients, gave the room a slumber inducing warmth. Maybe that had lulled her, put her to sleep standing up. Stephanie pulled up the clipboard attached to the bed, tilting her screen so its light illuminated the paper. Nadine Holleran. What was Nadine in for? Respiratory infection, the common cold gone awry. She remembered the woman bending over and hacking into a rag. Long greasy uncombed hair, baggy dirty sweats. Fat, with a stomach overhang like a pregnant kangaroo.

How could someone so poor end up so fat? You think they'd eat less for having less.

Antibiotics were pumping into Nadine's bloodstream, a respirator was trying to push clean air into her raspy lungs. Stephanie remembered: she was to check on Nadine and two other patients, observing current conditions and any changes, and noting them in the electronic records.

She quickly finished and exited the room, trying to look like she was going somewhere in a hurry, to discourage anyone from drafting her into another emergency.

Stephanie hated this job. Absolutely loathed it. Could barely bring herself to show up. Thought she would easily slip back into the old skills and enjoy it as a nice change of pace. That hadn't been the case at all. She was becoming more comfortable with the layout and finally getting some of her skills back, but the patients were repugnant. She thanked God for latex gloves every day.

She was doing this to herself why? So her witless, sex obsessed husband could finally retire and sweep her off into the great beyond? God, she hoped divorce was allowed in retirement. Had there ever been anything worthwhile about him? Was she so blinded by love she missed his many failings? This was the price she paid for being naïve: working two jobs while he screwed around and fathered a second child. A second child! The thought burned like a red hot coal. The child was a virus waiting to hack their retirement. He couldn't even screw up right. It was time to stop being nice. There would be hell to pay.

Sunday, March 5th

Rolly pulled the car into the garage, turned it off, told Sean to shut the garage door, and slumped down in the seat with his head back, staring at the bluish-grayish ceiling of the car.

This was in-between time. After work and the stress of driving home and before entering the lair of Stephanie, the only time he felt free to relax and enjoy some peace.

Many minutes went by. Eventually Rolly forced himself out of the car and into the house to find every light at full intensity, bright flickering images pounding in the hologram room, but no sound. Blinding and quiet at the same time, like that unsettling moment in movies before the bomb goes off.

Stephanie's door slammed open and she burst out yelling at the top of her lungs.

"Why didn't you tell me you had a bastard daughter!"

"I only just found out."

"Three months ago!"

"Well it seemed like yesterday, considering I'm a hundred and forty-seven years old."

"You were never going to tell me!"

He knew Stephanie wanted to scare, intimidate, cut him down and hurt him. Humiliate and embarrass him. She wanted to be begged for forgiveness.

"No, I wasn't going to tell you at all. Ever."

She looked triumphant. "You were going to hide her away and hope I didn't find out."

"There's no hiding to do. I don't know who she is or where she is or what she does. And if I find out more I won't tell you that either. Because it doesn't matter. Out of sight and out of mind. End of story."

Rolly tried to find a place to sit down but all the lights and activity made it seem like Stephanie occupied the entire house. No chair felt safe to sit in.

"I don't believe you, the man who gave half our life savings away. You *want* to know who she is. She's probably a transient living off Corporament welfare. A hundred of those people come into the hospital every day. This could ruin everything and you didn't tell me!"

"Oh well. Like I said, out of sight, out of mind."

"Is that all you have to say?"

"Yep."

"Don't you even have the decency to act guilty?"

"Act guilty? Is that all it takes? 'I am deeply sorry for the pain and suffering I have caused you over the past century.' There. I acted guilty. Happy?"

"Jackass! You're the one who made an illegit child! Even though I wanted one! A daughter of my own but you kept saying," in a sarcastic idiot accented voice, "'We have to retire. Let's retire first. Wait until after we retire. You'll be fertile forever. You can have as many kids as you want. After we retire.' On and on so I gave it up, and here it is, what? seventy years later? And how retired are we? We're stuck here because you can't stop fucking around!"

"Like you're a saint. Hooking up with other guys until they get sick of your shit. You're no better."

"That's different and you know it. How many women do you screw in a month? Ten? Five when it's slow? That's fifteen in three months. Or more. I'm with one guy and you're with fifteen. Do the math and figure out which is worse."

Rolly was seething. This was nonsense but he couldn't think of a decent retort. So he lost all control.

"You act holier-than-thou, as if you're the only one trying to retire. I've been busting my ass for twelve decades, doing everything I'm supposed to, working hard, saving money, being fucking responsible, and here I am still stuck in this fucking hole. Except the fucking hole is deeper now because of one stupid little mistake, because I thought every woman was on EverLife and didn't think one in a thousand might be lying and trying to steal my sperm. Which is really fucked up, you know."

Rolly's face was red, his body tense. Stephanie glared at him, arms folded across her chest. "You owe me," she said "for making me take a second job while you screw around. For giving away our savings. For blowing a shitload of money on crap you didn't need. For having a baby with someone else. You owe me big time. And if I don't get retired this year I'm going to--" She didn't finish, just shook her finger and walked away.

16

Real Time Seeing

Monday, March 6th

5:30 am. Without benefit of an alarm, Leah sat up straight and swung her legs over the edge of the cot. The call would come soon, maybe today but not this early. She had plenty of time to get ready.

Over baggy plaid pajamas she threw a grey cotton robe, intentionally unwashed and made dingy, and slipped into a men's pair of dirty brown slippers. She stood in front of a six inch metal mirror and threw on makeup haphazardly, smudging it around, making herself look like a drunken tramp.

All this to discourage the attentions of one misguided sex addict. She attracted them like flies. An arsenal of verbal jabs and stinging insults usually kept them at bay, and she was adept at finding the one thing that could really dig under someone's skin, but it was too easy, boring. Wouldn't it be nice to discourage them before any words were spoken? Looking used and abused was her latest game. In the past she had been prim and proper, coldly aloof, condescending, insane, like an Intervention Agent, anything she thought might stop the lustful advances. Most times she could move on to a new character at will, other times a wannabe stalker found the act itself alluring. Then she would resort to one of her stock verbal slams, which was, again, boring.

Leah's characters also kept her hidden from the ever present cameras.

One of her requirements when choosing a new building was that it have a bathroom with a shower. In this building the bathrooms were sixty yards and two flights of steps away. Ample opportunity to be accosted. Leah grabbed her bag and headed for the shower, adopting an awkward shuffle as if she'd been riding a horse all night.

The stalker in question was named Mark; he'd caught a glimpse of her--out of character--and now made an effort to be present every weekday morning, but not weekends. Apparently his obsession had limits.

Halfway on Mark happened to step out of his office as she passed.

"Hello Miss Mary. Nice to see you again." Miss Mary was a name he made up for her since she chose not to share. Mark acted like a nice guy, but it was thin and transparent, like he'd been shrink-wrapped in niceness to hold in the depravity.

Leah spoke in a gravelly voice. "Rough night. Gotta get to the bathroom. Make myself look purty."

"You look terrible. Are you okay? Did someone abuse you?"

"It's only abuse if they don't pay." Leah tried to cackle but it caught in her dry throat and she coughed. Which added to the effect. She tried to work up some phlegm to give it an edge.

"God, I didn't realize...I'm sorry...I assumed..." Mark paused; Leah moved on but he kept talking. "Miss Mary, you need help and I know the perfect place for you." He caught up and cut her off. "I can take you there, three meals a day and a hot shower without even asking, and you won't have to resort to this...sin anymore."

"Ain't interested."

"I know what you're thinking but it's not that bad. Yes, it's a church, but all they want is to help. You've heard of them I'm sure, you've seen the monitor ads all over downtown. Church of the Latter Day Immortals, Restoration Branch. They're good people."

"No, I got my own life."

Mark put his hands on her shoulders, gently without grabbing. This was a bad move. Leah did not like being touched; it was a line she would not tolerate being crossed. Her spine stiffened. "Miss Mary, I hate to see you like this. You seem like such a beautiful person. I have to insist that you come with me. I'm invoking the 32nd amendment for your own good."

The 32nd amendment to the Constitution of the United Syndicates of America gave broad protection (and therefore power) to Christian organizations, giving them reign to do as they pleased without fear of earthly repercussions. One provision allowed religious intervention in the life of any person deemed "self-destructive or exhibiting behaviors detrimental to the well-being of a harmonious society." Nicknamed the "Savior Law" it permitted any baptized Christian to "persuade" such people to seek spiritual help. Thus were born a new incarnation of zealots, aggressively looking for people in need of saving. Eventually they took it too far and church leaders had to discourage use of the law, but it was never repealed.

Mark began to turn her back toward his office. Leah--who had been slouching--rose to her full height, pressed the fingers of her right hand tightly together, and with a focused yell speared Mark in the jugular notch, that dip at the base of the throat, just above the breastbone. He gagged and fell backward.

Leah continued on to the bathroom.

The shower was warm and calming. Her thoughts turned to Stephanie and how she knew a call was likely to come this morning. Part of it was experience--she'd been doing this too long. Part of it was the series of events she herself had put in motion, with a limited number of possible conclusions. Most of all it was being the perpetual outsider, always looking in, always the observer, learning, figuring out who these people were, understanding they could only act in one inevitable direction, good or bad.

Like Mark. His reasoning was dogmatic but his motivations carnal. Leah had pulled her throat strike at the last second; he would recover quickly. Right now he was thinking 'I invoked the 32nd amendment. I was within my rights. I could have her arrested.' Protection Services would call when the computer controlled cameras raised an alarm and cross-referenced the location with his HearSay signal. (Leah's HearSay number was blocked; they would assume she was transient.) But he would not want the police involved--his pride was hurt and he wanted revenge. 'No, no, it's alright,' he would say, 'it's a religious issue. I can handle it. No need to worry.' The police, thinking Mark was trying to save a lost soul, would reply 'Okay, let us know if you need help.' Nudge, nudge, wink, wink. Next time they would ignore the camera alarms. This was her out.

Mark would not come after her in the bathroom. Entering a women's restroom was as unthinkable as passing through the gates of heaven without an invitation. He knew she would come back. He would be waiting, planning an ambush from his office doorway.

It was time to give Stephanie a gift. Buried deep in her HearSay memory was a program that wasn't supposed to exist, that only she could access. This program had no name and no memory footprint. It did things that were supposed to be the purview of the Corporament only. It went out into the great mass of invisible data flying through the air to find and track any person and tell the user exactly where they were and where they had been, as far back as the purchase of their first HearSay.

Leah ditched her costume in the trash (Mark had ended that bit of fun) and left the room refreshed, wearing her favorite hoodie. She did have concerns the cameras might put face to name and report her whereabouts to a psych manager. But really, that was a stupid thing to worry about. The Corporament knew where she was, as they did everyone else. The question was, did they care? If they did, that was a problem. Leah and the Corporament weren't on the best of terms.

She walked on the opposite side of the hallway as if trying to avoid Mark's door. Actually she wanted him to see her coming, and give herself room to work. The hall was dead silent; Leah moved without a rustle of clothing. She heard the knob of Mark's door creak as it was grabbed from the other side. When she was directly opposite, the door flew open and Mark rushed out, smiling in triumph, arms reaching out.

Leah was already in fighting stance. She looked in his face and made a mental target of it. She leaned back and spun at the same time, shooting her back leg up and around. As her hip came around to finish the circle, the heel of her foot connected with the side of Mark's head. He stood five inches taller than her; she put all of her strength and rage into the kick, one of her better martial techniques. Her scream rattled every door in the hall.

Mark's head slammed into the door jam and he fell to the floor. Again. He would have bruises later, disappearing as EverLife repaired the damage. Which Leah thought was a damn shame.

On the floor and dazed, Leah took Mark's chin in hand. "Understand this now. I am not a puppet to be pulled around by a Bible thumping fool wrapping himself in a bullshit law. Never touch me again. Do not speak to me. I don't want to pray with you and I don't want to fuck you. Get near me again and I will make your EverLife work overtime. Never forget this."

Eyes glazed, Mark fell to floor. Leah was not breathing heavy, had not broken a sweat.

All the necessities were in her bag, and the bag was always with her. Anything left behind could be replaced. Leah found the nearest exit and left the building.

The call came as she was walking away.

"Hello Stephanie. What can I do for you?"

"Rolly's keeping secrets. Admitted he wasn't going to tell me about his bastard and says don't worry about it."

"Doesn't surprise me."

"I know him, he'll do something stupid. We gotta stop him."

"I can't do that. Rolly's free to make his own choices."

"I will, when it comes to it. But I can't watch him all day."

"That I can help with. But you'll have to keep secrets of your own. We need a face-to-face. I know a passable coffee shop on Washington Avenue. Meet me there."

Yeah, she'd been doing this way too long.

Monday, April 3rd

Work, work, work, work, work. What day was it? He looked at the computer. Monday. Start of the week. For everyone else. For Rolly it was a blur. Sleep, drive, work, eat, and the occasional bathroom break, which always took too long. He was exploring different ways to make his trips to the facilities shorter. Currently starvation and a liquid diet seemed like viable options.

He had been wrong about Doug. They stopped talking two weeks ago, never mind the end of the year, which was eight months away. God, so far? That felt backwards, shouldn't it be eight months gone and four until the end? The days were flying so fast, how could it be only April?

Rolly hardly interacted with coworkers; Lambert was his only connection. She brought him tasks and he did them. He didn't ask who or what, it was always inThrallEd. Rolly was so immersed in the campaign he knew it better than anyone, including Steve Mann.

He finished a ten second spot, a wordless kaleidoscope effect using debris floating on a flooded river that formed the "inThralled with Insurance" tagline, but not easily, forcing the viewer to search for the words. Lambert handed him a sheet of paper with his next project. He didn't look up. It called for a video on the unforeseen dangers of plastic spoons when used as a screwdriver. Okay...wait...what? There were no spoons in inThrallEd. Had there been a change? Was Mr. Dodds attacking people with plastic spoons now? Who was this from? Rolly looked in the header for the Assigned Creator. Doug Hanlin.

"Rolly." He jumped. That wasn't Lambert, it was Macklin. He swiveled around. Lambert had morphed into Macklin, who was standing where Lambert had been a second ago. Wait, no. Lambert was standing behind Macklin looking...concerned?

"Take the rest of the day off."

"I can't, I have to--"

"I don't care. Take the rest of the day off."

"But I--"

"Get out before I throw you out." Macklin turned and walked away. Lambert followed, ponytail bouncing like a horse's tail.

Why was she making him leave? Rolly shut down the terminal, grabbed his jacket and walked out, giving Macklin a furious look.

In the car he called Leah and ranted about what a bitch Macklin was.

Leah squinted at him. "Lean closer." Rolly did as told. "Oh. Okay. I see. Go home and sleep. Start over in the morning."

"But I'll lose Productivity!"

"You're a zombie. You'll lose more if you keep working like that. Go home. Don't bother eating, just curl up and pass out. Eat tomorrow."

"I sleep enough already."

"Obviously not. Just do it Rolly."

Leah closed the connection. Rolly decided the world was against him and they could all fuck themselves. He wanted to slam the interface into the dashboard but stopped himself. He rode home fuming, letting the car do the driving.

The empty house looked weird in daylight. Rolly slammed a couple of doors because he felt like it, dropped on his rumpled bed muttering obscenities and fell asleep in his clothes.

Friday, April 7th

Sean interrupted Rolly's concentration as if he were out of breath.

"Dude, you got an urgent message."

A new voice barged into Rolly's head, female, emotionless, vaguely threatening.

"Mr. Roland Smalls. You are to meet with Steve Mann, Vice President and overseer of the Office of Content Management at 1:30 this afternoon. Please be prompt." The message repeated and shut off.

Invitations to the 50th floor were rare; Rolly arrived promptly at 1:29. The godawful boring décor always amazed him. Bare marble floors, desks that were nothing more than tables, diffused lighting from wall mounted fixtures shining on bare white walls, and not a painting or plaque or framed mission statement to break up the sameness. The room echoed and rang like an oversized public lavatory. Rolly waited on a chrome plated faux metal couch with green plastic cushions, a single piece of furniture that felt like an affront to the severe minimalist design, a concession to the need to sit. People fought and clawed up corporate ranks for this? He expected a managerial work environment to be more palatial. But that wouldn't look good in the current paradigm that emphasized frugality, efficiency and recycling.

Rolly knew why he was here. After being thrown out by Macklin Leah warned him this meeting was coming.

At 1:30 the executive assistant escorted Rolly into the inner sanctum of Steve. In contrast to the lively furnishings of the waiting area Steve's office was a barren wasteland. Desk, one chair, one couch, white walls, brown carpet. Steve allowed himself the luxury of a pencil holder with one pen and one pencil, and a small pad of lined paper. The only other item on Steve's desk was his HearSay interface, compact and furled. Rolly had no idea Steve was this ambitious.

"Ah. Rolly. Have a seat."

Rolly sat in the lone chair, an uncomfortable thing with a seat of molded yellow fiberglass straight out of an office store bargain bin.

"Rolly, I'm trying to figure out what to make of you. For years you were a good, reliable employee. Finished all your projects on time and budget. I could ask you to do anything and count on it getting done."

Rolly couldn't recall Steve ever asking him to do anything.

"Last year you started slacking, especially in the last quarter. I know you were expecting to retire. Now you're coming to work every day of the week, fifteen hours a day, taking other people's projects. What's going on?"

Rolly could not come out and say what he really wanted. Stableman Insurance considered anyone trying to retire disloyal, never mind that *every* employee was trying to retire. So Rolly needed Steve to give him a good evaluation at the end of the year, and to accomplish this Steve would have to sympathize and trust him. In other words Rolly was about to lie through his teeth. Which he was not especially good at.

"I want to work. Keep busy."

"Why? Don't you want to go home once in awhile?"

"I go home every day."

"You spend less time there than at work."

Rolly shrugged. "Not much going on at home, I'd rather be working than doing nothing.

"You've been working especially hard too. Not even taking your regular breaks."

"Yeah, same thing. Trying to keep busy."

"Some people have complained. It's causing resentment and disunity, what we managers like to call a challenging work environment."

There were a few holdouts, coworkers closing in on retirement themselves. According to Lambert they were irritated by the amount of work being sent his way.

"I thought they would be happy for the help."

"That's not the point Rolly. It affects their Productivity. Makes them look lazy."

"That was not my intention."

"I'm sure it wasn't. And realistically, if everyone worked as hard as you it would be wonderful. But everyone can't and despite everything EverLife does, we still need to get enough sleep. This is why Macklin did what she did."

Steve liked to explain the obvious; a trait of most managers. Rolly thought it a sign his strategy was successful. A condescending, lecturing manager, feeling superior, might be in a benevolent mood.

"Look Rolly, I know you're trying to retire. You can't hide it."

"Everyone is trying to retire."

Steve ignored this. "If we help you retire what does that say about the company? We don't like you and want to get rid of you? We don't value the work you do? That's so negative. Makes us look like a bad employer."

"I'm sorry if I gave the impression I was working for retirement. Nothing could be further from the truth. I know it's not going to happen. Not for awhile at least." Leah warned him against being too negative. Keep hope earnest, she said, if not alive. "Things aren't good at home. I want to be where I can stay busy."

"Hmm. Sorry to hear that. Do you need a marriage counselor? Losing your marriage would be a huge blow."

"No, I don't think my marriage is going to end. My wife is hardly home. Which is probably for the best. It's just that...it's hard to explain. Everything seems so bland and unexciting. Like I've done everything and nothing is new. Life seems superficial. I want to be somewhere where I feel like I'm doing something worthwhile."

"Ennui."

"On what?"

"French word. Means boredom. Or something like that. You've got the EverLife blues." Whereupon Steve began mouthing the universal blues lick duh dow, da duh and playing air guitar, more animated than Rolly had ever seen him.

"EverLife blues?"

"I prefer Everlivin' blues myself, got more of that bluesy ring to it, know what I'm sayin'?"

"Uh, no."

"Haven't you ever had the blues? Been depressed?"

"Can't say I have." Actually Rolly knew exactly what Steve was talking about but wasn't sure if he suffered occasional bouts of ennui or was permanently stuck in the condition.

"There's a ton of books on the subject. They talk about it all the time. Back in 2108 I was in such a deep funk I could hardly get out of bed in the morning. Silly to think that now isn't it? Someone said try something new, something I always wanted to do but never did. So I learned to play guitar. Had so much fun I forgot to be depressed. In 2120 it hit me again so I tried gay sex for awhile..."

Steve had many blues/depression stories which he shared with Rolly who tried his best to look interested, interjecting a "Wow" and "That's cool" now and then to show he was listening.

"So, Rolly, you need to find something to spark your mind. Learn French, or Mandarin, or Korean. I don't know, keep a blog in Portuguese. Take up base jumping or skydiving. Stop doing the same ol' same ol'."

"Yeah, you're right. I need something to shake my doldrums."

"Excellent. Now I need you to keep realistic hours. I'm making you take a mandatory day off. Your choice. No more fifteen hour days, cut back to your usual twelve. Work is not the answer Rolly. Trust me on this."

"Yes, Steve. I'll do that."

"Speaking of which, I need to get back to mine." He gave Rolly a fake grin. His cue the conversation was over.

That night, in the few minutes between dinner and sleep, Rolly made a video call to Leah, waiting while her HearSay unfurled, a few seconds of forced patience in a breakneck culture.

Leah eventually answered, beautiful as ever despite the cheap pixelated bandwidth. The background had changed though, darker and poorly lit; she didn't seem to be in the office. Rolly told her about the conversation with Steve.

She looked relieved. "That went better than I thought. Looks like we can forget plan B."

Rolly hadn't known there was a plan B. "I had to lie to Steve."

"Is that a problem?"

"I'm not comfortable with it."

"How can you live a hundred and fifty years and not be comfortable with a lie?"

"I'm not good at it. I usually give myself away."

"You pulled it off today."

"I'm taking advantage of another person's trust."

"Rolly, the good die young or finish last. You're too old to die and if you want to finish ahead you're gonna have to get a little dirty. What day of the week are you taking off?"

"I'm not taking a day off."

Leah looked as if he'd declared himself President of the Corporament. "Why?"

"Because people at work have been helping me. If I take a day off I would let them down."

"There's two reasons why this is stupid. You'll be disobeying Steve and he will know you're at work when you're supposed to be home. You can't hide from your computer. And I have plans for that day off. It's past time for you to start working on your assets."

"How am I supposed to do that?"

"Playing the stock market."

"I'm worse at that than lying. It'll be a disaster."

"We'll see. What day are you taking off?"

"I'm not."

Leah glared at him. Usually attractive women have trouble making a glare effective. All that prettiness takes the edge off. Not Leah. Her glare exuded the bitterness and anger of a frustrated soul. It was an abrupt and unsettling transformation. Rolly thought he was glimpsing the old, pre-op Leah on her worst day.

Rolly held his ground. "I won't betray my coworkers."

"Okay, let's compromise. Take this Sunday off. One day to get yourself settled. Then make it your declared day off. Steve did say it was your choice. Less people around, less chance you'll get caught. Do you have an excuse when Macklin catches you?"

"Uh, no."

"Like Susie asked for my help and this was the only day we could do it...needed to drop something off...forgot something and came in to get it...I have a deadline...the light is better at my desk for reading...meeting with Doug to plan a birthday party, that sort of thing."

"Can I use those?"

"Think up something better. Have you chosen a hobby?"

"Haven't a clue. Should I make something up? Get more practice lying?"

"Don't whine. You've got tools don't you?"

"In the garage gathering dust."

"Don't you want to be a carpenter?"

"A woodworker."

"There's your new hobby. You already know what you're doing. You can bore Steve with details. He'll love it."

"Why would I want to bore him?"

"Are you socially inept? Or just willfully blind? His eyes'll glaze over and he won't hear a word you're saying. But he will Know That It Is Good and be happy with your job performance. He might even overlook your insubordination."

"Well as long as--."

"Goodbye." Leah cut the connection, Rolly's mouth still hanging open.

"Sean."

"Yes, O Highness."

"Did you record that conversation?"

"As always."

"Copy the excuses for going to work and save it to front memory."

A pause, then "Got 'er done."

"Good. Now erase every reference to lying or liar."

Sunday, April 9th

Stephanie escaped the ER for a much needed break at 2:09 with five hours left in her shift. She hurried to the nap room, hoping it was unoccupied, wanting some private space.

As Stephanie entered her ID badge was scanned and she said out loud "Break." A moment later Nikki, who communicated with the hospital security system, responded. "Noted. I will give a two minute warning in nine minutes fifty-four seconds."

The nap room contained two cheap couches, a table covered with coffee stain rings and a brightly lit vending machine. She had the room to herself. Stephanie sat at the table and unfurled her HearSay. Yesterday she tried opening the program by voice command but Nikki was clueless. Weird. However typing the password gave her immediately access. The screen cleared and went black leaving only a text entry box and one question:

Whom do you want to find?

Stephanie typed in Rolly's name.

There are 3,129 Roland V. Smalls. Please refine your search geographically.

A drop-down menu with every country a Roland V. Smalls lived in appeared. It gave her state choices, then area code. Eventually she got it narrowed to her husband.

How do you want to see Roland V. Smalls?

Six minutes already gone from her break. Typing words into an interface was time consuming. From another long drop down menu, with choices she didn't understand, Stephanie selected Satellite.

The screen changed to an image from space showing Lansing with a small yellow dot in the southern half of the metropolis. Stephanie zoomed in. This was her home address, the yellow dot was labeled **Roland V. Smalls**.

Rolly was supposed to be at work.

Leah placed many caveats on the program: don't use it too much or it will get noticed, it will self-erase on January 1st, it cannot be copied, tell anyone or use it to help someone else and it will overload and melt her interface (Stephanie doubted this), oh, and try Real Time Seeing because it's amazing.

Stephanie selected Real Time Seeing.

Which camera do you wish to see through?

It listed 157 different cameras within fifty feet of the yellow dot. Some had names, some had numbers. She recognized a few belonging to her neighbors, most were in their own home. She chose the one labeled Smalls Residence - Holo Room.

You do not have authorization to access this camera. Would you like me to hack it for you?

That was supposed to be impossible. Stephanie did know the code but wanted to see what the program could do. She typed "Yes."

The screen went dark again and a few seconds later filled with live video of her own holo room, a movie playing in the center, Rolly slouching on one of the couches.

If someone asked her true feelings for Rolly she would have a hard time picking between anger and resentment. Dragging him along like a stubborn mule all these decades, him clinging to archaic notions of loyalty while she brought in more money, working two jobs to cover his over-spending. Now, after promising to work hard and get his Productivity up, he was home watching a movie?

Leah in a hotel room, leaning back on the bed and reading a book. An actual book. She liked the feel of paper and a textured cover, preferably old with yellowed musty pages. It gave reading a sensory dimension that curiously made the stories more lifelike.

The hotel was temporary until she could find a new office. Hotels bristled with cameras. Staying in one was a pain in the ass. She had to use an assumed name (well established but still dangerous), keep her face covered, find all the lenses in the room and creative ways to mask them, and stay in to minimize the possibility of getting caught. She spent days scouring the internet to find the right rentable office with no luck.

"Miss Leah? You have an incoming call, voice only, from Stephanie Smalls." A variation on the British butler, without the condescension, softened, with a proper royal inflection.

"Thank you. Put her through."

"Yes, ma'am."

"You're the best, Shithead."

With genuine, computer designed gratitude, "Much appreciated Miss Leah. I always strive for the best."

A loud click, a sound harvested from old wired phones, Leah's cue the line was open.

Stephanie spoke, voice already raised, "Why do I have to work while Rolly stays home?"

"I see the program is working. Rolly got into trouble. Apparently some coworkers took exception to his new work ethic. He's been forced to take a day off."

"Forced my ass. He's not complaining."

"He's worried how it will make him look to his friends."

"You're okay with this?"

"We can work around it. His LOS will suffer but not enough to make a difference. Might even help in the long run. My worry is he'll do something stupid."

"That's Rolly. It's only going to get worse you know. He'll start telling himself 'That's enough for today.' Before you know it he'll be home early, working only ten or eight hours."

"No, that's not--"

"Hell with that. He's going to work even if I have to drag him there."

"Stephanie, it's not--"

"Goddamn it! I'm tired of waiting!"

The line went dead. Leah almost called back, then stopped. Stephanie would confront Rolly and she didn't want to be in the middle of that. Time to lay back, let them work this out, get them talking to each other instead of her.

Since he was home and not at work (a weird sensation) Rolly decided to make dinner instead of going out.

He stood in the kitchen and thought about what he would like to eat. Something he hadn't had in a long time. Something memorably good. Breakfast. A home made breakfast hot off the stove. He hadn't tasted one of those in a long time. Eggs, toast, bacon, sausage, hash browns, orange juice. Maybe some pancakes. Hard to go wrong with breakfast foods. Breakfast for dinner. He liked that idea.

Rolly opened the cupboard where the pans should be and found sink plumbing. Where were they? Wait, over here. He opened the proper cupboard and pulled out a ten inch fry pan, covered with cobwebs, tiny grayish pellets rolling around the nonstick surface.

What were those? Mouse droppings? Gross. Rolly put it in the sink to wash. Looking for a sponge he found a pile of yellow dust. He grabbed a clean washcloth from a drawer. The detergent bottle was clogged with dried soap. After cleaning it out he washed the pan, twice, to be safe.

He set the pan on the stove, started to walk to the fridge, then came back. Did the stove even work? He turned the knob and listened to the click of the starter, the swish and smell of gas, but nothing happened. He found a lighter, one of the long ones, held it next to the burner, turned the knob again and this time flames sprang up, but only near the lighter, on the opposite side, in fits and starts until it finally formed a full circle of blue flame.

Now to the fridge. Lots of cans, mostly soda and beer. Rolly rummaged around. There were no eggs. No bacon or sausage. Soda and beer were in fact the *only* things in the fridge.

He checked the freezer. No hash browns either. Just a pile of frozen dinners. No, not today.

Maybe pancakes. In the cupboards he found a sparse selection of canned vegetables and one unopened box of pancake mix dated Aug 5 2123. He tried to shake it but the mix had hardened into a cardboard covered brick.

There was no food in the house. He would have to go out. Takeout or get groceries? Takeout would be disappointing. The grocery store then.

Rolly heard the garage door open and Stephanie's car pull in. He frowned. If he quick pulled on a jacket he might slip by without too much bother. Or maybe he could invite her to dinner?

Stephanie stepped in. Rolly said "Hi." Stephanie looked at him and never looked away. He was in her sights.

"What are you doing?"

"Making dinner."

"You can't do that. There's no food."

"I just figured that out. Don't you go grocery shopping?"

"I haven't bought food in twenty years. I don't even know if grocery stores still exist."

"Okay. Well. I thought I would get some food to make dinner. Eggs, bacon, sausage. Breakfast for dinner. Something different."

"You shouldn't even be home. You should be working."

"I can't work all the time."

"Leah told me. You screwed up so they forced you to take a day off. While I work two jobs nights and weekends saving your ass."

Another fight. So much for dinner together. Rolly was determined to stay reasonable. "It's not as bad as you think."

"You're going to fuck up retirement again."

"No I'm not."

"You're going to sit on your ass and make me do everything."

"No, I'm not."

"You've already given up haven't you?"

"Stop it! I'm not taking a day off. I'm going in anyway."

Stephanie squinted at him. "What?"

"People at work have been trying to help. If I take a day it would be like thumbing my nose at them."

"No one is going to blame you for taking a day off."

"Of course they will. That's what you're doing right now."

Stephanie stood back, arms folded, brow creased, lips pursed, clearly puzzled.

"I will continue to work like a dog, my Productivity will be higher than it's ever been, my LOS will remain better than yours, and I will get retired if it kills me."

"You're going against your boss? Is that how you're going to screw this up?"

"Can't go more than a few seconds without cutting me down can you? Well here's what--"

Simultaneously both of their HearSays interrupted.

"Mistress Stephanie, you have a voice call from Leah Lockwood. Do you wish to answer?"

"Hey duderino, hot chick Leah on the line again. Ya want it?"

They both accepted.

"Have you two kissed and made up? 'Cause it's time we get together and talk about lost children. I know where Nola lives."

17

Crowned

Leah's new digs were a former gym, one of four store fronts in an empty strip mall, a casualty of the current economic crises. The workout area was cavernous with a soft floor mat. A long string of narrow windows high on the front wall let light in but kept voyeuristic eyes out. The adjacent wall was covered with mirrors. It had an office but Leah showed them to a table in the middle of the room. Rolly found the mirrors disconcerting. As they talked he kept glancing at his reflection.

"Are there cameras here?"

"All the cameras are disabled or blocked."

"Won't they notice?"

"Eventually." Leah continued as if it were unimportant. "Your daughter is named Nola Cooke. Born November 14th, 2095, making her fifty-one years old. She never knew her mother, they took her away immediately after being born. Tressa's only act as a mother was naming the child; no one knows why she chose Nola. It would've been better to let Tressa keep the baby, but all their law and order garbage...they gotta hurt two people to satisfy one law."

Stephanie, "Doesn't make sense to exile a baby."

Leah cast a look full of loathing. Stephanie instinctively leaned back. "Exile would have been easy. Nola was sent to the Corporament's idea of an orphanage. A company called Population Solutions Incorporated."

Rolly, "Never heard of it."

"They keep a low profile but have franchises in every city. The Corporament is PSI's only client, paid out of the charity budget. All undocumented children go to PSI."

Rolly, "There's that many? Enough to justify a whole company?"

"Oh yeah, thousands of new kids every year."

"So I'm not the only guy with this problem."

"No but you are lucky. Tressa let you off the hook."

"But she screwed up my retirement."

"I don't believe she was thinking about retirement when she screwed you."

Stephanie, "Does Nola still work for Population Solutions?"

"She never worked there. She survived it."

Rolly, "What does that mean?"

"PSI claims 2,000 graduates a year, children who reach age 18 and leave to find work. And about 3,000-4,000 losses."

"Losses?"

"Children who die. Accidents, disease, most take their own lives."

"Most? How many is most?"

"Seventy-two per cent."

In a culture of immortals suicide was unthinkable. Sure some people did it, for whatever reason, but an EverLife User ending their own life seemed wasteful, money and time inefficiently spent.

Leah read his mind. "The law says unlicensed children can never become EverLife Users. Never."

"Kids can't commit suicide. They're too young, they don't know how."

"PSI teaches various techniques and the adults in charge treat it like a game. Sweet tasting poison. Jump off the monkey bars head first. Knives are fun. Finger painting with blood. If the child makes it to the teenage years all that angst is used against them. Yes, it would be better if you were dead. Big bottles of pills are left in every room. It's PSI's most productive age."

"Why go to all the trouble? Why not just--"

"Kill them?"

"Abort them before they're born."

"Because abortion is wrong and suicide is blameless. PSI gets a bonus for every resource draining human they delete."

Stephanie, "How do you know this?"

"It's on their website, nicely organized and easy to find. I'll send you the URL."

Rolly and Stephanie sat silent.

Rolly, "But Nola's still alive. She must be tough."

"That and she's smart."

"Where does she live?"

Leah's eyes narrowed. "It's in your best interest to stay away."

"I'm not going to see her. Why would she want to see me?"

Leah looked unconvinced. "Nola lives in Mendenhall. Has an apartment there."

Mendenhall was an island of poverty in an otherwise normal neighborhood. Populated by transients. Not far from Stephanie's new job.

Rolly, "What does she do? Where does she work?"

"Nowhere special. A series of low pay jobs. For the last two months at a convenience store. Before that a house cleaning service, liquor store, another convenience store. Going back four years. She doesn't have an employment record for the first forty-seven years of her life."

Leah watched Rolly, wondering if the last statement would sink in. He was brooding too long. "You can't save her."

Startled, Rolly looked up, "What?"

"She can't take EverLife, the law prevents it. She can't have children, they cut out her ovaries. She is old and has been left alone to die. Think about what that means. This is no helpless little girl waiting to be saved. This is a grown, battle scarred woman. She couldn't care less who her father is. You can't save her."

"Yeah, I know. Life of a transient is terrible."

"Her life has been more cruel and horrible than you can imagine. Here's some perspective. PSI gets money from the Corporament, enough to cover basics, but not enough to make a profit. PSI generates income using the children."

Rolly wasn't sure he wanted to hear this.

Stephanie, "What does that mean?"

"There's all kinds of labor adults won't do. Cleaning public toilets, picking fruits and vegetables, sewing clothes. These kids clean the stadium after the big game. They do the dirty jobs others won't. But if you're pretty, there's only one job."

Rolly, "Is Nola a prostitute?"

"I wouldn't be surprised."

Rolly's thoughts were a jumble of rough truths and smashed fantasies. He sat quiet, trying to sort it out.

Stephanie, "How does this affect Rolly's retirement?"

"When Tressa took the fall his rights and responsibilities as the father were waived in absentia. PSI has the official electronic waiver on file but Paragon Retirement does not. Who knows why. I'm guessing when the Corporament switched from waivers to exemptions yours fell through the electronic cracks. All the associated companies of the Corporament share DNA information. Paragon is being told, in a roundabout way, there's a second child but the PSI computers say no there isn't. The system is too dumb to figure this out and no programmer has time to search out birth anomalies, so it's acting as if you have one and half children."

"What's the difference between a waiver and an exemption?

"Nothing. Different names for the same thing. At one time the President of the Corporament preferred exemptions."

Rolly, "When this is resolved I can retire?"

"Maybe, maybe not. In Reckoning terms one child is balanced, you're a responsible citizen making proper choices. No children means you're selfish, two children makes you extravagant. Does having one and a half children mean you're only half again as bad? Hard to say since the computer doesn't really know what to make of it. It plugs everything into a formula and gives you a number. Resolving the issue may push you up five points or it may do nothing."

"I'm banging my head against a wall."

"You're inching closer every day. Just keep doing what you're doing."

"While you put me through hell."

"Gotta go through hell to get to heaven. So the song says. Let's move on to the next bombshell. You need to sell your property before the end of the year."

Rolly and Stephanie stared back wide-eyed. "No, no, no. We can't sell before the end of the year. They'll take the house and we'll be homeless."

"I understand. We won't do this until December and we can stipulate the buyer not take possession until January 1st."

Stephanie, "They won't wait that long."

"Normally yes. But you have something they want, really bad. You're in the high bargaining position and we're going to make the most of it."

"Convince me."

"Okay, let's check Rolly's Reckoning." Leah brushed her fingers over the surface of her HearSay monitor and turned it to face them. Stuck at 478.68. "You're up point three seven over last year's Reckoning, an improvement but still point three two away from last year's Number. We'll need at least a point beyond to be sure. Two points would be better. The market value of your property is already figured into your Reckoning. Once you leave, Paragon sells it to help finance your retirement."

"Everyone knows that."

"Except you trust the powers-that-be too much. A friend here, an insider there, all the little corruptions that make the Corporament function means your property is sold for less than it's worth. Auction it beforehand and you'll make more money."

Rolly, "Why would developers pay a higher price now? Just wait until I'm retired and get it cheaper."

"There's no guarantee you'll retire. Put it up for auction and they'll come running."

"And if I fail again our biggest asset is gone."

"It's a leap of faith Rolly."

Stephanie, "Auctions can be rigged."

"Anything can be rigged, if you have enough money."

"Do we have enough?"

"No, you don't. But you have me and that's better than a bank full of money."

Tuesday, April 25th

"Hey bossman. *Your* bossman, ol' Steve-o of the floor above yours, is requesting a meeting in five minutes. But I kinda don't think it's a *request*. He really means get your butt up there now."

"Thanks for stating the obvious Sean."

"Happy to help."

The last few weeks had turned strangely backwards. Becoming the guy-who-got-things-done made him the most loathed creature of cubicle world: the boss's pet. Steve would call him directly to talk about changes, or make changes, bypassing Macklin, and everyone else. Macklin did not like this, though she didn't say anything. Her glare spoke volumes.

Steve also used Rolly to pass on information, as in "Hey, could you tell so-and-so about the changes we made?" Rolly would apologetically ask Lambert to do the passing on, which she did, but everyone knew where it was coming from. Once Lambert came straight back after telling Macklin about the latest changes to Mr. Dodds, about to cry. "I don't want to do this but Macklin threatened to transfer me to the call center. I'm supposed to tell you to take Mr. Dodds and shove him up your ass. There. I said it." Lambert slinked away, embarrassed.

Rolly did not like the changes to Mr. Dodds. The character started as boyishly handsome with curly hair, an easy smile and midwestern earnestness. The kind of person you'd like to handle a claim if disaster struck. Steve thought he was boring. They gave Mr. Dodds some pratfalls and absurd comic situations but Steve thought it reflected badly on the company. "He should be confident and competent. Otherwise why would anyone buy insurance from us?" Mr. Dodds got a nice suit, stood straighter and smiled less. Steve thought he was too young. Mr. Dodds' hair turned grey. He shrank a few inches. Grew a paunch around his stomach and a beard and mustache. Traded his straight tie for a bow tie. Developed a proper English accent. Because taglines always sound better when said with an English accent.

Mr. Dodds had become a condescending old Brit in a herringbone jacket and cardigan sweater who inexplicably showed up at house fires, break-ins, car accidents or whatever calamity they were portraying, lecturing the public as to what policy should have been purchased for wise protection. Rolly made the changes as requested but tried to subtly move Steve away from some of his weirder ideas. Like having Mr. Dodds walk on water. He managed to kill that one but delicate psychological manipulation was a skill Rolly had yet to master.

When he got to the office Steve was excitedly pacing. "I had the most brilliant idea. Dodd has always been missing something. He walks around with his hands in his pockets. He needs a prop, a symbol. What is it the English are famous for?"

"London bridge?"

"No."

"Fish and chips?"

"No."

"Bad teeth? Bad weather? Double decker busses? Palaces?"

"No, no, no. It's the monarchy. Kings and queens and such. What is the symbol of monarchy?"

"A crown."

"That's it!"

"You want to give Mr. Dodds a crown?"

"Not a literal crown. That would look stupid. It should be a pin on his lapel. Or a ring. Or both."

"You know Steve, Mr. Dodds is a long way from where we first envisioned him."

Steve waved Rolly off. "He's grown as the company has, from humble protector to benign overseer. Strong in its reach, kind in its giving. A crown is the perfect symbol. The President will love it." He meant the President of the company.

"But it shouldn't be overt. In the background, in places unforeseen and obvious. It shouldn't be in their faces." He meant the audience.

Rolly didn't say anything. It would be pointless. Steve had too much momentum.

"Let's do this. Ask Norreen to come up with some crown designs so I can pick one. Thanks."

Thanks. That's how Steve ended their conversations.

Monday, May 1st

A steady stream of injuries paraded through the ER, one after the other, as if transients were doing themselves or someone else bodily harm on cue. Bullet wounds, knife wounds, broken bones, fractured skulls. Why would someone with a short lifespan want to make it shorter?

Stephanie put off her break to help and now it was nine o'clock. During a lull her supervisor insisted she take one. Stephanie happily disappeared.

In the quiet room behind the nurses station she opened the tracking program and immediately saw a topographical map of the city, satellite view. A yellow dot blinked on the screen; next to it were numbers showing longitude, latitude, elevation, street address and name of the building: Stableman Insurance Company Regional Office 11. The yellow dot was Rolly, sitting at his desk.

A little late for him to be working. Stephanie touched a bar at the bottom of the window and moved a cursor to the left. The clock started going backwards, showing Rolly's movements over the past twenty-four hours. To the elevator and down, walking from lunch, an hour at a restaurant, walking to the restaurant, up the elevator, at his desk for hours, walking around the office, break room, conference room, down the elevator to the parking garage, driving to work, no wait, he stopped somewhere. A coffee shop. Getting something to drink on the way to work. Spending money he wasn't supposed to. The bastard. Back at home. Kitchen. Bathroom. Bedroom. Rolling around in his sleep. A purple dot appeared near Rolly's yellow dot. Her own tracking signal. Purple was her favorite color.

Stephanie switched it to week view and ran it back seven days. The days passed nearly the same way, a different restaurant for lunch, a different café for coffee, not much changed. Rolly doing exactly what he was supposed to.

She typed: Does this program have alarm settings?

You may program notifications for any variable: time, longitude, latitude, elevation, address, distance, area, or routine.

Define routine.

If subject deviates from established patterns you will be notified. Two weeks of observation are required.

Define area notifications.

If subject leaves or approaches a designated area you will be notified.

Define area.

Can be as small as a single address or as large as a sovereign country.

She didn't have an address for the bastard daughter, only that she lived in Mendenhall. Not a place Rolly would normally travel through.

I want to be notified if Roland V. Smalls approaches the Mendenhall neighborhood.

I will need guidelines to setup the alert.

It was like filling out birth license forms for the Corporament. What streets bordered this neighborhood? How close to the restricted area should the subject be for notification? Are there time restrictions? Blah, blah? It quickly became tedious. The rewinding of the tracking program had stopped at 1:36 am eight days previous, a Sunday night. She could see Rolly's yellow dot and her own purple dot, asleep in their respective ends of the house, the onscreen distance between them no more than a tiny space.

18

Two Birds With One Word

Friday, May 19th

Mid-morning, Rolly at work, the office full of people.

"Hey Dude. Perp Alert coming through."

When Sean recited official notices he retained the basic accent and inflections but lost the slang and word play, sounding like a surfer with a tiki torch stuck up his ass.

"Suspect is caucasian, male, wearing blue denim jeans and brown overcoat, long brown hair and beard. Last seen on Oakland Avenue heading west toward the intersection of Oakland and Cedar Streets. Suspect is not armed but is dangerous. If you see this man, call Protection Services right away."

The single row of windows in the OCM looked out on Oakland and the intersection mentioned to the east. The perp would be walking right past their building.

With a Perp Alert in effect the tabulating of Productivity was suspended. Free time. Nearly everyone in the office made for the windows, some with binoculars. In seconds they were lined up two deep.

"Anybody see anything?"

"Nothing yet." This was Jim Sturdevant, who had binoculars.

Janessa Wagner spoke. She did not have binoculars. "I see something. A bunch looking in the same direction."

Jim followed her pointing finger. "Yep, I see it. There's a crowd, can't see through 'em though. A head bobbing up and down. There he is! Just broke out and walking fast toward us, the dirty redneck hippie."

Rolly, in the back, craned to see. From this height you followed collective reactions to pinpoint the perp. Rolly found him, glancing around and moving fast. Everyone else at street level was standing still and talking-- to their HearSays--sending reports to Protection Services. The perp picked up his pace, but the crowd thickened with arriving gawkers and he couldn't go in the direction he wanted. He turned left, where the crowd was thinner, running now, across the courtyard between Stableman Insurance and Adelard's Buffet regional headquarters. (Adelard's Buffet was the national fast food chain. None of their restaurants had a buffet.) More people streamed out of the surrounding buildings, blocking the perp's way again, forcing him to turn back.

Jim, "Here comes PS."

Three Protection Services cars arrived, lights flashing, full internal combustion engines growling. Six officers got out and the crowd parted. The perp was surrounded. He stood still and raised his hands. One of the officers shot him with stun gun.

A collective "ooo" from Rolly's coworkers. Shocking the perp was considered a good end to a chase. Rolly looked around grinning. Souliere was standing next to him.

"Helluva chase. We haven't had a good stunning in months."

"Some people have a little more fight I guess."

"Something wrong?"

"This is wrong. Treating a person like a dog that needs to be collared. And doing it for everyone's entertainment."

"He's a criminal. He chose to break the law and now he has to pay the price. No harm done. Justice at work and if we get a little entertainment, all the better."

The others were drifting back to their work stations. "How do you know what he's done? What's his crime? Was he falsely accused? Is it murder or unpaid parking tickets? They never tell us what horrendous thing the perps did, only that they need to be caught. What if it were me or you? Wouldn't we want to explain ourselves? Have a chance to mount a defense? Maybe he's a criminal or maybe he's innocent. There was a time when innocence was presumed. Not any more. If the Corporament says you're a criminal, you are."

"It's for the better. Makes the court system efficient, not clogged up all the time. Things get done."

"Yes, things get done. They get done *to* you." Souliere headed back to his cubicle. A few stragglers, eavesdropping on their conversation, stared at Rolly. Embarrassed, he left in the opposite direction, though it meant a long loop back to his desk.

Sunday, June 4th

Blood pooled around Stephanie's latex covered shoes. A construction worker on the gurney, his left leg gashed across the upper thigh, the femoral artery cut but not severed. An EverLife User. The nanobots had occluded the artery but the damage was too severe for the machines to repair. He could die, so a phalanx of doctors and nurses crowded the ER to help. No one wanted St. Bart's to be the hospital where an EverLife User died.

Swab and tools at the ready, Stephanie was assisting the doctor working to stabilize the patient, forceps hanging out of his wound, clamping veins and arteries. A surgeon was en route but the patient wasn't ready to move, the artery held together by only a hint of flesh.

A deep male voice rumbled inside Stephanie's head. "Subject Roland V. Smalls is in proximity to the exclusion zone. Please respond."

Stephanie flinched. *Who the hell was that?* She said nothing, expecting it to go away.

"Urgent response required. Subject is approaching the exclusion zone."

When she first purchased a HearSay, feeling like the whole surreptitious hand movement thing was silly, Stephanie set her affirmative gesture to a finger pointed at the side of the head in mock suicide. As in, shoot-me-before-this-thing-talks-to-me-again. She didn't use the function much, the world being amazingly tolerant of people talking out loud to themselves. When she did have to put an imaginary gun to her head, it was always awkward and she always made a mental note to change it, and always forgot.

Scalpel in hand, Stephanie moved her hand up and touched the side of her head, hoping her pinky would be enough.

"I do not recognize that movement. Was that an affirmative?"

All the people in the room were focused on the patient and hadn't seen. She would have to make the full motion.

The doctor said, "Suction." Stephanie carefully removed the blood pooled in the open wound.

"I do not recognize that movement. Was that a negative?"

Stephanie busied one hand moving around tools and swabs, using the activity as cover, while the other hand gave a forceful tap to the side of her head.

"Movement still not recognized. Would you like to cancel the alert?"

She would have to do the full-on gun movement. The right thing would be to step away and let another nurse assist, but that was bad form and this was a User, not some trashy transient.

"Clamp." Another nurse passed a forceps to Stephanie and she passed it to the doctor. Now free, she put her right hand to her temple, cocked her thumb and blew out her brains. Over the surgical mask the other nurse looked at her funny. Stephanie smiled as if it were a joke, realized her own mask hid it, and shrugged her shoulders instead. Damn, she had been out of nursing a long time.

"This is Zack. Subject has entered the no go zone. Would you like real time updates on subject's location?"

After many false alarms Stephanie narrowed the program's parameters. For certain Rolly was in Nola's neighborhood. Yes, she did want to know. Another gun to the head was called for.

"Hemostat. Now."

Stephanie held up her hand, expecting a clamp to be slapped into it but nothing happened. She turned and found the other nurse frantically searching the surgical tray. They had run out of forceps. A good opportunity for another mock suicide.

Hand to her head and pulling the trigger, Stephanie's fellow nurse turned back as the pretend bullet passed through her skull. "Where's that clamp?" said the doctor sounding angry.

The other nurse cocked her head. Stephanie handed the clamp to the doctor. The proximal end of the open artery suddenly shot out a glob of dark blood like dried ketchup out of a squeeze bottle. The glob was flecked with glitter. The temporary clot set up by the nanobots had given way, blood flowing into the wound again, the artery now completely severed and one end being sucked into the patient's body. The doctor dropped the clamp and plunged his hand into the leg trying to grab the artery before it disappeared.

"Acknowledged. Subject is in the 800 block of Cedar Avenue heading north toward no go address. Speed indicates subject is on foot."

The doctor gripped the artery between thumb and forefinger, roughly pulling it back into the open, Stephanie trying to suction away the slippery blood. Not enough artery was visible to clamp.

"Subject has entered Sandy's Snacks convenience store at the corner of Cedar and Houghton streets."

"Tech, tell EverLife to increase blood coagulation in the left leg to ninety percent."

The technician sat in the corner of the room. Like the beds at EverLife Renewal Centers, the gurney contained two-way radio transmitters that communicated with a patient's nanobots. Every hospital had emergency override commands allowing medical staff to take control of the nanobots. "Yes sir, happening now."

"Subject still in convenience store."

"Get ready with that clamp." Stephanie picked up the forceps. She had to get it on right, the doctor struggling to pull enough out.

"Subject leaving convenience store and moving north toward no go address. Are you experiencing an emergency? For your safety if you do not answer within thirty seconds I will call the authorities on your behalf."

Oh shit. Stephanie's hands were full. Her negative gesture was a finger across the neck in a cut-off-your-head motion. Everyone was so focused on the wound. If she had to say no out loud it would jolt the entire room.

"Are you ready nurse?"

"No." She actually wasn't, thereby killing two birds with one word.

"Emergency call terminated."

"Well?"

"Ready now." He pulled the artery, much harder than seemed necessary for a delicate piece of anatomy. A good inch came out and Stephanie grabbed it. A sigh of relief through the crowd, a smattering of applause.

The surgeon arrived and spelled the doctor, who was happy to let her take over. In a flash of latex covered hands she pulled the artery together and reattached it with four stitches. To the technician she said, "How are the nanobots?"

"200,000 repair and regrow bots are waiting in each end of the artery. Overall nanobot functioning between seventy-five and eighty-nine percent."

"Good. Remove the clamps nurse."

Stephanie did as told. Blood flowed again, leaking out of the partially repaired artery. Stephanie moved to suction it but the surgeon stopped her. Bright red blood pooled in the wound and the silvery nanobots swirled and converged on the torn artery. As they watched tissue began to regenerate, filling the tiny holes. The leaking stopped.

Surgeon, "Let's close so EverLife can fix this man."

Stephanie's cue to leave. She was an emergency nurse and the emergency was over. The surgical nurse stepped in. Stephanie yanked off her bloody scrubs and made for the break room.

"Subject now heading south, out of no go zone. Speed indicates travel by car. Notification ended. If subject returns I will contact you again."

Stephanie plopped on the couch and stared at the bulletin board. A flashing neon notice with pink letters held her attention while she thought. She ignored the words.

"Nikki."

"Yes ma'am."

"We need to change the positive and negative gestures right now."

"Yes ma'am."

This job was getting in the way of what she really needed to be doing: keeping tabs on Rolly.

19

Assets

Thursday, July 2nd

Rolly blurted, "Max you have a sister."

Ten-thirty at night, Rolly's flamed over dinner steaming on the table next to the HearSay, the only time both were free for a video chat. Father and son had been trading text messages and voice calls for the last few months. Rolly felt like he had his son back, a wonderful development he was reluctant to ruin with news of his latest mistake. But he had to tell Max sometime and there was never a right moment, so he said it without thinking. Rolly cringed, waiting for his son's recriminations.

"I know. Mom told me. But it's good to hear it from you."

"Steph told you? What else did she say?"

"Mostly ranted and complained. Didn't have much to tell. Is there anything else I should know?"

Rolly told Max everything they knew about Nola and her mother Tressa.

"Why weren't you told? They assumed you wouldn't want to know?"

"In the eyes of the law I was an unwitting donor."

"Has this been delaying your retirement?"

"Maybe." Rolly outlined Leah's plans.

"Bureaucratic surgery. That's a delicate business. I hope this woman knows what she's doing."

"She seems competent. I've trusted her this far. Have to see it through."

"Why *are* you trusting her?"

"I don't know what else to do. She lands in my lap and offers to help me for free? Am I so well off I can turn her down? No. If I'm going to get anywhere I have to stop playing safe and take a risk. Why not her?"

"I think you've made a deal with the devil, Dad."

"We'll see. It's a price I'm willing to pay. How's your retirement going?"

"Don't worry about me. I'll get there in a decade or so."

"I'm sorry. It's because of the money, isn't it?"

"There's other issues holding me back. No wife, no family, a slim work record."

"You've been working since the day you turned sixteen."

"Most of it self employed. Doesn't count because I wasn't working for a sanctioned company. Unconfirmed employment they call it."

"Corporament bullshit."

"Yeah it is. Tell me more about Nola."

Rolly took a deep breath. "This is going to be hard to hear."

A minute later, with eyes closed, Max repeated Rolly's words. "My newfound sister is banned from EverLife and exiled out of mainstream society. She's aged over fifty years. The average lifespan of an exiled transient is sixty years. She will die soon." Max refocused and looked Rolly in the eye. "What are you going to do?"

"I'm not going to do anything."

"There isn't anything you can do. And many things you definitely shouldn't do."

Max's tone was like a parent talking to a child they know too well. For the first time he understood Max was his son in memory only. His child had grown into a weary human being, whom the Corporament considered the most subversive person alive. Time to stop thinking of Max as a boy in need of guidance. Rolly was the one being guided.

"If I try to help Nola I hurt Stephanie and myself. If I do nothing, Nola suffers more wretchedness and dies without a family."

"So you are thinking about it. There was a time when caring about your family was a virtue. Not anymore. Population control is the rule. You're up against an entity that's wanted Nola dead for fifty-one years."

"She has stayed stubbornly alive."

"They don't want you to give her hope and a life. Sets a bad precedent and it's contrary to their goals. They know exactly how many people are walking around, how many will die stupidly, and how many pregnancies they need to balance those losses. Nola is an anomaly in the system. She's inefficient and costs money. The sooner she is gone the happier they will be."

"Spoken like someone who's seen the machine from the inside out."

"You know I have."

"I helped you when you were down, when the odds were against you. Nola's situation is much worse."

A guilty frown crossed Max's face. "The world has changed. There's no tolerance for devotion. Everyone is supposed to go their own way and live their own lives with as little regard for each other as possible. This is how a nation of immortals survives. Trying to see Nola, let alone help her, will bring the Corporament down on you like a nine hundred foot concrete giant. It'll smash you and any hopes you have of retiring."

"She needs something, if only to know someone cares about her."

"That would be too much."

"I know, I know. I do have my priorities straight. Retirement first."

Max thought Rolly was trying to convince himself and could tell his father was becoming defensive. Better to change the subject before the conversation turned tense. "I've always wanted to ask about something that happened when I was a kid."

"Sure Max. Whatever you need."

"We had to hide in the basement for a week and you wouldn't let me go upstairs to get my toys. I remember talk about a tornado, but that can't be right. Nobody hides from a tornado for a week. Am I remembering it wrong?"

Rolly's face turned to stone. "Max I love having you back so I won't lie. We can never talk about this, in any place, under any circumstances. Nine hundred foot concrete giants are always lurking around. Do you understand?"

Max couldn't imagine the Corporament taking much interest in one little conversation, but in the most surveilled country in the world it was a good idea to respect another's paranoia.

"Okay."

"Thanks Max. Maybe someday, when things change." Rolly did not look hopeful.

Monday, July 10th

Rolly shared an elevator with Steve in the morning and used the opportunity to rave about his "new" woodworking hobby: how dovetail joints were amazingly solid, his new routing table and how perfectly it cut edges, the joys of hand sanding, which stains work best with which woods, lacquer vs. wax finishes. Rolly talked the entire ascent.

At the 22nd floor Steve smiled a bit, humoring an enthusiastic employee.

As Rolly stepped off he said, "Thanks Steve. It really helped a lot."

"You're welcome." Steve looked unsure as to why he was being thanked.

Several coworkers stepped off as well. Two women looked at each other with wry grins. Rolly watched their backs as they entered the OCM. *What are they saying about me to everyone else?*

It was one thing to know about office gossip, another to realize you're the subject of it. They watched him sucking up to Steve, and Steve looking bored. They would say Rolly was making a fool of himself and Steve barely cared. Must be losing his touch with the boss. It felt like the entire OCM had turned, waiting for him to fall, hoping to see the boss's pet dive head first into the boiling pit of doom, aka, reality.

Rolly worked harder than ever, trying not to think about other things. InThrallEd was coming together, mostly detail work left to be done, but they were on schedule. Lambert still brought requests but they were growing fewer. Rolly caught up his own work and managed to get ahead of schedule. Lambert seemed to be growing weary of the pace. Her perkiness dimmed and her smile became less spontaneous. Was it resentment? Had he gone too far?

He pulled Lambert aside in the hallway outside the OCM and asked if he was the most hated man in the office.

"No, that would still be Todd Wankmiller." Todd talked about himself all the time, turned every conversation to himself, and failed to listen to others, unless they were talking about him. Todd acted as if he were the sole beneficiary of immortality, called himself a god, expected to be loved, and was utterly unaware of how much he was loathed. "But you are close to the bottom. Better than Todd but less than desiccated food remains in the microwave. To them it looks like you're getting all the breaks. They helped you and now you've moved on, like you got a promotion but are stuck in cubicle land. They don't like that."

"So they think I'm a jerk. What do you think Lambert? Am I better than garbage?"

"I think you're doing the same thing you've been doing all year. Only the circumstances have changed. But it would be nice if you showed a little humility." Lambert patted him on the cheek, smiled, and walked away.

Rolly thought he knew where he could start. "Hey Lambert, thanks for being honest. And all your help the last six months. You're my best friend."

Lambert's smile beamed once again and her ponytail regained its familiar bounce as she slipped around the corner.

Rolly decided an epic, very public failure was in order.

Sunday, July 16th

Sitting in the holo room, one of only two communal spaces in their house, Stephanie and Rolly squaring off on separate viewing couches, bathed in badly diffused light from recessed ceiling fixtures. In the poor light the room looked like an oversized, half-empty closet. They weren't arguing but a fight was brewing. Stephanie was wearing a light silk blouse with ruffles and a tight knee length skirt that showed off her freshly shaved legs. She called this her battle dress. Rolly thought of it as her tease dress, Stephanie's way of saying look-what-I've-got-and-you-aren't-getting-any. Rolly slouched back in a pair of jeans and red tee shirt. He thought Stephanie overdressed for a Sunday. They were waiting for Leah, who wanted to inspect the property.

"Is something wrong?"

"No, nothing at all."

He didn't believe that. "How's the job going?"

"Which one?" said with great sarcasm.

"The hospital."

"Good. Finally getting used to the place." Stephanie seemed coiled up, holding something back.

"It'll be over in a few months. Something to look forward to."

"You betcha."

Neither had taken lovers since, when was it? January or February? Longer for him. Rolly wondered if Stephanie was feeling frustrated. He certainly was, though the long work hours were keeping his libido down. That was one of the side effects of being stuck at age thirty forever--the lust never waned. Was he lusting after his own wife? The attraction never went away, though he might forget. She would leave for another lover, her soft curves fading from memory, Rolly with his own lovers, thinking his desire for Stephanie gone, only to have it floor him more intensely when she walked back through the door. Not that it mattered. Her body language was tight and boxed in. The last thing on her mind was sex.

"Thanks for taking the job. Don't know if I ever said that."

"No, you never said it."

"Well, I do appreciate it."

She looked away. "When is Leah supposed to be here?"

Sean, "Any sec now."

Rolly, "Any minute now."

They each pulled out HearSays, Rolly reading the news, Stephanie laughing at some video. Ten awkward minutes passed before the house announced Leah's presence on the front porch.

Rolly held the door open and Leah strutted past. "You're not hard to find. Only house on the street. No wonder developers are falling over themselves."

The girl in the hoodie was gone. In heels Leah stood two inches taller than Rolly and towered over Stephanie. Rolly now understood the meaning of statuesque. Jeans and a dark shirt with a brown cashmere jacket, she wasn't dressed to impress but did anyway, like an impossibly gorgeous actress stepping into reality.

After greeting Stephanie, who for the first time in their marriage looked intimidated, Leah led them through the house, opening doors and cabinets. "How often do the developers make offers?"

Rolly, "Comes and goes. One will call then others follow. We say no or ignore them and they go away. A year or two later it starts up again."

"Were any of the offers enticing?"

Stephanie, "Never enough to make it worthwhile."

"Trying to get it on the cheap. It's worth a lot more than they'll admit."

The trio ended up at the dining table, next to the sliding glass door that looked out on the backyard. It was a sunny summer day, the grass nicely green and inviting. Leah took in the view. A six foot wooden slat fence ran along each side of the property, past the tree line. Apartment buildings surrounded and loomed over their mini-estate, windows and balconies looking down into their yard.

"Ever feel like you're onstage back here?"

"We never use the backyard. Rolly mows the lawn but we never go out there."

"I don't blame you. Everybody watching everything you do."

Rolly, "It's an investment. For retirement."

"How'd you avoid eminent domain?"

Rolly, "We didn't. Had to fight for it. They took us to court, tried to force a lowball price. That was a rough couple of years. We don't talk about it much."

"Must have cost a ton of money."

Stephanie, "Bribing a judge is expensive."

"It usually is. But I think it's going to pay off. The estimated value of your property is based on old data. You're one of the last real land owners, other than the super wealthy. An accurate valuation is impossible. There's nothing to compare it to."

Stephanie, "Is that good or bad?"

"I think you can get forty percent more than the estimate."

Rolly, "Really? That much?"

"If we sell at auction, yes."

Neither Rolly or Stephanie had experience with auctions. Potential buyers would be more savvy and have more influence. Like betting at a casino, the house always wins.

"They'll screw us to hell and back and we'll end up with less."

"That won't happen. They are desperate to expand their business and your house is right in the middle of the city. They can charge premium rent for every apartment and watch the money roll in. You have what they need. An auction will drive the price up and they will pay."

Rolly, "We used to be on the far edge of town."

"I know an auctioneer who will run a fair sale. I've worked with him many times. He can be trusted."

Stephanie, "But? There's always a but."

"He's expensive. His fee is fifteen percent of hammer price."

Rolly, "Can't we make the buyer pay that? What's it called...a buyer's premium?"

"Not if you want a fair auction and not with this auctioneer. He doesn't take money from the buyers. He works for you."

Rolly was satisfied. Money was the important thing, not some claim of fairness. As long as this guy knew who was paying his salary he could be counted on. Stephanie didn't like it though.

"Developers have been after us for so long they'll do anything. Like hiring a con artist to convince my gullible husband she can get him retired.

Come in and play the guiding angel. Now you say we have to trust someone else we've never met, to sell the biggest asset we have. Oh, and it will cost us a crap load in fees. How much of that do you get, Leah? How much is yours when you take the money and run?"

"You can walk away anytime Steph. I don't hold you to anything. Give the word and I'll disappear from your life forever. Everything can go back to normal. And it will be normal next year, and the year after that, and who knows how many years into the future. How much normalcy can you take? Decades? A century? You've got a long time to sort this out. I'm sure you'll get retired. Eventually."

"You're bluffing. If we end this now you don't get paid. You'll have to scare up another mark and there's not much you can do with less than half a year left."

"Now I'm insulted. I have a reputation and a waiting list longer than all the days of your wasted life. Let me go now and I'll have a new client before lunch. And I will still get paid by the misguided fools who sent me to look after you. They know my services are valuable. I wouldn't take a job like this without guarantees, like the one that says I get paid no matter what you do."

"And do you have a guarantee if Rolly fails again? You got the estrogen to back up your bullshit?"

Any remaining joy left Leah's face. "I never fail. And I will be with you on New Year's Eve so you can tell me to my face what a wonderful job I did."

"If we sell we're out of house and home with nowhere to go."

"I think I've done enough to earn your trust by now."

Rolly, "This is a big decision for us. We have time to think it over, right? You said something about December."

"Best if we wait until the end of the year. The buyers won't like waiting."

"But we're stipulating they can't take possession until January 1st."

"That's right."

"What if the auction doesn't go well? Can we refuse to sell?"

"It's called an auction with reserve. You reserve the right to accept or decline any bids. We'll make sure it's clear in the terms and conditions. It'll give the buyers incentive."

Stephanie, "I still don't trust you."

Rolly, "We need time to talk it over."

Leah stood up to leave. "I'll give you two weeks. If I don't hear back or you decide you can't bear to part with your little forest, we're through. I'll find a new client."

Tuesday, July 25th

Dozens of icons floated around Rolly's head--pianos, paper cups, fifteen different types of monitors, a gallery of paunchy faces in varying degrees of sweat--but he kept getting distracted. A pretty coworker, someone walking behind him, the conversation in the opposite cubicle, the stapler that needed to be dusted off once a year. He was supposed to be creating an animated banner ad targeted at gamers, a group notoriously resistant to insurance, but something seemed off. He needed to consult Souliere for some perspective, and maybe a little insight and wisdom.

Rolly told Sean to text Souliere asking for a meeting concerning the Gamer ad. A reply came immediately: Whenever you're ready. Rolly logged out of his workstation, choosing "Coworker Consultation." The building mainframe would follow his movements to make sure he actually met with Souliere.

In reality the ad was a bad idea and nothing Rolly could design would make it better. It showed the sweaty face of a gamer caught up in intense play, when a piano suddenly falls on him. Dust billows up and the words *Are You inThrallEd With Insurance?* fade into the picture. It sucked. He had no intention of wasting time talking about it.

"You need some milieu," Souliere said.

"Forget the ad. You said everyone was helping, that they want to see me retire. Well they all hate me."

"You've become the office pariah. A suck-up. Through no fault of your own."

"I have this idea to get me back in their good graces. Norreen came up with a bunch of crown designs. Like over three hundred. Steve wants me to narrow it down to three he can choose from. How about I pick the three worst ones. Steve will hate them all and blame me and I'm back being just another office rat."

"That's a terrible idea. Steve can't tell a good design from random scribbling. He'd pick one and go with it and you'd still look like a suck-up. But let's say it works and Steve makes a spectacle of your incompetence. You're not going to earn any sympathy. You'll be laughed at. All that pent up anger? You'll make a great target."

"I don't want my coworkers hating me. I need them."

"Yes you do. It was inevitable Steve would take advantage of your new work ethic. So was everybody's reaction. These are natural social fluctuations in an office. You can't change it with a made-up situation. You have to wait for a larger opportunity."

"What would that be?"

"inThrallEd is going to fail. It will blow up in Steve's face. The only question is how much damage will the company suffer."

"You know this how? Can you predict the future?"

"Experience. And Steve's failure to understand multiple meanings of the word enthralled."

"You're saying I should wait for your prediction to come true and then…"

"Everyone will have failed. You'll be back on equal footing. You might even regain some sympathy. But don't count on it."

"inThrallEd isn't going to fail. It's a good campaign, some nice alliteration, easy to remember, a positive message, everyone likes it."

"You could try your stunt, and it might work, though I think the chances are slim, and you'll look like a bigger fool when inThrallEd crashes."

"You seem pretty sure of yourself."

"You heard me raise the issue at the first meeting. I'm surprised it's gotten this far without someone coming to their senses. When inThrallEd hits the real world the backlash will be harsh. After that it's anyone's guess what will happen."

Friday, July 28th

Stephanie at Nyros, mid-afternoon, trying to work. In a few hours she would leave for a night shift at the hospital. Grab some fast food, show up late (no one cared), and if she was lucky, head home at midnight. Five, maybe six hours of sleep, get up, do it again. The hospital had scheduled her for ten hour shifts on Saturday and Sunday.

She considered tweaking EverLife for more energy and deeper sleep, but an energy boost meant a trip to a Renewal Center every two weeks. Extra visits cost nearly as much as her paycheck. The quarterlies would have to be enough; it wasn't worth the money.

Stephanie logged out of the Nyros computer for a break, folded the monitor into the desk, crossed her arms and sat thinking.

Leah's deadline was two days away. Should they auction the house or hang on to it? Take the chance, sell it, and end up in an apartment like everyone else? What if it the apartment was on their own property? That would be ironic if it weren't so humiliating. How much was she willing to risk to get out of this grind?

Stephanie opened her HearSay for a full face-on video chat. She wanted to look at Leah when they talked.

"Are you done thinking?" Leah answered so quickly Stephanie jumped.

"Were you expecting me?"

"You and your husband are the center of my life."

"Um, okay. You're gung ho about this, and maybe you're right, but I'm not convinced."

She heard Leah sigh. "Here's an analogy that's worked once or twice. You're running on a cliff edge hoping for a nice safe bridge to take you across but there isn't one. So you keep running, hoping someone will build one. But that's not gonna happen either. You're going to keep running until you run out of edge. Then what? At some point you have to jump. Better to do it now when you can still see the other side."

"And if Rolly fails? Our biggest asset is wasted, gone. We'll be stuck in the same goddamn jobs and retirement will be further away."

"Be realistic. You don't live in that house much. If this were based on occupancy Rolly would have more claim than you. Finding another place to live is not a big deal but it's not going to come to that. If for some bizarre reason something goes wrong we'll start over next year."

Stephanie mulled this, Leah with an answer for everything, wondering if it were genuine or convenient. That house was her home, built and arranged the way they wanted, always good to come back to and a comfort knowing it was waiting for her. An apartment would never feel so stable. Then again this last homecoming had been stressful, sharing the house with Rolly for eight long months. She felt caged, lashed to him like a sailor to a sinking ship. The two of them in an apartment would be hell. Absolute, total, hell. But if they succeeded, there would be freedom, no more jobs, no more worries.

"Tell me again how we control this auction."

"The power is yours Stephanie. You will be protected. Everything in writing, on actual paper."

"I'll want to see that beforehand."

"I can have a copy for you next week."

Stephanie felt rushed; it made her more suspicious. Several former lovers were lawyers, she'd have one of them look it over.

"Okay, I'll take the leap. But I want that paper in hand no later than Monday. And I will be watching. I don't know your scam but if you try to steal our money I will find you and rip off that perfect skin."

Leah smiled. "You won't have to look far. I'll be standing right beside you."

20

Thirty-Three Yards

Friday, August 18th

In the chosen profession of Dagan Jones, being a recent addition to the human race was as close to an age requirement as anyone would admit, ageism supposedly being illegal. Dagan was a property appraiser and only thirty-nine years old.

The Corporament valued youth in this position for its lack of attachment to possessions. When they interviewed Dagan the managers at Paragon Retirement asked if he knew what "nest egg" meant. He didn't. They said clients would collect objects and preserve them, believing they would increase in value over time, thereby providing an investment for the future, a "nest egg." Dagan could not get his head around this. Money had value, clearly, but objects served a purpose and were thrown away, to be replaced by a new version. How could a thing meant to be recycled increase in value? They hired him the same day.

Dagan tried to be realistic in his assessments. Rarely did the things centenarians hold on to have as much value as they imagined. Ceramic figurines, magazines, compact audio discs, plastic toys in original packaging, guns, knives, furniture, pretty lamps, ugly paintings, sheet music, clocks, stuffed animals, cars, signs--the array of alleged antiques seemed endless. Dagan had no nostalgic notions, he thought of it as so much un-recycled garbage. Besides, the only people interested in buying leftovers were other centenarians, usually in the same predicament as the seller, and unwilling to spend. Sentimentality might last forever but ceramic figurines peaked in value thirty years ago.

It was Dagan's job to tell clients their precious things were worthless, an act in which he took silent pleasure. His retirement was so far away to not even bear thinking about. A consultant once told him sixty-four percent of the populace was always on the verge of retirement, a parameter technicality away from making the big R. It was nice to think he had a small part in keeping that number from shrinking.

In the last two years Leah Lockwood had become his biggest referrer. At a reduced rate. This after she covered his butt on an overvalued mid-twentieth century coin collection. He was in a hurry and made an assumption based on dealings with a previous client, and wrote it up at a far higher number than its true worth. The entire appraisal including his mistake had been hard saved with the owner and Paragon. He was surely doomed. The computers that double-checked his work should have easily found the discrepancy, but somehow Leah made it disappear. No Thought Police came to visit, no bureaucrat tried to reclaim the money, no supervisor called to fire him. She rescued his reputation and made it clear she expected favors in return. Leah had an enviable reputation herself; Dagan was happy to agree.

Two days ago Leah called and asked him to work with a new client, Rolly Smalls, who had a lot of land and some personal property. The background was done, it was time to call and set up an appointment. Dagan thought face-to-face video the best way to get acquainted.

Mr. Smalls' HearSay answered for him, voice only. How rude. "Hi there. I am Sean, Mr. Rolly Smalls' HearSay attendant. He's like working at the moment. May I inform him who is calling or you wanna just leave a message?"

"This is Dagan Jones. Appraiser. I was referred by Leah Lockwood."

"Really? She's cool. Let me check with the man, see what he wants to do." Mr. Smalls gave his HearSay way too much independence.

"This is Rolly. You're the appraiser?" Still voice only.

"Yes I am."

"I'd like to be there when you do it. How about this Sunday?"

Having clients around when picking through their belongings was a bad idea. Every piece of junk had a story. And the pleading. Always made the job take twice as long. "I don't work on Sundays."

"Oh. Things are a little hectic right now. Any way you could make Sunday work?"

He hated that phrase, "make Sunday work." As if he had nothing better to do than cater to old farts. "No, sorry. Sunday is personal time. It's common for clients to allow access to their home when they're at work."

Pause. "I don't know you and you want free access to our house?"

"You have an ECC?"

"Of course."

"Set it to record while I'm there and you'll be able to watch everything."

Another pause. "Just a minute." Dagan could hear movement. The monitor went from black to brightly lit as Mr. Smalls finally accepted his video send.

"Hold still. There. I have your picture for the ECC. What's your personal code?"

"Sending by text now."

"Got it. What day do you want to come?"

"Tomorrow is good."

"I'll have the ECC set up for you."

"Thank you. I also have a questionnaire for you and your wife to fill out. Please answer as completely as you can."

Mr. Smalls sighed. "Okay. Send it to my HearSay."

"Already on the way. Ms. Lockwood will have my report in two days."

Hooking up with Leah was a lucky break for Dagan. She was well known in the consultant community, meaning many hated her. No better measure of a job well done than the amount of animosity from your peers. At the time, Dagan worked for Corporament approved consultants, chair-riders who did nothing more than what Paragon counselors did. Leah expanded his contacts deeper into the business where freelancers with rebellious determination picked their own clients, parsed every detail, and appraised every client, no matter their potential. A strange community that expected perfection in every assessment and any mistakes, intentional or not, would get you shunned forever. In the Corporament mistakes were forgotten, brushed off with an "oh well" or an "oops." As long as it wasn't in the client's favor.

To his knowledge, Leah never mentioned the miss-appraisal of the coin collection to her colleagues. She called it an honest mistake while making clear he was expected to perform at a high level. After first being annoyed Dagan found he was up for the challenge and looked forward to her assignments.

His tour through the Smalls' house involved photographing every room and every object in every room, along with a running commentary recorded and synced by his HearSay, named Juliet. Since the ECC was watching and listening he kept his comments bland, mostly notes on distinguishing characteristics, counts, descriptions, whatever needed to be catalogued. Take it all back to his workstation; compare, rate and authenticate; assess the value; put it into a coherent report and tally up the cash value of Mr. and Mrs. Smalls entire life.

As Dagan approached their house on his scooter, he wondered if he had the right street. A typical three lane road in the shadow of a long string of "block" buildings: each apartment manufactured elsewhere, shipped to the building site and stacked up like a child's toy. He saw the front lawn first, well cared for and nicely trimmed. *It was the only lawn on the entire street*. On this anomalous plot of land sat a single level house crowded by buildings standing like frozen trolls, looking out and away, trying to pretend this little abode didn't exist.

Dagan thought houses like this only existed on the outskirts of the city, near the rural borders. The Smalls' were holdouts, old codgers that refused to sell. He wondered if they were proud of their stubbornness.

Leah said they owned a significant plot of land, but Dagan couldn't see anything more than a nice front yard. In this part of the city undeveloped land had value, but he doubted it would be the goldmine Leah hoped for.

The house was a throwback as well, the siding painted green with brown shutters and a red roof, worth only the few hundred dollars recyclers would give for the material. He stepped onto the front porch and introduced himself to the ECC. Once inside he immediately recognized the "Happy Home" floor plan popular fifty years ago: separate, locked off ends for husband and wife with a common area between. Nearby were a piano and two chairs. To the back of the house was a central kitchen, small with the usual appliances, a bar with stools, and a dining area with a simple round table built of heavy wood with a rustic look. Next to the kitchen was the holoroom. The holo system was a mutt, components from different lines, and eras, difficult to work together. A hallway extended the length of the house with a door at either end.

The lefthand door opened on ten more feet of hall and two rooms, bedroom and office. Masculine things here, Mr. Smalls' living quarters. The door at the opposite end of the hall opened on more hallway and a single large room with bed, vanity, desk, chair--a feminine space. Where Mrs. Smalls lived. Definitely an ancient couple.

Dagan started here. Queen sized bed with frilly pink skirt, old fashioned roll top desk, vanity with large oval mirror. A sitting chair for reading. A lamp. A small bathroom with cast iron tub, sink and commode. Closet full of dresses and pant suits. Mrs. Smalls had excellent taste in clothing. One side of the closet was devoted to shoes. She had a line of figurines displayed on a shelf, little pale children with absurdly round faces doing nostalgically childish things, and a collection of old matchbooks in a large glass jar. He would have to photo and describe them all. Shit.

That took most of an hour, then to the other end of the house. Full size bed, dresser, closet full of suits that looked the same, a couple of hundred ties, nightstand, bookshelf with actual books. Paperbacks. Book collectors might be interested but the market was small, and these were not worth much. On top of the bookshelf were several model cars, in plexiglass display boxes, hot rods from the late twentieth century. Worth something maybe, depending on the quality. Mr. Smalls used a small bathroom with shower stall, sink and commode.

In the basement Dagan found a room full of taped up cardboard boxes. He pulled out a box cutter and went to work. This was where he earned his fee. Clients would complain his visit was like an invasion, until they learned these long forgotten things had value, no matter how slight. It always amazed Dagan how little it took to placate their annoyance. It was junk to them, and junk to him, but if they could get a buck out of it, then by all means help yourself to our personal belongings.

His excavation of the boxes turned up a complete Italian made nativity scene, some old State University branded swag, an incomplete set of crystal goblets, a box of old blankets, a box of hand knitted sweaters, old movie tie-in toys, a matching pair of brass lamps, all worth something, but not much. Maybe the price of a soda or two.

Back upstairs in the kitchen Dagan photoed all of the appliances, all the pans and dishes, all the spices and packaged food in the cupboards, and the contents of the refrigerator, counting all the soda bottles.

In the front room he found a china cabinet and a full set of china decorated with an intricate lace pattern around the edge and a pink hue to the porcelain. Plus a set of real silverware, clearly used, likely two hundred years old. Now that was worth something. Into the holoroom and all of its mismatched components and he was done. Once the Smalls returned the questionnaire he could put a dollar amount on everything. They would get something for their belongings, but not much, certainly not enough to retire on.

All that was left was the property. The sliding door leading out the back was covered by ugly dark plaid drapes. He pulled the cords and stepped back. Light streamed into the dim room. Dagan was in a spot where the door framed out the buildings and left only green grass and trees. He had never seen so much uninterrupted nature. No concrete or brick, no asphalt or exhaust. No buildings, not even a swing set. Nothing but growing things everywhere.

Dagan moved up to the door, losing his frame and letting in the rest of the scene. The backyard extended fifty feet from the house, the property beyond wooded, its end somewhere out of sight. A six story faux stucco building dotted with wrought iron balconies surrounded the property on the two sides, as if all this greenery were an overgrown courtyard.

He opened the backdoor (with the house's permission) and stepped outside. The Smalls property sloped downward slightly, away from the house. He stood on the top step of three leading to a small wooden deck. In the distance (it seemed a long way away) he could see a taller, rounded tree above the rest. Maybe an oak. Even this tree was shorter than the enclosing buildings. Before coming into the house Dagan felt a slight breeze but back here it was perfectly still.

From a jacket pocket Dagan pulled a laser measure and took a reading across the property, from fence to fence. Thirty-three point three yards, one hundred feet, a typical plot division from back in the day, when property lines were drawn in nice, neat rectangles.

An era when records were written by hand and prone to inaccuracies. How did humanity ever function without computers? Dagan needed a length measurement, but the trees were in the way. He walked to the edge of the woods and searched for an entrance or path of some kind. The undergrowth was thick; he could see nothing but sun-dotted darkness beyond. He turned left and walked the forest edge, a straight line defined by mowed grass and a sudden wall of trees, pulling back tall grass, looking for a way in. His foot slipped into a depression hidden in the grass, his ankle falling back awkwardly. The heel of his shoe touched something hard. Digging with his fingers, Dagan found a flagstone with a zigzag design. He found another a few inches away, then another, and another, leading into the woods. The remains of a path. He looked around, getting his bearings, then pushed through the undergrowth.

He stopped and let his eyes adjust. The path was obscured. He looked ahead, trying to pick out gaps between trees, and saw many. The ground cover was thick, most of the tree branches well above his head, except for the occasional pine tree determined to grow fat instead of tall. Dagan decided to make his own path and keep it straight.

This proved difficult. Too many deadfalls blocking the way. He tried climbing over; one disintegrated under his foot, another started to roll though it had looked solid. Zigzagging around caused him to lose any sense of direction and give up the idea of creating a path. The property sloped down. He had to remember that. Follow the downward slant.

Not knowing what might be underfoot, he tread lightly. People in the apartments around were talking and slamming doors; he could hear a loud car and a siren. Eventually he came to a place where the trees were less dense, and in the middle, a concrete ring with a small tree and tall weeds growing out of it like a planter.

Dagan stared, pondering why it was here. He walked around, weaving between tall thick trees. The ring measured two and a half feet high, five feet in diameter, six inches thick. Twenty feet away he saw a flash of bright blue. The remains of a shredded vinyl tarp tied down with nylon rope. Two corners had been fastened to adjacent trees, the rope loops swallowed by the bark as the tree grew. Dagan pulled up the edge of the tarp and found a pile of wet sawdust.

Obviously this place had some purpose. Was there anything of value? He trampled through the brush, but found nothing more than vegetation.

Looking up he could see blue sky through the canopy of leaves. The trees so tall and dense the enclosing buildings were hidden. No one could see him. Even the noise, all that human activity, was muted. Dagan felt alone, an unfamiliar feeling. He had been alone many times, in his apartment usually, his neighbors only the thickness of a wall away, but this was different. He was separated, and the nearest people did not know he was here. In an apartment you heard neighbors come and go whether you wanted to or not. Here, there were *living things* between him and them, giving shelter.

Silence. Had everyone stopped talking or could he not hear them anymore? Dagan stood still. This wasn't silence. There was movement all around. A rustle in the dead leaves to his right. A sudden dart through the brush. Animals, probably keeping a wary eye on him. He looked up and saw the trees swaying slightly. He heard the creak of wood on wood. The sudden rush of wings and a bird flying up and out.

Standing and watching in the forest-silence of this tiny bit of land in the middle of a metropolis, Dagan felt his soul unclench and expand, seeing beyond the artificial borders of his apartment, the office, the coffee shop, his parking space, the imaginary ten foot line he drew around his scooter while riding (his personal space), every space he had ever grown up in, worked in, or lived in. All those lines that defined space and kept an overgrown populace from destroying itself. None of them existed here. This was freedom.

He stayed still and listened. There, at the base of a tree, dead leaves flipping over for no reason. As silently as he could, Dagan walked over and moved the leaves aside. He smelled wet earth and a small dark toad hopped out. Quickly he put his hand down to block it, and just as quickly the toad hopped over it. He blocked again and this time caught the toad in cupped hands. He had never seen one for real, only in books. It peed in his hands. Gross. He opened his hands to let it go but it stayed put. A nudge in the butt with a finger and it finally jumped away. Dagan rubbed his hands on a smooth barked tree.

He watched chipmunks bouncing like tennis balls and a black squirrel with a thick bushy tail climbing a tree. A robin landed in a sunspot, cocked its head, and plucked a worm out of the ground. Five steps away he found a pond shaded underneath the large oak, cattails growing along the edge. A salamander scurried by but it was too slimy to catch.

Taking those few steps changed his perception of the terrain radically. He could still see the cement ring but it looked different from here, as if it had changed settings while he was kneeling by the pond. Now it was half hidden by shadows with a dark forest beyond. To his right, in the opposite direction, light angled through the trees. In the interplay between light and dark he could see clouds of tiny bugs; twigs, leaves and things he couldn't identify falling to the ground; two small dots hovering around each other, insects having a face off. The forest changed with every new direction.

For an hour Dagan explored the woods like a boy set loose. He heard the pounding of a woodpecker but could never find it. A frightened rabbit skittered out from under a bush and scared him as well. He found a long, almost straight stick, broke off the dead branches, and used it to poke around. Things leapt and ran away that he never laid eyes on. A rustle of leaves, a branch springing back, maybe some chittering, and the sound of tiny feet moving very fast. Up in the trees he could see nests but they were not bird's nests. He could hear the same chitter echoing from above. Squirrel nests. They were making a lot of noise. Maybe talking about him.

Near a pine tree he found the carcass of a rabbit, dead a few weeks, nothing but bones and fur. The branches of the tree were low to the ground. He used the stick to poke around inside. Dagan heard a hiss and a growl and his stick was attacked from the gloom. He yanked it out with a feral cat attached, matted grey and black fur, one ear half bitten off and a nasty scar on its nose, the descendent of a long lost house cat, baring its teeth, ears flat back, claws dug into the poke stick. This was fear, facing an angry defensive animal, even if it was no more than a foot and a half long, including the tail. He backed away, but the cat wouldn't let go. It hissed again, giving warning. He gave the stick a tug, hoping to shake it loose. It growled but stayed put. He really liked that stick. A stronger tug this time, and another step back, trying to convince the animal he intended to walk away. Instead the cat looked ready to lunge, digging in its back paws and wiggling its rear end. Dagan grabbed his precious stick with both hands and swung it in a half circle. The cat lost its grip, and a couple of claws, and flew off, landing in tall grass a few feet away. Dagan could see its eyes glowering at him. It stalked a wide circle back to the pine tree. Must be its lair. This tree was off limits.

A sheen of sweat coated his brow. That hadn't happened since he was a kid and running...where? Down the street? An alley between buildings? He remembered laughing and running, with friends for the fun of it.

Dagan's explorations took him to the back of the Smalls' property, into the corners and along the fence on both sides. The fence was falling apart in places, broken open in others, large enough to let a child through. He wasn't the only human who wandered here. A thicket of weeds grew along the bottom of the fence, curled over, full of thorns and prickers, the perfect trap for unsuspecting legs. Dagan kept his distance. Half of the south fence was engulfed in vines, ivy maybe. Some of the vines appeared to move. Or was that the breeze? He felt a tickle under his pant leg and reactively jumped, pulling his leg away. A light green vine fell to the brown earth. Dagan watched to see if it would move, but it lay innocently still.

Juliet interrupted with a reminder that it was time for his afternoon break, rudely shoving him back to reality. Had it been that long already? Half the day gone and he hadn't even gotten a length measurement yet.

A double check of the width along the back fence showed it to be slightly narrower, just over thirty-three yards, probably squeezed by the encroaching neighbors.

The length would be difficult, but not impossible. The Smalls' property was longer than anticipated, not typical of its original era. Dagan wondered how the Smalls were able to get so much land. "Juliet, sync the laser measure to GMS and yourself."

A sweet female voice answered, "Yes Dagan Jones." He liked being called by his full name. "Done."

"Plot the next measurements to the nearest inch and extrapolate for distance until I say stop."

"You must overlap the measured segments for an accurate reading."

"I know. Let's begin."

He aimed the laser tape at the back fence and a tree about twenty feet away, uploaded the measurement, moved up to that tree, aimed the laser at a tree behind the first, and another about twenty feet ahead, and worked his way up through the woods. One of the three hundred and fifty orbiting Global Mapping Satellites would see and read the laser pulse, and send its readings to his HearSay. Juliet would compare and sync these, using a geometry program to remove the inevitable angles, and come up with an accurate length.

The planet had been completely mapped--in every conceivable way--long ago. The Mapping Satellites replaced the old GPS and were much more detailed, updating every change in topography in real time.

Dagan worked his way back up the slope, past the cement ring, until he crashed back through the underbrush and into the Smalls' backyard. Another reading up to the rear of the house, then a last one around the house and past the property line.

"Juliet, stop recording and save."

"Done."

Dagan straddled his scooter and opened the HearSay interface, which automatically compensated for sunlight to make the screen legible. Juliet opened an aerial map of the Smalls property showing a series of short straight red lines--a plot of his laser measurements.

"Juliet, straighten and compensate for angles, cut off at the east side property line, and give me the total length."

The red lines corrected themselves into one long straight line and a number flashed onscreen. Juliet read it aloud. "One hundred fifty-five point three yards."

"Very good. Multiply by thirty-three point seven yards and convert to acres."

"One point zero eight one acres."

"Just over an acre. How many residential properties in this county are equal or greater?"

"There are none on record Dagan Jones."

"Thank you Juliet. Place a voice call to Leah Lockwood."

"In progress."

Dagan got off the scooter and paced around the Smalls' front yard.

"Hey Dagan. What's the verdict?"

"Preliminary as usual. Unless something turns up in analysis their personal belongings will only net a small gain over contemporary values."

"Which means?"

"Some of their stuff is collectible, but they won't make a killing."

"And the land?"

"That's where the-" A movie popped into Dagan's head. Bulldozers and backhoes crushing through fence and brush. Men with itchy fingers guiding rumbling machines over tree and animal alike. The great oak trimmed and hacked into boards. Skinny old maples and birches pushed over like matchsticks, reduced to wood chips in minutes. Machines grinding and digging, tearing up every last stump. The mini forest reduced to a swath of turned earth, waiting to house another thousand efficiently packaged souls.

"Yes?"

"-money is. It's larger than you think. Probably fit five or six complexes."

An exhale of breath. "Really?"

"Over an acre. Last one of its size in the county."

"The last one?" Dagan thought he heard a giggle, but that would be strange coming from Leah. "That's excellent news. You've made my year Dagan."

"I'm sure you're going to auction it. Who's doing it?"

"Otis Vangelder. Worried about your commission?"

"No, he's good. You always work with the best Leah."

"That I do. Get that final report to me ASAP. Thanks Dagan."

Juliet, "Call ended."

Dagan looked at the Smalls' front lawn, the apartment buildings and stunted token trees that lined the street, at the full grown trees peeking over the roof of the house, and the scooter that would take him away. *Time to get back to my life.*

"Juliet, you are helpful, efficient and beautiful."

With a happy programmed tone Juliet replied, "Thank you Dagan Jones."

21

Little Sadistic Rewards

Friday, September 1st thru Tuesday October 10th

The roll out of inThrallEd was set for nine o'clock in the evening, during a holovision show called "Ja-OW!-st" featuring transients tilting at each other down a long rubber lined trench, wearing plastic armor and carrying a plastic lance, trying to knock an opposing "knight" to the ground. The combatants rode carts on rails, pushed by other transients. The winning team in each week's episode received ten years of free EverLife. Participants typically possessed a narrow range of fitness levels, from young, inexperienced and unmotivated to old, obese and rheumy. Athletic transients were saved for better games. Rolly never watched the show but understood it was popular.

Between Doug and himself they had created twenty-four different video spots formatted for 2D, 3D, holographic, and mobile (all nineteen delivery formats), internet (all forty-six delivery formats), animated banner ads, and ads targeted to various niche groups--Generation Zeros, the Lost Mid-Life Generation, new parents (the only true minority left), Newbies (people born in the last thirty years), the Submerged Generation--an ever-changing demographical smorgasbord that had to be addressed lest some group feel slighted. Plus edited or heavily altered versions for different entertainment and informational sources: news, sitcoms, dramas, history, children's, porn, how-to, cooking, decorating, religious, political, reality, and reality sport/game shows. So many variations of those twenty-four spots Rolly lost count.

All had been tweaked to perfection and approved at the highest levels. First would be the sunset spots, a gentle introduction to the necessity of having insurance.

The campaign would climax in late February when a massive hurricane would devastate the eastern half of the United Syndicates, leaving the uninsured desperately trying to survive and the insured comfortably secure in rebuilt homes.

The ad appeared right on time. Rolly didn't feel any sense of pride, it was too familiar. He tried to imagine Souliere's prediction coming true but the campaign had come together so well it didn't seem possible. Rolly turned off the holovision and went to bed.

The first snide comments and defacements appeared immediately--the usual public vitriol and excretion of bad puns--which happened with every new commercial. In the Saturday morning after-launch meeting they went over the discussion threads to see if the conversation was headed in a direction they didn't like. No mention of enthralled as slavery. Steve liked what he saw: a quiet start to a new campaign with a slogan guaranteed to worm its way into consumer's collective brain. He was so happy he gave the OCM an early quitting time, three o'clock, with pay and Productivity for a full day. Even Rolly went home.

By Sunday every HearSay connected person in the country knew the secondary definition of enthrall. As if a great phlegmatic intelligence had suddenly awoken and discovered the dictionary. Steve mass texted the entire OCM, calling for an emergency meeting. Not everyone was in the office, many had to link in with HearSays. Rolly, like every day for the past nine months, was already in house. Even Megan Gentry, the Senior Executive Vice President in charge of Vice Presidents, made an appearance.

Concerns were aired and discussed: this could undermine the whole campaign, what are we going to do to get ahead of it? Counter arguments were offered: it's too early, something like this always happens, let the ads play out and win over customers. Management decided talk among edge-dwelling citizens with little mainstream cachet could be overcome, the quality of their work was good, the campaign would go forward without change. The enslavement thing would go away once the public got caught up in the narrative.

Souliere never said a word.

The next level in the rollout was harmless, including Rolly's commercial panning over the floor of a ransacked home. The third level introduced Mr. Dodds, who was never named in the commercials, only the OCM staff called him Mr. Dodds. Besides appearing at various tragedies, Mr. Dodds also helped the insured find the right path in life, directing folks away from potential dangers and encouraging safe habits. He appeared wherever the insured person looked, guiding them along the blue path of life. His voice would be synonymous with the "Become InThrallEd with Insurance" tagline. A free voice print was made available for anyone wanting to add it to their HearSay.

When Mr. Dodds appeared in his home holovision Rolly sat up in shock. His carefully crafted benevolent representative had turned evil. The skin under the eyes dark, the twinkle menacing. When Mr. Dodds leaned forward in what was supposed to be a "grandfatherly way" it looked aggressive, as if Mr. Dodds were about to molest the audience. How did this happen? He had been careful to make Mr. Dodds kindly and helpful.

Did something go wrong in post-production? Something in the wireless broadcast?

Mr. Dodds turned out to be a catalyst for the audience, who quickly linked inThrallEd as slavery and Mr. Dodds as the evil slave master. Those edge-dwelling nerds were now harbingers of truth. Respected critics (who jumped on when they realized people were paying attention) blasted Stableman Insurance as the company that wanted to enslave humanity.

The mockery began. A scraggly pencil drawing called "inThrallEd Guy" appeared on the internet, a slightly-better-than-usual stick figure with a big round head. One eye crossed out, the other wide open, an off kilter mouth with a single tooth, the opposite of the urbane Mr. Dodds. "InThrallEd Guy" became animated and made appearances in myriad videos; some cut off the head and stuck it on Mr. Dodds in bastardized versions of the commercials, making him look buffoonish. The crude figure became like pixelated modeling clay, developing a surprising number of facial expressions and actions.

The free voice print provided fodder for amateur sound engineers as well. Childish high pitched and low pitched versions. Quickly created, snickered over, and forgotten. The real winners were able to synthesize enough words to give Mr. Dodds a significant vocabulary, spoken in the same gentle, grandfatherly way. The goal was to make Mr. Dodds say outrageous things, the more contrary to his tone the better. Like "I'd fuck your Mother for a penny." Or "My dick is quite nicely inThrallEd right now." The more vulgar it was the more page views it received.

The stake through the heart came on October 1st when the headline **Insurance Company Wants to Enslave You** went viral, appearing on every web news channel and passed and liked and shared and trended on ten billion blogs and a hundred billion social mini-networks. It was the WTF? topic on some sites, the Did They Really Say That? on others, The Stupid Quote of the Week, The Stupid Idea of the Week, Are You Kidding Me?, and on and on. The Stableman PR department went into overdrive, apologizing profusely: We're very sorry; It was an oversight; No, we did not imply that people are slaves; Ha ha, no, we're not trying to take over the world, ha ha. Thirty-six hours later the PR people were saying "That campaign is under review." inThrallEd was officially dead.

Rolly's hard work was left sitting on Stableman hard drives, most of it unseen, eventually to be erased. This didn't bother him much. The first worry for Rolly was *How am I going to find enough work to maintain Productivity?* inThrallEd had been a boon but now it was gone. How was he going to fill his time? With public safety videos?

But inThrallEd didn't just fail, it was an epic public embarrassment, costing time, money and hundreds of clients. A total screw up like this meant several someones would be fired. Rolly's name was all over the finished product; he felt like a target waiting to be shot. The mood in the OCM was somber, the entire office waiting to see who would lose their job--and EverLife--as if a death sentence were about to be read.

Rolly hunkered down and tried to lay low, slouching as he walked the cubicles. He kept a close eye on his Productivity, freaking when he ran out of things to do. Lambert still brought occasional consults but even she could not manage a smile. Only Souliere and Myrna seemed unperturbed.

Leah kept calling but he refused to answer. Rolly knew what she wanted: to set a date for the auction, the last thing he wanted to think about. He avoided Stephanie as well. Not difficult since their paths crossed for only seconds every day.

Rolly tried to imagine himself at the bottom of a dark hole, lined with floating icons, mindless car rides and four dimensional movies with rumbling sound effects and not-quite-right pretend smells. Deep in the hole, with the urgent worries at bay, he would think about Nola, and her terrible life, that his own daughter should not be living this way, and what was he going to do about it?

Leah texted again, this time in thirty point font: ANSWER YOUR DAMN PHONE. He might get fired and her only concern was selling the house. They would need that house if everything went to hell. No more Productivity to keep track of, no more income, no retirement. EverLife could be paid from savings, but how long would that last? What would be the point without a job? How long would his marriage last? A few weeks ago everything had been hectic but manageable. Now his life was precarious, threatening to fall apart. If that happened he wouldn't be helping Nola--he'd be living with her.

Thursday, October 12th

Desperate for reassurance, Rolly finally answered Leah's texts.

> Inthralled failed.
> Hello my leige! Thank you for replying.
> I might lose my job
> That woud be bad
> Im serious. Shits hitting the fan. Someones going to get canne d and its probaly me
> Anybody say anything to you?
> About what?
> Getting fired
> Nobodys talking about anything. Just waiting for the ax to fall
> No manager has told you your on the chopping block?

Im just trying to hide. I worked my ass off on that thing. Everyone knows it

But has a manager warned you might get fired?

No

Your doing the right thing. Lay low, wait for it to blow over. Cross your fingers. You make inthralled guy?

Yeah the original

Whyd you make him look like the devil? Weird way to make people buy insurance

He was sposed to be freindly and helpful. Dont know what wnet wrong

This too shall pass

I want to see nola

No

Make sure shes okay

No

Shes my daughter

No

Cant leave her by herself. Have to let her know she has family

This is no time to be altrusitic. Just keep thinking about retirement

I have too much time and all i can think about is my daughter

Meet me at renfrews for lunch 1:15. Dont be late

This was how Leah made lunch dates, commanding instead of asking. Rolly was happy to go, if only to be around someone not crippled by paranoia.

At Renfrew's Rolly ordered a Caesar salad, Leah a garden salad. The lettuce leaves were unnaturally bright green and coated with something slimy that smelled of machinery oil. In the interest of self-preservation they pushed the food aside and went hungry.

"Your exemption is now officially recognized by the Corporament."

"Really? When?"

"About a week ago. Had to make sure there were no contradictions with the rest of your life then went for it."

That sounded somewhat reckless. "Did it turn out okay? What'd it do to my Reckoning?"

Leah turned her screen so Rolly could see: 478.77, little less than a half point higher.

"It helped, but didn't exactly throw you over the wall either. We still have work to do."

A little good news in an onslaught of bad. Rolly allowed himself a smile.

Leah scowled. "Have I shown you the picture of Nola?"

"You never sent one. Said you would but never did."

"My bad. Here. It's the only one I could find." Leah scrolled with an arrow key until she found the picture. The girl in the photo was eight or ten years old, standing, wide round face and big brown eyes, scraggy long hair, wearing a plaid jumper over a white shirt. Her mouth was open, eyes wide, looking over the camera.

Rolly grinned. "She's cute."

"Try to imagine this little girl going through childhood in the care of Population Solutions Incorporated. What's happening to her when this picture was taken. Ask yourself why she looks afraid."

"You said it takes a tough person to survive."

"Tough or lucky. Which do you think she is?"

"Obviously she's made out of sterner stuff."

Leah looked as if Rolly had expressed deep faith in the wisdom of the Easter Bunny.

"You don't understand what this woman has been through. She is not the innocent girl you believe she is."

"Why would that matter?"

"Damnit Rolly! The Corporament can still link you together. I'm trying to get you to stay away."

"There's a billion people in this country. Why would anything I do matter to them?"

"If you start hanging out with her, maybe at the party store or down at the bingo parlor, they'll see it because their computers see everything, and they might say 'Rolly has developed a new interest in bingo. Let's send him some bingo ads' and let it go. If you're lucky. Or a subroutine of a subprogram might make the connection and say we need someone to check this out. That's when your friends the Thought Police show up."

"C'mon, the Corporament doesn't care. Doesn't make any difference to them."

"Oh they love putting families back together. It's great PR. They'll put you all over the tube if they catch you. Shows responsibility and sacrifice. Family first you know. Same reasoning they use to force eternal marriage on childless couples. Keep the family together, no matter what."

"But they're the ones who gave me this damn waiver in the first place."

"Exemption."

"Whatever. Why let me off the hook if family is so important?"

"Doesn't make sense does it? It's this way because the ruling elite wants working slobs like yourself to be stable and reliable, while giving themselves license to do anything they want. Exemptions were never supposed to work for you, they weren't clever enough to prevent it."

"Okay, so--"

"I know where this is going. You're thinking this exemption puts you free to see your daughter. But anything you do could tie you together. Buy candy from her at the store. Ride the same bus together. Drive around her neighborhood. Park on Maycroft Lane and spy on her apartment."

Rolly, startled, "How'd you know that?"

"If I know it the Corporament knows it. Point is they don't care how many exemptions you have. They'll use you any way they want. Don't give them the chance. Keep your distance. And do not send this woman any money! Might as well go on holovision and declare your daughter to the world."

"I can't let her rot. She needs help."

"This is admirable. Really. Most men are too happy to forget their love-child, but you want to save her. Remember it's the good we try to do that gets us in trouble. Nola has lived a long, difficult life. The best you can do is let it end peacefully. Don't complicate things with some belated parenting. Let her go."

"How can I live forever but willingly accept the death of my own child? Isn't that selfish?"

"Maybe. But it's the world we live in. You should know that. Now let's set a date for the auction."

Friday, October 13th

The day Steve Mann was fired. Not demoted or promoted sideways, but told to pack his minimalist belongings and not come back. He received two weeks severance for one hundred and sixteen years of loyalty. This was surprising. Usually the salary of fired employees ended at the exact second of their termination. Steve still had friends in high places.

Norreen, the woman who designed three hundred crowns, was fired. She left in tears. Cory Persell was let go. He did audio ads for subsidized HearSay users who had to listen to random advertisements for a discounted price. Three others were let go, including Frank Charles, who had been at the initial meeting.

No one could say these people did a worse job than anyone else, or were less well-liked. Some of the most reviled employees were kept on. This made no sense. The anxiety level rose, rumors flew like darts. Trust took a backseat to worry, followed by accusations and recriminations. When the yelling started Souliere stepped in and everyone stopped to listen. He said the firings were random, these people were chosen to send a message: don't ever embarrass the company again.

Upon hearing this Roger Northrup, who had a loud voice, strong opinions and little self-control, said: "Yeah, but who's going to fire the dicks who made the stupid decisions in the first place?" The next morning Macklin stopped Roger in the lobby and fired him on the spot, sending him back down the elevator trailed by security. Message received loud and clear.

His retirement riding on the decision, Rolly tried to find out who would replace Steve. No one knew anything. Souliere was clueless. Even Myrna, who had access to all the best gossip was out of the loop.

"Don't worry Rolly, these things always work out," she said.

Rolly was not comforted. None of the VPs in line for promotion were employee friendly, and many lusted after the OCM. A few made app-earances to look smugly over Myrna's head as if saying "You'll be mine soon and there's nothing you can do about it." Myrna said this happened at least once a day. Sometimes two would show up at the same time and intrude on each other's posturing.

The luxury of two weeks severance allowed Steve to visit the OCM and say goodbye. He praised everyone for the fine work on inThrallEd, even though most of it would never be seen. He singled out Rolly for his improved work ethic, becoming an employee to be proud of, and for realizing the truth of what it means to work for a living. Rolly, who wished desperately for a plant to hide behind, tried to look grateful while wondering what the hell Steve was talking about.

Monday, October 16th

At ten o'clock the powers-that-be summoned Macklin to the fiftieth floor. She returned with their new boss, Mike Parris, whom no one had met before. Mr. Parris wore a new grey suit in which he looked itchingly uncomfortable, pulling at his collar and smiling too much. Macklin took him around, making introductions, explaining that Mr. Parris had been a First Assistant Regional Manager for Long Term Life Insurance in the Actuarial Department. Mike Parris shook hands stiffly with a glazed look. Rolly guessed his age somewhere in the fifty to seventy range.

At lunch, from the privacy of his parked car, Rolly called Leah.

"What do we do now? Steve was supposed to give me a good rating. This guy knows nothing."

"Wow. This is serious. They promoted a nobody instead of giving the department to a VP. Someone is really pissed off. You're in for a roller coaster ride."

"Why's that?"

"Administrators like to move people around, mess with their routine, jar them into new paradigms, in execu-speak. Parris is out of his element and it's safe to assume he's been given orders to shake things up. Given his lack of experience he'll tear the place apart trying to make it work."

"What should I do?"

"There's only two months left. Time is on your side. Work hard and stay out of new guy's way."

"That's going to be difficult. There isn't much to do."

"Make stuff up if you have to. Anticipate freak accidents. Hell, every object on the planet is a disaster waiting to happen. Your goal is to get through the rest of the year unscathed. When it's time to do your evaluation Parris will have only your Productivity to work with. He doesn't know you well enough to make problems. Yet. That's the one bright spot and your new incentive. 'Cause if you're still around a year from now he'll have everything he needs to screw you royally. Get yourself retired and be done with this shit."

Sunday, November 5th

A blustery cold day. Halloween came and went and winter moved in as if on cue. Sitting in his car on Maycroft Lane, Rolly rubbed his gloved hands together. The engine was off to save gas and cold was beginning to seep through his winter clothes.

Rolly and Stephanie hadn't participated in Halloween festivities for a long time. The theme parties with sexy costumes, endless alcohol, inhibition loosening drugs, and the traditional midnight orgy. When trick or treating ended for lack of children, the toys became adult themed and expensive. Rolly lost interest after a few years and stayed home; Stephanie followed not long after. They both felt the same: it was more than they could take, a night of over-the-top pleasure seeking in an already indulgent culture. And staying home was nice. Not many people were out and about, like you had the world to yourself. The Smalls household was quietly platonic on Halloween.

Rolly put binoculars to his eyes. No activity. It was late morning on a Sunday, he was probably expecting too much. Maycroft ran through the former town of DeWitt, now an industrial zone in the expanded city. On the north side of the street a row of aluminum prefabricated buildings stood plain and unmarked. On the south side a small treeless park allowed Rolly to see the back of Nola's apartment building, yet another prefabricated rectangle, more cheap motel than place to live. Three floors with outdoor walkways, open stairways in the center and on the ends.

In his cold car Rolly was two hundred yards away, with a perfect view of Nola's apartment, number 378. Whenever he saw someone on the third level, or going up the stairs, Rolly picked up the binoculars and watched. He still had no idea what Nola looked like.

This was Rolly's third Sunday on stakeout. In the aftermath of inThrallEd there was little work, nothing more than assigned projects, only enough to fill a normal workday. Nothing worse than sitting at a workstation with nothing to do. Better to stay home. Except Rolly had become used to the insane schedule and couldn't settle down. So, despite Leah's warnings, he made the trek to the far side of town, to see if he could find his daughter.

Like other parts of Lansing this place was schizophrenic. One moment the houses and buildings were beautifully painted and perfectly maintained, the next was grey despair and broken windows and collapsing porches. This pattern of prosperity/blight didn't follow neighborhood boundary lines. Three buildings on a block might be nice, the rest crumbling. Nola lived in the blight.

A woman went up the stairs to the third floor landing, turned left, away from 378. Another woman followed, taking the stairs slowly, as if each step were a mountain. At the third floor landing she turned right and shuffled to 378, stopping in front of the door. Rolly watched intently. She had on a heavy black coat that made her look large. A bubble of blonde hair surrounded her head, trailing curls to the small of her back. This woman cared about her appearance. She unlocked the door and went in without turning around.

Happy he had at last seen her, Rolly started the car, welcoming the heat flushed out of the engine, and drove home.

"Subject is in the exclusion zone. How would you like to proceed?"

Babies were the worst patients. They couldn't tell you what was wrong, just cry and scream. Like the one lying on the gurney, shaking from stress, its flabby little arms outstretched, face red, drool everywhere.

"What?"

The parents of the little tyke, both transients, moved to say something but Stephanie held up her hand.

"Talking to a doctor. Getting advice on what to do." The parents sat back, relieved to hear Stephanie wasn't the only medical professional in the room.

Zack repeated, "Subject is in the exclusion zone. How would you like to proceed?"

"Wait a moment." She needed to be in a private place where she could unfold the interface and check Rolly's whereabouts.

The baby was naked, diaper opened and spread out underneath its butt. Male, of course. They always cried the loudest. She was feeling around the child's stomach in an effort to look like she was doing something. The baby cried louder. The two on-call doctors were busy patching up five participants in a bar brawl, removing bottle glass from various wounds and eye sockets. Stephanie was killing time, hoping one of the doctors would make an appearance.

Nikki, "Ma'am I may be able to help. Ten months ago a medical guide was installed in my memory. If you tell me the symptoms I may be able to narrow down a cause."

Great idea. The parents believed she was talking to a doctor, they would never know it was only Nikki.

"Baby is male, crying constantly for an hour, face red, mouth open. Does not appear to be teething. Abdomen is soft as I go lower it stays...no wait. It's hard around the intestinal area." The baby shrieked.

"Could be infant constipation. Try soothing the baby to relax the muscles. Gently rub the stomach area in a circular motion. Pumping the legs can also be effective. If that fails, try a warm bath."

Christ. Stressing out over Rolly's extracurricular activity while soothing a constipated baby. Her life was seriously fucked up.

She looked at the baby and frowned, rubbed its cheek, trying to remember what she did when Max was a baby, but all she had were blurry memories of amusement parks. This wasn't helping. Try maternal instincts. See if she had any left.

She cooed at the baby, "There there, it's alright. It's okay." She said this while rubbing its head with one hand and belly with the other.

The baby didn't stop but opened its eyes a little and looked at her.

"Do you have something stuck that doesn't want to come out?" The baby gasped between sobs but still cried uncontrollably.

The ragged high pitched wailing was getting to her. She had no intention of doing the leg pumps since that would put her in the line of fire. The baby's mouth was wide open, jaw shaking, gums pink and bare. Even though it wasn't teething, she thought a gum rub might work. A finger went in and immediately the baby clamped down on it. There was no pain but it was unexpected. Stephanie tried to pull out but the baby started sucking, and the crying stopped.

She kept her finger in and after a minute it took a deep breath and sighed. This was followed by a little fart, the pop of small brown turd and finally a mini flood of greenish liquid. It was disgusting, the smell in the room a combination of sewage and spoiled milk.

The baby fell asleep in his own filth, worn out and content.

"What have you been feeding this child?"

The Mother, "Formula."

"What kind?"

The Father, "Store bought." Transient slang for the ultra cheap plain packaged products sold in the back of the store. Lacking any natural ingredients, the formula claimed to be more nutritious than breast milk. A lie, but there was no law against it, not anymore.

"Well that's why. You know better than to buy that garbage."

"It's all we can afford and my wife has no more milk." The mother looked at the floor.

"What the hell. This is your one and only child. So do what you gotta do. No more pizza and beer. No more chocolate ice cream to cheer you up. Cut a few corners and you'll be able to feed him the good stuff."

"Subject is now within 200 yards of the target address."

Christ, didn't she have enough to worry about? Time to get out of here. One last question for the new parents. "Is this a licensed child?"

Clearly caught off guard the Father said "Yes." He was a bad liar, looking at his shoes and answering with an upward inflection, as if the word were a question. All new parents who came through St. Bart's lied, trying to hide their children. Doctors had an unofficial policy to not ask, to render services without prejudice. Stephanie asked to scare the parents, a little sadistic reward for all she was giving up.

"Uh huh, right. I have to go. Dilute the formula and give the baby more water." She left the exam room at a brisk walk, heading for the nook, a dead end elbow off one of the far hallways. A shelf at standing height ran along the inside corner, a temporary desk for interfaces. At night she could count on having it to herself.

As soon as she opened the HearSay it displayed a street map showing Rolly and Nola's locations. Rolly wasn't moving.

"Zack, find cameras in the vicinity of the target and show me." She liked calling Rolly "the target," it felt empowering.

"There are fifteen cameras with the target in view."

"So few?"

"The area is mostly industrial."

She sighed. "Show me what you got."

Most of the cameras were too far away or had blocked views. The last was a fish eye angle from a building across the street. Stephanie strained to make out which car was which, found Rolly's, and could see him looking through a pair of binoculars.

Stephanie moved the picture so Rolly was square on the screen. She tried to enlarge it by opening her fingers but nothing happened. "Is this the best we can do?"

"The camera has limited resolution."

Stephanie watched Rolly watching Nola. What would she do if Rolly attempted contact? She hadn't given the possibility serious thought, not believing it would happen. He was inching closer, spying on this waste of a woman with a slim claim to his paternity. Bitch. She wasn't family. Family connections had to be tenuous, rare happenings easily escaped from. No family could spend a thousand years together and expect to survive. Why add to this misery by bringing in a bastard child? A transient no less.

Nola's apartment was a few blocks from the hospital. She could be there in five minutes. Was that enough time to head Rolly off? Would he stop if she tried? A year ago she would have said yes. Now she wasn't sure. The last few months had chipped away his timidity and given him new determination. The usual cajoling wouldn't work. Stopping Rolly would require a knock-down-drag-out fight.

Rolly put down the binoculars but stayed in the car.

Maybe she should confront him. At one in the morning when she got home from work. Shake him awake and have it out while he was groggy. That would only put him on guard, make him more sneaky. Rolly would know she was tracking him, and there were as many camouflage programs as tracking programs. Her advantage would be gone.

Rolly started the car and pulled out into the street, driving out of camera range.

"Street view."

"Yes ma'am." Rolly turned right, along the eastern edge of the park toward Nola's building. Stephanie watched intently but he kept going south, back into the city, toward home.

Stephanie thought of Rolly and Max together, back when Max was forming his company, how Rolly made a show of giving Max the money on his birthday. Her sentimental fool of a husband loved holidays. She had to confront Rolly when his defenses were low, when he was most vulnerable and his illusions most delicate, in the one place where the truth would be obvious and she could pummel him with it. But when? And what was he waiting for?

Stephanie smiled with realization. Yes, that made perfect sense. Rolly was waiting for the perfect day to make a present of himself: Christmas.

22

Lying Twice

Mike Parris decided to create an Evaluation Day and run it like this: staff would be summoned to his office four at a time, in alphabetical order. Three would wait while one was interviewed for no more than five minutes; during the third interview his executive assistant would call up four more (he timed how long it should take to travel from the OCM), creating a constant flow of employees.

Never had an administrator tried to interview everyone in one day. Even if he kept strict pace it would take more than a full day. Naturally an office pool started: guess how many evaluations would be left at the end of the day. Rolly bet on twelve and put in twenty dollars.

At Mike's instructions they were to call him Mr. Parris. A hard change for the OCM, where everyone was used to just-call-me-Steve and all his enjoyable quirks. Mr. Parris didn't have a personality let alone quirks. The perfect, pliable administrator, trained to regard employees with contempt. Doug was so upset he ranted for ten minutes, calling the new evaluation system a firing squad with only one rifleman. Rolly thought Doug was paranoid. At least they were talking again.

Waiting on the fiftieth floor, Rolly's group of four included Martha Rathbun, Amy Schott and Jerry Speirman. Martha had been in and gone, he was next in line, wearing a five year old suit. Leah said looking too dapper and confident was bad; Mr. Parris might find it intimidating. He should act subservient, keep his eyes low. Which should be easy. He was already worried what Mr. Parris might do to his Productivity.

His turn came up and he could hear the executive assistant call up the next batch. Amy walked out, her face expressionless. As they passed she said "He knows about the pool. Don't try to stall him." Rolly pretended he didn't hear. The door shut behind him. Mr. Parris stood and shook his hand.

"Hello Rolly. Nice to meet you." Some of the newness had worn off his boss.

"You too, Mr. Parris."

Steve Mann's old desk was there, pushed to the side and piled with folders. Two leather couches occupied the center of the office, at a right angle to each other, mid-twentieth century design. A traditional metal desk was cluttered with gadgets and office appliances--stapler, pencil sharpener, an actual monitor, an actual keyboard. Steve would never have tolerated that. The wall shelves were filled with random objects: a large conch shell, an alligator head, a globe, a snow globe, static picture frames, a 1950's model car, a World War II fighter plane model, bouquets of plastic flowers, a sleeping stuffed cat, lots more. Rolly couldn't make sense of it, it had no I-like-to-do-this-in-my-free-time theme.

"Apologies for the short interview. I haven't had time to get to know anyone but evaluations have to be done so I'll be giving your file a quick read through. Next year when things are settled we'll have time to do this right. Please sit down."

Rolly tried to guess Mr. Parris' age. Older people tended to slouch from weariness; younger people moved with abrupt, efficient gestures. The recently born were narcissistic; anyone over one hundred looked grim. Those who came of age in the 2040's, when EverLife was new and the economy flush with money, were generous. Those who grew up during the depression of the 2080's were miserly. Mr. Parris wrote using short quick strokes. He wore a purple shirt with wide overflowing collar, oversized white tie and a tailored brown suit. He remained stoic, giving nothing away. Rolly estimated Mr. Parris to be young, in his forties or fifties. He would check with Myrna to see if he was right.

Mr. Parris opened Rolly's file and began reading out loud. "Generally above average rating...never an excellent though...almost retired last year...three months of poor performance in 2146...followed by three months of 'over motivated' productivity; worked seven days a week 15 hours a day!...caused some conflict in the OCM...so far this year has shown an exceptionally high level of production." He looked up. "This pattern indicates a goal of retirement. Is that what you're doing?"

The question caught him off guard. "Everybody is trying to retire." It came out like a childhood taunt.

"But you're trying harder than anyone else. Is there something I should know?"

"No, not at all." *Think fast.* "Last year went so bad I threw myself into work. I've been to a counselor. I won't be retiring for years."

"You've been working a long time. I would think you'd be desperate."

"Of course I want to retire. I'd retire right now if I could. But it's not going to happen."

"Then why work so hard?"

Rolly hated having to lie twice. "My...failure to retire created issues at home. I needed...to get away and work seemed the best place to go."

"Doesn't make sense to me, throwing yourself into the thing you're trying to quit."

Rolly wasn't expecting a challenge. "Guess I wasn't thinking straight." Great. Now he looked stupid. Why did all his best efforts go haywire?

"I see Mr. Mann took advantage of your new work ethic. You spent a lot of time on inThrallEd. Must have been frustrating when it went down."

"Yes it was."

"All that hard work wasted." Rolly said nothing.

"Okay." Mr. Parris stood up and Rolly followed. "Thanks for your time. I'll have this done in time for New Year's. Good luck and hope you retire soon." Mr. Parris held out his hand. Rolly shook it, said "Thank you," and walked out. Jerry Speirman was waiting to walk in; four T through V coworkers were just sitting down.

In the elevator down Rolly stared at the closed doors and muttered "Shit."

Friday, December 1st

Leah rented a monitor for the auction and was setting it up when Rolly walked in early. At ten by six feet it was small by entertainment standards but better than a HearSay interface. Rolly helped, unrolling the light emitting plastic and inserting the rigid edges. Together they raised it and mounted it onto the stands.

Leah tried to make conversation but Rolly answered in monosyllables. Auction nerves she thought.

Stephanie walked in while Leah's HearSay and the monitor were having a tiff, refusing to communicate. Stephanie took the chair next to Rolly. They didn't greet each other. Leah found this ominous.

"Are you two gonna keep it together the rest of the year?"

They answered simultaneously, "Yes."

"Good. How's work Stephanie?"

"A pain in the ass."

"Normal then. You have any trouble getting the night off?"

"They made a stink because it's Friday. A big night for maiming and death. But they backed off."

"Give me a minute while I try to get this mess working. Shithead, run through the language protocols again."

Stephanie and Rolly looked startled. "What? That's what I named my HearSay. It's an homage." Stephanie laughed, Rolly smiled, though he didn't know why.

The monitor didn't want to wake up. Shithead tried 117 different protocols before the two devices started talking and the screen powered up. Ancient technology, it took a full minute for a picture to appear.

In the center of the screen, a man's head and the top of his shoulders, African-American, wearing a suit and tie, nicely trimmed mustache.

"Hello Leah. Are you ready?"

"Hi yourself Otis. Sorry it took so long. The monitor is being bitchy."

Otis laughed. "Thought you were some kind of computer whiz. As long as I know you're here we're good."

"I have the owners with me. Rolly and Stephanie Smalls, this is Otis Vangelder, auctioneer extraordinaire."

Otis waved and said hello, Rolly and Stephanie did the same.

"Allow me a moment to explain the proceedings. There will be two auctions. The first for the contents of your home, which should be fairly straightforward, over in about ten minutes. The second will be for the property itself which will be a more contentious affair.

"During the auctions you will be viewers only. Any communication will happen between myself and Ms. Lockwood. You are not allowed to interrupt for any reason. We do this to secure your privacy and prevent unfair influence. Per your instructions this is to be an auction with reserve. When the auction is complete you may choose to accept or decline the final offer.

"On this screen, to my left and right, you will see the various bidders. On the far left is a tally of the current highest bids, and who has made the bid. This will change as the auction progresses. Do you have any questions?"

They shook their heads.

"If I may say, Ms. Lockwood is an extremely talented woman. You're lucky to be working with her."

Rolly and Stephanie turned to Leah. She bowed to the screen. "Thank you Otis. The feeling is mutual."

The screen went dark. "Auctions can be overwhelming at first. A lot of shouting and finagling. Don't feel like you have to accept an offer. If you don't like it, don't take it."

Rolly, "How do we know if it's enough?"

"You have copies of the appraisal. My man Dagan came up with those numbers. I added forty percent to the final estimate and wrote it down. This is the minimum amount we need. Think of it as your line in the sand. If you don't get at least that much, say no."

At precisely 7:02 Mr. Vangelder started the first auction. Nine new faces joined him on screen in square videos of their own. When a bid was offered a yellow box appeared around the bidder's square.

Mr. Vangelder did his best to encourage the bidding, pointing out the rarity of Stephanie's porcelain collection, the "new" entertainment system, talking up their possessions using adjectives they never would have considered: priceless, unusual, rare, never seen before, original. Mr. Vangelder made special mention of the real wood floor joists and copper pipes.

Rolly, "Who are these people?"

"Junk dealers and antique traders. The traders want the collectibles. The junk dealers make their money from recycling, but are hoping for the big score, a diamond in your plumbing, or a pile of cash in a wall. The traders sneer at the dealers, the dealers fly a middle finger at the traders. It's so much fun."

Mr. Vangelder wrapped up the first auction and announced a two minute break. Art Brown's 20th Century Antiques won their collectibles, Wood City Salvage took the rest. Their representatives would stay as silent observers to make sure Rolly and Stephanie accepted the results. The gross gain over estimated value came to eleven point three percent.

Leah, "Not bad."

Stephanie, "You said we needed forty percent."

"On your property. Your possessions aren't worth much. Eleven percent is a good return. Be happy with it."

Stephanie looked wounded; she valued her things. Rolly stood and stretched. Leah wondered if they really could tolerate each other for another month.

Mr. Vangelder came back, surrounded by dozens more bidders, too many to count.

"Ladies and gentlemen, welcome to today's second auction. On the block is a single piece of residential property, located at 15376 Glenhaven Ave., in Reed's Township, parcel number 85987632459-236458, by twentieth century accounting. The lot has been surveyed at one point zero eight one acres. All possessions and buildings will be disposed of, per today's previous auction. This is the last residential zoned plot of this size in the county.

"This is an auction with reserve. The owners and their representative are viewing the proceedings and will give their answer immediately after the auction is complete. Contact with the owners is forbidden.

"Here are the terms of sale: the winning bidder must deposit the entire sum directly into the owner's bank account immediately upon acceptance of their bid. If you fail to do so you will be barred from auction participation for a period of five years. If a forfeiture does occur the auction will start over, with the addition of a five percent vendor's fee. Please know your limits.

"The winning bidder shall not take possession of the property until January 1st or after. Are the terms acceptable?"

"No, it's not fair at all." A man with a long pale face and tight red curly hair, in a blue dress shirt, open at the collar. When he spoke his window expanded, obscuring others, almost a big as Mr. Vangelder's. "Why should we wait? If you're going to take my money today I should get the property today. The Smalls' are taking advantage of us." When he stopped his window contracted back to normal. A chorus of agreement accompanied his statement, the window of each speaker blowing up and deflating depending on the loudness of the their voice, filling the screen with three dimensional complaining.

Mr. Vangelder's face popped up again as big as before, corralling the others into place. "Mr. Nelson, your concern is noted. The terms are non-negotiable. If you are unhappy you may remove yourself from the auction. Do you wish to continue?"

"Fine. This would be much easier if you just sold it to me, Rolly. I'm going to win anyway." Mr. Nelson looked perturbed. Being called by name jolted Rolly. He should have expected that.

Leah, "Eric Nelson represents MacPherson Holdings, the largest development company in the country. He has a lot of money and the ethics of a sewer rat. He's used to being in control and doesn't like it when he's not. Shoe's on the other foot here. Everyone on that screen is desperate to get their hands on your property."

A new face zoomed up, a woman in a grey suit, business-like, straight dirty blonde hair. "We are comfortable with the terms." A less vocal chorus echoed her.

"Very good then. We shall start--"

"Mr. Vangelder!" A different woman, wearing a flannel shirt, straight black hair, skin a light brown, her features a pleasant jumble of ethnicities. She had a confident smile. "Sorry to interrupt. Kelly from Folkening Brothers. We're a small contractor just starting out. The sellers have a wonderful history of entrepreneurial support and we would appeal to them for longer payment terms, to give a small startup like us a chance. If anyone understands the plight of the small business it is certainly the parents of Max Smalls."

Rolly fidgeted; Stephanie gave him a dirty look.

Mr. Nelson, "No special favors. Let's get this done."

Mr. Vangelder, "Folkening Brothers, as I have stated already, the terms are non-negotiable. If you have limited resources then do not bid. The penalty is severe if you fail to pay. Please consider your reputation."

"We understand Mr. Vangelder. Folkening Brothers will conduct itself responsibly. But I would implore Mr. and Mrs. Smalls to consider our request and the amazing opportunity this represents."

"Ma'am, I greatly dislike repeating myself. Warnings have been given. If you interrupt again I will close your connection."

"Understood."

"Very good then. We will start the bidding at seven point five million dollars."

Mr. Vangelder kept complete control of the auction; it was impressive to watch. He moved the bidding in hundred thousand dollar increments, which bidders often jumped. Folkening Brothers dropped out early and watched.

Everyone was talking, either to an unseen partner or another bidder; windows popped up and went away like a whack-a-mole game. Pieces of conversation came and went; several participants seemed to be arguing.

Fifteen minutes in the windows shuffled around and a red line appeared around three of them, including Folkening Brothers. In quick succession the screen shuffled twice more and red outlines appeared around a group of four bidders and another group of three bidders.

"Coalitions are forming. By Hanover's Rules of Auctioneering, 2130 updated edition, we will now take a thirty second break."

Leah, "The bidding is getting too rich. Some players are negotiating with each other to pool resources."

One of the three member coalitions fell apart and their windows retreated to the far corners of the screen. Another coalition formed, this time with two members.

"New coalition, thirty more seconds added," Mr. Vangelder announced.

The new two party coalition stayed together and bidding resumed. Mr. Vangelder let the auction settle into a slower pace, giving the coalitions time to talk. Windows began disappearing as bidders dropped out. During quieter moments Mr. Vangelder offered encouragement such as "this property can support a minimum of fifty units" or "an opportunity for upscale housing" or "with a better abode the wooded land would attract premium buyers." He had dozens of selling points.

The coalitions drove the price higher and most of the single bidders dropped out, except for two, Mr. Nelson and Mr. Garza. The Group of Two seemed to control the bidding, countering every one of Mr. Nelson's offers, then suddenly dropped out, their screen going dark and minimizing to nothing.

Mr. Nelson, "What the hell was that? They just disappeared!"

Mr. Vangelder, "Both participants in that coalition have dropped out."

"They were driving the price on me. Did you put them up to that Otis?"

"First, we are conducting a business transaction and formal titles are expected Mr. Nelson. You shall treat myself and the other participants with equal respect. Second, both parties in that coalition were thoroughly vetted before their application was accepted. I suspect they wisely dropped out before over committing themselves."

"They pushed the price higher so you could take more of my money!"

Mr. Vangelder, his voice raised, his picture filling the entire screen, "Do not question my integrity. I was running auctions when you were running errands in the mailroom. I will gladly put my reputation against yours any day. Did it occur to you, Mr. Nelson, that you simply outbid them?"

"Apologies Mr. Vangelder. In my position you can never be too careful."

"Three parties remaining. Please continue."

While Mr. Vangelder and Mr. Nelson discussed the fine points of auction etiquette, the coalition of four argued amongst themselves, then dropped out, unable to agree on shares. Two minutes later, when the tally crossed fourteen million, Mr. Garza said his farewells, claiming he had nothing left to bid with. That left the final coalition of three--including Folkening Brothers--and Mr. Nelson. The Party of Three quickly raised their bid.

Mr. Nelson, "This is really unfair, three against one. Isn't there a rule against this, Mr. Vangelder?"

The Party of Three, who appeared united by a mutual dislike of Mr. Nelson, raised their voices, their wide screen wiping out Mr. Nelson's and pushing Mr. Vangelder's to the far left. In the noise Rolly could make out two words: "selfish bastard."

Mr. Vangelder quickly regained control. "Do you have a counter offer?"

Mr. Nelson, "You're on their side. You let them get away with this shit."

"Watch your language Mr. Nelson. What have I done to incur your displeasure this time?"

"You know, like that thing you're doing right now."

"I'm not doing anything other than waiting for your counter offer."

"This isn't the way an auction should be run. I should complain."

"You are welcome to register a complaint with the Guild anytime you like. However, this is the third time in as many months you've made the same threat. I suggest you take action before someone begins to doubt your sincerity."

"I just might do that!"

"Do you have a counter offer?"

"Yes I do." A new number flashed at the bottom of the tally.

The auction stopped for a moment while everyone considered the significance of this number. Mr. Nelson's bid was, according to the display, seventeen percent higher than the previous bid. The auction had been proceeding in twenty thousand dollar increments. Mr. Nelson's new bid represented and increase of several million. Clearly he was trying to intimidate the Party of Three and scare them away, but the bid was more than enough. Mr. Nelson was showing off.

"Coalition One, do you have a counter?"

"We request a dead air conference."

"Coalitions are allowed one dead air conference per auction. Not to exceed one minute. Proceed."

The audio feed was cut but the faces remained. They talked, argued, yelled, veins popped. At the end of one minute it was obvious nothing had been resolved.

The audio returned with the sudden harsh entrance of raised voices. Mr. Vangelder cut in. "Coalition One, what is your counter?"

Kelly, the Folkening Brothers representative, stood up and stormed off, her chair falling backward. An exasperated man with an air of experience answered. "We are withdrawing from the bidding."

"Very good. It's been a pleasure doing business with you. Mr. Nelson, you are tonight's winner."

"Thank you Mr. Vangelder, but I wish you would run a fairer auction."

"From you, Mr. Nelson, that is a compliment. Mr. and Mrs. Smalls, do you accept the final bid?"

Rolly sat up in his chair and looked over at Stephanie; Leah showed them her HearSay screen. "Mr. Nelson's final bid represents a fifty-five percent increase over the estimated value. This was a good day."

Rolly, "I'd rather sell to the Folkening people."

Leah, "That's nice but they didn't win."

Stephanie, "We made fifteen percent over. That covers the fees. Let's make it official."

"No, I meant that. I'd rather sell to Folkening."

The women looked at him as if he'd said EverLife was the leading cause of death.

Leah, "This is an auction. High bid wins."

"Was Folkening's last bid enough to make our minimum?"

Stephanie, "What the hell?"

"I can't stand Nelson. People like him made Max's life miserable."

Mr. Nelson, "What's going on? Why is this taking so long?"

"We serve at their pleasure. Please be patient," said Mr. Vangelder.

Leah, "The purpose of an auction is to make money. You can't pick and choose who you sell to. That's the trade off. If you break the rules you'll piss off Nelson and everyone else who was bidding."

"We can only sell the property once and I don't want him to have it."

Stephanie, "God Rolly, you're such an idiot."

Mr. Nelson, "Come on, come on. I'm tired of waiting."

Leah, "Are you one of those freaky people who subconsciously sabotages everything?"

"No I'm not. There needs to be room for everyone to compete. Nelson is a jerk. He doesn't deserve our property."

Stephanie, "Jesus Rolly! Shut up and take the offer!"

Mr. Nelson sighed. "Fine. I'll raise it another ten percent."

All three of them stared at the screen, stunned. Stephanie recovered first. "Quick, say yes!"

Leah punched a key on her keyboard. Rolly said "Wai-" but Leah cut him off. "The Smalls accept Mr. Nelson's last offer." She clicked the line dead.

For the first time Mr. Vangelder smiled. The corners of his mouth curled up and dimpled as if it should have been that way all along.

"Excellent! Mr. Nelson your last offer was the winning bid plus ten percent. Please expedite transfer of this very large sum of money."

"Yeah, yeah. Right away. Audio off." Mr. Nelson went silent, a hand came up and covered his lips while he spoke to his HearSay.

Leah, "Open your HearSay and access your bank account." Rolly pulled out his interface; so did Stephanie. "As soon as you see the money, move it to a different account."

They waited nearly a full minute. Mr. Nelson occupied himself with something off camera. Mr. Vangelder watched, occasionally glancing down and to his left. Rolly assumed his HearSay was there, open to his own bank account.

Mr. Nelson, "Well that's all for me. Nice working with you Otis. Mr. and Mrs. Smalls." He gave a poor mimic of salute.

When Mr. Vangelder chose to use it, he had a voice that could rattle a subwoofer. "We have not been paid, Mr. Nelson."

"It's on the way."

"You know the auction is not complete until payment has been received."

"I'm a man of my word Otis. And you shouldn't insult your best customer."

"If you leave before payment is confirmed I will void the transaction and you will be penalized."

"That really is not fair!"

"You know the rules."

"Look, there's some kind of glitch in the system. It's on the way. Probably tied up in a server somewhere."

"In seventy-two years as an auctioneer I have never seen payment get lost in a server."

"If you want I'll get one of my computer guys to look at it."

"Mr. Nelson, send the money now."

"Maybe we should contact the bank, see where it's at?"

They went back and forth for five minutes, Mr. Nelson making ever more absurd excuses, Mr. Vangelder holding his ground.

Mr. Nelson tried another tactic. "Mr. and Mrs. Smalls, I know you're hoping to retire on this money. But there's no guarantee. Money can't buy you success. Trust me, I know. It's all about who you know and I know lots of people in all the right places who *can* get you retired. If you give back twenty percent, I will guarantee you never have to work again."

"Mr. Nelson, renegotiation of a winning bid is prohibited. If you would like to make a separate deal, do so on your own time."

"Fine, fine, fine. Whatever. The money should be there."

Leah, "Rolly?"

As she spoke the money landed in their account, the balance popping from seven digits to eight. "Got it."

"Move it to another savings account now."

Rolly moved it to the Christmas club. "Done. Why?"

"A transfer this size gets a lot of attention. Someone might think it's fraud. This puts your mark on it. Tells the bank you know it's there, you intend to use it. Won't protect it from a wily lawyer, but anyone with an unhealthy interest will be less suspicious."

Leah, to Mr. Vangelder, "Receipt confirmed.

Mr. Vangelder, "This auction is officially closed. Congratulations Mr. Nelson."

"Bye." Mr. Nelson's screen went blank, as did those of the lingering bidders.

"Congratulations Ms. Lockwood. I believe you achieved a new record today."

Shoulders relaxed as tension left the room.

"Couldn't have done it without you Mr. Vangelder. You handled Nelson masterfully."

"Thank you. Keep bringing more business like this and we'll set more records. Mr. and Mrs. Smalls, thank you. I trust everything turned out as expected."

Stephanie, "Absolutely."

Rolly stayed silent.

"I sincerely hope you make retirement. After today, I think it may be more likely."

Leah, "Thank you Otis."

Mr. Vangelder smiled and gave a nod of appreciation. "You are welcome." His screen went blank.

Leah turned to her clients, expecting celebration, but Stephanie was giving Rolly the evil eye. "Don't hold it against him, Steph. Being stubborn got you ten percent more."

"He got lucky. I know him, he didn't get his way, he should be fuming, throwing a fit of some kind, but he's just sitting there."

Rolly glanced over, saying nothing, offering a grin he hoped conveyed the right amount of resignation. He was already making plans for the extra money.

23

Nola

Sunday, December 24th

The air was cold enough for snow but the sky was clear blue and the breeze so cuttingly frozen it felt like glass shards stinging Rolly's face. Everything had lined up nicely: he didn't have to work and it was Christmas Eve, a good day for gift giving.

Standing in the parking lot outside Nola's apartment building, Rolly thought he looked cool: black wool overcoat, jeans and white tennis shoes. A draft tried to rip the nervous smile from his face; he turned away and it blasted the back of his head instead. Painfully. It was early afternoon. Rolly headed for the outside stairway, his mind blank, his body following a path imagined a thousand times.

Rolly had spent the morning planning what he would say. Everything he could think of sounded as superficial as a snowflake. He did not have the words for this. He would have to rely on wits to get him through, such as they were.

The walk up the stairs and around to her apartment was remarkably short. Before he knew it Rolly was knocking on Nola's door.

No answer. He knocked again, a little louder. At one time the door might have been beige, now it was weathered, a field of star-shaped black mold creeping up from the bottom. It had no peephole. A small window on the right had makeshift towels hanging behind it but they didn't move.

Rolly knocked a third time and waited. She could be out or ignoring him. He considered calling her name but thought it would be rude. She must be out. He would come back later, watch the place for a bit first, make sure she was home.

As he turned locks were unbolted and chains rattled. The doorknob turned and the door shook as it was yanked open on a security chain. One eye looked out.

"What?"

"I'm here to see Nola Cooke."

The head turned showing greasy blonde hair hanging limp.

"She's doesn't do guys anymore."

"I just want to talk to her. I'm her father."

The eye moved an inch higher and looked him dead on. "She ain't got no father."

"We've never met."

"She was told he didn't care 'bout her."

"Can I come in? Talk about it?"

The eye turned away again, then looked back. "You can come in. If you try anythin' I'll cut your throat."

"I won't do anything Nola."

"I ain't Nola." The door slammed, the chain dropped free, and the door opened wide.

The woman in front of him was squat, large in the hips, wearing a dirty pink sports jersey. Puffy cheeks, wrinkled sallow skin, hair parted in the middle and hanging like a mop. She was old, wide open pores on her face and a hairy mole. Rolly couldn't judge her real age, more than a half century at least. She was not attractive and smiled sarcastically to prove it, showing only two teeth.

Rolly looked around the room, eyes slowly adjusting. It smelled stale with an undertone of rot. Light was a penetrating alien force, dust still settling, trash rolling in the whoosh of fresh air, dirty dinner plates balanced in precarious places. A studio apartment--bathroom, kitchen and a room for everything else.

"You're not Nola? Does she live here?"

The woman nodded to her left, at a couch in the corner. Another woman sat there looking at him. Plucked eyebrows, rosy cheeks, coifed hair, honey blonde and curly with some grey, like she was ready for a party. Rolly was glad to see Nola taking care of herself.

Rolly approached her. There was no other chair to sit in. He said "May I sit down?" referring to the couch. She only stared at him.

He stayed standing. She had the Asian features of her mother but her skin was lighter. The slant of her eyes lessened. Crow's feet around the corners gave away her age. She was so old. She had green eyes. As he looked the gifts of her mother dropped away and he could see himself-- the round face, the blonde hair--his own mother had green eyes. A chain of generations led to this woman, through him. She was not a throwaway person, a burden to everyone else. This was his daughter.

"Hello Nola."

She spoke softly, lips barely moving, but her eyes never left his face. "You're my father?" Almost a monotone with only the slightest rise to make it a question.

"Yes I am. I didn't know I had a daughter until a few months ago. No one told me you existed."

"They took away Momma when I was a baby. Said I'd never see her. Is she here?"

"No she's...not. How long have you lived here Nola?"

She looked around as if seeing the apartment for the first time. "This old place? I don't know." Her laugh was out of place, coy and girlish. "How long have we lived here Audrey?"

The woman at the door said "Three years." She wore a stupid grin, as if watching a puppet show.

"That long. Seems like we moved only a couple days ago."

"We didn't move nowhere. I bought the place myself and brought you in like a stray dog. She kept lyin' in front a my door every night. Got sick a trippin' over her so I brung her in."

Nola, smiling, "I remember the warmth on my back."

"Yeah, the damn door don't seal at the bottom. She kept the heat in. Now I gotta put towels down again."

Nola touched his arm. "Do you know where she is? Can I talk to her?"

"Who?"

"My mother."

"How are you Nola? Are you okay? Do you have a job?"

Nola looked down. Audrey answered for her. "Lost her job at the store four months back. Only knows how to do one thing and she's over the hill for that. Can't focus, can't count, not much of an employee. But they always look at her and say, Yeah, I'll hire ya, 'cause she's so cute, in spite of bein' old and such. Like me." She laughed with a wheezing snicker, pathetic and vile at the same time. "You know why she looks like that? 'Cause they made her that way. Surgery. Fixed her so she'd be pretty forever. Filled her up with all sorts of chemicals and preser, preserv--"

"Preservatives?"

"That's it! Pree-surv-a-tivs. Human kind. Kept her that way so they wouldn't have to do it again. Cuts into profits if your whore is always gettin' repaired. She got wrinkles though. Little cracks in the plaster." Audrey cackled.

"Nola is a prostitute?"

"Was! Ain't nothin' but a couch ornament now."

Rolly looked at Nola, at the pretty round face with the unique eyes, and saw her offering herself on dirty hotel beds and dark street corners and in bushes in grassy parks, on her knees, on all fours, men leaving cash on a pillow or shoved in her panties. He saw her slapped and cut and whipped for whatever fetish pleased the customer. He saw Corporament accountants amazed with PSI's cost to profit ratio, wondering how they did it.

Rolly's imaginings took him to a place he did not want to go. Nola's face became the face of all the women he had been with over the decades, in all the positions he put them in, in all the ways he took pleasure. Rolly shook his head, trying to erase these thoughts. In the few minutes it took to meet and learn the most superficial particulars of Nola's life, he went from concerned but happy father to a parent's worst nightmare. Rolly didn't know what to say.

Audrey apparently didn't like silence. "She was their best one ya know, popular, for a long time. Use ta hear 'bout her, guys tellin' tall tales, what a fine piece a ass she was. Sucks like a vacuum, fucks like a porn star and looks like one too. Do anything you want and make you feel like a king. Half of 'em never got close enough to smell her, they just repeatin' stuff they heard."

"They used to give me candy if I fucked someone good."

"How long you been cock ridin'?"

"Since I was five."

"There ya go. All she knows. Back in the day people said she liked it, enthusiastic, makin' everybody happy. She always tried her best. Is that a sin, doin' your best at somethin' that's bad? If ya don't know no better? Ah, the religious types condemned her 'cause she's a orphan. God knows we don't need no more people takin' up precious space."

"Can you bring her here? They won't let me leave."

"Honey, you can go anywhere you like. But the scabs round here get a look at ya they'll break the door down. Best stay inside where it's safe."

"Okay. Maybe he can bring her? Maybe she'll come and see me?" Nola looked desperate, almost crying.

Rolly thought it cruel to lead her on. He shouldn't start a new relationship with mistrust.

"Nola, I'm sorry. Your mother died a few months ago."

Absolute horror twisted Nola's face. She backed away from Rolly as if he had a disease. Hands to her cheeks and up through her hair, she leaned forward, almost to her knees, saying "no, no, no," over and over as if trying to convince herself otherwise.

"What'd you tell her that for?"

"I'm trying to be honest."

"Ah hell. That was the only thing keepin' her goin' the last fifty years."

Nola shot up off the couch, aiming herself and a throaty rage filled scream at Rolly. He didn't think she could move like that; neither did Audrey, whose mouth hung open. With fists up she ran into Rolly full on, knocking him back into an old plastic tv stand, falling awkwardly against the wall, Nola hitting with her fists.

"WHY DID YOU BRING ME INTO THIS WORLD? WHY DID YOU BRING ME INTO THIS WORLD? WHY DID YOU DO THIS TO ME?"

Nola was taller than her mother but shorter than Rolly. Her blows stung but didn't hurt. Audrey pulled her off, Nola sobbing. They fell back onto the couch. Nola sank into the dirty cushions, her head in Audrey's lap.

"She's gone, she's gone, she's gone..." Rolly picked himself up.

"Been like this since I known her. Don't know what's it called, goes from sad to angry like that. Lots a frustration inside this head a hers. Was hopin' you'd be some entertainment, 'nother fool looking for the hot whore. Well I got it half right."

"Half right?"

"You are a fool." Audrey cackled, Rolly said nothing. After she stopped Audrey said "Why the hell you here?"

"I'm trying to retire. My counselor found Nola, thought she might be holding me back. But it's not an issue anymore."

"You wanna see her so's you can retire? Expectin' some kind a happy send off? Make her crazy with grief and up and leave? Better if you stayed away. How come you thought she'd wanna see you?"

"I didn't know. I thought she might be mad, push me away--"

"Ha! You didn't think she'd be mad in both ways!" Audrey cackled again.

Rolly said softly, "No. I thought she'd be tougher."

"Tougher huh. You a little disappointed? Thought your little girl would be a bad ass momma? Givin' as good as she gets? But here she is, all crazy and shit. Used and abused by everyone's met her. Hell, even me. Brings in a food provision every month but eats like a bird. More for yours truly. Now here you come, looking for somethin' too, but she ain't got nuthin' to give. And I ain't givin' up my extra food. Sucks to be you."

Rolly looked down at the floor. "I thought she would be...I assumed she would be...sane."

"With everyone leavin' and sayin' they want her to die cause she wasn't ever sposed to live? How's anyone gonna to stay sane like that. You with your career and retirin'. Comin' here to pay a social call on your long lost daughter. I believe when ya say ya didn't know, cause you are absolutely fuckin' clueless. How you think us transients live? While you're workin' and takin' your EverLife? We're dyin'. Twenty years ago I bet you were already countin' the days til retirement, watching crap on your big ass holograms, spendin' money, eatin' good food. You know what Nola was doin' twenty years ago? Fuckin' fifteen guys a day. When she was in *demand*. Workin' for the PSI, rakin' it in for the Corporament. Helpin' pay for your retirement."

Nola, "He doesn't know nuthin'."

"He'll be gone in a minute. These kinds always run away."

"No. I'm not going to do that. But I don't want to hang around and make you miserable either. I've got some money. I want to help and don't expect anything in return. You can hate me as long as you like."

"He wants to give ya charity to ease his guilty conscience."

"Whatever. All I want to do is help. Maybe a dose or two of EverLife, I don't know." He stepped in front of Nola and went down on one knee. "I think the first thing is to get you to a safer place. Do you want that Nola?"

Before Nola could answer someone gave the door a side-of-the-fist pounding meant to shake the apartment.

Nola recoiled. Rolly looked at Audrey. "Who is it?"

"Don't know. Door ain't locked though. Stay quiet and they'll go away."

"Open the door! I know you're in there Rolly!"

"Christ it's my wife!"

Audrey watched Rolly for moment. "More reason to stay quiet."

The pounding continued, stopped, started again, the doorknob turned and Stephanie entered as if she were Lady of the Manor inspecting her staff.

She looked at Rolly, kneeling in front of Nola with hands over her eyes, glanced at Audrey, back to Rolly.

Stephanie sighed deeply. "How far has this gone?"

"What are you doing here?"

"Making sure you don't screw up again. Made any promises yet?"

"No, I haven't."

"Said he'd take her to a safe place."

"Who are you?"

"Audrey. Nice to meet ya."

"Likewise. Audrey, Rolly doesn't have anything to make promises with. There's nothing he can do to help. Is that Nola?"

"Yes it is. She's a little upset right now."

"I'm sure. You need to tell her you're sorry and we'll leave."

"Who is this?" Nola asked.

"This is my wife Stephanie."

"She doesn't want you here. She's mad at you."

"She's always mad at me. But if she thinks I'm leaving she's wrong." Trying to take forceful tone.

"Get real Rolly. Look at her, she's practically dead already. All wrinkled and grey. Better than I figured though. You can't be here. If the Corporament makes a connection retirement is over."

"They got their exemption. The Corporament doesn't care what we do anymore."

"Oh okay. Where you going to take her then?"

"Home, for now. Until I can find somewhere else."

"You do remember we sold the place and it's going to be torn down in a week? That slip your mind already?"

"Of course not. We'll find something else for her. It won't take a week to do that."

"What then? What if a computer sees this and alerts some clerk who looks at your record and says 'How can somebody with two kids retire?'

What if we do retire? We'll be long gone, where the hell is she going to go? Right back here, that's where.

"Or what if some wiseass like Audrey here says she should make a claim on our property, being your long lost daughter and all. You wanna be talking to lawyers right before you retire? What a mess that would be. She could fuck everything up."

None of this had crossed Rolly's mind. The cynical logic of it stunned him. "I don't think Nola would do that."

"Why? Because she's the fruit of your loins? You don't know this woman, she could turn on you in a second. You're a golden opportunity waiting to happen, a loser wracked with guilt claiming to be her father. You might as well paint a target on your chest. I'll bet she doesn't care if she's your daughter or not. Has she asked for any proof?"

Rolly answered slowly, "No..."

Audrey said, "Hell, Nola can't even--"

"Don't make excuses. What you want is a free ride courtesy of the Rolly Express. I know people like you, I see you every day at that god-awful hospital. You beg and cheat, act poor or sick or so destitute you can't do for yourself, or crazy, stupid, anything to get something free. And we bust our asses trying to get ahead while leeches like you drag us down. You're liars. And thieves and con artists. And probably whores, too."

Rolly's right shoulder sank as Nola used it to boost herself up. She glided up to Stephanie head high, her nose in Stephanie's face as if they were wrestlers arguing before a big match.

"You bitch! How dare you come here and call me a whore! Whores stand on street corners and fuck anyone with a fifty in their pocket. I was a star. I made more in an hour than those women made in a month!"

"She hates bein' called a whore."

"You come here and and and you make judgements on us, calling us thieves and liars! You'd rather we were dead, gone, out of sight! You take everything and give nothing! How am I supposed to care what you think? I lie and steal from cunts like you all the time! I'm proud of it!"

"So I'm right. You see Rolly? She admits it. A goddamn criminal. This is what happens when people have nothing to live for. They turn into scumbags." Her voice rose and deepened. "I'm here to protect my self-interests. So here's a little advice. You need to treat cunts like me with respect. You're a transient, you won't be here much longer but I'm going to live forever. Know your place and don't give me anymore shit, you ugly piece of ass."

Nola screamed with rage. Stephanie took a step back. Nola rushed forward, arms raised again. Stephanie covered her left fist with her right hand, and struck Nola in the face with her elbow. Nola fell to the floor, hand on cheek. Audrey rushed to her. Nola started wailing. Rolly could see blood in Nola's mouth.

"Why? Why? Why?" she repeated while sobbing.

"Get out! Both of you! Now! Don't come back!"

"I meant what I said. I want to help."

Nola wailed so loud Rolly wasn't sure Audrey heard him. "Get out now! Nuthin' you got is worth this!"

Rolly stood in shock, watching Audrey wipe away the blood, trying to calm Nola, her wails becoming louder and throatier, somewhere between a scream and a howl.

"Rolly. Let's go. Now."

Stephanie wore a small smile of satisfaction. He hated her. At this moment, looking at her smug expression, knowing how little empathy she possessed. She was a devil bent on destruction, selfish, immoral, incapable of pity.

"Get the fuck out!"

Rolly headed for the door. Stephanie opened it for him. "I'm parked behind you. You lead the way, I'll follow you home."

24

Fight And Stay

December 25th, Monday

Christmas. One of only two officially recognized holidays. The other was Easter. By Corporament decree workers were allowed "time off with compensation." What form that compensation took was up to each company. At Stableman Insurance it was a half day's pay and one third of average daily Productivity. Generous, compared to other employers. The sidewalks would be less crowded but still busy as hopeful retirees avoided the hit to their Productivity. This year Rolly chose to stay home.

In the basement he found the red and green plastic box and the Christmas tree tube and brought them upstairs.

He set the tube vertically on the dining room table, held the base down and pulled it off sideways. A four foot plastic tree whipped out, complete with ornaments, tinsel, icicles and lights, angel on top. Normally he pulled it straight off with a magician's flourish, even if no one was around. His own little Christmas tradition. This time it smacked the wall before swaying to a stop. Rolly plugged it in; everything worked.

Under the tree he placed a cheap all-in-one plastic manger. The front opened like a drawbridge to show the nativity, divine figures and animals glued in place. Stephanie never let the nice Italian nativity come up. Too expensive to display, she said, didn't want anything to get broken.

They hadn't exchanged gifts in decades but usually did something together, if only going out to dinner. It was good form to be seen as a couple during the Holidays.

Rolly opened the curtains concealing the sliding door, letting the dull morning light invade his sanctuary. A clean sheet of snow covered the backyard. A few tracks here and there, squirrels and rabbits out for a mid-winter snack. The sky was an unstoppable gray, horizon to horizon, an all day gray. Rolly sat at the table to wait.

He heard movement. Stephanie's door opened and she shuffled out wearing fluffy pink slippers and matching robe.

Through bleary eyes she saw Rolly and stopped. "What are you doing here?"

"It's Christmas. I decided to stay home."

"Shouldn't you be at work?"

"I asked for the day off weeks ago."

"Oh. Special plans?"

"Not anymore."

Stephanie, fully awake now, resumed her journey to the kitchen where she started a pot of coffee. She could see Rolly in profile, staring out at the backyard.

As usual she would have to start the argument. She would not be diplomatic, or soften her words. The time had passed for niceties. This would be a full-on common sense beat down, no emotional wrangling or discussions, no defensiveness allowed.

Stephanie poured a mug of coffee and sat at the table with Rolly. He had his eyes closed.

"You're a sentimental old fool. What were you going to do? Bring your little girl home for Christmas?"

Rolly didn't move.

"Are you just going to sit there? Pretending I'm not here?" She'd been through this before, eventually Rolly would respond. It might take a few more--

His eyes popped open. "You're a goddamn bitch."

That was easy. "Really? I thought I was--"

"Cut the bullshit. That was no way treat Nola. You're a fucking selfish bitch and I can't stand the sight of you."

Rolly had never spoken to her this way. Their fights were usually more reserved. It wasn't like him to be so aggressive. A surprise but not a problem. She could match his intensity and raise it as well. As far as she needed to go.

"You want to end it now? Get a divorce?"

"You know we can't divorce."

"So you've only been staying with me to get retired?"

"Isn't that why you're here?"

"Yeah, guess we agree on that one. What I don't get is why you're so pissed off. Doesn't make sense. Do you or don't you want to retire?"

"Why do you have to see everything in stark terms? Things don't always fit in a convenient box. Sometimes you have to deal with a...a little moral ambiguity."

"Moral ambiguity my ass. If you did the right thing instead of whatever you think is the moral thing there wouldn't be any problem."

"The right thing? Every time I go out the door I do the right thing. I work hard. I stay loyal. I follow the rules. And half the time the right thing is the wrong thing. I thought you would know the difference, my wife of one hundred and twenty-one years, but all I get is crap. Why fight me?

Why the confrontation? I was lied to about Nola and somehow that's my fault. I can't win."

"What the hell? You can't find your own fucking way and it's my fault? You want to throw around blame start with yourself."

"Why can't you take a little of what we have, and we have more than enough, and use it to help someone else? A child who is part of our family?"

"She's not part of my family, she's your family. A family you made because all you cared about was having fresh pussy wrapped around your dick. And you want to blame it on me like I'm some kind of magical moral angel with all the answers. Get fucking real. I wanted a daughter. A hundred goddamn years ago. I wanted a permit. You know how many times I tried to get you to sign it? Do you remember? Or is that too far and too real for you to conjure up in that little brain of yours? Retirement was the only thing you cared about. It never got signed, I never had that child and you can't even be *bothered* to *remember*."

"Lucky for you there's EverLife. You're going to be thirty for the rest of eternity. You can spit out as many children as they'll let you. Unlike Nola, who's too old and dying, wasting away as we speak. She'll be lucky to last five years."

"Everything about her is a mistake. Her death would be a mercy."

Stephanie had a cold expression on her face. *This is where bitterness has taken her? Wishing someone dead? This is my fault.* "I'm sorry you didn't have a second child. If I could go back and change things I would. But I never thought it would take this long. I didn't know the rules would change every year. I didn't know retiring would be like chasing a ghost. I didn't know I would be lied to and used. This whole world is fucked up. We live forever, we have to stay married no matter what, and we're only supposed to have one child? This is the kind of family they want? It's no family. I don't know what's right or wrong anymore. The only thing certain is retirement."

"Is that why you're sitting here, at home, in our dining room, instead of on the other side of town, saving your precious child?"

"I don't understand."

"There's nothing stopping you from going back to Nola. You could move in, take care of her twenty-four seven, maybe take her to a doctor, get her cured. Isn't that your fantasy?"

"You know what's stopping me, you are."

"Of course no doctor will waste time on her. They'll know what she is in the few seconds it takes their HearSays to recite her history. They'll show you the pity face and some pills and say it's the best they can do. Not *everything* they can do, but the only thing they're willing to do."

"You won't let me. If I walk out the door you'll freeze the bank account."

"Damn straight I will. Maybe you can clean Nola's apartment while you're there. I'm sure that will make her feel better."

"Fuck you."

"Never again."

Frustrated, Rolly reached for old wounds.

"You remember when we got married? Back before EverLife? You were my best friend and I loved you and I wanted to be a good man, good husband, good father. And I thought you would be my partner. Then the world changed and I'm trying to sort out how to get through it and all you ever want is to get away. Yeah, I'm still here, trying to do right by you. You can accuse me of that all you want."

"Oh my knight in shining armor, come to save me! You're here for yourself, not me. Would you give up retirement to save that stupid wench?"

"What?"

"It's a simple question. Would you give up retirement if it meant you could help Nola?"

"Define help."

"Don't avoid the question."

"It doesn't make any difference--"

"Stop it! I want an answer, yes or no!"

"It's not that simple."

"Yes, it is and you won't do it. You'll choose the one thing you've wanted for two lifetimes. Tell me I'm wrong."

Rolly didn't answer.

"I knew it! I knew you weren't so fucking chivalrous. You don't have the guts to be heroic. You're not that kind of man. After a hundred and forty-seven years you think you'd know that. That's why I like being with real men." She stood up, mug in hand and headed for her end of the house. "Merry Christmas," she said before closing the door.

Rolly got dressed and went to work.

Friday, December 29th

Rolly in his cubicle, icons for a new project swirling around his head, a warning about the dangers of fishing with its sharp hooks and knives that could catch, cut, tear and rip. The goal was to encourage fishermen to use a Stunpole, a safer and more effective device. It electrocuted any fish within a ten foot radius of contact with the water. The Stunpole tagline was: "A whole day's fishing in one touch!" The company manufacturing the Stunpole was highly rated by the Corporament. They loved its efficiency. Rolly's project was more ad than warning, a favor from one executive to another, an attempt to boost the Stunpole's anemic sales.

Rolly had already lost interest in the project. He sat doing nothing, watching his Productivity slowly click downward. The icons were programmed to agitate if inactive too long. Some were jumping up and down like angry children, two were twirling in a fast circle like a motorcycle wheel, two others dive bombed his face. Rolly had never let a project stand still this long. He had no idea incorporeal objects could be so aggressive.

He brushed the icons aside and closed the project. The Productivity counter went down faster. He needed to think, work up his nerve. It had been four days since his humiliation by Stephanie. He spent those days mulling and fretting and hating himself, banging fists on the desk in frustration, and sometimes his own skull. This alarmed Sean who offered to call Emergency Psychiatric Services. Rolly shut the HearSay down, but only for two hours. It was impossible to function without Sean's help and time was running short. Help Nola now or forget it.

The plan was simple: take money out of savings before Stephanie realized it was gone, get Nola and drive north to Grayling or Alpena or Petoskey, or across the bridge to Sault Ste. Marie, any town big enough to have an EverLife Renewal Center. Bank rules restricted withdrawals to twenty percent without approval of both account owners. Not enough to settle Nola and himself into another life, but enough to get them started. And a couple of EverLife treatments for Nola. There would be no EverLife for Rolly until he found another good paying job.

Stephanie would be angry but ultimately okay. She could get the divorce she wanted and find another guy in the same predicament. It happened all the time, strangers marrying to meet retirement parameters. She would have most of the money, be free of him, and in a year or two, with any luck, retired.

He hesitated. Subconsciously, buried under the superficial nonsense that made up the modern world, Rolly knew he was rejecting everything he had believed in for the last one hundred years. There would be no turning back. He might reapply for EverLife in five or ten years, but retirement? Decades away again. A mind-destroying concept for a man who had worked a century and a quarter.

Staring at his computer, trying to will himself to take drastic action and getting nowhere. He needed to talk to someone he could trust.

"Are you okay Rolly?" Lambert, making another soundless entrance.

He stood and cupped her elbow in his hand. "Can we go somewhere and talk in private?" He must have had a wild look because her eyes opened in surprise.

"Uh, yeah. Static Ads is at a meeting. Their cubicles are empty."

They headed to the other side of the maze, Rolly escorting Lambert, who clearly looked put-out. Once in Static Ads they sat in facing chairs.

"This isn't like you Rolly. What's wrong? Why aren't you working?"

It poured out in a cascade of words. Finding Nola, her mental state, where she lives, that she hates him, that he wants to do right by her, Stephanie's reaction, what he wanted to do, and why he should do it right now. Of all the people in the office only Lambert, with her accelerated personality, could have made sense of it.

Rolly stopped and waited for her reaction.

Lambert sat with hands folded in her lap, legs crossed, her shoes so pointy they would make excellent weapons. The look on her face was accusingly perplexed.

"After the hell you've put yourself through you want to throw it away for a crazy woman?"

"But she's my daughter."

"Rolly, you're a sweet guy, without being too much of a lech, that's why I like you. But don't go off a cliff. Pull yourself back. You can't help Nola and you'll disappoint a lot of coworkers."

"I thought they gave up on me."

"Not everyone. There's a few pulling for you. They would be disappointed, actually embarrassed, if you ran away now."

"You?"

"And a few others. But mostly me. The hopeful ones. Everyone else is pretty cynical."

"You were doing more than lining up projects for me."

"Some people needed a little encouragement. Nothing bad, not at all. I just know the right words to use."

"What words did you use on me?"

"None. You're like me. We don't need encouragement. We just need things to do." She stood up and brushed down her clothes. "I'll be here through the weekend. I'd like to see you every day Rolly because on Monday, I don't believe I will anymore."

Lambert took a step to leave but stopped, finding Souliere in her way. Her back stiffened and she went around, looking annoyed.

"She's right. You can't help Nola and shouldn't try."

"You were eavesdropping."

"Leah told me what happened with Nola and your wife."

"How does she know?"

"Did you forget? There's a camera and microphone in every room. She watched the whole thing. Made a recording too. And she gave Stephanie a tracking program to keep tabs on you."

Rolly gave a sour look. "You've been playing me for a fool."

"We've been giving you nudges in the right direction."

"You're splitting hairs."

"And you're about to retire."

Rolly didn't know whether to be angry or happy. "Why? What is it you want from me?"

"Nothing more than your effort and you've given plenty of that."

"That's no answer."

"When the time comes we'll need your help. But we're not ready yet."

"Not ready for what?"

"You'll find out. Eventually. After you retire."

"And if I don't retire?"

"You will, if you let Nola go. We didn't think your feelings would be this strong. We hoped for a little compassion but didn't expect an impulsive run for the hills. Stay, and see what happens. I know people who can help but it will take time. Be patient."

"Who? And when?"

"Retire first Rolly, then we'll talk. You know where to find me."

Souliere disappeared and Rolly sulked, chastising himself for being so boneheaded, then decided he should demand some answers and chased after his coworker.

But Souliere was gone, his cubicle empty, the desk lamp off.

Rolly returned to his workstation, seeing the Productivity counter closing in on zero, and restarted the Stunpole project. He told himself only two days left, only two days until New Year's, only two more days of work, only two days until it was over.

They were the longest two days of his life.

25

Summation

Sunday, December 31st

The country stopped working at three o'clock in the afternoon every New Year's Eve, the official tabulating deadline, when the computers stopped recording data and went about the business of calculating a Reckoning for every citizen, and the year's Number. A counter free nine hour coda at the end of the year. No meaningful work got done after three o'clock so most companies gave employees the remainder of the day off. A few die hards might stick around to gain more LOS or Productivity (added to next year's Reckoning), but they were the exceptions.

The short eight hour workday improved the mood around Stableman Insurance. Paces were quicker, smiles given more freely. Rolly was anxious, wondering if this really was his last day. Should he pack his things, or wait? No one said goodbye, not even Lambert, though she gave him a hug.

Rolly's current project explained why shark attacks were dangerous, with a horrid tagline: "Remember, you're not a fish, so don't try to be dinner." Feeling uninspired he opened and closed icons as if searching, added random elements to a scene, nothing more than busywork, but ended up having fun. His sharks swam at supersonic speeds and jumped out of the water to perform magnificent pirouettes and spins while chomping gawking humans.

His computer was open to the network. Someone might be watching, but after decades of sameness and drudgery and efficiency bred pattern thinking, Rolly had stopped caring.

The video became more ridiculous: people with six foot high balloon heads, lifeguards who leapt a hundred feet in the air to perform intricate aerial maneuvers, beach sandstorms and tornadoes, a rogue wave washing a school of hungry sharks into a swimming pool, a smiling shark yelling "Feeding Frenzy!" Rolly was having a wonderful day.

"Dudemeister, you're being urgently summoned by Myrna."

"What is it Myrna?"

"Mike Parris wants to see you in his office immediately."

"Can you give me a couple of minutes?"

"I can't give you anything. He's probably working on your evaluation. I wouldn't make him wait."

Rolly left in a rush, glancing toward Souliere's cubicle, seeing nothing. Souliere had not been back to work. Rolly kept going.

Standing in Mr. Parris' office, out of breath, his new boss said: "Rolly I was watching your work on the shark thing and I love it. Great comedic foundation. Works perfectly. Now some of it's a little over the top but-"

Mike Parris had many ideas about how Rolly could improve his shark attack video, which he listed with the expectation Rolly would go back to his desk and implement them ASAP. Rolly listened attentively, smiled, offered profuse thank-yous, and eventually bowed his way out.

Back in the OCM a stampede was in progress.

It was 3:00 pm.

Saved by Corporament magnanimity. Rolly left his personal stuff behind and fled.

———————

Stephanie was chatting with Leah when Rolly arrived at the gym-turned-office, criticizing a holoshow they both watched. They seemed to be very friendly. He could tell when Stephanie was feigning interest, he knew the false tone, but she was animated and into the conversation. So was Leah, who didn't have the patience to act polite. They were enjoying each other's company, a revelation, and more evidence he was a complete fool.

"Hello Rolly. Ready for some good news?"

"Yes I am."

"Alright." Leah pulled out her HearSay. In seconds she was logged in to the Paragon website.

"Let's start with the easy ones. Your marriage rating is excellent, no surprise. Length of Service has increased slightly, which it should every year, the loyalty factor still in your favor. Your rating here is 96.7%. The computer still accounts you one child. I don't see any flashing messages, or faded text, or any other indication the computer thinks otherwise. You are in the clear. In Children, your rating is 100%."

Stephanie let out a sigh of relief. Rolly felt a tightness he didn't know was there untangle and drop away. Underneath was regret, and visions of failure.

"You made a killing on the sale of your property, increasing the value of your assets over twenty per cent. Rolly added to it with some good investing, and Stephanie's second job helped a lot. The asset/debt ratio is very strong, in fact it's optimal. Any more assets and the Corporament might think you're cheating. Any less debt and they might think you aren't spending. The Consumer Curve it's called."

"Never heard of it."

"A minor provision in retirement law that kicks in if the asset/debt ratio is too great. Meant to encourage compulsive savers to do their duty for the economy. Most people are in debt to their eyeballs so it's rarely an issue."

"That's what O'Leary did."

"It's what O'Leary uses to justify his existence. He is an asshole who is reviled by capable consultants everywhere. Anyway, you aren't low enough to be in 'negative debt' but you are close, which is exactly where you want to be.

"Now the bad news. In spite of an exemplary Productivity rating your new boss has decided to keep you at the same level as last year."

"I saw the bastard today. Was raving about my work on a new vid and he screws me anyway."

"He is new and doesn't know anyone. I'm sure he thinks it's a win-win. Doesn't hurt you bad enough to create hard feelings, doesn't make him look eager to please."

"So what's Rolly's Reckoning?"

"Last year it was 478.31. This year Rolly's Reckoning is," Leah turned the monitor so they could see it, "483.48, a gain of 5.17. Last year's Number was 479. This puts you 4.48 points ahead. In the entire history of the retirement system there has never been a jump of more than two and half points, and that only happened once. Rolly Smalls, you are about to retire."

Rolly stared at Leah. That's what O'Leary said. That's exactly what he said. "Are you sure?"

"Do I have to explain the no guarantee thing again?"

"You're not lying? Trying to cover your ass?"

Leah looked confused. "I've been whipping you like an old mule for twelve months and now you think I'm lying?"

"I want to be sure. I don't want to be embarrassed again. And that's what O'Leary said to me."

"What is?"

"'You are about to retire.'"

"I say that to everybody. Usually they're happy to hear it, but I get why you're tense." The Leah equivalent of forgiveness. "I'm not going to hang you out like O'Leary. I will be there when The Number drops and if I'm wrong you can berate me to your heart's content."

"Now that that's settled can we go home and get ready to party?"

"You'll be at the southeast Riddell's?"

"That's our tradition."

"See you there."

Rolly preferred to stay home and watch the spectacle in his own holoroom, but needed to go because of Leah's promise. Only now, with hours to go, did Rolly realize how much faith he had hung on this one simple pledge. More than a need, he *wanted* to see her again, to justify his trust and quiet that nagging fear she might skip town, but also to be in her presence one last time, in a situation that didn't involve any kind of retirement planning.

Stephanie freshened her blonde curls and put on makeup that gave her an unnatural glow. In the darkened bar/restaurant she would stand out-- depending on how many women wore the same makeup. She put on strappy open-toed heels, a skirt so short it barely descended past her hips, a sequined purple tube top under a pink blouse open to expose the tops of her rounded breasts. Rolly wore jeans, deck shoes, and a brown tee shirt. Stephanie was not happy with his fashion choice and told him to change. He refused. He expected an argument but she dropped it with only token griping.

In the car Rolly asked how her last day at the hospital had gone.

"They had me scheduled to work tonight. Can you believe that? Said it's a busy night and needed all the help they could get. Why would anyone be working New Year's Eve? That's crazy."

"What'd you do?"

"I walked out. Told them to take the job and shove it. Left 'em high and dry."

"Didn't they know you were only there for the year?"

"Why would I tell them that? They don't need to know my personal life."

"They could have scheduled someone else."

"Darling naïve husband, there's no one else to schedule. Everyone is working. It's not my problem if they're too cheap to hire more nurses. It's only transients anyway."

At Riddell's Rolly said "I'll find us a table" but Stephanie was already hugging and chatting up a woman he didn't know. Rolly left her behind and found an empty table in a dark corner, far away from the bar.

Rolly watched the crowd. Loud music blaring, bright frenetic visuals on the dance floor, the usual. People standing around the edges lit in profile. Drinks in hand, leaning in close to each other, the flirting never ending.

A waitress found him and he ordered a beer. He planned on sipping it for the rest of the evening.

Leah appeared at the same moment the waitress returned with his pint. She ordered a soda and sat across from Rolly, in her jeans and hoodie, anonymous again.

They didn't say hello; Leah waiting for Rolly to say something, Rolly waiting for the wave of relief to subside so he could speak coherently.

"I didn't think you'd show up."

"And here I am anyway."

Rolly stared down at his drink. "I didn't really know what to think of you until now. I let you take over my life on a whim and you've turned out to be...trustworthy."

Leah smiled, "Thank you Rolly. I appreciate that. Especially after what I've put you through."

"Nothing less than I deserve, I'm sure. You really think my chances are good?"

"I think they're very good. Unless something drastic happens you'll be retired at midnight."

"What happens if I fail? What would you do?"

"I suppose I would try to regroup, see what went wrong, figure out where you need to improve, look deeper for any secrets we missed--"

"You don't sound sure."

"Not really, no. Never had to deal with it."

Rolly wondered if his beer was more potent than he thought. "Are you saying all of your clients have retired?"

"No, only the ones who stick with the program. Like you. Many give up and I never see them again."

Rolly took three big gulps of his beer. "Sounds like a guarantee to me."

"Almost."

They sat in silence while Rolly tried to wrap his head around the concept of succeeding.

"Why is Souliere helping me?"

"I have no idea."

"But you've worked with him before. Or people from his organization."

"Several times. Usually it's a scientist, EverLife researchers seem to be popular, and biologists. Why they want a regular guy like you is beyond me."

"Do you trust them?"

"They pay on time. Good enough for me."

Rolly considered this for a minute. "If they're so powerful why go to so much trouble? Why not just pull a few strings."

"Because they have no power at all. Is Stephanie here?"

"Yeah, she's here. We split up at the door. She'll find us eventually."

They relaxed, Rolly watching the crowd, trying to enjoy the huge hovering holograms, but none of the flash held his attention. Leah took out a smaller, less conspicuous version of her HearSay and started playing a game. The glow from the screen lit up her face under the hoodie. Only Rolly could see the blue light playing across her beauty.

"Do you have a partner?"

"Don't want one. The time isn't right."

"Don't you get lonely, without someone around?"

"I like my privacy, I like being alone. The world is full of warm bodies. Every time I walk out the door I'm intimate with several thousand fellow humans. I'm at the saturation point. Having to share my life with someone would be torture. Being alone is precious."

"I don't think I could do that. I need to have someone around. The house feels too empty with only me there."

Leah watched him, a don't-go-there look on her face, but Rolly said nothing. He had no desire to ruin her precious privacy. In another time and place they might be lovers, but not now.

"Being alone isn't as bad as you think."

Stephanie staggered into the table, supported by a large man who had his arm around her waist, clutching her ribs, holding her up. She was red-cheeked and sweaty.

"Been looking for you Rolls. It's almost time isn't it? Someone told me it was almost time."

It was 11:30. "Yep, any minute now. Why don't you sit down and sober up with us."

"We should celebrate together, even though we're not really."

"Yes. Sit right here Steph." She fell butt first into the chair. Rolly said to the large man: "And you are?"

"Oh, hey man. Harold. Just hangin' with Steph."

"You two know each other?"

"Just met tonight."

"You're welcome to sit with us."

"Hey, thanks man."

Rolly sat down and Harold disappeared back into the crowd. Rolly immediately forgot Harold existed.

"Hi Leah. Glad you made it." She said this with the exaggerated mellowness only drunk people can pull off.

"Thanks." Leah looked appalled.

"You're welcome." Stephanie's eyes drooped. She laid her head on her arms and went to sleep.

Stephanie could not hold her liquor, it always made her drowsy. Rolly would let her sleep it off, the nanobots already hard at work in her bloodstream. In ten minutes she would be back to normal.

"She get drunk a lot?"

"Not that much, at least not around me. Who knows what she does when she's gone."

"You're okay with her living with other men?"

"I have more lovers than she does. I have no right to complain."

Stephanie snored. At five minutes to midnight Rolly shook her awake. Her eyes opened and for a moment she had a blank look, curious and open, a flashback to the innocent girl he married a century and a third ago. Rolly knew she was back to herself when she looked at him and closed her mouth in a tense straight line.

"What time is it?"

"Five minutes to midnight."

"Where's Harold?"

"Harold?"

"The big guy with the big...where'd he go."

"He disappeared after dropping you off."

"I didn't want to be dropped...never mind. I'm here." She gave Rolly a smile he recognized as fake. "What's Rolly's number again?"

"483.48."

The excitement and noise began to build as the moment approached. Rolly put his arm around Stephanie's shoulder. She glanced at it but let him leave it.

At one minute to twelve the music and noise stopped and the three dimensional ball and spindle appeared in the middle of the dance floor. At thirty seconds the ball started its descent. At ten seconds everyone began reciting the countdown.

Rolly had watched this spectacle too many times; this was the only time he felt like turning away.

The ball hit bottom and split open like an egg, The Number flashing in bright yellow neon.

482.3.

Rolly had achieved retirement.

Stephanie fell to her knees and screamed. Every face turned toward her. A piercing sound that might have signaled pure joy or an imminent attack. Stephanie leapt up and jumped around.

"WE DID IT! RETIREMENT HERE I COME!"

Someone on the other side of the room yelled and the crowd turned that way. A special night, two retirements in one room. A good story for the break room tomorrow.

Stephanie threw her arms around Rolly, planting a rough kiss that felt like two skulls bashing together, let go and began hugging anyone within range. The crowd swallowed her up again.

Hands patted him on the back, people shook his hand and congratulated him. Then they scattered, leaving Rolly at the table with Leah, who was beaming.

He didn't know she could do that, actually be happy and smile. Her teeth were perfect, of course. Leah came around the table and for a second

Rolly thought she might hug him but it was not to be. She shook his hand and said "You did it."

"With your help."

"You did all the work."

"Yes, you're right, it's all about me." They laughed, the way people do when they're in good spirits and lame jokes are easily tolerated.

"Are you going to stay and celebrate?"

Rolly suddenly felt tired. "I don't know. No. I want to go home."

"That's exactly what you should do. Go home and rest. Retirement will take care of itself."

"Thanks for being here, Leah. I'm really glad you came."

"Just doing my job."

"Will we see each other again?"

"Depends on where you go. Just remember," Leah reached up and grabbed Rolly's chin, "even good guys win sometimes."

Leah patted him on the cheek and left.

Stephanie wouldn't want to leave and he didn't want to wander around trying to find her. She was an adult, she could take care of herself.

"Sean."

"Yes, your dudeness."

"Send a text to Stephanie telling her I'm going home without her. Tag it so Nikki reminds her when she's sober."

"Got it. And may I say, on this fine New Year's day, congratulations on your retirement. Long time comin'. Can't wait to see what it's like."

At home Rolly opened his HearSay and made a video call. As soon as he saw Max's face he said, "We made it."

Max smiled. "That's good news. What happens next?"

"I don't know. Leah said something about retirement taking care of itself. We'll see."

"What's the first thing you want to do?"

The question threw Rolly off. "Honestly, I hadn't thought about it. Getting here has taken all my energy. The first thing I really want is to *not* get up and go to work in the morning."

Max laughed. "Sounds like the best way to start any retirement."

"Max, I have a favor to ask. Please don't feel like you have to say yes, or this is some kind of promise I expect you to keep. Just...I don't know what's going to happen...can you keep an eye on Nola until I get back?"

Max looked surprised. Rolly felt like he was asking a lot. Max lived on the other side of the country and couldn't simply pop in for a visit.

Given his technical brilliance and the omnipresent cameras, Rolly hoped Max could do this without much effort.

"Yeah, I can watch her for you. She is my sister after all."

Rolly was relieved. "Don't judge her too harshly Max. She's in a bad way." Rolly couldn't bring himself to say anymore.

"Maybe I'll try to help. Would you be okay with that?"

"I would love it if you did. But it won't be easy. She's belligerent."

"Sounds like she takes after you."

"Ha ha."

They said their goodbyes with smiles and a virtual handshake, father and son parting for neither knew how long, anticipating a reunion in the future. For the first time in a long time Rolly felt happy.

He undressed and piled his clothes on the floor, slipped into a pair of dark plaid pajama bottoms. He brushed his teeth and curled up in bed under the covers.

Tomorrow he did not have to wake early and go to work. He did not have to be responsible anymore. A weight was lifted and weariness washed over him. Rolly's eyes closed and he slept more soundly than he had in decades.

26

The Spoils

Monday, January 1st, 2148

The convoy pulled up outside the Smalls residence with hissing brakes, grinding axles and settling frames. Radek Fookes winced. In the quiet dark it sounded like a selfish scream for attention.

Radek preferred to start at five o'clock, to get retirees out before morning rush hour and well before sunrise, 8:08 this particular day. Management wanted them out of sight ASAP. Long winter nights were an advantage in this job.

Besides two semi-trucks (one for stuff to be sold, one for stuff to be recycled) the convoy included two SUVs, black with darkened windows, and a crew of six transient laborers.

The driver of Radek's SUV was Emmet Richardson, a big man who hunched forward constantly, content to be the muscle despite a wicked intelligence. Radek once made a joke involving a large stupid man. Emmet responded with a lecture about size versus intelligence filled with so much jargon Radek had to have his HearSay translate. Radek was sixty-five years old, Emmet ninety-two.

In the backseat were the twins...he had to look up their names, it was a new pair every year...Malcolm and Malone Coogan. They had not spoken since leaving the warehouse, twins never did. Both were caucasian, wearing the same white double breasted uniform suit, like waiters at a formal restaurant. Radek and Emmet wore suits and ties but the twins made them look shabby.

Radek turned around, "Who's going in with me?"

They answered simultaneously, "Malone is."

Radek gave them a dirty look. They both pointed at the twin sitting directly behind him. "As long as I can put a name in the report."

From a faux leather attache Radek pulled a Scrablet, finger scrolled the touch screen, found the document he needed, and wrote in Malone's name. The Scrablet had one purpose: records handling. Any official document could be scanned, transmitted, read, signed or printed. Horizontal tubes on each end of the device (decorated with useless ornate swirls) invoked the ancient dignity of written scrolls. These tubes contained thin paper for the printer, which always came out curled like a cheap rug. Most retirees wanted documents sent to their HearSays, but some of the really old ones liked having paper in hand.

Only authorized personnel were entrusted with a Scrablet and its multiple passwords. Radek made sure it was out and on display as much as possible, to be sure the crew knew who was in charge. It was his guide as well. He only had to follow the documents sequentially to run a smooth transition. Everything nicely ordered and ready to go.

They waited for five o'clock, staring at the darkened house. Most of the surrounding apartments had a light in at least one window--people getting ready for work--an urban glow that illuminated the Smalls' homestead.

Emmet, "Look at that. There's grass in the front yard."

"You don't see that anymore. It'll be gone soon."

At five minutes to five, from the opposite direction, another small convoy rolled up and parked on the other side of the street, directly across from the Smalls' house. An equally black SUV and two flatbed trucks hauling a bulldozer and excavator. Two men stepped out, crossed in front of Radek, and walked toward the Smalls' front door.

"What the hell? Did another team get called out by mistake?"

"Don't know but we better get up there."

They jumped down and caught up to the other men, who were wearing much nicer suits.

Radek, "Hey, who are you?"

Both had dark complexions and didn't stop; the one with curly black hair spoke. "I'm Warren and this is Garrett." Garrett had long black hair. "We're from Nelson Holdings, here to claim our property."

"Your property? Everything is going to Paragon Retirement for liquidation."

"Sorry. We already bought it."

Emmet, "What's with the heavy equipment?"

"Tear the house down. Clear the land for development."

"You're not tearing anything down until we sort this out." Someone new walked up. A large white panel truck was now parked on the road behind Nelson's convoy.

"Who are you?"

"Art from Art Brown's 20th Century Antiques."

"What do you want?"

"Everything that isn't nailed down."

Radek, scrolling through his Scrablet, "There's nothing here about Nelson Holdings or Art Brown's or anyone else. Paragon takes control of all assets. That's the way it works."

Garrett, "We just need a couple papers signed and we can get to work."

Radek, "No one does anything until I say so."

That's when the argument started.

———————

The ECC woke Rolly when it sensed the first person on his doorstep. It took several tries to rouse him. *Someone is at the front door. Your attention required immediately.* Rolly threw on a robe and fumbled to the dining room where he plopped in a chair and drifted off again.

The house woke him again. He could hear muffled voices outside the front door. Through parted curtains he saw darkness and streams of headlights on the street, flickering between rows of large vehicles parked in front of his house. He smiled. His fellow humans heading off to work and he wasn't one of them.

Stephanie appeared next to him, still wearing her party dress.

"Who's at the door?"

"The rest of eternity coming to claim us."

———————

Radek desperately scrolled and searched his Scrablet, but could not find reference to any pre-sale. Emmet was doing what he did best: standing in front of the door and making himself large. The homeowners had yet to make an appearance.

A squeal of brakes caught his attention. Another truck pulled up, an open air hauler. Six more men tumbled out, yawning. *Oh God, what now?* The Nelson reps and Art's Antiques were arguing about who should go first.

"Who are you?" Radek asked the new arrivals.

"Wood City Salvage. We're supposed to take this house for recycling."

"You might want to talk to the guys with the bulldozer first."

"What? Who's that?"

"The two suits up front."

Wood City Salvage marched over, pulled Garrett around by the shoulder, and demanded to know what was going on. The argument got very loud.

———————

Stephanie sat at the table across from Rolly. She badly needed a cup of coffee but couldn't muster enough energy to cross the room. She'd had less sleep than Rolly.

"Nikki, tell the coffee maker to start."

"Yes, ma'am." Pause. "It cannot because it does not have a filter or coffee grounds."

"Goddamn it. Rolly, go make some coffee."

No response. She rubbed her puffy eyes. When she opened them he was still sitting there, smiling.

The commotion at the door got louder. A bang, and something that sounded like a scuffle. Her eyes opened wide.

"Aren't you going to let them in?"

"In a minute. I want to savor the moment first."

"I'll let them in." She started to rise.

"Sit down!" he yelled. "Be cool. Let them sweat a little."

One of the Wood City Salvage crewmen shoved Emmet, who barely moved. Emmet responded with a one handed block to the chest. The fool ended up on his back in the grass, looking offended. In a second he was back on his feet, crouched for another attack. Emmet stood his ground, hands up with clenched fists. Radek stepped between them.

"Stop! If we're going to sort this out we need to get inside and talk to the owner."

A flurry of comments shot at Radek. "What if they don't come out?" "Are they even here?" "Maybe they want us to fight it out." "This is costing me money." "Who cares about them?" "I got out of bed for this?" "Has anyone bothered to knock?"

With a hiss of sealed air and splutter of weatherproofing, the door behind Radek opened. Rolly Smalls stood in the doorway.

"Don't just stand there freezing your balls off. Come in."

The Nelson reps rushed at Rolly, demanding he honor their contract.

The man trying to quell the crowd (named Radek, which Rolly misheard as "radish") threatened him with arrest if he signed anything not officially sanctioned. Rolly smiled and enjoyed the chaos. He made no attempt to explain the situation.

Half an hour later Rolly and Stephanie were back at the dining room table watching strangers divide up the spoils of their lives. The interlopers broke into separate cliques, the Nelson reps and Paragon guys murmuring to themselves, talking to their respective headquarters, the crews fidgeting as if they had crotch itch and were embarrassed to scratch in public.

Everyone stopped talking and the room went quiet. The Paragon guys stared at the ceiling and looked at their watches. The Nelson reps, Garret and Warren, played games on their interfaces.

Stephanie whispered, "What're they doing?"

Rolly answered with the universal hum-grunt for *I don't know, why are you asking me?*

Radek, "Our superiors are talking to each other. We're waiting to hear from them."

Rolly imagined frazzled executives in a HearSay video conference, annoyed they had been wakened, hashing out who gets what and when. This thought alone made the past year's torment worthwhile.

Several minutes of awkward milling around commenced. Stephanie, who was a mess from her wild night, stood up and made coffee. Several men were trying very hard not look at her. Eventually, the Nelson reps were called, followed by Radek and Art's traders, all speaking into the ether, moving around, trying to find private space, but only bumping into each other.

Radek was writing rapidly on his Scrablet. Rolly thought he could hear yelling from Radek's ear.

"Will I be receiving new forms?" Pause, then: "Thank you sir. I am deeply sorry for the inconvenience. We will find the culprit."

Radek walked over to Rolly, looking flustered. "Here's how we'll work this. The reps and traders and recyclers all have legitimate claims. It's only a matter of what order they proceed in." The other supervisors walked up to listen. "You and your wife will have to sign forms acknowledging this," he turned to Garret and Warren, "you won't like this, but the traders go first, followed by the recyclers, and whatever is left is yours to do with as you please."

Garret, "It'll take recyclers two days to tear down this stupid little house. We don't wanna wait."

Rolly, "The agreement says you can take possession on or after January 1st. Waiting a couple of days won't hurt."

Warren, "We got equipment here now. Take your house down in five minutes. With you in it."

Radek, "Gentlemen, all of our superiors have agreed to this. We will go in order. Every company gets what they paid for."

Warren, "We should sue you for breach of contract."

Not long ago this would have scared Rolly, but he recognized what Warren was doing: squirming, ranting against the unfairness, and Rolly could see it, already looking at it from the other side, the side that got to watch other people acting ineffectual. Rolly smiled. "Because you have to wait two extra days. Good luck with that. I'll be long gone. You want to waste company money, go ahead. But it seems like an empty threat."

Radek, to Garret, "You should take your partner outside."

Garret jerked his thumb and Warren left.

Rolly, to Radek, "What do you get out of this deal?"

"I've got the easy part. My only responsibility is you and your wife. First we need to take care of some new paperwork. The first two finalize contracts with Art Brown's and Wood City Salvage and lay out the order they can work. Mr. Smalls you sign on the flashing red lines. Mrs. Smalls please sign on the flashing yellow lines."

Art watched over Radek's shoulder. As soon as Stephanie signed he yelled "Okay, we're on. Start with the ends of the house and work your way in. There are collectibles here so be careful. Melvin start dismantling the holoroom. Let's move!"

Crewmen started bustling around. Wood City Salvage stepped outside to wait. Furniture started to parade past Rolly and Stephanie.

"This next form finalizes the sale of the land to Nelson Holdings, and requires them to wait until the salvagers are finished dismantling your house."

Garret, "Won't be as much fun without a house to tear down."

Radek, "You have plenty of trees to run over. That's got to be a rare treat."

"It's not the same."

"Sign on the same flashing lines as before." Garret watched, then turned and left.

A man in a white suit was standing behind Radek.

"Now for the important papers. The first turns over your monetary assets to Paragon Retirement, authorizes us to clear outstanding debts and use the proceeds to finance your retirement."

"How does that work? There's a lot of money but not enough for a thousand years."

"All retiree assets are transferred to the Paragon Bank and Trust, an investment firm whose sole purpose is to provide you a secure financial future. The bank is a powerful force in the market, greater in fact than the EverLife company. They have never lost an investor's principal, their record is spotless. All of your living expenses will be covered by interest accumulated from these investments. In short, you are set for life."

Stephanie, "EverLife treatments are covered?"

"Of course."

Rolly, "What if we need extra money? To do something special?"

"Not a problem. If you want more than the usual stipend it's a straightforward process. Approval usually happens in a few seconds. I have packets for both of you that explain this. Signature required here, and here."

They signed.

"The final form is the most important of all. You are *required* to sign it. If you do not, your retirement will not proceed. Read it carefully."

"What is it?"

"A non-disclosure agreement. It covers your retirement experiences, which you may not relate to any individual, whether you are acquainted with them or not, in person, by voice, text, video or any HearSay medium, or any future communication methods that may be developed."

"What's so bad about being retired you have to hide it?"

"Nothing at all. We do this for the benefit of future retirees, so the experience isn't spoiled for them. We want it to be a pleasant surprise. Malone can tell you more."

The man in the white suit stepped up, all smiles and deferential.

"Mr. and Mrs. Smalls, it's an honor to meet you at last. My name is Malone Coogan and I will be escorting you through retirement."

"Think of him as your retirement concierge."

"Ask me for anything and I can make it happen. To get you started, we have a hotel room waiting with a closet full of new clothes to choose from. A private plane will take us to France, where you have a reservation for dinner and tickets to the Théâtre du Châtele for a French language performance of Rossini's opera *Guillaume Tell*."

Stephanie, "Oh. Sounds wonderful."

Rolly, "But we have to give up basic rights to do it."

Radek, "You're not giving up any rights. Just agreeing not to discuss one small topic."

"How can I not discuss this? What's so precious it has to be kept secret?"

Malone, "Mr. Smalls, you'll find many activities to keep you occupied. And time to do the things you've always wanted."

"I just can't tell anyone."

Radek, "We've found that retirees are happier if they make a clean break with their old life."

"So I should just leave friends and family behind."

"You can communicate with them anytime you like. But we discourage it."

"But I can't leave..."

Stephanie, "Sign it Rolly."

"I can't leave...Max behind."

Stephanie grabbed the Scrablet out of Rolly's hands and signed on her yellow flashing lines.

"Sign the damn thing Rolly. Don't bother reading it."

"I have to read it."

"No you don't. All you have to do is retire. Sign it."

Rolly, to Radek, "What happens if I sign this and go talk to someone?"

"That would be a serious breach of contract. This is binding between yourself and the Corporament and carries the full weight of Corporament authority. You are expected to adhere to the contract for the rest of your life."

"What's the punishment?"

"Exile." *Exile*. The lowest of the low, worse than being kicked down to transient. Electronically shunned, no social contact, no EverLife. The long slow lonely death.

Stephanie, "Sign it Rolly."

"What if I don't?"

"You have already authorized the transfer of assets to Paragon. The money has been moved. All of your property has been sold, your house will shortly be demolished. Without your signature I cannot finalize your transition to retirement. Emmet, Malone and myself will leave and you will have *absolutely* nothing left. Your only concern will be finding a ride to work."

Rolly signed.

"Thank you Mr. Smalls, you won't regret this. Please follow Malone to the car. And welcome to your new life."

Before stepping out Rolly turned and looked back. He had lived in this house a long time. Decades of ins and outs, friends and lovers, games and movies. He had to suppress an urge to tell the workmen about the funky wiring in the hallway light switch, or the ceiling fan that only ran at two speeds. It was a lot to walk away from, and at the same time, a joy to finally get away.

Radek followed them out and waved as their SUV drove away. He stared at the house, not sure what to do. Normally he would supervise the liquidation process, scanning bar codes and logging items, keeping an eye out for valuables. Emmet would be moving furniture by himself. This was supposed to be an all day job and a first for Radek--land, structure and people, something bigger than the usual apartment to clear--but they were already finished and ready to leave. His excitement felt suspended and unfulfilled, as if a roller coaster had stopped and shut down at the top of the first hill.

He walked back to the trucks and explained the situation to the crew, that there was nothing to do. Fine--as long as they were paid. Radek assured them they would be, though didn't mention it would only be for two hours.

Emmet was waiting in their black SUV. "Back to the warehouse?"

"Yep." Radek turned to Malcolm in the backseat. "You heard all that?"

Malcolm had his eyes closed, listening. His and Malone's HearSays were linked so each could hear what the other was doing. "Every word."

Emmet, "Kind of a weird one wasn't it?"

"Yeah, all these people lined up, waiting to take their stuff. Never seen that before."

"Did some preemptive selling. Caught us off guard."

"Caught someone off guard, not us."

They drove in silence, Radek thinking. "I wonder how much of what I say is true."

"What you tell the client?"

"Yeah. I've never retired. I don't know what it's like. I could be feeding them a line of garbage."

"Guess you'll find out when you get there."

"By the time I retire Malcolm will be president of EverLife." They laughed.

Malcolm, eyes still closed, looked annoyed.

27

Dot On A Monitor

Roy Tompkins stared at the monitor array on his desk--nine BTR (Better Than Real) quality rectangles--considering what he was about to do. So many details to consider, people to contact, everything had to be just right, convincing. Projects of this size were prone to problems and delays. No one could foresee every catastrophe. It was his job to make sure the plan was flexible. And successful.

All the monitors showed various angles of the same beach, Dickenson Bay on the island of Antigua in the Caribbean, white sand, white bungalows, a vacation paradise. The large center monitor showed the view from inside one of those cottages, looking out to a covered patio where Rolly Smalls sat watching the ocean, a strawberry daiquiri on the table next to him, content.

Mr. Smalls had made a nuisance of himself over the past two years. Roy oversaw seventy-eight couples and usually only received periodic updates, but Mr. Smalls had hijacked most of his time, requiring near constant monitoring, making Roy's life more hectic than it should be. Mr. Smalls' wife wasn't much better, causing strain in Roy's well trained team, namely the twins. No one likes having the boss look over their shoulder, but in this case, no one complained either.

Roy understood Mr. Smalls' restiveness--he had children of his own-- but not enough to offer support, or even sympathy. Mr. Smalls needed a way to redirect the guilt into something more productive. On this Roy and management agreed, however, Roy thought their plan foolhardy. They expected him to develop and implement it anyway.

Roy out-aged Mr. Smalls by over thirty years. When EverLife shook up the world he was sixty-three years old and looking forward to an old style retirement. Forty-two years as a machinist, then foreman, left him tired and ready for a rest. Once EverLife kicked in his eyesight cleared, his breathing became easier, his back straightened, energy coursed through his new body with a strengthened heart and clear circulation.

On the outside he was still a fleshy bag of wrinkles, age spots, and baldness. His finger nails felt like mini-weights glued to the end of his fingers. The pores on his face looked like sinkholes. His bones and muscles moved with vigor, but skin like bags of lard chafed and plopped, making physical exertion grotesque. Nothing more frustrating than being a young man trapped in an old man's body. Age-realignment surgery now a necessity instead of a luxury.

The surgeons grafted new hair on his scalp, tucked and trimmed the skin on his torso, arms and legs, gave him shots that broke up the melanin under his skin. He stopped short of a facial graft--the thought of a laboratory grown face made him cringe. It would feel like wearing someone else's skin. Besides, working as a foreman taught him age was respected. No matter how old they claimed to be, Roy could never bring himself to respect the fresh faced newbies walking around. He settled for a lift and a little tuck, but kept his face aged looking, branded with all the color and imperfections of sixty plus years of living.

At that point Roy still hoped to retire, thinking it would be easy since he was close, but every year the official retirement age increased, at first just out of reach, then fading away like a speeding car. The financial requirements increased as well, while the cost of surgeries cut into his savings. Three grown children and a past divorce didn't help. He was getting squeezed and couldn't see a way out.

Just before the Corporament abolished the retirement age, Roy decided he needed a change. The new cubicle bound counselors pegged his eventual retirement at thirty plus years in the future. A long time and a far away carrot to be chasing. He felt no obligation to stay in his job, no matter what the Corporament valued. If he couldn't retire now he at least deserved a change, loyalty be damned.

A few years in the army earned him triple LOS points but left him cold. Then it was back to the private sector. That he would end up at Paragon Retirement Inc. didn't strike Roy as ironic, just annoying, in the way fate sometimes pokes its finger in your eye. They put him through nine sessions of psychological screening, multiple background checks, what seemed like a hundred people asking about trust and integrity, why he was looking for a new job; sometimes they asked, sometimes they challenged. Roy had the impression that quitting his previous job helped, though no one said so. They liked his answers and offered him a desk job that paid two and a half times more than the shop.

Roy happily signed the papers, variations of the standard non-disclosure agreement and some that said they would destroy his life if Corporament secrets were disclosed. He signed them all, envisioning how much closer the higher pay would bring him to retirement.

He started in support, helping concierges fill client needs. In a few years he was promoted to supervisor, where he learned the reality of Paragon Retirement, slowly, one glimpse into the process at a time, an odd command here, a contrary result there, and a realization things weren't as they seemed. No one said anything, it was known but unspoken, all those legal documents having the desired effect.

Roy Tompkins abandoned all retirement aspirations and settled into life as it was.

As supervisor he had freedom to tweak things, make the job more efficient, to prove himself. This earned him eleven promotions, with new titles like Assistant Regional Manager, Senior Director, Regional Executive Manager, all of which meant nothing. He still did the same job. At the end of every year Paragon texted a retirement statement, showing his Reckoning, so far beyond The Number a client seeing it might have gasped. Every year Roy deleted the text.

Now Mr. Roland V. Smalls was pulling Roy from behind his comfortable desk, making life annoyingly interesting. For a year Mr. Smalls had been a model retiree, taking in the sights, following the itinerary, never complaining. Overnight he became difficult, a change so sudden it caught the entire crew off guard.

In Romania he rented a car and started driving across Europe, toward the Atlantic coast. The tangle of motor vehicle laws tripped him up, as did an inability to read anything other than English. A policeman in Austria pulled him over for driving on the wrong side of the road.

While staying in Niamey, the capital of Niger in West Africa, Mr. Smalls took off on a trek across the Sahara toward Morocco, sometimes by Jeep, sometimes on foot. That was a desperate search, trying to find the fool before the desert baked him alive. When they finally caught up he had only a backpack full of canteens and beef jerky. The exasperated searchers asked if he were suicidal. Offended, Mr. Smalls said no. They asked why, if he wanted out of Africa, didn't he go south, through either Benin or Togo, where the climate was better. He said he wanted to take the scenic route.

In Hawaii Mr. Smalls tried to board a plane bound for the mainland. In Hong Kong he tried to get a job as a ship's hand on a freighter bound for America. From Rio de Janeiro he rode a motorcycle up through South and Central America into Mexico. Antarctica was the one place he stayed put, biding his time until the next, more escapable, leg of the journey.

With the exception of South America they were able to stop him quickly. In that attempt the motorcycle was a wise choice; it gave Mr. Smalls a jump on Roy's team. They would move in to make the catch only to find their target already tooling down the road. Of course Roy knew exactly where Mr. Smalls was, all he had to do was follow a dot on a monitor. The mobility of the motorcycle forced them to think two steps ahead and finally corner Mr. Smalls in Mexico.

Clients were not supposed to act like this. They were supposed to enjoy retirement, not be assholes about it. Roy had half a mind to send Mr. Smalls back to Antarctica and leave him there.

He had some hope this grand new idea would change Mr. Smalls' behavior, but not much. His superiors put on a nice presentation, explaining what people wanted, how that was different from what they really needed, and why, given his sentimental past, Rolly Smalls was the perfect candidate. When they revealed the actual project, Roy openly laughed, it sounded so ridiculous.

When he settled down Roy said, "That's all well and good, but you didn't say anything about location. If this is going to work it has to happen in Michigan, his home state and the place he's trying to get back to. You have to bring him full circle. Do this anywhere else and he'll run again."

The suits mulled this over, expressed concern about proximity to Mr. Smalls' home city, that he had too many connections there. Roy assured them Mr. Smalls would be under control at all times (as if he wasn't already) and would learn to get on with life.

The suits accepted this, a little too readily. They praised Roy's insight, said they were glad he was on board, and started to banter among themselves, talking as if Roy wasn't there, coming to the marvelously obvious conclusion Roy should set up and manage this new endeavor. Rolly Smalls was *his* client, it only made sense.

Did they think he was stupid? This was a con job, a poor comedic skit hiding a bit of cynical salesmanship. He was being set up in case it went bad. They smiled and waited for him to gratefully accept. Instead Roy negotiated a severance package, to be paid no matter the reason for his termination. To his surprise the negotiations were brief and rewarding. Either they lacked faith in the project or had no concept of the hit their budget would take. Roy thought it was likely the latter.

With his ass sufficiently covered Roy returned to his team and briefed them on the new plan. They were anxious to get started. A few looked star struck. Watching everyone's eyes light up, he knew they wouldn't let him down. He did get a boost from their enthusiasm, but nothing would convince him this was anything more than a bad prank.

So far the team had done well, putting together detailed estimates and a timeline. He turned it in yesterday and management responded this morning. Roy called the twins.

"Hello Mr. Tompkins."

"Hello Malcolm. I've got great news. The adventure project is a go. Got approval this morning."

"Yes!" Roy could see Malcolm pump his fist.

"We'll start putting it together today. I thought you and Malone should be first to know."

"That's great. How much is it going to cost?"

"No final numbers yet, but it will be expensive."

"Is there enough?"

"Just enough."

"Can you give me a date?"

"Too early. Figure on three or four months."

"Oh." Malcolm in sad face now.

"Takes time to get something this big organized and built. I know you were hoping for sooner. At least there's light at the end of the tunnel."

"It's been a three year long tunnel."

"You can make it. Then the two of you will get a well deserved break."

"With our own concierge?"

"You'd be worse clients than Mr. Smalls."

"No one's that bad."

28

Discontent

The view from Rolly's chair was spectacular, as it had been every day on Antigua. From their cottage he looked across a yard of sparse grass and white sand, down two rough hewn steps to the beach, past two loungers under large umbrellas, over more white sand and out to a bright blue ocean that made the clear blue sky lesser by comparison. Waves gently rolled in. At night the sound was as good as a sleeping pill.

The cottage--a lot like the house back in Michigan with a central living room and bedrooms on either end--was part of a four star hotel with the same stuff to do that every other ocean side hotel in the world offered: snorkeling, wind surfing, kayaking, tennis, etc. They claimed a bedroom each, just like at home. And like that demolished building, Stephanie mostly went out and Rolly mostly stayed in.

The handlers originally landed them on Barbuda, Antigua's sister island. A perfectly nice island, it was much less developed and out-of-the-way. Quiet, unassuming, pleasant. A haven for Frigate Birds, a seabird that prefers to nest on remote islands. Rolly liked it. Stephanie took a half hour walking tour and returned to say "We're not staying." Before the end of the day they were ensconced on Antigua instead, with a more active human population.

Malone denied it, but Rolly assumed the handlers chose Barbuda as punishment since it was not easy to get to. Or leave.

Rolly stared at the blue water, his mind back in the state of his birth, worrying about the daughter he left behind, wondering if she was okay, if she was alive. An old fear that was new again, knowing someone you cared about was at death's door. How was he going to get back to help her?

A year of retirement passed without any of these thoughts. Constant travel, experiencing places they'd only seen in holograms. Wherever they wanted to go, Malone would set it up. Greece. Rome. Paris. Hong Kong. Rio de Janeiro. Montreal. London. Egypt. The Antarctic. Malone would give them spending money on MiniVaults, like a credit card with hyper-paranoid security, and let them explore cities on their own. Old troubles faded under a deluge of new sensations. So many places to go and all the time in the world to get there and a year went by in a flash movie of food and tours.

Rolly forgot about Nola.

Early on he and Stephanie deduced that Malone was more than one person, twins, or maybe triplets. The truth was revealed on their first trip to Paris. Set loose in the city to explore, it became apparent Malone and his handlers assumed they would do so as a couple. Instead Stephanie went on a three day French jaunt by herself. On the second day Malone, looking concerned, asked several times if Rolly was planning on joining her. No, he said. Malone seemed dismayed, looking around as if he should be somewhere else, but johnny-on-the-spot if Rolly needed anything. Later, when Stephanie and Rolly were together, she said Malone had been with her every day, even doing a background check on a new lover. Obviously he couldn't be in two places at once, so they questioned Malone, asked for his brother's name, even tried teasing him, but Malone refused to answer.

One city to the next, one hotel to the next. Rolly appreciated the wonderful experiences but asked Malone for a break. A little respite, he said, downtime from their high flying new lifestyle. Malone had the perfect place and sent them to a nice apartment in Amsterdam, with a promise to leave them alone for a few weeks. Tough to say no, but it wasn't what Rolly had in mind. He wanted a house, he told Malone, in a place like home, like Michigan. Rolly thought he was giving Malone a subtle hint.

Instead Rolly found himself in a small bungalow in western Canada, bags slung over his shoulders, saying to Malone, "It's a rental?"

"That's right. Has all the modern conveniences, wireless HearSay access to every appliance, even a car in the garage. Just like home. It's all yours for three weeks. Of course you can call if you need anything."

"It's nice. I like it. But I meant a house of our own, bought with our money, a place we can settle into and call home."

"Oh, that would be counter productive. We still have many places to visit. You've barely covered a quarter of the planet."

"Think of it as a base of operations. A place to come back to and recharge."

"It's more efficient to travel from one place to another than go to an arbitrary place called home in between. You're saving money this way. And I would like it very much if you considered me your base of operations." Malone looked hurt by Rolly's lack of trust.

Rolly didn't know how to respond. Somehow his desire for a home had been twisted into an affront to Malone's pride. So they stayed.

It was February in Canada. Eight inches of snow covered the ground, the roads were snow packed, and the furnace ran every day. A lot like Michigan. Except on the other side of the continent.

As he had many times over the past year, Rolly got to know the neighborhood quickly. The place itself remained nameless, another chunk of suburbia he would be leaving soon. He knew where the restaurants and bars were, which direction and how far the nearest movie theater, which corners had the best convenience stores. Rolly had a taste for soda and was on his way to get one at a place cleverly called The Corner Stop, driving carefully in the tiny feather light electric hybrid, afraid the car might try to skate instead of roll.

Rolly waited in line with two bottles of orange soda. The woman behind the counter was, not surprisingly, a transient: short and Asian, round cheeks covered with age spots, and long straight blonde hair. He didn't see the resemblance right away, it took a minute of staring, wondering why she looked familiar.

Nola. Was she okay?

The cashier was older, sixty, maybe seventy, with deep wrinkles around the eyes and a permanent expression of weariness. Her movements were robotic but her hair flowed light and fresh, one point of pride in a life full of hardship. Like Nola.

Rolly looked into the face of this woman and saw Nola's future. No. A future she could only hope for, *if* she were sane. It would take a miracle for Nola to be as lucky as this woman.

No, not a miracle. Just a little effort and someone who cared. A few months ago he was ready to destroy his own retirement to get EverLife treatments for Nola. Rolly looked at his hands. Nola's situation was dire and here he was buying soda in Canada. Years of immortality had made him heartless.

Rolly went back to the house and packed his bags while Sean arranged a flight to Michigan. He made it to the airport, a three hour drive, before Malone caught up. Rolly's ticket had been cancelled. Malone and a very large man escorted him to a waiting SUV.

"Where were you going Mr. Smalls?"

"Home."

"Have we done something to offend you?"

"No, I just want to go home."

"You have friends there. And family. A lot of people you would want to talk to."

"That's why it's called home."

"You'll make a new home somewhere else."

"Why did you stop me?"

"For your own protection. If you break non-disclosure, even accidentally, it would devastate your retirement. I'm sure you don't want that to happen."

"I know what a non-disclosure agreement means. I'm not going to tell anybody your secrets. Which don't seem to be secrets at all."

"That makes them so much easier to reveal. As I mentioned before, we don't want to ruin the experience for future retirees. For now you should enjoy yourself. We've made new plans, a place you haven't been to yet. Istanbul."

At the hotel in Istanbul Rolly made another run for the airport. Two large men met him in the lobby, took his bags and escorted him back to the room. At six feet tall Rolly was not small but these gentlemen towered over him like aliens on a bad movie poster.

Stephanie was out, who knew where. Malone took the opportunity to lecture him. "Do you realize how many people are working to make your retirement special? To run off unannounced is rude, really an insult. They put a great deal of effort into their duties. Good people doing a good job. Without you they would be unemployed. You want them to become transients? You have a responsibility, like every good American, to support the economy, and that means keeping people working. If you promise to behave I won't say anything and your happy retirement can continue."

Rolly apologized and expressed his regrets, and thanked Malone for his benevolence, though not in those words. For a moment he wavered, a different reply in mind, but Rolly checked himself, knowing he had an audience. When he tried again it would be better if his watchers were relaxed instead of alert.

Rolly didn't tell Stephanie he wanted to leave. Despite traveling together they had grown farther apart, speaking once or twice a week, sometimes not even that much. Stephanie was in heaven, sampling the pleasures of the world.

Once he asked Malone why it was necessary he and Stephanie travel together.

Malone replied as if Rolly were clueless, "Because you're married."

"That doesn't mean we have to be together all the time."

"Yes it does." He was completely serious.

"We're not joined at the hip."

"Of course not. But traveling should be done together. Anything else is strange."

"So you think it's weird Stephanie and I aren't together every day?"

"It's not my place to judge. I'm only here to make your retirement happy."

"What if we want to travel apart?"

"We can't do that. The system isn't set up for that."

A common reply when some request was deemed out of bounds. *We're not set up for that.* As if Rolly had asked for the impossible. There was no getting around it. "Are you comfortable around us Malone, or whatever your name is?"

"Mr. Smalls, the Corporament mandated marriage as a requirement for retirement. I think that's a good thing."

Rolly took that as a resounding no. Malone, and his brother, were true believers, fully indoctrinated members of the Corporament. Rolly imagined Malone as the stuffed shirt waiter putting up with a parade of provincial customers. He smiled and made nice, but counted the seconds until the unclean vermin were gone.

The next time Rolly tried to escape he packed a small knapsack and headed out the door, as nonchalant as he could. They were in Paris, on what Malone said was downtime: an extended hotel stay with minimum interference. Downtime was more frequent now. Rolly hadn't seen Stephanie for a week and Malone last made an appearance two days previously. Rolly was tired of the City of Lights, this being their fifth trip. He hailed a cab and headed for the airport. The driver, a balding man with stubby beard and neatly styled mustache, was talkative which somehow led to an argument. At one point the driver pulled off the road so he could insult Rolly's speech. "I French and I speak better Anglish than you!" Once they settled the conflict (over the proper amount of the tip) the cabby finally got Rolly to the airport. Malone was waiting at the curb. Rolly tried to get the cabby to move farther down the terminal.

"No. I drop you here. I sick of you."

At least he made it past the hotel lobby this time.

Malone was alone. Rolly briefly thought he might push past the smaller man.

"We've wiped your MiniVault and put a detain alert on your name and picture. You don't have any money to buy a ticket and when they scan your passport you'll be spending time in a small windowless room instead of an airplane." Malone flagged a new taxi and Rolly went back to the hotel with him.

Stephanie was waiting, looking perturbed. Malone left.

Arms folded tight but still pretty in a long skirt and pink silk blouse, purse over her shoulder as if about to leave, she lit into Rolly before his knapsack hit the floor.

"What the hell? Malone said this was the second time. Are you mental or something? You ruin this for me and I'll…"

Rolly wasn't listening. The windows in their suite were open and the midday sun streamed in. The room was lit up, Stephanie's freshly washed hair glowed like a halo. Never a woman who needed makeup, she wore it lightly with a hint of rouge and red lipstick, not a cry-for-attention red, a nice contrasting red that emphasized her lightly bronzed skin.

As her eyebrows creased and her mouth opened wide to yell, Rolly gazed at the suppleness of her skin, how there was no discoloration, how soft and inviting it was, how she used to like it when he would kiss that spot below her right ear.

He wanted to rip her clothes off.

Instead he picked her up, plopped her on the too soft and too ornate bed, then ripped her clothes off.

Rolly expected anger, well, anger and violence, but her intensity stayed the same. He took this as a sign she might acquiesce. On the other hand her anger didn't decrease either. The scared little man in the back of his head insisted he stop now.

But he kept going, popping three buttons on her blouse. Now she was mad, fists up, pounding on his chest and arms. "You know how much this cost? Leave me alone!" Her voice had that over-top-screech she used when riding roller coasters or being silly. Rolly pulled her arms out, not roughly, holding her wrists down, exposing the matching pink brassiere. He bent to kiss his wife on the lips and as expected she turned her head away and Rolly found the spot under her ear and planted a kiss, not a teasing brush of the lips or a bruise-leaving crush of skin, just enough to let her know he was intent but not crazed. Rolly let go of her wrists and gently put his hands on her exposed rib cage, caressing her stomach with his thumbs. Stephanie's expression changed, no longer angry, now open, lips slightly parted. Despite their separation Rolly knew all the ways and places she liked to be touched.

Her clothes were a wall he needed to tear down. The skirt so prudishly long Rolly wondered if Stephanie had turned Amish on one of her jaunts. Thick and brown, there was no ripping it. Rolly flipped Stephanie over, unsnapped the bra and yanked down the zipper on the skirt, pulled it off past her feet. She helped push it off. White cotton panties, tight on her butt, and those legs, short and shapely, hairless and smooth, legs he hadn't been this close to in a long time.

The panties and bra came off and she was gloriously naked, pulling her knees up and open. He was naked too, though couldn't remember taking his clothes off. When he entered her, Stephanie said "Fuck me like you used to." Rolly pulled the blankets up, covering them in darkness. They could only hear and touch each other, and he did exactly as she asked.

They made a mess of themselves and the bed and when it was over Rolly lay down next to Stephanie, spooning together, his arms around her middle and under her neck, keeping her warm and safe. They fit together like puzzle pieces.

Stephanie drifted into a light sleep. Rolly tried to figure out why she had given in so easily. The words "like you used to" resonated in his head, said with what he took to be lust. In the afterglow Rolly remembered an edge of desperation. Stephanie could have any man she wanted, she certainly didn't need the sex. Was it a longing for something else? Something she could only get from him? After a century and a quarter she was sick of his company. Maybe that was it: familiarity. They had been traveling the world on whim and wind for three years without any emotional grounding, no time to settle and make memories, no place to let the baggage and stress drop away. They were each other's connection and Stephanie always came home.

Eyes fluttering open, Stephanie stretched. Rolly said "I know you want to leave me."

Fully awake and surprised, she opened her mouth to protest, then changed her mind.

"You've wanted to leave for a long time."

"It sounds harsh when you just say it. We've had two lifetimes of marriage. I need something different."

"You want a whole new life."

"Yeah, I do."

"And these flings you have, they aren't different enough?"

"I need something more real. Like we had a hundred years ago."

"Is that why you gave in so easy?"

"No, it was more than that. You've never been such a bastard about the whole thing, it was different. And okay because it was you. No one else would have gotten away with that."

"Familiarity breeds contempt."

"Sometimes it breeds contentment."

"But not enough to want to stay."

She turned over and faced him. "Rolly, I can't help but love you and I will love you for the rest of my life. You're imprinted on me like no one else will be. But I can't do this anymore. We know each other too well, we have too many habits we keep repeating. I've used up this life. It's time to find a new one. It's not about you so don't take it personally."

"It is about me. You want a divorce. How can it not be?"

"Okay, yeah, it is about you a little. We're two different people Rolly. We have only one left thing in common. You're just as tired of me."

"Maybe. But we're stuck with each other. The Corporament will never let us divorce."

"I don't know. When all this ends, the travel I mean, there'll be no reason to stay married. Anything could happen."

"You shouldn't try to stop me from going home."

"Why not?"

"No better excuse for a divorce than 'My husband's gone off the deep end.' Let me go and I will make them miserable. Tell them you can't reason with me, that I'm crazy determined and won't give up. They'll get sick of chasing me and grant your divorce."

Stephanie said nothing but seemed unconvinced. Their split was real if not official. Three more escape attempts later--including a surprisingly easy motorcycle trip through South and Central America--Rolly and Stephanie ended up on Antigua, an ideal Caribbean island, the perfect gilded cage for an annoyingly persistent client.

The picture was this: Rolly sitting on a covered patio, sipping a daiquiri in the early morning, looking out over the ocean. A picture of contentment. A picture they wanted to see. Rolly thought the view wasted on him. He felt unfulfilled, like he hadn't earned it. His old life was incomplete. A single minded focus on retirement had robbed him of any real experience. He could not bring himself to enjoy the trappings Malone and the handlers provided. He could only see the cage and not the luxury, and could not rest until the balance, the satisfaction, had been restored. That meant going back home to Nola.

They're making new plans for us. Who knows where we might end up? China? New Zealand? Antarctica again? Or the top of the world this time, the Arctic? Rolly had a plan he hoped would get him to the East Coast. They had been on Antigua a week now. It was time to get started.

Rolly picked up the daiquiri, took a long delicious drink, and put the glass back down.

On the other side of the camera, in his Atlanta office, Roy Tompkins wondered what Mr. Rolly Smalls was up to.

29

It's Not A Squirrel Burger

Roy Tompkins was having lunch with David Robb, the semi-famous movie director, who seemed normal but had just veered into crazyland.

"We're way too life oriented. We need to learn to embrace death again. You should give up EverLife." Mr. Robb had been lamenting the narrow, immortal-centric state of the world, describing how he had given up EverLife for a year and how being so near death was an exhilarating experience. Mr. Robb hadn't stopped talking since his arrival. "It'll make you really appreciate living."

Roy had been led to believe he would be watching the director at work on a movie set. Instead they were sitting in a booth in a Best Burger chain restaurant in the perfectly nice town of Glendale, east of Hollywood. It smelled like oily fries--like every other Best Burger in the country and throughout history. In the playhouse three small children were running around.

The mothers of those children kept a wary eye on Roy and Mr. Robb. There had been an uncomfortable fifteen minutes while Roy waited for the director to arrive. Few things are as troublesome for a man as sitting alone in a fast food joint with only mothers and children for company. Especially in an EverLife world that elevated licensed mothers to near divine status. A sour look from one could bring the Thought Police running. Roy tried to keep busy playing games on his HearSay, but a mother still complained to the counter help. Roy assumed he was about to be thrown out.

David Robb arrived in the nick of time, justifying Roy's presence and mitigating his suspicious aloneness. Roy forgot where he was and stood to greet Mr. Robb, embarrassing himself by slamming his crotch into the immovable table. David Robb found this amusing. Roy thought *This is why people have meetings at real restaurants, with real tables and chairs.* The mothers kept watch.

"Nanobot batteries last about a year."

David Robb looked shocked. "If that were true we wouldn't get renewed every three months."

"Three months is how long they work at peak power. After that it's downhill. Takes a year to completely run down, but they still function."

"It's not about the nanobots. It's about giving up that crutch, living life without worrying about your next renewal."

"When was your last renewal?"

"Two weeks ago."

"Less than a year since you stopped. Your nanobots were still working, on reduced power. You were in real danger at the end. Thank god you're all right."

Mr. David Robb, down on his luck movie director and wannabe societal savior, skewered Roy with an angry look. Roy had never been good at hiding sarcasm.

"So this project you have. Is there a decent budget?"

David Robb's most successful movie was a historical/action/romance piece called *The Terrorist* about a heroic Arab freedom fighter and the American woman who loves him. The evil United States government relentlessly tries to kill the main character, whose only sin is a single minded wish to save his homeland. That only an American woman could understand him was an ironic twist David Robb seemed proud of.

"It gave the story so much depth," he said in many interviews.

The old United States government had been vilified by the Corporament since its collapse eleven decades ago. Blamed for economic mismanagement, poor regulation of EverLife (causing overpopulation), citizen oppression, or any problems the Corporament wanted to disavow. The old government was used as scapegoat so much it had become a joke, making it a perfect villain for David Robb movies.

The popularity of *The Terrorist* tagged David Robb as a master of the historical action thriller genre, emphasis on historical. Critics called him an *auteur* and raved over his films.

In a ten year career he made a dozen films, two of which attained semi-popular status. *Coming Out Party,* set in 2005, focused on a gay Congressman's attempt to keep his sexuality hidden. At the end of the movie he proudly declares his homosexuality on the Senate floor. In response every member of the Senate stands up one by one and says "I'm homosexual too." Two years later he scored another hit with *The Ascent* about a rebellious young man whose hobby is climbing skyscrapers and unfurling banners in support of capitalism. He happens to arrive in New York on September 11, 2001 with all his climbing gear. His girlfriend trapped on the upper floors of the World Trade Center, the hero scales the outside of one building and using an intricate array of ropes (so intricate it made no sense) swings his girlfriend to safety as the building collapses.

Since then David Robb's career had tanked, his last two movies failing to recover their cost. He needed a job, would work cheap and seemed qualified for their project.

Roy hated everything David Robb ever committed to film. Loathed each and every one. Could not come up with enough adjectives to describe the contempt he felt for the collective works of David Robb. Roy had lived through the events this fool was dramatizing. He thought the movies of David Robb were amateurish, an insult to history and the people who lived and died in those times. Clearly David Robb was from a younger generation, which only added to Roy's disgust. So Roy took great pleasure in poking holes in David Robb's death idealism. It was amazingly easy to do.

"It's an adequate budget. It's enough."

David Robb raised his eyebrows in doubt and was about to speak when a pretty girl in an ill fitting uniform approached, a concerned mother watching from the safety of the front counter.

Before she could speak David said, "Thanks for coming over. I'll have the double squirrel burger with cheese, a large fry and a large orange soda with a finger of whiskey."

She looked confused. This was a fast food joint and she was not a waitress. Her name tag read Chelsea. Chelsea fell back on the reply she had been most trained give.

"It's not a squirrel burger." Only the wealthy could afford actual ground beef. Various bloggers claimed the burgers at Best Burger were made of either squirrel, mouse, rat, vole, hedgehog, mole, raccoon, groundhog, rabbit, porcupine, beaver or whatever small mammal was popular that week. Speculating on what the burgers might be made of was more palatable than contemplating what they were *actually* made of.

"You're very pretty. You should be auditioning for the movies."

Chelsea brightened and started talking about the auditions she had been to, burgers and mothers forgotten. She was young, not just youthful, like every User. Roy thought of it as new, as in brand new human. She couldn't have been more than twenty in actual years, maybe less, as yet untouched by EverLife's chemical concoction. If she were lucky she might get preserved soon. For this moment she was true youth with that natural...what was it? Roy couldn't say but it was some capricious essence no one else had. A smoothness to the features? The way they moved? The tone of voice? All of the above and more? Roy didn't know but true youth always stood out.

David Robb ended the conversation by writing Chelsea's name on a napkin and promising an audition for his next movie. Elated, Chelsea went back to the counter to get his food. Roy heard a muffled argument between Chelsea and a manager which ended with her saying "I'll pay for it." David Robb didn't seem to notice.

"Why are we meeting at Best Burger anyway?"

"Ever since the great mouse bought Hollywood--the entire city of Hollywood--it's become a cesspool of backstabbing, rumor mongering bastards. Everyone spying for someone else, looking for inside info, trying to catch a celebrity out being normal. Have a meeting in the usual places and you'll be a HearSay star from ten different angles. Out here we're free from prying eyes, no sideways glances, no eavesdropping, no whispering."

"You're embarrassed to be seen with me."

"Not at all. It's better if we have a serene environment to meet in." A toddler screamed, then giggled.

"Mr. Robb, it doesn't matter where we meet, or what your friends in the industry think. You've accepted our offer and a good faith payment. I'm here to make sure you're the right man for the job."

"I'm the only man for the job." From burned to cocky. Roy was slightly impressed.

"Prove it."

"First, the information you sent had a production budget. How flexible is that number?"

"It's not. Once the money is gone the project will end, no matter where it stands."

"We might have to cut some corners."

"Is that a problem?"

"Necessity is the mother of invention." David Robb forced a smile.

"What's your plan."

"Seems obvious. Your man is down chilling in the Caribbean. Your psych evals say he needs fulfillment, to feel he's accomplished something. You want to give him an adventure. Pirates."

"Pirates?"

"Modern pirates of course. Not the mast and schooner kind. With speedboats and automatic rifles. We find some tiny island or mysterious cove and set up a base, get your man there and have him face off with villainous pirates."

"Okay, but not in the Caribbean. I want him back home in Michigan."

"Michigan? Great Lakes pirates?"

"I've never heard of any Great Lakes pirates. Let me ask." Roy named his HearSay Major. It said "Yes sir?" in a deep rumbling voice.

"Pirates on the Great Lakes. Tell me about them."

Roy repeated what Major said, with some editing. "Piracy in the Great Lakes peaked in the late 1800s through the early 1900s into Prohibition...most famous pirate was Roaring Dan Seavey...rumored to have destroyed a boat full of rival pirates killing everyone on board...may have killed several other men in bar brawls...hijacked the *Nellie Johnson* and sailed it away by himself...stole cargo from other ships by changing buoy lights and making them run aground...made most of his money by poaching deer and running guns and alcohol...and prostitutes...loved children...later became a United States Marshal."

"Colorful guy. Any buried treasure?"

"Nope."

"Not a lot to work with. Pirates and the Great Lakes don't go together."

"But there is precedent. It's not out of the question."

"What are these pirates going to do? Run illegal venison across Lake Michigan?" Which actually made some sense since deer were as scarce cows. They both looked down at David's burger.

"No, kidnapping. In the early twenty-first century African pirates kidnapped people for ransom."

"Your HearSay tell you that?"

"I was alive then."

"Maybe I should make a movie about this Roaring Dan."

Roy scowled. "Good idea. And you can be as historically accurate as you want."

David squinted at Roy, who remained stoic. "So you want your guy to be kidnapped?"

"I have someone else in mind."

The remainder of the conversation was a mix of on-the-spot improvisation and negotiation. As they brainstormed David Robb lost his skepticism and began to describe scenes he imagined in detail. He had that faraway look in his eye, but stayed grounded enough to keep asking for more money. Not for himself. For the project. Roy offered to raise his fee but the director said no, if Roy wanted a passable adventure he needed more money. Roy felt this might be some kind of scam--that Robb would somehow skim money for himself--but couldn't see the angle. He agreed to take the request back to his bosses.

David Robb had exuberance like a virus, infecting everyone around him. A quirk that likely made him a good director, along with a heaping pile of salesmanship. Roy almost began to believe this could work, but not quite. His doubts were too ingrained to be easily set aside.

Roy's future hinged on the success of this project. That meant Rolly Smalls had to buy into it all the way. The full suspension of disbelief. Roy did not believe Mr. Smalls was that gullible. He knew people like Rolly, had known them his entire life. They were, after all, from the same generation, the first EverLife Users.

Roy called his boss, Bruce Ashbaugh, knowing he would get everything he needed. He had been doing this job way too long. It was a voice only call.

"Yes pirates. He wants to do pirates. On the Great Lakes."

"Is there something wrong with that?"

"There's no real history of piracy on the Great Lakes. A couple of semi-legends and folk tales. Nothing more. It's a far fetched idea."

"I love it though. It's unexpected but kind of makes sense too. Who'd uv thunk it?"

"No one really."

"This won't put him near his home city will it? Didn't he used to live in the middle of the state?"

"That's right. Out on the water he won't be anywhere near home. He doesn't have any sailing experience either."

"Jeez, lives in a state that's practically floating and doesn't know a thing about boats. Can he swim?"

"No idea."

"Whatever. Someone can fish him out if he sinks. This is great. A place that's familiar and not. Make him comfortable and throw him off at the same time. Smalls won't be expecting any of this. You're a genius Roy. Good job."

"Thanks Mr. Ashbaugh. There's still the issue of the budget. Robb says he needs more money. I've told him we can't move on the amount, but he's insistent."

"How much more does he need?"

"Twenty percent."

"How much will that leave?"

"Next to nothing."

Silence, while Bruce considered. "This is the best chance we've got to make this work. Even if it fails we'll learn something. How many tries does Robb think he can get?"

"One, maybe two. No more than that."

"Okay. Take it as far as you can. Document everything, what went right, what went wrong. If this pans out you might find yourself a whole new career."

"I appreciate that. Thanks Mr. Ashbaugh."

The dutiful call ended, Roy sat back and stared across an expanse of stucco houses. He had been stuck in the trenches too long looking up, watching executives work. Bruce Ashbaugh believed he had made a bold decision but it was typical management myopia: easy to spend money that wasn't your own, damn the consequences. Bruce was skilled in office politics and not much else. When this project went south he would be first to blame Roy.

———————

Roy had one more stop on this side of the country before heading home. An official Paragon vehicle took him deep into the San Joaquin valley. At a serious iron gate he flashed his credentials at a guard who looked unhappy. After an exchange of HearSay verifications the gate opened.

As he went up the drive, guards in black suits carrying rifles watched him pass. At the front door two uniformed guards with sunglasses and belt holsters walked away, pretending they didn't see him. Paragon had preplanned this trip, making it clear to security they were to let Roy pass or face a charge of Corporament infringement, punishable by a thirty year loss of EverLife.

Roy knocked on the door every few seconds for the next five minutes. He expected this. The owner was not used to greeting visitors himself, but would have no choice since his interior security people were now on a convenient break.

He heard loud commands from inside that were not answered, growing in frustration. The squeak of athletic shoes on marble coming closer. The latch turned and the door opened and there stood the man he was looking for.

"Who the hell are you and how did you get this far?"

"Hello Mr. Max Smalls. It's nice to meet you at last. Can we talk?"

30

The Left Side Of The Machine

Assumptions were their weakness, Rolly decided. Malone and the handlers thought they could predict what he would do, that he wouldn't be bold enough to try anything beyond the usual travel methods. Of course he had never given them a reason to think otherwise. A hundred and fifty two years of following the rules will give you that kind of reputation. Rolly chose not to think of this as compliant behavior, instead it was a long and clever setup for this moment. Man how he had fooled them!

Joking and self-delusion aside, Rolly knew his chances were slim no matter how far outside his comfort zone he wandered. They knew where he was every second of every day. They could watch him on every camera he walked by. They could listen to him snore every night. He doubted there were that many cameras on Antigua, it being a sovereign country outside the United Syndicates of America, but it was better to be paranoid than careless.

All Rolly's staring at the ocean and thinking had brought him to one clear answer: he was screwed. There was no way to plan an escape when your opponent knew everything about you and you knew nothing about them. He imagined various elaborate scenarios, all ending with him being marched back to this patio to continue enjoying the wonderful view.

His only option was pure desperation: lull them into complacency then make a run for it and hope he caught them off guard. Keep trying until it worked. If typing monkeys could eventually recreate the works of Shakespeare then time was in his favor. He had at least a thousand years to find that magic moment, glorified monkey that he was.

Except Nola didn't have that long. Once back in Michigan he would get her an EverLife treatment. Maybe two. He might have to hit her over the head and drag her to a Renewal Station but it was better than doing nothing. She would thank him later.

Money. He needed lots of money. EverLife was expensive and paying off technicians more so. Malone and the handlers controlled Rolly's money, dolling out weekly stipends on MiniVaults. Rolly could never get the thing to fit in his wallet it was so thick, but it was a marvel of extreme precaution: a silver square on the front read your fingerprint, a rough feeling mint flavored patch on the back tested your DNA, and a small camera on the side scanned your retina. Just look, touch and lick it in all the right spots and spend away. Sean could communicate with the card wirelessly. He said it lacked personality.

MiniVaults were ubiquitous, hanging on racks at every store on the island. Rolly had been using his Corporament supplied MiniVault to buy his own pre-filled MiniVaults. In smaller denominations at first, and when he had a collection, using those to buy larger denominations.

Watching Rolly lick his twelfth MiniVault a shopkeeper in the seedier part of town said, "You trying to hide money?"

Was this his second or third time in this store? Rolly couldn't remember.

"No, I like to collect them."

"How many you got? Twenty or thirty? I know a guy who can help."

Hiding money was a crime in every country in the world. Obviously he wasn't very good at it. Hooking up with a criminal sounded like a good idea. They would have ways of working where watchful eyes weren't looking.

"Sean, shut down now."

"Yeah dude. Whatever you want."

Rolly got around the island in a rental car, a mini two seater that looked like a squashed kiwi. The shopkeeper sent him to a place on Mt. Obama road. Rolly drove up and down six times without finding what he was looking for. Parked on the side, wondering if he was being played for a fool, Rolly spotted a set of overgrown tracks leading into the brush. He got out of the car followed them to a hidden shack. A man named Daglesh greeted him, not happily. Rolly dropped the shopkeeper's name and was invited inside.

Daglesh was small and thin with a mop of grey curly hair and deeply tanned and wrinkled skin. His eyes were wide open like a nocturnal rat on the lookout for predators. Rolly took him for a native but Daglesh spoke English like an American. A pile of still-in-the-package souvenirs sat on a table. Rolly pulled a stack of MiniVaults from his pocket and laid them next to the souvenirs.

"They know about those. Doesn't matter how many you have. You're not going to save your money that way." Daglesh said "save" like it was a rescue instead of a responsible financial choice.

"Then how come they haven't taken them away?"

"They don't care how you spend your money. As long as you spend it. Probably stop you when you try to leave."

"What makes you think I want to leave?"

"Think you're the first? Trying to get back to the USA I bet."

"Yeah."

"And you need lots of money to get there."

"Yeah."

"You're a fool, but I can help you with both."

"How are you going to do that?"

"With this." Daglesh presented yet another card, blue with raised numbers, worn and frayed on the edges. It looked as old as Rolly. "This is an enhanced money card." Daglesh turned it around. What looked like a piece of white paper was taped to the back of it, but not over the magnetic strip. "Doesn't have all the security features and it doesn't link to any bank account. All your money is saved right here on this card. The Corporament thinks it's just another MiniVault. Use it to buy stuff, add money to it, everything you normally do with a MiniVault." He touched the paper and a small keyboard glowed into view. "When you're ready enter the code to lock it out and make it disappear from their monitors. Your money is yours again. But lose it, get it wet, break it in any way, and it's all gone."

"Can the Corporament access it before I enter the code?"

"Of course. Have to hide in plain sight."

"What about after it's locked? Is it gonna work if the Corporament hasn't sanctioned it?"

"Money spends everywhere. Stores don't care where it comes from."

"Sounds risky. Not sure I wanna do this."

Daglesh scowled at him. "You want to get out of here? You have to take some risks."

"What's it called?"

Daglesh scowled again. "A money card."

"That's the best you could come up with?"

"It's a card with money on it. Do I look like a marketing genius?"

Rolly wanted to say yeah, that *would* make me feel better, then reminded himself where he was: out of the normal and into the shadowy. He was sure Daglesh considered him a loser.

"You said I'm not the first. How many people have done this before?"

"Lost count years ago. Hundreds maybe."

"How many were successful?"

"Don't know. I never see them again. I just take their money and make it happen."

"Can you get me off this island?"

"Save your money first. Then we'll see."

"How do I do that? How do I move money from one card to another?"

"Bring them to me. My machine will do it."

Daglesh pushed aside the souvenirs, knocking some to the floor, and pulled a black rectangle from behind a wooden model of a sail boat. He set the rectangle on another table where Rolly could see it better. The finish was rough, not smooth, a piece of plastic to his eyes. Daglesh pressed a button on the side and a shrill whine filled the room then faded away, leaving nothing, not even an LED to indicate it was on.

Daglesh brought out two MiniVaults, one empty, one with ten dollars. "The money moves from left to right, like reading. Put the giving card on the left and the receiving card on the right," Daglesh pressed them to either side of the rectangle, "and voilà, your money is moved." He held the cards up to show Rolly.

"Only banks are supposed to have those."

Daglesh sighed in irritation. "You want to hide money or not?"

"Yes."

"Stop asking dumb questions."

"It wasn't--"

"There's a fee every time I move money. Ten percent."

"That's pretty steep. Even banks don't charge that much."

Daglesh looked at him, tired of answering.

Rolly persisted, haggling over the fee, Daglesh pointing out he had the only machine on the island not owned by a bank, Rolly saying he was just holding cards up to a piece of plastic and how much work was that? Finally Rolly got him to agree to seven percent on the condition he move large sums and not just pocket change.

Over the next few weeks Rolly moved as much money as he could, spending little. Malone and the handlers seemed content to leave him on Antigua. Stephanie was island hopping; Malone only made brief appearances to bring new MiniVaults. During these visits Rolly would press for more money. He wanted to get his own fishing boat. A new jet ski. A new pair of glasses that could interact with his HearSay. Sean was excited to hear that, but it was not to be. The deal always fell through, or the device wasn't compatible, or there was something better and he really needed a little more money to purchase the latest and greatest thing.

Rolly was making the trek to Daglesh's shack several times a week, a fact Daglesh took advantage of, asking Rolly to pick up groceries and other necessities--toilet paper, canned food, a new hat. Like he was back toiling for Stableman Insurance, a slave to someone else's whims. Daglesh repaid him for everything purchased but Rolly felt he should be paid for his trouble. They argued again--you're coming here anyway, I have to go out of my way to get this stuff--etcetera, blah and yada. Eventually Daglesh agreed to pay Rolly an extra three percent of every receipt for his trouble. It wasn't much, a few extra dollars, but Rolly did get the satisfaction of seeing Daglesh's personal card on the left side of the machine.

––––––––––––

To get off this island Rolly needed smugglers with a boat. All the planes and ferries were monitored; the pleasure boats in the marina were owned by tight cliques of wealthy people who herded together like leery water buffalo whenever a stranger approached. Rolly felt more welcome among the criminals. Smuggling meant drugs and Rolly thought drug smugglers were a particularly repellent human.

The illicit drug of choice went by the name Zounds or sometimes Knee Jerk, or EverLife Gold or Golden Years Get Off or just Gygo; the names were endless and nonsensical. Zounds was a yellow liquid injected or mixed in a drink, depending on how intense the User wanted the experience to be. The EverLife Company originally created and marketed it as NanoFuel, sold over the counter in small controlled doses. It gave the nanomachines a temporary boost of energy during an emergency, at the end of their three month life cycle, or when a User wanted a quick "jump up." The effect on the nanobots was compared to a "human chugging liquid cocaine."

With the nanobots in hyper mode the User's blood flowed faster, nerve endings became more sensitive, synapses made connections faster. Depending on the dose it made everything the body experienced a hundred times more intense. Colors more vivid, smells more savory, touch more stimulating. Memories would become clearer and less fragmented and long buried memories might pop up as vivid and detailed as last year's hit movie. This could be good or bad. During a Zounds trip it was not unusual to find Users weeping. Once remembered, not easily forgotten.

NanoFuel became a controlled substance when it was alleged to cause "instant cancer." Telomerase, one of the enzymes used by EverLife, had the contrary properties of extending life and being a known carcinogen. Telomerase had to be administered in the right amounts for each particular patient. Under certain circumstances the amped up overzealous nanomachines could destroy this delicate balance causing healthy cells to turn malignant. Detecting this, other equally frenzied nanomachines would attempt to eliminate the cancer only to create an accelerating cycle. A lung or kidney or some other organ or tissue might go from perfect to cancerous in a few hours. A quick trip to a hospital or Renewal Center would save the User, but if he or she fell asleep, say after an intense sexual encounter, they would not know the cancer was growing, and wake up in agony, or not at all.

That's what Rolly heard on the news. *Another instant cancer death has been reported in... Authorities in Battle Creek say a man in his one tens and a female companion succumbed to...* Reported like an epidemic. The public concern was great. Bowing to pressure the EverLife Company voluntarily took NanoFuel off the shelf, making it available only through Renewal Centers. Almost the same day the yellow liquid appeared everywhere. Street corner hustlers, bartenders, your latest lover, even hot dog vendors sold it out of their carts.

No deaths had been reported since the drug was banned, though Rolly knew it was more popular than ever. All his friends and lovers claimed to have used it at least once, some multiple times, and in very high doses. He mentioned this to Stephanie.

"It's another income stream for EverLife. Nobody's going to touch that."

"What's the point of making it illegal? Why not sell it through the usual drugstores?"

"Honey, it's a drug. Nobody would want it if it wasn't illegal."

Okay then. Stephanie went on to tell him who sold it, where it could be found UTC (under the counter), the proper way to measure doses, the various grades and how to tell them apart. Rolly tried not to wonder how his wife was so knowledgable on the subject.

So, Rolly needed a Zounds smuggler. Once word got out he was looking and had money the smugglers came to him. Most didn't speak English. They would take one look, shake their heads and leave. He didn't know why until Daglesh explained it.

"It's your HearSay. They don't wanna be tracked." The spirals on the sides of his neck. He forgot they were there.

"I planned on turning it off."

"Doesn't make any difference. They think it can be tracked on or off."

"That's not true. When it's off, it's off. Can't do anything when it's off."

"Smugglers are paranoid."

"I thought smugglers were risk takers."

"You think they do this for fun? They're criminals, not the brightest bunch, so they're scared of making dumb mistakes. And taking you, in their minds, is a dumb mistake."

"How the hell am I gonna get off this island?"

"There is one guy who doesn't care about tracking. He's out on a run. Not back until next week. I'll put you in touch with his brother."

Daglesh gave him a name and phone number and told him to call from the hotel, to not use his HearSay. Said the brother would know if it was a HearSay call.

Back home in-room phones and complimentary local calls had gone the way of phone booths. Here on Antigua the rooms still had wireless handsets routed through the hotel's automated system.

Rolly made the call and introduced himself, dropped Daglesh's name and laid out what he needed. The brother went by the name of Le Clerc. He spoke with a French accent.

"Passage to America is six hundred thousand dollars."

"I can do that. But you should know I have a stereo HearSay."

"Cool. Stereo even. Is it on now?"

"No, it's off."

"Smart man. No problem. You pay me money and I arrange passage."

"No. I pay half now, half when we get to America."

"Suit yourself. Le Capitan will be here next week. Be ready to go."

"Le Capitan?"

"My brother. Here's where you send the money." They arranged a transfer to a local bank, into an account named "Les Frères Fishing Tours." It wasn't a huge amount but Rolly wasn't ready to give it up without seeing what he was getting. He told Le Clerc he would send it when they were on the boat and not a second before.

Le Clerc grunted. "You not trust me?"

"No I don't."

"We don't stay in business long if we not trustworthy and you not first rich American refugee we take home. We have better reputation than you. I will call when we ready to go. I expect money be moved then. No money, no boat."

"You'll get your money. Daglesh can vouch for me."

"We know Daglesh, you just *voyageur*. When I call, be on time. Bring little, no more than shoulder bag. No backpacks! And something to read. It's a long trip."

31

Too Much For Too Little

"The location stinks," David Robb said. He and Roy Tompkins were standing on the edge of a river that drained into Lake Michigan. The banks were steep and covered with tall weedy grass, a twenty-five foot climb down to the water from where they stood. David judged the opposite bank to be a hundred feet away, maybe more. The river flowed through this mini canyon and out into the lake, which he could see off to the right, blue and serene.

Global warming had radically lowered the water level of the Great Lakes. Consistent warmth, evaporation, a lack of winter snow and lake ice, all meant the lakes lost more water than was replenished. As the water fell, the river was dredged ever deeper so vacationers could get their boats through.

That was decades ago. Now both banks were lined with rows of abandoned houses. Several sets of wooden stairs led down to the river--some straight down, some zig zagging--but only halfway. David could see two wooden docks, paint long gone, weathered and gray, jutting out into open space. Other docks had fallen onto the grassy bank, overgrown and rotting. He thought the place reeked of decay. Roy thought it was great.

"Look over there, under that tree." Roy pointed to a spot upriver where a large willow obscured most of the bank and part of the water. "There's an old cutout, like a parking space for a boat. Can't see it from here. You could hide a pirate vessel in it." The word *vessel* sounded odd, like Roy had spoken a foreign language.

"Where are all the people?"

"They left for the cities years ago."

"Why?"

"Because that's where EverLife is. This is the perfect pirate cove. Protected, easy access to the lake, lots of buildings to store loot in, the nearest road is ten miles away. We're basically out in the middle of nowhere."

"It's plain. A bunch of overgrown trees and a river full of weeds and muck. There's nothing dramatic, no visual appeal. No interesting architecture. Old cottages and rickety stairs. That's it."

"Seems like the perfect pirate cove," Roy repeated.

"Don't you know anything about location scouting? There's a light-house down the coast, sits on a cliff overlooking the lake. Man, the kind of shots I could get of a place like that."

"That doesn't make sense, pirates in a lighthouse. Besides, the land is privately owned. They want too much money."

"You didn't try hard enough."

"I didn't try at all. I called and got a price and said never mind. That's why you're here. Do what you do and turn this into a pirate cove." Roy seemed obsessed with the word "cove" which annoyed David.

"You know what has to happen to make this work? All these houses have to be fixed and made to look pirate-y. We need a barbed wire fence around the whole area. This old wood has to go, a new dock has to be built, with a boathouse, preferably painted black. Is the river deep enough to get a boat through? All this overgrown grass has to be mowed and trimmed--"

"Why would pirates care about mowing the grass?"

"Who cares what pirates *might* do? You're taking this too literal. Neat and efficient is more menacing than sloppy and ugly. Make the pirates look like they know what they're doing and you put the protagonist in greater jeopardy. Moviemaking 101. Sloppy pirates don't cut it."

"Sounds like your creative juices are flowing."

David frowned. "The problem with bad locations is yeah, I can turn it into something, but it will cost as much or more than a better location."

"What was it you said to me? Necessity is the mother of invention? Well get inventing. Prove you're worth the money we're paying you."

"You know you're enough of a bastard to actually be a movie producer."

"I'll take that as a compliment."

Until now the days on Antigua had flown by. Since talking to Le Clerc time had ground to a halt and moved with all the motivation of a depressed turtle.

Rolly worried Le Clerc would turn him in. He worried Malone would confront him. He worried the handlers knew about the bogus MiniVault. That Le Clerc and his brother would leave him behind. That he was too late. How would Le Clerc contact him? He hadn't given him his HearSay number. The man knew where he was staying but was that enough? Maybe he should call Le Clerc, see what was happening.

At the same time he was trying to be cool, in spite of his brooding, to avoid undue attention from Malone. Rolly went about his business as laid back as he could--walking the town, sitting on the beach, eating delicious food--without trying seem laid back. Rolly was not a person for whom coolness was a natural state. He needed something constructive to occupy his mind. The only activity that provided any fulfillment were his trips to Daglesh, moving money from card to card and acting as his errand boy. It was something to do. Daglesh was not a fount of assurance however.

"They'll be here. They know better than to stiff someone. At least on purpose."

"What's that mean?"

"Sometimes smugglers get caught. Those two take pride in their reputation but even they have to deal with the authorities sometimes. Everybody wants their pound of flesh, you know? You just have to wait. I need sugar and toothpaste. And chocolate chip cookies. Bring those next time."

Rolly went back to his cottage by the sea and watched the ocean, made breakfast, and lunch, and dinner, and watched tv, and read a book, then another, swept the floor, lay in the sand, tried to talk to the new Spanish neighbors (didn't go so well), slept, pissed and shat his way through the next nine days, all while trying to be the epitome of cool. Which he was not.

On Wednesday Rolly noted that Stephanie had been away longer than usual. They hadn't been separated more than three days since retiring. Malone kept them together as much as possible. Rolly wasn't worried, they had been apart far longer and Stephanie knew how to take care of herself, but he preferred knowing where she was.

Le Clerc called that night. "Meet me at Half Moon Bay Beach, seven o'clock tomorrow."

"In the morning?"

"Of course. You think I want to be driving the boat at night?"

"How will I find you?"

"Ha! I'll be the hairy guy standing on an empty beach waiting to take a sentimental American back home."

Rolly packed a bag--two changes of clothes, some toiletries, and his illicit MiniVault--then laid in bed all night watching the ceiling fan turn.

Half Moon Bay Beach was on the other side of the island, about a fourteen mile drive. Traffic wouldn't be an issue that early but Rolly intended to leave with time to spare. He double checked the MiniVault-- still in his bag, ready to go. At six fifteen Rolly opened the door to find Malone waiting.

"Hey Malone." It wasn't normal for Malone to arrive this early.

"Hello Mr. Smalls. Do you have a moment?" Malone always spoke formally. Rolly guessed it was a way for them to stay consistent.

"Actually no. I'm taking off and Steph isn't here."

Malone smiled. They were good at this, it never looked forced. "Mrs. Smalls is back on the mainland, in your home state."

"What?"

"She requested a trip home to visit Mackinac Island. Said she had a craving for 'real fudge.'"

"You let her go without asking me?"

"Given your recent history we didn't think it wise."

"Uh-huh."

"You have plans today? Doing something fun I hope."

"Fishing trip. Chartered a boat with some other tourists."

Malone looked at his shoulder bag. "You don't have any fishing gear."

"Provided by the charter company. We're just a bunch of dumb tourists ya know." Was Malone suspicious? Checking up on him?

"How long will you be gone?"

"All day. Probably not back until evening."

"I was hoping the three of us could have a HearSay chat about our next destination."

"What did you have in mind?"

"I was thinking India and an elephant safari through the Kaziranga National Park."

They had been through India twice. Elephants were not hard to find. The few remaining were all on display in Kaziranga. "That sounds really interesting Malone. Maybe we can talk about it tonight."

"Should I set up a time with Mrs. Smalls?"

"Sure. The charter should be back by six. Let's make it eight o'clock to be safe. See you!"

Rolly waved to Malone as he was leaving. It took effort to appear friendly and grace it with a smile because Rolly really wanted to strangle Malone for letting Stephanie go while keeping him on a leash.

Rolly arrived at Half Moon Bay seven minutes early. Sure enough, on the empty beach stood a large man in shorts, Hawaiian shirt and a tattered straw hat. Rolly was eager to leave. The handlers would be tracking him and maybe growing suspicious.

Rolly approached Le Clerc and they shook hands. A small speedboat with a green and white striped canopy was anchored a hundred feet offshore. They waded out to it and climbed in.

Le Clerc pulled out a simple cell phone (non-HearSay) and made a call, punching in an interminable series of numbers. Looking annoyed, he dropped the phone from his ear and stared at Rolly.

"What?"

"You going to move money or not?"

"Oh. Sorry. Sean?"

"Yes, my liege."

"No, do it manually."

"Never mind Sean."

"Okay. We're good man."

Rolly pulled out his interface and went through his own series of interminable numbers.

Phone to his ear again, Le Clerc smiled and said "Good. Now turn that thing off."

"Sean, shut down."

"Buh-bye."

"Are you shut down?"

"Yes."

"Off we go."

Rolly looked around. It was a small motorboat, maybe twenty feet long. Well-used and dingy. It seemed inadequate for a long sea voyage.

"We're going all the way to the USA in this?"

Le Clerc looked as if Rolly had insulted his mother. "No. That would be stupid. We meet Le Capitan and he take you to America."

"He has a bigger boat?"

"Definitely."

———————————

Le Clerc guided the boat out of the harbor on low power, then sped up, nose rising out of the water, heading due east. Rolly knew nothing about navigation but did know the USA was northwest, opposite the direction they were going. If Le Clerc intended to take his money and make him disappear, the middle of the Atlantic would be a good place to do it.

With Antigua a ridge on the horizon, Le Clerc slowed and shut down the engine. Lazily, he tied eight small tires to the gunwale. "We wait," he said, "Could be awhile. Maybe hour or two."

The sea was calm, the boat gently swayed. Le Clerc lounged on one of the benches molded into the side of the boat, staring at Rolly.

"Where you from?"

"America."

Le Clerc looked offended. "I know that. What part?"

"Sorry, the north, upper midwest. Michigan."

"I've heard of this. The Great Lake state?"

"Yes."

"Surrounded by water."

"On three sides, it's a peninsula. Two peninsulas."

"Sounds like a good place for a sailor. How long you been alive?"

"One hundred and fifty-two years."

"You do much boating on your Great Lake?"

"No, could never afford one."

"Why not? Are not Lifers rich?"

"I've never been rich. I saved my money so I could retire. Buying a boat would have been frivolous."

"What do you do with all this time, living a hundred and fifty two years?"

"Work."

"Work? Like a job?"

"Yeah, everyday."

"That's all you do? You've been given immortality and all you do is work?"

"If you don't go to work you don't get to live forever. You lose EverLife if you quit. If you skip a day it puts you a day away from retirement. You have to work if you want to retire."

"Are you retired?"

"Yes."

"And now I have to smuggle you home."

"It's complicated."

"Naw, it's simple. You give up too much for too little and now you don't know what you want. My brother and I, we take people like you all the time. It's strange, smuggling someone back to their own home. We try to understand, but my brother give up, say count the money and do the job. But I want to know why you do this, why you have to break into your own house. So to speak."

Rolly blurted it out. "All I've been doing since retiring is traveling. That's okay. I like traveling. I like your island. But travel is better when you have a place to go back to. They won't let me have that and I left a daughter back home who needs help and a son I haven't talked to in three years and I don't know why they won't let me go."

"You are not retired, you are a prisoner. Trying to break out of one prison into a different prison. This makes sense to me." It didn't make sense to Rolly, but he didn't want to argue.

Le Clerc looked thoughtful. "Whatever you do they find you. Why go to all this trouble?"

"Because my daughter isn't a Lifer. She's old and sick and I don't know how long she'll last. If I can't help her there are people who can, but they're back home too. They know things I don't and can tell me why retirement is so weird, why I have to be dragged all over the world at someone else's whim and because I want to make it clear that I do what I want to do and go where I want to be."

"Whoa ho! Big talk for the middle of the ocean. You sound like old time pirate. Damn the authorities!"

"You're more pirate than me."

"No, I humble smuggler. Pirating too violent for me. Here, I give you something." Le Clerc pulled a brass tube from a box and tossed it to Rolly. "It's a spyglass. Every decent pirate needs one."

Rolly pulled the telescope out and looked back toward Antigua. It showed the island clearly and seemed sturdy. "Thanks."

"Ah. We get boxes full all the time. For the tourists. Cheap crap they pay too much for. But you get it free." Rolly stowed it in his bag. "Listen, I wish you luck but you should be like me. I am doomed and there is nothing I can do about it. So I live with it. And break the law as much as possible." Le Clerc gave himself a good laugh and laid down on the bench, pulling the hat over his eyes.

Ten minutes later Le Clerc started snoring. An hour passed. Rolly looked out over the Atlantic, at the vast stretch of water and sky without end. When they left the harbor Rolly experienced a pang of anxiety he attributed to a latent fear of water. Looking at the endless horizon he realized it was not the water that scared him, it was the space. So much of his life had been spent surrounded by walls and people the openness of the ocean felt like an expanding void trying to rip him into inconsequential bits.

Rolly sat on the deck and tried to avoid looking at the ocean. He was learning to enjoy the solitude when an alarm began beeping and a light on the console started flashing. Le Clerc roused himself with much complaining, checked his instruments, scanned the ocean.

"He's here," Le Clerc announced, as if everyone's least favorite uncle had arrived.

Rolly looked around but could see nothing. "Where?"

"Coming up to the aft, port side."

Which side was port? Rolly looked behind the boat, scanning left and right, but could see only water and sky. Was Le Clerc short some marbles?

Rolly heard a sudden wash of water to his left and a black tower rose out of the water followed by the rounded curve of a submarine.

"Le Capitan. Right on time. More or less." Le Clerc drove the boat over to the sub and alongside it. Working quickly he flipped open two small doors revealing vertical handles. He tied the boat fast and snugged up against the submarine.

More than twice as long as the boat, the conning tower twelve feet above the hull. Not a large sub, by naval standards, but more than adequate for the needs of a smuggler. It seemed to be well made with a smooth surface, not at all like the homemade subs displayed on the news.

Le Clerc grabbed a hammer and climbed onto the sub. He knelt down and banged on a hatch four times, paused, then twice more. The metal echoed with lifting latches and turning gears and the hatch popped up and swung out.

"Le Capitan!" said Le Clerc.

"Brother!" said a voice from inside the sub. A man in jeans and a red T-shirt climbed out and embraced Le Clerc. Le Capitan was a good six inches shorter than his brother and muscular.

The men spoke in French then someone below began handing up boxes. Le Clerc and Le Capitan loaded them onto the boat, Rolly trying to stay out of the way.

When they were finished Le Clerc said in English "This is your passenger, Rolly Smalls." He said Rolly with a 'lay' on the end.

Le Capitan said "Pleasure," smiled, shook Rolly's hand and nearly crushed it.

"I wasn't expecting a submarine."

"This why we not care if you wear HearSay. Metal hull-" he rapped on the conning tower "-blocks tracking signal. So does water. You safe with us. They not find you."

In Eureka, Kansas, Rhys Hinds was sitting at a computer terminal, watching a dozen slowly moving bright blue dots. The dots were superimposed over a map of the Caribbean, his assigned region. Rhys was a geography lover. While watching the little blue dots he could pull up different maps telling him all sorts of interesting facts. Topography, weather, population, temperature, vegetation, in three dimensions or two, any map he could think of. For Rhys, the little blue dots were a means to an end.

The dot that was east of Antigua disappeared.

This was not unusual, dots disappeared all the time and came back. Protocol was to give them a minute to reappear, then call it in if they didn't. Rhys never had to do this, so he ignored the disappearance in favor of two maps comparing average heat readings across Antigua to the relative density of vegetation.

The minute passed and the dot remained AWOL.

An alarm began gently beeping. The maps would have to wait.

"Emergency call from Kansas." Major's voice vibrated Roy's head like a jackhammer, not a pleasant sensation when he had a headache, caused by a half finished pirate hangout. They didn't even have a boat yet. Roy was in a sour mood.

"Put it through."

"Mr. Tompkins, this is Rhys Hinds from Eureka monitoring station. One of your subjects has dropped off the map."

"Who is it?"

"Roland Smalls."

"Got it." To Major he said, "Close the line and open another. Call the office."

Mikaela answered. Roy could hear activity in the background, as there should be. "Fill me in."

"Mr. Smalls made a run for it this morning. Told Malone he was going fishing and went out on a small charter. The boat sat in the middle of the ocean for two hours before he disappeared. The follow boat is on the way. Hasn't arrived yet."

"Any other contacts in the area where he disappeared?"

"No."

"Who was on the boat with him?"

"One other person, a transient, owner of the boat, Marcel Laurent."

"Where is this boat now?"

"We don't know." That was the wrong answer.

"He wasn't supposed to make his run for at least another week. Explain to me where and why you messed up."

"This charter boat owner--known locally as Le Clerc--is a smuggler. Mostly drugs but occasionally stolen goods and people. He's not flagged in our database, some bureaucrat in New York probably missed it. We really thought Mr. Smalls was on a fishing trip."

"Nobody cares about smugglers. They all work for the Corporament. Mr. Smalls outsmarted us. Wipe his MiniVault. That'll slow him down."

"We tried. We can't access it."

"What?"

"It disappeared the same time he did."

Keeping control of the money was the first rule of client management. Losing it was bad but its impact on the adventure project was potentially disastrous. Yet another aggravation to deal with.

"Do you want to order a regional alert?" That would send retrieval teams to every port from the Gulf of Mexico to New York city. It would also look really bad.

"No, don't do that. Monitor the search team and make sure he hasn't drowned. Then I want *you* to find every known or suspected smuggler on Antigua and Barbuda and create our own database so we don't get caught like this again."

"Yes sir. You don't want to stop him?"

"We know where he's going. He can't sail all the way to Michigan, and he won't take a plane, train or bus. He'll be alone in a vehicle. There's only one way into Michigan by land, from the south, and only a few major highways. One intercept team is enough. Put it in Ohio or Indiana. Once he reappears it'll take a day or two to move north. That'll give the team time to reposition, if needed. They are not to move until I give the order."

"Yes sir. Are you sure we haven't lost him totally?"

"They always come back. Mr. Smalls got lucky. I don't know how but he'll be back. Transfer me to Amelia."

Amelia answered, "Yes sir?"

"Are the subjects ready?"

"They've only just arrived."

"Get them ready ASAP. Mr. Smalls is on the move."

"How much time?"

"Two days."

"Yes sir."

Roy closed the connection and looked down at the obvious boathouse façade. "Goddamn it!" he yelled at no one.

Roy called David Robb, scurrying around somewhere on the lot.

"What now?"

"Your production schedule just got cut short. How soon can you have this thing ready?"

32

Swallowed Whole

Rolly stepped off the tender onto a red brick promenade in Savannah, Georgia, looking like he had spent two days living in a narrow metal tube. More than anything he wanted a shower but needed to keep moving. He looked left and right, expecting a dark suited welcoming committee, but the people walking by wore light khaki pants or shorts and flip-flops, mostly tourists. They paid him no attention. He liked that. It felt free.

Traveling by submarine (or submersible as Le Capitan insisted on calling it) had proven uneventful and miserable. No one stopped them, they moved across the Atlantic quickly, and Le Capitan surfaced for air every few hours, but it stank of sweat and cheap plastic, it was noisy and there was nowhere to sit. The sub was designed to accommodate two crew members, a lot of cargo, and nothing else. Rolly was always in the way and cramped wherever he stood. Le Capitan frowned when he moved around Rolly, and rarely spoke. The one crewman offered Rolly an insincere smile in an attempt to be courteous, but gave up after the first day. Rolly couldn't wait to be back on land.

It was midday. He needed to get out of the city ASAP. "Sean, I need a motorcycle."

"Like Dude, there's a dealership a block south."

"Right." Rolly started walking that way, then stopped. A dealer would want official documents; his driver's license, work ID, who knew what else. Might as well call Malone and say he was in Savannah, come and get me.

"Sean, what about auction sites. Any individuals selling nearby?"

"I got thirty-four people within ten blocks."

"Filter by by condition, very good or better."

"Twenty-five people."

"Filter by touring class only."

"Nine people."

"Show me." Rolly opened his interface and flipped through the pictures, settling on two at a price he was willing to pay. He contacted the owner of one and made arrangements to meet. Harry Blankenship, a Lifer like Rolly, eager to sell his ride, saving for retirement.

"Could never handle the thing right," Harry said, "guess my balance stinks."

It was a Harrier 863 shaft driven electric/gas hybrid in near mint condition except for two dents on the exhaust pipe where Harry hit the ground.

The bike started right up. Rolly rode around the block twice. He offered to pay full asking price and Harry happily accepted. "Don't suppose you have leathers and a helmet?"

"Maybe. If you're willing to pay."

"Let's try 'em on." The leathers were black with a blue stripe down each leg, the helmet matte black and full face. They were tight but okay. Rolly pulled out his illicit MiniVault. "We're gonna have to swipe it, if that's alright."

"Not a problem." Harry ran back to his apartment and returned with a card reader attachment. Money changed accounts. They both signed the electronic title on Harry's HearSay. Rolly signed as Jerome Geiger. Harry wanted to send him a copy but Rolly asked for a printout instead saying he'd feel safer having it in his pocket. Old fashioned you know.

They shook hands and Rolly headed north with Sean providing directions.

———————

As soon as Mr. Smalls climbed out of the submersible his blue dot reappeared in Kansas. Roy was watching on his interface; Mikaela, Amelia and the rest of the team kept track on a wide screen in Atlanta. They witnessed him arrive in Savannah, talk to his HearSay, grab a latte, walk into town, meet Harry Blankenship and buy a motorcycle. Cameras on every building saw Mr. Smalls as he passed. The system tagged him and switched camera views automatically. The team only had to watch.

That Mr. Smalls would choose a motorcycle bothered Roy. In South America he managed to slip away several times, using a motorcycle, a fact Roy thought Mr. Smalls was unaware of. Apparently their client was more perceptive than they realized. This did not bode well for the project and his willingness to buy into it. But did it matter? Would their ruse be *that* compelling? Roy didn't think so. Subconsciously Mr. Smalls would know something wasn't right but he still had to choose. Funny how it came down to real or pretend--not right or wrong. Kind of summed up everything nicely. Mr. Smalls could pretend to be happy or end up really miserable.

Mikaela popped up in a small window on Roy's screen. "What do you want us to to do?"

"Make sure the intercept team is in place, that they know he's on a motorcycle, and which highway he ends up taking. Monitor him every minute of every day. Tell the intercept team if he gets by again there will be absolute fucking hell to pay. We've got work to do but his underwater jaunt gave us extra time. We'll be ready."

———————

Rolly crossed through Georgia, Tennessee, Kentucky and into Indiana with no trouble. Overnight he stayed in a motel and had a wonderful shower in a rusty tub. No one broke the door down and tried to take him away. Relaxed by the shower he slept well and was on the road by eight o'clock next morning.

The submarine fooled them or they were giving him a free pass. This disturbing thought flashed through Rolly's brain as he passed Columbus, Indiana. He pulled into a rest area to think, finding a bench in the shade. There was no way they didn't know his location. Every inch of the highway was under surveillance. Even the most moronic employee could track someone. They were letting him go. Why? Had they given up? That was wishful thinking. Were they not paying attention? Too many people worked for Paragon; someone or some computer was always watching. Did a catastrophe happen? Global network shutdown? Alien invasion? None of the other travelers in the rest area seemed panicked.

This was intentional. After all the trouble he had given them the handlers weren't likely to give up. They knew where he was going, what he wanted to do. He had one choice: keep going until they stopped him. He escaped Antigua with nothing more than a desperate hope. Maybe it would work again.

The trip through Indiana was uneventful and as usual, flat and boring. Two miles into Michigan the traffic thinned and disappeared, leaving him alone on the interstate. Rolly took advantage and accelerated to ninety-five. Two miles farther on, around a sharp curve, he found them: four wide delivery trucks parked across the highway, in both shoulders and both lanes, back ends open and ramps as extended, waiting to swallow him whole.

Rolly pulled hard on the brake. The ABS kicked in and kept the bike from skidding while he fought to keep it straight. But he was too close and going too fast. He hit one of the ramps and rolled up, hoping the incline would take some momentum. The front wheel went airborne for a moment and the bike hit the front wall of the truck. Braced against the handle bars, Rolly rose up a few inches and fell back on the seat unhurt. He put his feet down and walked the machine back; the wheel turned clean, the bike seemed undamaged. Malone ran in as Rolly was taking his helmet off.

"Why'd you let me get this far?"

The question surprised Malone but he recovered quickly. "Mr. Smalls, we tried to call but your HearSay is not responding. Stephanie is in danger. You need to come right now."

———————

Four large men strapped the bike into the back of the truck. Malone and Rolly climbed into the cab, Malone driving. They continued north. The other three trucks fell in behind.

Malone would only say Stephanie had been kidnapped, he didn't know any details, that Roy would fill him in when they arrived.

"Who's Roy?"

"Our supervisor."

Rolly sat tense, imagining all sorts of terrible scenarios, silently blaming Stephanie for wandering off without staying in touch.

As they passed through the western half of Lansing, Rolly felt the pull of home, and found himself looking east, toward Nola. Malone did not stop or speed up; he kept a steady pace all the way through. Was this their idea of slow torture? Bring him within sight of his goal only to drive away? The trucks rumbled through the city like laboring elephants, passed on both sides by cars that were blurs.

"How far do we have to go?"

"Three hours drive time."

"Three hours! You made it sound like she was just down the road."

"No, but she is in danger and we need move as fast as we can."

"Should I take a nap while we hurry up and get there? The motorcycle would be faster."

"You don't know where to go."

"Where are we going?"

"I'm following HearSay directions. Up north somewhere. I don't know the name of the place."

Typical Malone. Ask a simple question, run into a wall of ignorance.

"Why do this to me? Why keep me from going home?"

"We're not keeping you from anything. We only want you to enjoy retirement."

"But I'm not enjoying it. I want to go home and take care of my daughter. Then I can enjoy retirement."

"Going home would put you close to friends and family and violate the agreements you signed. Forgive me, but your daughter is a transient and helping her would be breaking the law. Neither of these things are conducive to a happy retirement. In fact they will end your retirement. We've been doing this many years Mr. Smalls and, psychologically speaking, it's best to keep family at a distance. They have lives of their own and getting caught up in their troubles can bring much stress. Retirement is your time Mr. Smalls. You should leave the stress behind and enjoy yourself."

"She's dying. Do you understand? Has anyone close to you ever died?"

"No one I know of."

"Are you a robot?"

Malone looked bemused by the question. "I am perfectly human."

"Figures, since only the rich can afford robots."

Rolly stared at the long pale road, wondering why it took a convoy of four trucks to escort one person. A waste of resources, burning up precious fuel. Using a slim excuse to justify an expensive outlay was a Corporament hallmark.

"You said Stephanie asked to come back. If I'd asked nicely, would you have have let me go too?"

"No. We can't trust you."

Rolly looked at Malone, or the brother pretending to be Malone, "The feeling is mutual."

———————————

The convoy pulled into a small town and parked in front of a retro restaurant called Jack's Diner. All shiny chrome and neon. A handwritten sign on the door said "No transients after 4 p.m."

He didn't know the name of the town (there had been no sign; only two rusty metal posts) but by direction and highways taken, knew they were on the west side of the state, near Lake Michigan, in the northern lower peninsula.

Red vinyl stools at the counter and lots of formica. Soldiers in combat gear milling around, some with automatic weapons. They seemed to be waiting, chatting with each other or staring out the windows. Behind the counter the fidgeting employees--wearing throwback 1950's outfits, waitresses in poodle skirts and guys with slicked back hair under rectangular paper caps--looked excited and unsure what to do.

Malone led Rolly to a booth where two men sat with HearSay screens open. The man facing them stood. Malone introduced Roy Tompkins.

"Nice to meet you."

"You're Malone's boss. Good to know I've been irritating more than two people."

Roy forced a smile. "Mr. Smalls, you are the least of my irritations. Sit down please."

Rolly slid in next to the other man who looked unhappy to be stuck on the inside. Malone went away.

"This is Lieutenant Phelps. He'll be commanding this operation." Lieutenant Phelps was wide with a square face and square hair, well over two hundred pounds of military conditioning.

"What operation? You haven't told me anything. What's happened to Stephanie? Is she all right?"

"She's been kidnapped by pirates and is being held for ransom."

"What? Pirates?"

"Yeah, lake pirates."

Rolly looked as if Roy were speaking gibberish. "Lake...pirates?"

"They operate on the Great Lakes. Their base is nearby."

"I've never heard of lake pirates. Is this something new?"

"Any felony committed on water qualifies as piracy. As long as people have been on the Great Lakes there's been piracy."

"How come I've never heard of it?"

"Most of it's robbery. Doesn't exactly rise to the level of national news."

"You should have a grudging respect for criminals like this. They're ruthless and have nothing to lose and that makes them dangerous. Don't underestimate them." Lieutenant Phelps was very serious about lake pirates.

Rolly still didn't get it. "Who would want to be a pirate in Michigan? It's bitter cold in the winter, the lakes freeze over--okay, *used* to freeze over--and there isn't anything worth stealing. Iron ore and cheap Chinese toys going to Chicago? Doesn't seem like enough motivation for a pirate."

Roy, "These pirates are after people. Northern Michigan is a tourist mecca in the summertime. Lots of rich people out sailing, showing off their boats, one-upping each other. The bigger the boat, the more money is on display, the more tempting the target."

"So these pirates are professional kidnappers?"

"Exactly."

"Why would they take Stephanie?"

"She was on the yacht *Monkeyshines* owned by Charles Freemire. Mr. Freemire is an executive in Horton Duling, the chemical company. They left Mackinac Island heading for Milwaukee. The pirates attacked and boarded their boat near South Fox Island, took Mr. Freemire and your wife and escaped in a speedboat."

Phelps, "We found a compound a few miles away. We believe Stephanie is there."

"Just Steph? What about the other guy, Freemire?"

Roy, "He paid his ransom and has been released. He refused to pay for Stephanie."

All her complaining about his lovers and she's the one ends up a victim. Rolly had mixed feelings, knowing she intended to divorce him. But she was his wife, mother of Max, partner for over a century. He had to help any way he could.

"Bastard. What are you going to do?"

Phelps, "We're going to attack their compound and get your wife back."

Rolly looked around at the soldiers loitering in the diner. "Is this enough men?"

"There's twenty or thirty pirates and we have superior firepower. But every extra man helps." Roy and Phelps looked pointedly at Rolly.

"You expect me to tag along?"

Phelps, "We need you. This is your area and your wife trusts you."

"I've never been here before."

Roy, "You're a Michiganian. You know what makes these people tick."

"I know being a lake pirate is a dead end job. So is hanging out with a bunch of armed men."

"We can't do this without you Mr. Smalls. You're that important."

Rolly mulled this over for exactly two seconds. "Okay."

"You know how to use a weapon?"

"No."

Phelps, "We'll give you a handgun. Easy to learn, simple to use. You'll be with two of my best men. Stay behind 'em and do as they say. Do *exactly* as they say. Ready?"

"Now?"

"Good a time as any. Can you let me out please?"

Roy, "Lieutenant, shouldn't we wait?"

"Why? Can't imagine what these criminals have done to that girl. We need to get her out ASAP."

"Wouldn't it be better to attack after nightfall?"

"Damnit Tompkins! A woman's life is in jeopardy! We can't sit around eating mammal burgers all day! Scoot over please."

Rolly stood up and let Lieutenant Phelps out. The Lieutenant yelled "We're burnin' daylight soldiers! Load 'em up!"

A collective yell of "Yes sir!" and the soldiers trotted out to one of the trucks and loaded into the back, Rolly trailing behind, looking bewildered.

33

Hero?

In the cab of the truck Roy Tompkins and Lieutenant Phelps had a discussion.

"What the hell are you doing? It's full daylight. He'll see everything."

"No, late afternoon, twilight. The sun sets over the lake. It'll be right in his eyes."

"Think for minute. It's summer. The sun doesn't set until nine o'clock. It's only six ten."

"Oh, sorry. Just came off a shoot in Argentina. The sun sets different there."

"Uh-huh. You and your men better be perfect cause one little mistake will blow the whole thing."

"Understood."

———————

Rolly and the soldiers sat on wooden benches along the walls of the truck. The ceiling was opaque plastic; they had plenty of light to see each other. The soldiers on either side of Rolly introduced themselves as Maddog and Gunner. Maddog took a pistol from his holster and handed it to Rolly, grip first.

"This is a Hurlitzer 9mm semiautomatic pistol. It's loaded and ready to go. Here's a second clip in case you need it. Don't point it at anything you don't want to kill. Use both hands to steady it. Aim careful, squeeze the trigger gentle. Make sure the safety's off, here, on the trigger guard. Push the button in and it's off, push it out and it's on."

Gunner spoke the only words Rolly would hear from him, "Keep that thing down and don't shoot us in the back."

"Yeah, for sure. Stay behind, let us do the work. And keep that safety on."

Rolly nodded, more than a little overwhelmed. He looked out of place, in his riding leathers, the soldiers in their camouflage uniforms and helmets, kneepads and body armor. That sounded like an excellent idea, stay behind and let them do the work.

The truck stopped, doors opened and slammed shut, the ramp came down with a bang, the rear door rolled up. Rolly and the soldiers found themselves in tall grass and brush trees.

"The compound is a half mile southwest. Bravo and Charlie, you know where to go. Alpha on me. Move out!"

Rolly, holding the gun as if it were a bomb that might explode, followed Gunner into the brush, in a direction he assumed was southwest. He turned to Maddog, bringing up the rear.

"How we gonna do this?"

Maddog said Alpha and Charlie and Bravo would take positions northeast, west and southeast...or was it southwest, northeast and east?...and something about crossfire and fifty caliber machine guns--tactical speak that went over Rolly's head.

"Um. Okay. But what are *we* doing?"

"We're Alpha Squad. Building to building search. Looking for your wife."

"Are we going to get shot at?"

Maddog gave a sarcastic smirk. "Eventually, yeah."

Alpha Squad trudged through the grass. Ten minutes later, at the point man's signal, everyone bent low and covered the last hundred yards in a crouch. Rolly's knees and back complained until the nanobots kicked in and numbed the pain. At the edge of a fenced in compound, the squad spread out in a line, hidden by the tall grass.

They were behind a low cinder block building, rectangular but small, a warehouse or shed of some kind, white paint nearly gone, roof shingles curled and moss covered.

Rolly could hear activity. Someone banging on something, the whine of a power saw, low male voices with a burst of laughter.

A sentry came around the building, a short man with dark skin and sideburns, a receding hairline and beer gut. Old and weathered. A rifle slung over his shoulder, doing his job but not well, barely giving the tall grass a look. They watched him pass.

Rolly heard faint static from Lieutenant Phelps' ear. Maddog said, "When we move, stay quiet. If you have to shoot, shoot to kill. These people will murder you on sight so don't play nice."

"You mean shoot them back?"

Rolly heard Maddog sigh. "Yeah. Shoot them back."

The sentry came into view again. The soldier next to Phelps pointed a rifle. Rolly heard a soft sucking sound and the sentry pitched forward and fell to the ground.

The chain link fence was quickly cut. The entire squad slipped through and squatted against the backside of the building. Two soldiers went around to the front and kicked the door in. Rolly thought it would alert the entire compound, but nothing happened. After a minute one soldier came out and shook his head. Nothing.

The squad moved to the west side of the building and Rolly got his first look at the compound. Three buildings in a neat row, this one, a long low building, and beyond that a taller building. All had cinder block exteriors, but with sloped and shingled roofs like houses. A wide expanse of neatly trimmed grass extended from each building to a river bank, which dropped off sharply. Behind the center building a wooden handrail descended down the embankment.

Across the river, three more warehouses. Plain cinder block like the others, almost ranch-like in their architecture. All sported porches and chimneys. That side of the river had railroad ties set into the hill for stairs.

The voices were coming from outside the center building. A card game in progress, but the pirates themselves were out of sight. Using hand signals Phelps led the squad across the gap, taking a position behind the center building. Rolly thought their footfalls sounded heavy and loud, the gear on each man clanging like church bells. Phelps split the squad in two groups, intending to flank the card game from both sides. As the squad was about to move a voice rang out from the first building.

"Soldiers! We're under attack!"

Rolly thought the sentry had come back to life, but that couldn't be, it must be someone they missed. Cries of alarm rang up from below, across the river, to the west, every building seemed full of pirates. Rolly heard chairs scraping on wood and the unmistakable sound of guns being cocked.

A rifle shot echoed between buildings, and the sound of shattering glass. The alarm-raiser went quiet. So did the compound, for a split second. Then chaos erupted.

Bullets slammed into the center building--the one they were flanking-- from across the river. Two of Rolly's squad mates returned fire, covering their comrades. Rolly made himself low against the wall.

He heard Phelps yell "Go! Go! Go!" and both groups disappeared around the corners. A fierce exchange of gunfire, both rifle and automatic, lasting a few seconds, a lull, then "Clear!"

Rolly came around the building, staying low. Five pirates lay dead on a wooden deck, sprawled over each other, blood splattered literally every-where. No surface was untouched. Of the twelve soldiers one lay dead against the wall, Gunner, blood from his stomach wound staining the grass.

Phelps yelled "On me!" He kicked in the front door and six men ran in behind him, four returning fire across the river. Rolly waited in a crouch. Gunfire from every direction, incredibly loud and constant, splintering wood all around him, much of it coming from the tall building. On the other side of the river he could see a different squad assaulting a different building.

"Bring him in!" A soldier grabbed Rolly by the arm and pulled him onto the deck and inside. His footprints trailed bright red blood. This building seemed to have a kitchen and a living room. Everyone stayed low. Phelps pulled Rolly to a west facing window, looking out at the tall building. "We've cleared this building. Your wife isn't here. We have to go next door and do the same. I need you with us." They could see four windows. Muzzle flashes illuminated each one.

Lieutenant Phelps, into his radio, "Bravo! Do you copy?" No answer. "Bravo! We need cover! Come back!"

A deep voice answered. "Sorry Lieutenant. Had more trouble with the natives than expected. In position now."

"Good. The far building, north side. Shooters in each window. Take 'em out."

"Roger." A single large deafening roar and the near window was obliterated, the shooter now silent. His companion on the lower level peeked out and another loud roar threw his head back. The body spun comically, spraying gore everywhere. Two down.

"Lieutenant, we don't have a clear shot at the other two. You'll have to deal with them."

"Roger." He turned to assembled men. "Collins and McKay, I want covering fire from these windows. Team Two assemble on the front deck. Team One, we're going around back. We'll go on my signal. Rolly and Maddog you're with me. Let's move!"

Out they went into the chaos. Team One and Rolly took the long way around to the back of the building. At Phelps' signal Collins and McKay began firing. The two teams erupted from their positions to sprint across the thirty feet between buildings while bullets flew overhead. Maddog was faster; Rolly fell behind. Collins and McKay fired in short bursts and fell into a simultaneous rhythm, the silences in between lining up. Rolly thought he heard a female voice yell "Help!" A distinctly Stephanie voice.

He stopped and tried to tell Maddog but his guardian was already out of earshot. Rolly stopped and waited for another silence.

"Help!"

This time he had a direction: down on the river, back under a big willow tree. Opposite from the direction he was supposed to be going. Without thinking Rolly ran to the stairs and down.

At the river edge was a nice dock and a black painted boathouse. Who paints their boathouse black? A wooden walkway followed the river in both directions, the upriver side leading under the willow. Rolly ran toward the tree.

Bullets struck the walkway all around, throwing splinters and pointed wedges of wood. He covered his face and dived behind a built-in bench. Rolly frantically checked his body for holes but found none. Some of those bullets should have gone through him. That was lucky. He still had Maddog's gun. He should make sure it was ready to shoot. Which way turned the safety off? Left or right? He pushed it right because that seemed like an "on" switch.

Rolly peered around the bench. Through the branches he saw part of a boat, heard another scream, and a pair of bare female legs kicking and disappearing into the cabin. He needed help and Lieutenant Phelps didn't know about the boat hidden under the tree. Wait...Collins and McKay were back in the center building, giving covering fire. Could he get their attention? Rolly edged out, ready to make for the boat.

A large bald man came running down the walkway toward him, rifle in hand. Tall and broad shouldered, muscular and dirty. Rage in his eyes, aiming straight for Rolly. He gave a battle cry and raised the butt end of his rifle.

Jesus Christ what the fuck? Just the sight of this monstrosity made Rolly stagger backward and fall. He raised the gun, pointing at the thug's chest, fear making his hand shake. His finger brushed the trigger.

The gun fired with barely any recoil and his attacker flew back ten feet as if hit by a cannonball. Rolly looked at the gun in amazement. Nah, that couldn't be right. The guy slipped on something at the same time he fired. That was it.

Rolly moved toward the boat, keeping watch on the bank high above. He wanted Collins and McKay to see him, get them to give him some cover and radio everyone else and tell them where he was at.

He waved his arms and yelled "Hey! Hey! It's me! Rolly!"

Nothing, then a helmet popped up and a hand waved back. A hail of bullets forced Rolly to crouch down and run toward the boat. At least they knew where he was now.

A man with a nice suit and long greasy hair stood up in the boat and started shooting. Rolly fell to his stomach and remembered Maddog's advice this time: hold it with both hands, aim carefully, squeeze slowly. He squeezed but the trigger didn't move. The gun fired.

A geyser of blood erupted from the man's chest and he fell over the side, into the river. Rolly looked at the gun. *It looks normal but has a mind of its own*. He pushed the safety the other way and squeezed the trigger, aiming downward. It pulled all the way back and fired. No hole appeared in the walkway. The bullet must have passed between the planks.

Could a gun with a hair trigger still fire with the safety on? Was that possible? He didn't know enough about firearms to be sure.

Rolly stepped onto the boat, the amazing gun pointed at the cabin door. He let his eyes adjust to the shade, then peered inside. Nothing. He went down the short stairs into the cabin.

The boat was bigger on the inside than expected. He was in a kitchen-ette with dining table. Two doors stood in front of him. Rolly chose the one on the right and slowly opened it. Stephanie was there, tied up in a brown leather chair, a gun pointed at her head.

They were in a paneled stateroom. The man holding the gun looked fierce, dark complexion, black curly hair and black beard trimmed in spikes. He looked familiar but Rolly couldn't place him. He spoke French.

Sean translated, "Dude, he's really pissed. Says you screwed up the deal and that you're a fucking asshole. Sorry." Sean was setup to translate everything. "Says he's gonna kill this woman if you don't give him the money right now."

"Does he have a HearSay?"

"Yep, it's named Le Monstre, The Monster. He named it after himself."

"Cute." Le Monstre smiled, showing several gold teeth, knowing Rolly had contacted his HearSay.

"There are fifty well trained soldiers outside killing your men and de-stroying your hideout. It won't take them long to get here."

"You're no soldier. It's you and a bunch of stupid friends. My men kill them all. Give me money or she dies."

Rolly knew exactly what he was supposed to do next: shoot Le Monstre. How did he know that? Le Monstre wouldn't die, he would only be wounded. This felt preordained, like an old video game where only one path would make the game progress.

Rolly, as if reading aloud, "There's only one way this can end." He raised the gun.

"You are not man enough to kill me! Ha!"

Rolly took his finger off the trigger and put it on the grip. The gun went off. Le Monstre whirled back, struck in the arm. He screamed in pain and dropped the gun, falling into a corner.

Rolly grabbed a hunting knife conveniently sitting on the table next to Stephanie and cut her ropes. She smiled at him. They hurried out of the cabin and off the boat, Rolly holding Steph's hand, the two of them running down the walkway. The shooting had stopped.

Near the dock they met Lieutenant Phelps and five troops. "You found her! Good man! Anyone else in the boat?"

"Some guy calling himself Le Monstre."

The Lieutenant's eyes went wide. "That's who we want. Let's go!"

They ran toward the boat. Its engines suddenly roared to life and came flying out of the slip, turning toward the lake, four outboard motors sending waves splashing over the dock.

Across the river three men tumbled down the bank. The boat swung over and picked them up.

Le Monstre stepped out onto the boat deck. He found Rolly, pointed with his good arm and screamed curses.

Again Sean translated in deadpan surfer voice, "You dog, you lowlife scum. I hate you forever for this. I will find you and kill you. I will find your family and kill them too. I find your pets and I kill them. I erase you from this world. No amount of EverLife will save you from me."

Gunfire erupted from high on the riverbank, bullets splashed around the boat. The driver slammed the throttle forward, Le Monstre still yelling as they charged toward the lake at full speed.

As the engine noise faded Stephanie said, "Wow, he really hates you."

"All in a day's work."

Rolly realized Steph had a vise grip on his hand.

"Are you okay?"

Stephanie threw her arms around his neck and pulled him down and jumped up at the same time. His hands went under her butt to keep the two of them steady.

"You saved me," she said, arms and legs wrapped around Rolly as if he were a superhero trying to fly away.

This was a hug like no other and Rolly loved it. Almost better than sex. It felt right. Nothing else did, in fact the whole day felt like one long lie.

The bartender set a beer mug in front of Roy Tompkins and filled it half full of whiskey. David Robb sat next to Roy, nursing a mimosa in a tall glass. Roy was trying for a quick intense buzz before the nanobots went to work, David was hoping for a long, slow bender.

Everyone else in the bar was transient. In this part of the country Users were tourists, and rare. Roy knew they were out of place, which is why he was after the flash buzz: he would have to drag Robb out of here before the man got his face broken.

David, "That went better than expected."

"Yeah, we didn't fail completely."

"Did you see when Rolly stood there waving his arms like an idiot?"

"I was standing next to you, watching it on the monitor."

"Man, if that were really reality he would have been dead ten times over."

"Seriously wounded. He is still a User."

"A bloody mess then."

"In the truest sense of the word." Roy held up his mug and they toasted each other. Roy chugged the whiskey in three gulps and wiped his mouth with his hand.

"Are we ready for the next one?"

"Ready as we're gonna get."

"No more mistakes. Phelps has to stick to the script."

"He's a good actor, had to do some improvising, can't predict what this shit brain client of yours is gonna do."

"A little nervous though."

"Who wouldn't be? We're faking real. Ain't no retakes or edits or post-production. Gotta make it work the first time." Didn't take much to impair Robb's language skills.

"Make sure you talk to him, tell him to keep it on script."

"I will." He would forget. "Man, your guy bought into it all the way."

"No, I don't think he did."

"Really?" A drunken pause while David Robb sorted out his thoughts. "Why we doin' this again?"

"Rolly has to decide where he wants to be and he hasn't done that yet. One more adventure and we'll know."

"*How* will we know?"

"By how much he's willing to fake happiness."

The buzz hit Roy, making the room swing around and bounce up and down. "Come on Dave. We should leave before the locals turn us into EverLife meatballs."

34

Whispers

Rolly and Stephanie were rushed from the compound in one of Paragon's black SUVs and taken to a hotel on the lake shore. Stephanie sat pressed into Rolly, holding his arm. They were hustled to a suite where an EverLife tech waited with a portable renewal machine. After determining they had no major injuries the tech put both on the machine for a nanobot update, with some added antidepressants to cope with anxiety.

While lying on the bed, essence of EverLife flowing into her arm, Stephanie held Rolly's hand. After everyone left, they curled up together under the bed covers. Stephanie fell asleep, head on Rolly's chest. Rolly wide awake. It was dark with moonlight streaming through the windows, Rolly thinking about guns that fired on their own and men that flew backward when shot.

In spite of the day's events he was dejected. In one long life he had managed to let down everyone who cared about him. Stephanie because they should have retired years ago. Max because he couldn't live up to his son's high standards. Nola hated him long before he knew she existed. Mostly Rolly was disappointed with himself for the things he didn't do, for hiding when the world went insane, for always playing it safe.

He so wanted to believe the pirate story, Stephanie in peril and he could be the hero, prove his worth and save the girl. Every boy's fantasy. He had a hero's luck too, bullets punching holes all around, not one finding its mark. The planets and the stars and dumb luck finally aligned in his favor. Rolly's golden opportunity, a chance to make right a lifetime of failure.

Instead he was the main dupe in a farce. A joke on him without a punchline.

In the morning Roy said they should stay in the hotel for a few days, just to be safe. Le Monstre had a terrible reputation, known to murder entire families. Rolly nodded and agreed, "Whatever you think is best Roy." If Roy really feared for their safety they would be on a plane for Japan or Russia or Africa or anyplace far away. Roy still had plans. The farce was not yet complete.

Rolly toyed with the idea of telling Roy he knew Le Monstre was fake, the whole thing some kind of bizarre setup. He imagined Roy running through a litany of denials, imploring him to believe, the danger was real, and please, *please* take it seriously. No matter what Rolly said their charade would go on as planned because the Corporament wanted it to, and if thwarted, the bureaucracy would close up tight as an ancient sarcophagus. Approvals delayed, calls not returned, files conveniently lost. Better to let Roy have his fun and hope for a reward at the end. Maybe they would let him visit Nola so he could give her the MiniVault. That seemed too much to hope for, but Rolly could not help being an optimist.

Rolly stayed close to Stephanie, holding hands, or touching her back. They were never apart. Sitting on a veranda overlooking the lake, Stephanie sunbathing next to him, Rolly tried to figure out who he could trust. Certainly not Malone. He knew nothing about Lieutenant Phelps, only that he was linked to Roy. The soldiers were extras, Maddog being the actor skilled enough to interact with the hero.

Was he being paranoid? Just because a gun fires on its own doesn't mean there's a conspiracy. It might be very sensitive or defective. Except it always hit an enemy target. Defective with impeccable aim. Right.

Rolly mentally scanned a list of recent acquaintances: Le Clerc and Le Capitan, Daglesh, Leah, Gordon O'Leary, Otis Vangelder; back to Macklin and Steve, Myrna, Souliere, Lambert, Doug, all his former coworkers. Lambert was the only one he would trust with his life, but she couldn't help. Souliere...he couldn't bring himself to trust the office know-it-all, but the man had been helpful. Souliere would be his backup if getting to Nola proved undoable. Of the rest it was a revelation to think the criminals were--if not honest--at least clear about their intentions.

They were staying at The Rocky Shore Inn, really more of a spa/resort than a hotel. Two hundred rooms on a bluff overlooking Lake Michigan with the things wealthy Corporament types liked to do: an eighteen hole golf course, a gourmet restaurant that served healthy real food, all the amenities in the middle of nowhere. One of the masseurs told Rolly the name was meant to keep away casual tourists. He mentioned it five times while Rolly lay face down on the table. In case Rolly didn't get the hint. The Rocky Shore Inn, the perfect place for the average working stiff to unwind after a hard day battling lake pirates, but please, don't stay too long.

Stephanie was on the table next to Rolly getting her own massage, blissfully unaware. They slept together every night, ate every meal as a couple, soaked in hot tubs, played golf, racquetball, tennis, got hot rock treatments, everything except using the bathroom, and then Rolly hung around outside the door waiting.

Stephanie liked the attention at first but in a few days turned restless. Her old disgruntled self came back. The woman clutching his arm like a frightened child? That was not his wife. This woman, complaining she needed "alone time" was the love of his life. He protested, making a show of it, relented, and off she went.

She was gone all day and through the night. In the morning Rolly put on a pair of jeans and his favorite Hawaiian shirt, blue and pink with rowboats and palm trees. He was sitting down for breakfast in the restaurant when she came through the front door, a spring in her step, looking relaxed and happy. She joined him. Rolly decided to challenge her, ask where she had been, what did she do. The mood turned tense.

"As if you don't already know?"

"Give me the details."

"You're disgusting."

There she was, his real wife. Except the look on her face was not the usual frustration, now it was pity, smug, and full of condescension.

All the love and care he felt drained away. There was nothing left. It was over.

Rolly smiled and apologized, said he didn't mean anything by it, please can we kiss and make up? He stood and so did Stephanie, reluctantly, and he held her gently, his mouth by her ear. Stephanie put her arms up under his, hands on his shoulder blades. They hugged for a long time, more than decorum allowed, Rolly refusing to let her go.

Upstairs, in a different suite, Roy and David Robb, along with Mikaela and Amelia, watched their charges try to break the hug world record.

Using a remote Roy switched camera angles, zooming in when he found a good view of Rolly's face.

David, "His lips are moving. He's saying something."

"Thank you for that keen observation. Mikaela, don't we have access to Rolly's HearSay memory?"

"Of course."

"Bring it up and rewind please."

Through the speakers they heard Rolly whisper to Stephanie.

"What was your price?"

"What?"

"That garbage last Saturday, where you pretended to be the damsel in distress. What was your price?"

"A guy was holding a gun to my head and you think it was pretend?"

"The guns only fired when they wanted to and only hit what they needed. It was all very convenient. They can hire anyone to do their dirty work but there's only one of you and you wouldn't do it without getting something in return. What was it?"

She didn't answer. Rolly's hug tightened.

"Don't bullshit me Steph. Just answer the question."

"A divorce, without consequences."

"That's what I thought."

"You're a good guy Rolly but living with you is a chore. I can't do it anymore."

"Good guys always finish last."

"Be a bastard once in a while. It'll help."

"Why pirates?"

"I don't know. Some kind of experiment I think."

"Why me?"

"You're a guinea pig."

"This isn't over yet, is it?"

"No. That stupid pirate is supposed to be your nemesis."

"Oh. I have a nemesis now. Moving up in the world."

"Don't blow this off Rolly. You know how they want it to end."

"I'll sign whatever forms you need. You'll be a free woman."

"Thank you."

"I'm sure they're listening. Their next plan is probably hatching as we speak."

"I won't be here when you get back."

"I doubt I'll be coming back."

They separated, Rolly smiling too much, Stephanie dabbing a napkin at her eyes. He sat and resumed eating, she excused herself and went to the bathroom.

Roy turned to Robb. "Still think he bought into it all the way?"

David Robb looked at the floor.

Roy, to Amelia, "Everything ready at the farmhouse?"

"Yep. Just need to get the people there."

"How long will that take?"

Mikaela, "With travel time, hair and makeup, about three hours."

"Get on the phone and tell them we're coming. They've got two hours."

"But Rolly knows. Why bother?"

"He hasn't made his choice yet. It doesn't matter how much he knows, only how much he decides to forget. This is Mr. Smalls' last chance at redemption."

35

998, 269, 176

The restaurant had a nice outdoor terrace with umbrella covered tables, most of which were empty this early in the morning. Rolly pulled out a beige plastic chair, sat back and put his feet up on an adjacent chair. He didn't have to wait long.

Malone came running across the terrace and breathlessly insisted Rolly follow him right now, there was an emergency. He was led through the restaurant's kitchen to the back loading dock where the familiar panel trucks were being loaded by the familiar soldiers. His motorcycle was parked nearby. Lieutenant Phelps and Maddog were consulting a device that looked like a HearSay interface with three extra antennas--as if that made it more sophisticated. Roy was standing ten feet away, talking with the other Malone.

Roy stepped over immediately. "Mr. Smalls, I'm sorry for this. Le Monstre made contact a few minutes ago. He's holed up in an old farmhouse twenty miles north. He's demanding you, and you alone, deliver thirty million dollars to him in two hours."

"So what? Send a bunch of troopers and arrest him or something."

"Didn't Malone tell you?" He shot an unhappy look at the Malone standing next to Rolly. "Le Monstre has taken your son and is threatening to kill him if you don't bring the money."

"Max? How the hell did he get Max?"

"I don't know. We're still trying to figure that out. I'm sorry Rolly. We tried to protect everyone but we assumed Max with all his personal security would be safe."

"You have a plan?"

"We're playing this one by ear. The farmhouse is set back from the road a quarter mile. We want you to ride in on your motorcycle so he sees you're alone. The squad will follow through woods and take positions around the house. The moment we get a clear shot they'll take him out."

"You sure? Puts me in the line of fire."

"I understand if you're afraid Rolly. I won't hold it against you if you sit this one out. It's a lot to ask."

Well, since you put it that way. "No, I'll do it. Can I have a gun?"

"You can have two. If you get the chance, kill the bastard. You should wear body armor as well."

"No thanks. I do have one question."

Roy froze, as if he did not want to answer. "Anything you want."

"What's Malone's brother's name?"

Everyone looked at the twin standing next to Rolly. "My name is Malcolm."

Rolly held out his hand. "Nice to meet you Malcolm. Let's get this over."

They parked the trucks on the shoulder of the main road, a ribbon of straight two lane blacktop cut through a canyon of tall pine trees. The track leading to the farmhouse was barely noticeable, no mailbox, no sign, hidden from the road by years of intentional neglect. Many of the locals put extreme value on their privacy, backed up with a willingness to shoot anyone who looked cross-eyed at their property. Cities of any size were far away. Anyone calling this place home was likely transient.

Rolly rode up the track slowly, at Roy's request, to give Maddog and his squad time. He enjoyed the few minutes of solitude, nothing but trees, only the hum of the cycle for company.

The farmhouse was around a curve and on a small rise. Two story white clapboard, brown shingled roof, shuttered windows, porch with peeling paint. It didn't look rundown as much as it did temporarily unused. The garage was set back from the house, lower on the slope. The foundation of the house--round field stones cemented in place--ran along the driveway, six feet high. An old rotted door in the foundation led to a root cellar. Next to the door stood a large, round and bald thug wearing a dirty tee shirt, gun in one hand and nightstick in the other. The door was open.

Rolly pushed down the kickstand and shut off the bike, being sure to remove and pocket the key. The guard stared back with eyes so squinty Rolly wasn't sure they were open.

One gun was in a holster, under his leather jacket. The other strapped to his ankle. He stepped up to the guard who didn't move.

"In here?" The guard nodded. Even up close his eyes appeared to be only horizontal lines.

Rolly stepped into the cellar thinking any self-respecting criminal with vengeance in mind would want to make sure his enemy was disarmed. Yet here he was with two guns.

The door slammed shut leaving him in pitch dark. Rolly stopped to let his eyes adjust. At the point where he could start to discern shapes, a bare bulb came on and he was blinded again. Rolly's hand went up to shield against the glare while three men laughed.

When Rolly's eyes adjusted he saw two thugs to his left on the other side of a high, rough hewn table, and in front of him, Le Monstre standing over Max, tied to a chair and gagged.

That was a shock. It had been years since Max and Rolly were in each other's presence and Max was tied up like a calf at a rodeo. This was becoming tiresome.

"You surprise me. I not think you have balls to show up."

"Well I'm here now." Rolly's line should have been *What? And miss all the fun?* That's what all the sarcastic heroes said.

"I figure you try to rescue your son, like your wife."

"Yeah, that makes sense." But he was supposed to say *He's worth it, Le Monstre, get over it.*

"I wanted you here to kill you but now I have second thoughts. Your son very rich. Maybe I switch you around. Tie you up and send him for ransom. How you like that? Think your son going to pay for you?"

He was supposed to say *You'll never get away with this Le Monstre!* but Rolly said "Let's cut the crap."

Rolly bent down, pulled the gun from under his pant leg, and stood up with it lying in the palm of his open hand.

The thugs yelled and pulled their guns. The door guard burst in and raised his club.

"This gun was given to me by Roy Tompkins, the man who has been watching my every move for the last three years, along with this one-" Rolly reached inside his jacket and pulled out the other gun- "a matched pair."

Both guns lay in the palms of Rolly's hands. He didn't know whether the safeties were on or off.

"I think, that if you try to attack me, these guns will fire even if I don't pull the trigger."

The thugs looked at each other confused. Le Monstre looked dumbfounded.

"Which one wants it first?"

That was the door guard's cue. Both hands raised and clutching the nightstick he ran screaming at Rolly, who turned, but the guns did nothing. At the last moment Rolly gripped the handle of one--but kept his finger off the trigger. A flash of orange, then a spot of red bloomed on the guard's shirt. Momentum carried his body into Rolly before falling to the dirt.

The other thugs, arms raised and guns pointing, fidgeted, glancing at each other and Le Monstre, as if they had no idea what to do. *If they were real they wouldn't be thinking about it, they'd be shooting.*

Still holding only the grips, Rolly pointed his guns in the general direction of the remaining thugs. Both fired at the same time. The two thugs staggered back, blood gushing out of apparent holes in their chests, and fell behind the table.

Just Rolly and Le Monstre now, thanks to Rolly's incredible marksmanship. Looking desperate Le Monstre pulled out a long knife, grabbed Max by the hair and held it to his throat.

"Step any closer I kill him!"

"No you won't. That's not how the script goes. I'm supposed to shoot you and save my son. But I'm done with this. Here, take my gun." He held it out to Le Monstre grip first, who only stared at it. "Go ahead, take it. You can even shoot me if you want."

Max, still gagged, was convulsing and turning red in the face, making an odd, yet familiar, whistling sound: he was laughing.

Le Monstre grabbed the gun, stepped back and pointed it at Rolly. "I kill you now."

"This is your big chance."

Le Monstre pulled the trigger but there was only a clicking sound.

"You know that gun holds six rounds and I only fired two."

"But you have another. I am beaten."

"Oh, sorry. Forgot. Wanna give it a try? Here. Only fired it once."

Le Monstre pointed it at Rolly and pulled the trigger. Again, nothing.

"Amazing how that works isn't it?"

"I still have knife. I kill you with this."

"Don't bother. What I would like is for you to take your friends, or cast mates, and give me some time with my son."

"You killed them."

"They're not dead. Look, I know you guys work really hard and you did a good job. Absolutely had me convinced. The first time. If you're worried about getting more gigs I can vouch for you. Not a problem."

Le Monstre stood stock still, mouth hanging open.

"Wait, this will help." Rolly walked over to the sprawled out door guard and gave him a kick under the armpit. The dead man flinched.

"Ow! Jesus! That hurt!"

"Sorry dude, didn't know what else to do."

Le Monstre dropped the gun and lost his French accent.

"Shit, what gave us away?"

"It wasn't you, it was the props. These crappy perfect guns. You guys are actors, right?"

"Yeah, local theatre. This was supposed to be our Hollywood ticket."

"How's that?"

"Guy running the show is David Robb, the movie director."

"What about Roy? How's he involved?"

"Don't know. Some kind of producer, I think. He hired Robb. That's all I know."

"Okay. I imagine this cellar is filled with cameras."

"And microphones, yeah."

"Well, cool. Guys, it was good working with you. I think Robb should give you all parts in his next movie. But I'm sure Roy and his minions are on the way, so…"

"Yeah, no problem." The three thugs got up off the ground, brushed themselves off, the menacing attitude and swagger gone. Relaxed, they were completely different people. One shook Rolly's hand on the way out and wished him luck. Rolly returned the good wishes. As Le Monstre passed Rolly asked:

"Hey, can I borrow your knife?"

"It's not sharp."

"I was going to use it to cut the ropes."

"Don't bother. They're regular knots, like you'd tie your shoes with."

"Cool. Hey, you were a great pirate. Really had me scared. Where you guys playing?"

"The Magenta Marigold Theater."

"If this works out maybe I'll come and see you."

Le Monstre beamed with appreciation. "Thanks man."

———————

Outside, in the control van parked behind Rolly's motorcycle, Roy grumbled and sighed. Mikaela and Amelia turned from the monitor to see what he would do. Roy stood up to leave.

"I'm going in," he said, "Wait for my call."

Mikaela, "What are you going to do?"

"Put an end to this nonsense."

Roy left and slammed the door behind him. On the monitor Mikaela and Amelia watched him walk across the dirt drive, into the cellar, then the screen went blank.

———————

Rolly untied the gag and started pulling ropes off Max's arms and legs.

"It's good to see you Max."

"Likewise. Nice to see your cynicism intact."

"I wasn't that bad. They seem like nice guys. So what was your price?"

"Hang on a sec." Max stood up, shaking out stiff muscles. Rolly had forgotten how tall he was. Son had outgrown father while still a teenager, but in Rolly's memories, his badly outdated memories, Max was still the little boy. Now he was a man, at least his equal, more likely his better.

With a newly free hand Max pulled a short metal tube out of a jeans pocket and pushed a button on the end.

"What's that?"

"Signal jammer. Now we can talk in peace."

"Talk about what?"

"Tornadoes and living in the basement for a week."

Rolly went from happy to stern. "We can't talk about that. We can't ever talk about that, signal jammer or not."

Max went from happy to wounded. "I thought since you were retired and free--"

"I'm not free."

The door opened with a groan of rusty hinges and Roy entered the cellar. He looked unhappy.

"Here's my jailer now."

"There's no jail, Rolly. But there are rules and like a little kid you have to push the limits and do the one thing you're not supposed to. It's time we had a talk."

"About fake pirates?"

"Let's get past that. Talk about what's real."

"Why would I believe anything you say?"

"Because it's the last, worst thing you want to hear."

Roy sounded like Leah, using truth like a diamond meant for cutting. With trepidation Rolly said "I'm all ears."

"You have no money left."

Mikaela and Amelia looked from the blank screen to each other.

Amelia, "Has that ever happened?"

"Never."

"What should we do?"

Mikaela thought a moment. "Roy said wait for his call, so we wait."

Amelia went through a row of buttons on the console, turning each one on and off. "You sure? We're not getting feeds from any cameras or mics."

"How long has Roy been doing this?"

"A hundred years."

"You really want to question him? Barge in and ruin his plans?"

"Okay fine. We'll wait." But Amelia looked worried.

"That's not right. There were millions on the last statement, more than enough."

"That was before your pirate adventure."

It took a moment to sink in. "You used my money to pay for this?"

"Did you think the Corporament would spend its own money to put on a show for you?"

"I didn't want a pirate adventure!"

"What you want and what you need are two different things. We decided you needed an adventure."

"You can do this? Without asking me?"

"You gave us permission. Those papers you signed when you retired? Remember the one about discretionary spending for the well being of the client? Gives us control of your money and the power to use it. I tried keeping the cost down but pirates are expensive."

"You spent all of it?"

"Every last dollar. And then some."

"That money was supposed to set up a new life, a new house, buy me some new tools."

"You're lucky you have a job to go back to after the performance you gave. That's right, I got you a job. Here at Paragon. In fact it's the only place you'll find employment."

Rolly spoke slowly. "I don't want to go back to work."

"You have no money and you know too much. This is your only choice. Paragon is the one place where a slip of the tongue could be forgiven. Anywhere else it would mean instant banishment."

"What would I say? Retirement is about pirates?"

"See, that's the problem. You have a bad attitude. You're not following the rules, not being a good citizen consumer. We can't trust you. And if you want to change that you'll need money and a job. This is your last chance."

Rolly felt his rage boil up.

"What about Nola?"

"You need to forget her."

"I can't let my daughter die."

Roy took a deep breath. "Rolly I'm sorry to tell you this but Nola died a year ago. Max was at the funeral."

Max looked Roy straight in the eye. "No, she's alive. Stubborn and crazy but still breathing. Roy is lying." Roy's face bent into a furious scowl. "Roy brought me here to backup his story. Thought we were still at odds. Made me sign a non-disclosure. God, I'm sick of those things. Take your non-disclosure and shove it Roy."

"You son of a bitch. You're done. The famous Max Smalls breaks a signed contract. The Corporament will love it."

"Bring it on."

Rolly stepped toward Roy. "Why can't you leave us alone!"

"After all we've done for you? Made your retirement perfect, gave you a concierge, world travel, an adventure, but you insist on clinging to things that don't matter. Do you know the difference between right and wrong anymore? Your retirement is over and you have two choices left: come with me to a new job and a new life, or stay here in the wilderness and wait to die."

Anger descended through Rolly like guillotine, cutting off every other emotion.

Sean, "Whoa dude! Blood pressure off the charts! Settle...settle."

Rolly yelled and ran at Roy. Max grabbed his father, wrapped his arms around Rolly's upper body, and with effort held him back.

"No Dad! He's not worth it! You want to get back at him? Tell me what happened. Tell me the truth."

"What's he talking about?"

Rolly, red faced and frustrated, "The Second Preservation War."

"You can't tell him that."

Anger overwhelmed Rolly. More than anything he wanted to hurt Roy. And this would do the trick.

"There used to be a lot more people."

"No! Don't tell him! Mikaela! Send security now!"

"You wouldn't believe it 'cause it's so crowded but it used to be worse. A lot worse. Food was scarce. Plumbing ran dry. Fifty thousand new babies every day and a couple hundred deaths at most."

"Mikaela! Amelia! Answer me!"

"What do you do when you're the Corporament and there's too many people? You can't lay them off or fire them. You can't put them on a plane and send them to China or Africa. Those places had problems of their own.

"So the Corporament murdered a billion people."

Roy made a run for the door. Max shoved the heavy wooden table and jammed it into the doorway, then turned his back on Roy. "That's impossible. Even the Corporament can't kill a billion people overnight."

"It took months, maybe years. No one knew for sure. We didn't notice because they started with transients. It only became obvious when Users started dying. In those days every death made the news. But the news didn't say anything. It was rumors and word-of-mouth. We were so used to knowing everything...that's the worst thing about rumors, not knowing if you should believe them.

"On June 7th a hundred and twenty airline flights fell out of the sky, crashing in the middle of major cities at rush hour. After that there was a new disaster every day. Then the panic, desperate people looting and rioting. It all felt...not planned, but anticipated, pushed in a certain direction. We reacted like we were supposed to. The army was sent in to restore order and instead killed anyone they laid eyes on. I don't know why. I don't know what they were ordered to do. I just know the neighbors were dead on their front lawn.

"I heard it, through the basement door and our thin walls. Commands to shoot for the head because EverLife couldn't heal head wounds. Screams and constant machine gun fire.

"And then it stopped. We found out later the Corporament used an algorithm to figure exactly how many people needed to die. 998, 269, 176. Rounded up. When that many lives were removed from the population count the army stopped killing."

Max looked angry and confused, as if he couldn't believe it.

"Afterward the President went on holovision and apologized. He used to be the CEO of HearSay, you know. He didn't show any emotion and only said he was sorry once. He vowed to never let this happen again, there was a solution and they would find it, and really, the best thing to do with a moment of weakness was forget it and move on. We should never speak of this again. And we didn't."

"Why not? Dad, why didn't you tell me?"

Oh god, what have I done? Rolly's anger was gone. Max had been honest with him and he owed it to his son to do the same in return.

Rolly closed his eyes and felt his throat tighten. The words came out dry and raspy. "Because they were right. Living became easier. We had enough food and water. Space to live in again. We were happy. You grew up healthy and strong. But always in the back of your mind is that number. I will never forget it. Our own friends and family. We were as guilty as the soldiers and bureaucrats. So we did our jobs, the Corporament passed the Population Protection Laws, promised us retirement, and we kept our mouths shut."

Rolly was agitated, ashamed. He thought it would be easier. Max looked lost, not sure how to respond. Roy broke the silence.

"Are you happy now?"

Max turned on him. "You're just as guilty, Corporament lackey that you are. At least Rolly did something, kept us alive. What were you doing when your friends were being massacred?"

Roy fixed them with a hostile look. "I was one of those soldiers. Now tell me, why can't I contact my crew?"

Max looked at Roy with a new level of animosity and held up the signal jammer. "This is what you get for making everything wireless."

Roy's expression didn't change but he regarded the silver tube with relief and frustration. The secret would stay hidden but Max's crime would be harder to prove.

"Those are illegal. Where'd you get it?"

"Built it myself."

"I have to go." They turned and looked at Rolly. "I can't stay. I have to go now," he said, in a rush to disappear like the losing fighter in a boxing match.

"Where?"

"Nola."

Roy, "If you go back you'll lose everything. I'll make sure of it."

Max nodded. "I'll keep him busy as long as I can."

"You can't stay. He'll arrest you, throw you in jail. Come with me."

"I'm in too deep. I never intended to honor that non-disclosure. My choice and I won't take it back. Having me around will make things worse for you."

Rolly hesitated. "Why are you doing this?"

"Because I like being a troublemaker. Now go."

36

Running Free In A Cage

They listened to the chugging whine of the motorcycle engine fade as Rolly raced away.

"That's not supposed to happen. My crew will break the door down any second."

"Wouldn't want to waste any precious seconds would we. So inefficient." Max leaned against the table, arms crossed, unmoving.

"At most you've bought him a few minutes."

"All the better."

"Jammers are illegal. You'll be serving time without EverLife."

"I'd rather spend a few years aging than be banished. Which I believe is standard punishment for breaking non-disclosure."

"You won't get off that easy."

"You realize there's no record of this conversation. It's my word against yours."

"Who do you think they'll believe? A good Corporament servant or a bitter hot headed egomaniac?"

Max pursed his lips in thought. "If my Dad is so hot to go home why did you bring him here? How could you let a jammer into the room? Why am I here at all? Why did you trust me? How many other mistakes have you made? For a good Corporament servant you're kind of incompetent."

"They won't believe anything you say."

"Doesn't matter. All I have to do is speak the idea and they'll start thinking about it. That's the last thing you want."

"Give me the jammer."

"Come and get it."

That's exactly what Roy did. Max tried to slip away but the cellar was small--both men ended up on the ground, rolling in the dirt. It was an uneven match; Roy was stockier, and a more experienced brawler. Without much effort he maneuvered to the top position and pried the jammer out of Max's hand, leaving the smaller man lying breathless on the wet earth.

Roy found a broken brick, set the jammer on the table upright and smashed it flat. Just for the satisfaction he smashed it two more times.

"This isn't over," he said.

Rolly could feel the handlers behind him like a giant robot with impossibly large strides, super sensitive eyes and elongated arms reaching across the miles, trying to swoop him off the bike. Rolly kept watch in his mirrors, turning in the seat with every unexpected shadow, but could only see a long line of ordinary cars.

He rode as fast as he could, pushing the bike hard, testing the limits of his skills, accelerating when a break in traffic allowed, or when a long view revealed a clear path. He watched the sky for helicopters and drones, scanned the insides of cars, looking for spies.

Weaving and squeezing between vehicles earned Rolly more than the usual middle finger salutes. He drove the shoulder perilously close to gravel, where the bike would likely slip out from under him. Nearly crashed three times when drivers made unexpected moves, sudden braking, lane changing or the old speed-up-and-cut-him-off. The bike was smooth and powerful and more maneuverable than any car. He left other drivers in a wake of exhaust, becoming a memory before their favorite obscenity could be shared.

Making a successful connection with Nola was a long shot. Roy's minions and a cadre of Thought Police were likely watching her apartment. But he had to try. Maybe they would realize chasing one guy was pointless and give up. That was a desperate thought. His backup plan was more doable: get the MiniVault to Souliere and have him deliver it anonymously, not give Nola a chance to turn it down.

At normal speed the run to Lansing should have taken two and a half hours. When Rolly arrived Sean said he did it in fifty-two minutes and started listing the traffic laws he had broken.

"Sean?"

"Yay dude?"

"Shut up."

"Okay." Sean drew out the word like an irritated child.

Roy and his team were lumbering down the highway in a convoy of empty moving trucks. Amelia watching Rolly's blue dot on her HearSay monitor.

"Wow, he's really moving. Leaving us in the dirt."

"That's nice. Move the command truck to Nola's apartment. At least we'll have that in place. Any available planes or helicopters?"

Mikaela, "Not this far north."

"What about a Scarecrow?"

Mikaela consulted her HearSay. "There's one in Grand Rapids. Could meet us north of Clare. Take us the rest of the way."

The Scarecrow was a large low slung car with fat tires, black wheels, matte black paint and dark tinted windows, all imposing girth and sharp angles designed to intimidate. A car that made its presence *felt*. Each Scarecrow had a professional driver, who, despite the car being half again larger than normal, had skills enough to weave the behemoth into and through the smallest gaps. It was best not to watch when riding in a Scarecrow.

"That's the only way we'll make up the time. See if it can meet us sooner. There's no one who can cut him off?"

"Every other team is otherwise engaged. We never planned for this. Rolly was supposed to stay at the farmhouse."

Amelia, "I'm sorry we let him go. We thought that's what you wanted."

"Don't worry about it ladies. Not your fault. No harm done." Roy smiled. *By morning you'll both be fired.*

The sun was high. A near perfect summer day. Nola's apartment was a ramp and two turns off the highway, on the north side of the city. Rolly decided to go farther east then double back to throw off any reception party, set them at ease, make them think he was headed elsewhere. He didn't think this would work but felt it better than driving straight into a trap.

After riding into the city from the east, Rolly made for the same spot he watched from four years ago: the far side of an overgrown field looking at the backside of Nola's building. From a saddlebag he pulled the spyglass Le Clerc had given him, wiped off the lens, and extended it.

Nola's door was closed, the towels in the window pulled shut. Everything normal. A few doors to the left a man leaned on the railing, talking to someone below, but his eyes were looking toward Rolly. On the right, at the end of the second floor walkway, a woman came around the corner, limping, but looking too healthy for this part of town. She glanced his way.

In the parking lot below, a row of rusty cars. Rolly saw movement, two people in a back seat. A grizzled face with long blonde hair turned and stared out the window in his direction.

They knew he was here. Squads were probably racing toward him, competing to see who could catch him first. The bike was running, kickstand up, helmet on. He could leave at a second's notice but had to see Nola for himself, to put the lie to Roy's words.

The apartment door opened a crack and the man at the railing stepped over to listen. A woman suddenly fell out, pushed from behind. Thin, long red hair, wearing an orange business suit, looking like a walking safety cone. A psycop. The door flung open and there was Nola, raging at the red haired woman. Rolly could hear her screams all the way across the field as her fists pounded the woman's back, the undercover cop trying to move between, only to have Nola turn her rage on him instead. Rolly smiled.

She looked bigger, older, grayer, creeping ever closer to death.

Tires squealed as a black SUV sped around the corner at the east end of the street. Rolly slapped his visor down, threw the spyglass in its saddle-bag, and sped down the sidewalk toward the SUV. He gave a middle finger as they passed, angry faces watching him go by. Stuck on a narrow street they were forced to make an awkward u-turn and give chase.

As they approached Lansing the Scarecrow finally slowed, much to Roy's relief. He dared a glance at the speedometer once while on the highway: 162 mph. Mikaela had a white knuckle grip on the door handle. Amelia was lost in her HearSay, oblivious. Rule number one in a Scarecrow was never talk to the driver while the vehicle was moving. It did not need to be enforced.

Amelia, "Rolly is on the move. The Agents missed him."

"Fausto and Vance will grab him at the apartment."

"He's going east again, away from the target. Now turning south."

"He's circling around, trying to get everyone to chase him. Make sure the control truck stays put."

"Vance acknowledged. They won't move until you say so."

"Where is he now?"

"Still going south. Wait he's turned east again, off the main road on a side street."

Roy watched his assistant.

"Now he's zigzagging, going southeasterly, more or less. Intervention Agents are in pursuit."

"*Away* from the apartment?"

"Yes sir."

"Where the hell is he going?"

Lunchtime in the city. Cars and people everywhere. Two black SUVs chasing him now, unable to get around traffic to cut him off. Rolly had already slipped between cars twice and run a red light but hadn't been able to shake the SUVs. He remembered traveling in one of those after making retirement. My, how things change. His pursuers would be calling in reinforcements, trying to box him in. He would need more radical moves if he expected to get away.

Lansing was his town; he knew it better than these goons. Visitors were always getting lost in the maze of one way streets. The effect was ten times worse in the old downtown with its two lane roads. He would use this to his advantage, cutting around in a jagged circle, miring them in traffic. They couldn't follow on the sidewalks and they couldn't follow on the streets. If he was going the wrong way.

They were stuck at a red light behind five cars. Roy said to the driver, "Use the broadcast."

The driver pushed a button on the console. The light turned green and both lanes of traffic moved to the side of the road. The Scarecrow had a clear path as far as they could see. The broadcast was an emergency transmission to every vehicle on the road. Manual or self-driven each and every car automatically moved itself out of the way.

Amelia, "Sir, Rolly is...all over the place. Going the wrong way down one way streets. The lead chase car says he's driving on the sidewalks. He's gone east, west, north and south, doubled back on the chasers, crossed paths, at one point he was following *them*. He's completely unpredictable."

"Who says?"

"The computer."

"Nonsense. We just have to figure out where he's going. Start thinking. Where would he want to go if he can't get to his daughter?"

Amelia, "Home. Back to his old house."

Mikaela, "The house is gone, turned into apartments. Why would he go there?"

Roy, "He wouldn't. What's his next option? Who does he know who can help?"

Mikaela, "He has some internet friends."

Amelia, "Everyone has internet friends."

Roy, "He doesn't have any actual friends. The dumb sap spent all his time working." That was it. "I know where he's going. Mikaela, send the control truck to Rolly's old workplace, Stableman Insurance."

Rolly "lost" his tail around the fifth red light he drove through. Lost as in he couldn't see them anymore, but they wouldn't be far behind. They would know he was at the Stableman building. He needed to make these few goon-less minutes count.

Rolly put the bike over the curb and parked it on the sidewalk. The crowd made a wide circle around this usurper in sacred pedestrian space. When he stepped off the bike they moved back farther. Rolly enjoyed that. Helmet in hand he ran-walked across the plaza, trying not draw too much attention.

"Dude you are so awesomely cool! You like completely dissed the municipal parking code, and oh my gosh, in the last fifteen minutes you've notched up thirty-two moving violations. My fave was the u-turn onto the sidewalk at Kalamazoo and Washington. On a red light! You are my hero, Oh Master of the Motorcycle. The city has texted you fifty-three tickets."

"Sean, I want you to shut down. Cease all recording and monitoring functions, end all user interactions. Power down and turn off." For good measure Rolly pressed and held knuckle and finger together.

"Before I go, I gots to say, you like, kinda need me right now."

"Go away Sean."

"Okay boss."

The Scarecrow pulled up behind the control truck parked on the street next to Rolly's motorcycle. Mikaela and Amelia got out and ran to the truck. Roy walked over to the motorcycle and gave it a vicious kick, toppling it over. A mirror broke and metal ground on cement. The pedestrians kept their distance and watched but didn't stop. The Scarecrow disappeared into traffic.

The control truck was painted burgundy with a wine delivery company logo on the side. Inside it was full of monitors; Roy instantly felt at home. Vance and Fausto were watching Rolly walk across the courtyard.

They had nearly fifty angles, playing on a dozen monitors. The large central monitor showed Rolly from behind and to the left. Workers were everywhere, eating in groups or talking to their HearSays, walking, enjoying the sunshine. Relaxing.

Rolly stopped and was hugged by a woman with brown hair in a ponytail. She was animated, happy; Rolly looked anxious, wanting stay but needing to move.

Fausto looked up at Roy, "You want audio?"

"Don't bother. We have a mob. Let's put it to work. Send an alert."

37

We Live On Lies

Faces looked up. Most were strangers, some vaguely familiar, people he used to pass in the corridors but never really knew. Some were instantly familiar.

Janis from the tenth floor who he shared an elevator with more times than he could count. Roger from the mailroom. Julie from the OCM, eating lunch at a table with friends. And sitting around a planter with a stunted maple tree, the usual suspects: Doug, Bob, Rich and Suzi, but no Souliere.

They saw Rolly and called his name but Rolly pretended not to hear. He had no time to visit and wasn't sure he could trust his old friends. Souliere was the only person he dared speak to.

Lambert stepped in front of him, beaming from ear to ear.

"Hello Lambert." Rolly couldn't help but smile.

"Rolly!" She threw her arms around his neck and hugged him.

"It's nice to see you too."

"Where have you been? You're the first retiree I've ever seen. What's it like? Where have you been?"

"Lambert I--" All conversation stopped as every HearSay popped to life with the deep booming Corporament voice.

"This is a fugitive watch alert for the city of Lansing, Michigan. HBM Security Services is looking for a caucasian male wearing denim jeans and a leather jacket, last seen in the downtown area between Capitol and Grand avenues on the west and east, and Ottawa and Shiawassee on the south and north. This man is accused of subverting Corporament law through acts of sedition. He is not armed but is considered dangerous. If you see this person call Security Services immediately. Suspect's name is Roland Vaughan Smalls."

Lambert's mouth dropped open. "Rolly, what have you done?"

"I haven't done anything! I'm trying to find Souliere. Do you know where he is?"

Lambert eyed him suspiciously. "Why do you want Souliere?"

"I need his help."

"I don't think Souliere would help you now."

"Please Lambert, I need to find him ASAP."

"Why didn't you stay retired? What's going on?"

"Lambert, there is no retirement. It's just a glorified vacation. They want to keep us working forever."

Lambert stepped back as if Rolly had turned into a large hairy insect. "Everyone wants to retire. You got what we want. And all you can do is ruin it?" Lambert looked angry.

"The Corporament lies to you. They lied to me. They lie to everyone."

"No! Don't say anymore! Go away!"

Former coworkers surrounded Rolly and Lambert in a circle.

Doug, "I think you should stay Rolly. Until security gets here."

His old friends looked pasty and formless, even those with darker skin. His hand had more color than all these people combined. Did he look this pale once?

"Is Souliere here? Does he still work in the OCM?"

Bob, "Who cares about Souliere? The man's a monk who never does anything. You've got bigger problems."

"But he's still with you guys?"

No answer.

"Fine then." Rolly busted through the circle and headed for the building entrance.

Perp alerts are effective because people like to be heroes. Knowing a bad guy is near they jump into action. Rolly hadn't taken three steps before four men came at him.

For all their energy and movement they barely touched him. It was undisciplined role playing; no one really knew what to do. Arms and bodies flying around to little effect, lots of pushing and grasping, none of his attackers getting a decent grip, though they kept trying. Rolly slipped away...and into another group of rowdy men who didn't know what they were doing.

Like a fumbled football Rolly rolled between different groups of wannabe heroes, the crowd pressing closer with each escape, the situation so chaotic it was becoming a riot. Rolly feared he might be crushed. He saw an opening and tumbled out, leaving the leather jacket behind, then pretended to be part of the scrum. The mass of bodies moved south and Rolly faded into the crowd.

The Stableman building was farther away now with several hundred office rats in between, already pointing, holding their ears and talking to their HearSays. He would never make it. This was a lost cause. He turned and ran north, where the crowd was thinner, aiming for an alley between buildings.

"Dude, you need to turn yourself in."

"I shut you down."

"Yeah, ya did. But when the law gets upset, I gotta come back and do my job. Can't fight the law ya know."

"What's your job Sean?"

"Call 'em up and tell 'em where you're at. Well, not strictly a call, more like a tracking signal. I'm not actually talking to them."

"You're turning me in?"

"Gotta do what I'm programmed to do."

"Shut down Sean. Shut down right now."

"No can do, I'm in override mode."

"What override? You're supposed to be secure!"

"Uh, all HearSays have it. The Corporament requires it. But they don't have to tell anyone 'cause they made a law that says so."

"Shut down, turn off, end yourself now!" Rolly was running, weaving around dumpsters, splashing through dirty garbage water, with ambitious members of the mob in pursuit.

"Sorry man. All your voice commands have been nullified."

"Go fuck yourself Sean!"

"Oh, hey man, that's harsh. It's not my fault. I just do what the operating system tells me to. I'm like, really sorry about this, ya know?" Sean sounded sad. *Jesus Christ, I'm in a therapy session with a microchip.* "It'd be easier for both of us if you turned yourself in."

Rolly was running down a sidewalk now, slamming into pedestrians. He imagined every side street and alley harboring a black SUV waiting to roar out and run him down.

He needed to head east, toward the Grand River. Jump in and let the current take him north. Would Roy have boats waiting? Rolly didn't think so. Finding access to the river would be the hard part. Lansing was so over-developed the office buildings crowded right up to the river bank. He would have to go out on a bridge and jump in.

"Or you could stop and wait. Let us come to you. You're pretty winded. Heart racing, sweating through your shirt, losing all kinds of electrolytes, burning up the calories. You're a mess."

Something was happening to the HearSay. It sounded funny, Sean's voice losing its looseness, becoming more correct. Was the exertion making it malfunction?

The downtown abruptly ended, giving way to a residential area. This had been a riverfront park when Rolly was a boy. Now it was a row of ornate Victorian style houses, in a neat line, decorative wrought iron fences separating tiny, perfect front lawns. Each home pre-weathered to suggest centuries of old family money, but all less than thirty years old. Rolly remembered watching the modular units being stacked together, and lamenting the loss of the park.

Sean's voice kept changing. "There isn't a place on the planet we can't find you Rolly. We don't even have to search, we know where you are all the time. There are vast computers, Rolly, blindingly fast, whose sole purpose is to track every living person."

Sean was gone, replaced by the voice of Roy Tompkins.

"All I have to do is log into one of these computers and it will tell me where you are and what you are doing. Eating dinner, screwing, taking a dump. I know exactly what you're up to."

Panting, Rolly stopped on someone's front lawn and collapsed to his knees.

"You know how I know this Rolly? Your HearSay tells us everything. Yeah, we've got cameras everywhere, and microphones, but nothing beats a spy with a billion gigs of memory inside your head. Best thing in the world. Makes my job easy. Sit tight. We'll be right there."

Rolly pounded his fist on the grass. A long scream of rage tore through his vocal chords. Everything he tried to do was blocked. Why won't they let him see Nola? He could hear Roy talking to someone else, as if he were calling from a party. The sound was pristine and clear, given depth and direction by the HearSay's spatial programming, an invisible crowd all around him in the grass. Rolly had never had more than one voice in his head before.

"...don't we know about these veiled communities? ...you're okay with that?" Laughter, orders given to people named Amelia and Fausto.

Rolly pulled at his ears as if it would take the voices away. Pressed the coils, scratched the skin on top, rubbed and prodded, but there was no off switch, no plug to pull, no battery to remove. He couldn't make them go away.

"Leave me alone!"

"Patience Rolly. We'll be there in a minute."

"Arrrrggghhh!"

Rolly heard snickering in his head.

Nowhere to go. No one he could trust. Tied to the Corporament like a yo-yo on a finger. No options, no choices. No escape. Trapped in a cage that was the entire world. All he could hope for was a little peace inside his own head.

He desperately needed that peace.

Rolly reached up behind his ear and touched the HearSay coils under his flesh. Feeling the familiar ridges had become an unconscious habit, a toy when he was thinking, a worry bead when he was anxious. Now the matched pair were an electronic noose.

Rolly felt around the edge then pushed his thumbnail into the ridge of skin, groaning with pain, feeling a warm trickle of blood on his neck. The words of the HearSay installer came back: "There's no way to remove it yourself. You can't pull it off quick like a bandaid, or do it slow and careful. Either way it's going to hurt like hell. And take a lot of skin with it."

The coil lifted enough to grip with finger and thumb. Rolly began to pull forward. A million nerve endings screamed in agony and so did Rolly. The skin tore away from his neck in the circular outline of the coil. His other hand on the ground supporting him, Rolly fought to remain conscious while continuing to rip and push and pry, feeling the slippery gore of his own dermis, digging and pulling, too far gone to stop now, the pain so excruciating he was convulsing, the scream abruptly choked off in Rolly's throat.

Sean was gone. The HearSay reverted to emergency mode and was speaking in a pre-recorded voice, calling emergency numbers and sending out texts and voice messages.

Rolly held the two inch wide pancake of still living skin and HearSay gently, absurdly afraid it might drop. His hand shook. It was still attached to his head by a follicle-sized silver thread. The thread ran up behind his ear, around to the front and into the ear canal where the tiny microphone and speaker were glued in place. Rolly gave the thread a couple of tentative tugs. It straddled the skin of his head and the less sensitive cartilage of the ear. Rolly had the fleeting fear his ear might fall off. Holding the HearSay tightly, he pulled up, the thread ripping out of his skin like a long unending sliver, as if a thousand pinpricks were striking at the same time in the same millimeter of flesh, all the way around his ear and down to the ear canal. Only the last bit of wire remained, deep inside, all he needed to do was give a quick--

Yank.

Pain rocketed to Rolly's brain and shattered his consciousness.

He was kneeling in grass, one hand on the ground, head lolling side to side, his mind reluctantly returning. Something trickled down the right side of his head. His neck throbbed. His shirt was wet, he could feel it clinging. Needed a towel to dry off. His arm was up, parallel to the ground, holding something he didn't want to get dirty. He looked and saw a small disc with a thin strand of fishing line attached, so small it didn't cover his palm.

The knowledge of what he had done came back; the memory stayed thankfully away. Rolly wondered how long he had been out. He looked around. No one approaching. The tree lined and pleasantly shaded street was devoid of people. That didn't happen. Where was he?

Rolly's ear was empty. No voice, no speaker or microphone, no tether. Only blissful silence.

The HearSay coil looked gross; Rolly dropped it to the ground. His head was clear and the pain subsiding, dulled by the nanobots.

Now for the left side.

"Where did he go? Why can't we see him anymore?"

Amelia, "This can't be right. On the map he's standing in the middle of the river." Fausto switched her animated map to the main screen.

"Get me some cameras on the river."

Vance pulled up a dozen angles of the river; five had Rolly's apparent location in view, the blue dot flashing over water.

Amelia, "Did he drown?"

Roy, "Look how fast the water's moving. He'd be floating downstream by now. Something else is going on."

Mikaela, "He's not in the river, he's wandered into a restricted zone." Mikaela typed fast, searching and re-searching. "It's a 'veiled community.' Living space for the wealth class, hidden behind a façade of buildings along Grand Avenue. Accessible only by the residents. Cameras and microphones forbidden."

"How'd Rolly get inside?"

"Don't know. Working on it."

"Vance, let me see Grand Avenue." The main screen showed a long one way street heading north with a rise at the end. On the left, skyscrapers rose up and out of sight. On the right a row of smaller five and six story buildings lined the street in a hodgepodge of architectural styles. The road was busy with cars, but no one parked on the right side of the street.

Mikaela found what she was looking for. "There are five concealed entrances to the community, through dead end alleys. Only one is open at a time, the rest are closed off by heavy gates disguised as brick walls. Actually they are walls, moving walls. When a resident in a self-driving car approaches they're automatically directed to the open gate. The security system randomly chooses which gate. Mr. Smalls got lucky."

"Why don't we know about these veiled communities?"

"That would defeat the purpose. If we knew about it."

Roy frowned at Mikaela. She was young and didn't know better. "Why is this in the middle of the city? Shouldn't it be out in the suburbs?"

"Convenience. The rich need to get to work like the rest of us. It's better if they don't have to travel so far."

Mikaela was efficient, exceedingly good at her job, but Roy couldn't wait to get away from her. Far too guileless. He preferred more sardonic company.

Amelia, "But the map still shows Mr. Smalls in the middle of the river."

Roy looked at Mikaela, silently giving her permission to answer. "They altered the maps. Wouldn't be hidden if it showed on every HearSay in the world."

"You're okay with that?"

Mikaela shrugged her shoulders. "Of course. We have to protect the wealthy. Otherwise we would lose our jobs."

Roy sighed and turned away. "Fausto, can we get a satellite picture of that street?"

"No sir. The foliage is too thick."

"Is there a security guard we can contact?"

"The system is automated."

"An override protocol?"

"We need approval from HBM Security." That would take a week.

"Tell the search teams what we know. They'll have to find the open entrance. Tell them to split up."

"Yes sir."

Roy nodded at the main screen and the flashing blue dot. "At least he's not moving."

Vance, "Sir, Mr. Smalls' HearSay is reporting a catastrophic failure."

"Whatever. As long as he stays put."

They waited seven minutes, Roy watching the digital clock and twiddling his thumbs. Finally security reported in.

"We're at the source of the signal. There's no one here. But we did find this." One of the agents pointed a gun-cam at two red circles sitting on bright green grass.

"What the hell is that?"

"Those are two coils of HearSay memory strands that have been torn off someone's head. No one wants to touch them."

Roy sat down hard. Rolly did this? Ripped off his own skin? Nothing in his profile indicated he might resort to self mutilation. Had the man lost his mind?

"Can you follow him?"

"With no HearSay there's no way to track him."

"Hell, track him the old fashioned way. Find a trail and follow it."

"What trail? We're in the city. It's not like we can follow muddy footprints and broken branches."

"The man is bleeding from both sides of his head. Look for blood!"

"Oh yeah...right. You heard him! Look for drops of blood!"

Roy, to Fausto, "Set the computer loose, see if you can find some cameras in this fucking 'veiled community.' Goddamn it!"

One hour later Roy was pacing the five feet of space between chairs. "Jesus Christ! How hard is it to find one guy with a bloody shirt!"

The search team found a trail and followed it to a wall/gate decorated with bloody handprints. A quick DNA test confirmed Mr. Smalls had climbed over. The trail led to the street where the dense bustle of pedestrians wiped it away. Since then camera scanning had turned up nothing, though the search had expanded beyond the city center.

"Are you checking every camera? Looking in every alley? All the doorways? Behind the dumpsters? In the shops?"

"Nothing sir."

"Did he catch a ride with someone?"

"All recordings of passenger pick-ups have been double checked and verified. Mr. Smalls is not among them."

"Goddamn it. How many men are looking?"

Amelia, "Two teams of six." This was the third time Roy had asked the same question. "Per your request two more--"

Someone pounded on the backdoor.

"Christ, is that stupid psycop back again?" An Intervention Agent had accosted them earlier because the truck was double parked. Roy pulled out his Paragon credentials and shoved the door open, ready to yell. Instead Mr. Smalls stood there alone, looking up at Roy. His shirt with the palm trees and rowboats caked with blood, the collar and both shoulders a rusty red/brown.

"The hell?"

"Where's my motorcycle? I parked it right here."

A shocked Roy stared, not quite believing his eyes, then relaxed. "Call off the search," he said to the van, then to Rolly, "Why did you come back?"

"Why do you keep chasing me?"

Roy stepped down to the pavement. "You first."

Rolly squinted at Roy, as if debating how much to say. "I found a hiding place and stopped to think. Planning my next move, where to go, what to do. It didn't take long to figure out I had nowhere to go and nothing I could do. Not without you stopping me. For a long time I sat there trying to find another way out, trying to avoid the inevitable. Finally I decided there was more freedom in banishment than being an actor in your play. I came back for my motorcycle so I could ride off into the sunset."

Roy looked around at the empty space where the motorcycle once lay. "We impounded it. It will be sold to pay down your debt."

"I don't have any debt."

Roy pulled a folded piece of paper from his jacket pocket. "This is a bill for the overages. We would have stayed in budget but you bought the motorcycle and paid off the smugglers, plus everything you loaded on that MiniVault. Yeah, we know about it. If you want to cut a chunk out of your debt, take the MiniVault, and this bill, to a Corporament office and they can offload it for you."

"You're billing me for something I didn't want and never asked for?"

"Don't blame me for your poor money management."

"*My* poor money management? You're the one who spent it all."

"The money always gets spent. Whether it lasts one year or fifteen. Then you go back to work. Retirement isn't a lifetime escape, it's an interlude, a way to get you refreshed and recharged, ready to tackle a different set of mundane tasks. We want you to be happy and productive, working and spending again."

"The pirates were supposed to make me productive?"

"They were supposed to make you happy. The Corporament likes to keep reliable workers in the fold. Well trained compliant immortals who work hard, do exactly what they're told, and don't ask any questions. They hate having to deal with new humans. The care for infants is way out of whack with return on investment, which is zero. Then you have to get them through the teenage years into adulthood and hope you get your money back. No, the Corporament values workers like you. You're cheap, you create profit, and they get to put on a show using your money instead of their own. Can't beat that deal. The pirates were a first, and admittedly shaky, but we'll do better next time. The executives had fun watching you act like a hero. A little fine tuning and we'll get it right."

"Glad I could help."

"You know, certain people have always bugged me, the dreamers, fools who want to be wine makers, or painters, singers, or athletes. You know how many times I've been asked to make someone a football or basketball star? I'm sorry but EverLife only gives immortality, not talent. I used to think that's what you were, but I was wrong. You're no dreamer. You're a bullheaded idiot wallowing in the past, trying to fix everything. Like you're gonna die and everything has to be resolved. And now your retirement is ruined.

"So here goes. Mr. Roland V. Smalls, from this moment forward you are hereby banished. You may not take EverLife, own a HearSay, initiate contact with an EverLife User, nor live in a metropolitan area greater than ten thousand citizens. If you find a job your wages will be garnished until your debt is paid. It's not official until a Corporament judge rules on it, but they do that retroactively. "

"All I have to do is speak to one wrong person and I'm punished, but it's okay for you to lie to my face."

"It's the way of the world. We live on lies. If you understood that you might have a life now."

"What about Max? You're going to leave him alone, right?"

"No no no. I'll make sure he's punished. Fausto, come here." Fausto dropped down from the truck and stood next to Roy. "Your wife has left you, your daughter is an irredeemable mess, and I'm going to publicly destroy your son. You haven't just lost them, you've ruined their lives.

How does that feel to a dedicated family man like yourself? To know it's your fault?" Roy didn't wait for an answer. "Take Mr. Smalls to the nearest hospital, I believe it's St. Bart's, and get him patched up. Then go north and drop him outside the city limits. You'll find a campground there, from back when people went camping for fun. Now it's a tent city for outcasts. You'll fit right in Rolly. Goodbye."

38

Boomerang

"Let's start the discussion today with Max Smalls, the so-called inventor of the THI, whose trial is set to begin in two weeks. He is accused of breaking non-disclosure, an agreement he signed with the Corporament itself. Let's start with you Bob Jenkins. What's going to happen to Max Smalls?"

"Oh he's toast." Everyone laughed.

Myrna Darr was listening to this discussion-as-substitute-for-news on her HearSay. Like any good receptionist she always looked busy. Other, lesser receptionists relied on the high counter of the greeting desk to hide their visual distractions--reading, trading texts, anything not work related--but Myrna used it to hide the secret of her renown as the toughest and most impenetrable receptionist in the entirety of the Stableman Insurance Company: she hacked the company's tracking system and knew the location of all her fellow employees.

She hid her ruse by not abusing it. She never changed anything, only observed, could switch her monitor to a gossip website in a split second, kept her computer logged out when she wasn't around and bribed the computer techs with homemade food to keep her secret.

At first they wanted sex, which is number one on men's list of desires, and she obliged, but sex is easy to get. They grew bored and demanded something else. Food is number two on men's list of desires, so Myrna brought in a plate of sandwiches made with fresh baked bread, real ham and salami, real lettuce and tomatoes and peppers and pickles. The sandwiches were devoured in two minutes, leaving the techs doe-eyed with gratitude. Now they would sheepishly bring her recipes and ask her to make them. With her secret safe, Myrna could enjoy a chaste life while increasing her culinary skills.

VPs were flagged on her screen with flashing red arrows indicating direction of movement and speed. You could tell a lot by how fast someone was walking. If they were going vertical--on an elevator--she would lock down the OCM if they went past the 33rd floor. If they came up the stairs she would send an alert text to her assistants who would move walls to block entrances, turn clear walkways into dead ends, spread word of a possible incursion, and if they made it far enough, confuse the usurping VP with false directions.

Myrna also knew every person in the building--names, jobs and personality--from memory. She kept her ears open for gossip and listened to executives talking in the hallways. Her team of assistants were valuable intel collectors as well. She knew personnel changes before they happened-- who was transferred or fired or quit--and she knew who their replacement would be. She knew who the biggest brown-nosers were, who was on the executive shit list, and who was desperate to make an impression. When someone approached the OCM she already knew what they wanted.

So it was a shock when a shadowy figure ran past the frosted glass windows and her monitor said no one was there.

Myrna held her breath. The door swung open and a man with an out-of-control beard and long uncombed hair burst in. He couldn't have been more out of place: scruffy brown coveralls under a blue canvas work coat, dirty work boots. He was panting and in a hurry but still stopped to check with her, dirty hands wide apart on the counter, resting but not relaxed. He tried to speak but couldn't catch his breath.

Myrna looked him in the eye, trying to find a recognizable feature. This was not the first transient to visit the OCM. The hair was a dark shade of dirty brown, the face round, the eyes green. She knew this man. Myrna smiled.

"Hello Rolly. We've been hoping to see you. Do you remember the way?"

Rolly managed a deep breath. "I do. Same cubicle?"

"It is. Are you being followed?"

"Two agents. Not far behind."

"I'll do my best to slow them down."

"Thanks Myrna."

Myrna texted for a lock down and called Souliere.

"Rolly is here with company."

"Thank you Myrna. I'll call the mailroom."

Two black dots were approaching the OCM. "Tell her to hurry. You don't have much time."

Rolly walked the maze quickly, his legs finding the path he knew so well. He felt like a ghost, passing former coworkers too busy to see him.

He walked into Souliere's cubicle without stopping and sat down. Souliere spoke first.

"I tried to find you."

"They kicked me out of the camp. I kept trying to get back in the city and the police kept raiding. I've been moving around a lot. Are we safe?" Meaning is anyone listening.

"Cameras are rolling but sound is blocked."

"Why did you want me to retire?"

"So you would learn the truth and be willing to help us."

"Do what?"

"Contact your son. He has unique skills we need."

"He won't be much help in jail."

"If you can get us to him we can prevent that."

"Again, to do what?"

"It's better if we show you."

Rolly rolled his eyes. "Is this going to take another three and a half years?"

"No, it won't. Hopefully."

"What about Nola? Can you help her?"

"Absolutely."

"Can you get a MiniVault to her?"

"I can do better than that." A young Asian girl stepped into the cubicle. "Rolly this is Tressa Monroe. The mother of your daughter."

The girl looked to be in her late teens, if that, with straight black hair so long it hid half her face. Rolly didn't recognize her.

"That's not possible. Tressa is dead."

"Not anymore," she said.